PRINCES OF NEW YORK

PRINCES OF NEW YORK

A NOVEL BY
ROBIN LESTER

Print ISBN: 978-0-7867-5557-8
ebook ISBN: 978-0-7867-5558-5

Distributed by Argo Navis Author Services

Distributed by
Argo Navis Author Services
www.argonavisdigital.com

TABLE OF CONTENTS

TOM'S NEIGHBORHOOD

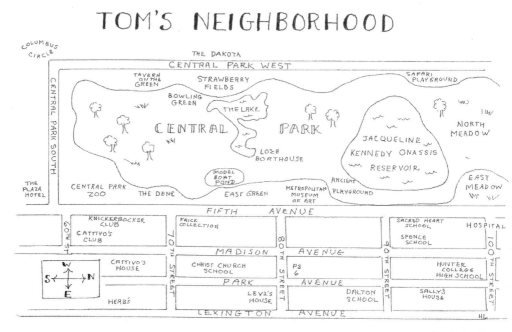

By Helen Lester

PRINCES OF NEW YORK

Because the world is mostly evil, a prince who fails to act because he is concerned about principle, sooner effects his ruin than his preservation. Hence it is necessary for a prince who wishes to maintain his position to learn how not to be good.

Niccolò Machiavelli, THE PRINCE, 1513

"Swift action trumps palsied principle."

THE PRINCE,
Translation by Robert George Cattivo, 2006

WINTER, 2006

CHAPTER 1

The head of Christ Church School got up at his usual five on a foul winter morning with less confidence than he wished he had. He was at his desk by six-thirty and the world beat a path to his door. Some even beat on his door.

The school's lawyer was first at seven with his impatient knocking and a dire report on the student newspaper. The careful man had previously offered Dr. Tom West only legal advice so bound by contingencies it was unusable. This time, however, he couldn't contain himself. "It's too late for a retraction, so the only possible mitigation might come if you dismissed the staff — that whole reckless bunch!"

Tom caught the "reckless bunch" — the three school newspaper editors — for an emergency meeting as they were stashing slushy parkas into their lockers. They settled in his office with mugs of coffee as a ferocious wind rattled the antique windowpanes. He knew them well, but that knowledge complicated his thinking. Two of the three were looking for a father; the third was trying to escape from his.

"I've got bad news," West said. "It's about that special report on the Central Park horses you ran this year — we may get sued over it."

The head reached for a file on his desk while the editors looked at each other in disbelief. "Central Park Stables is threatening legal action over your attack on the condition of their carriage horses."

"But that was my favorite story," said Catharine "Cat" Balewe, the *Christ Church School Chronicle* editor. "People loved it! All those big eyes, soft noses — abused!" Unnerved by the head's steady gaze, her eyes drifted to his familiar rumpled hair, tweed sport jacket, and corduroys.

"Cat, let's get serious," said Tom with a partial scowl. "It comes down to

5

this — our lawyer asked if we could back up your claim that, among other choice phrases, their horses are 'sickly brown bags of bones.'" He looked over at Matt Ernst and Maury Davis. Neither boy could hold his eye.

"Holy shit! Sorry, Doc," Cat gulped. "See, we all agreed we needed to get that story out. Have you seen the broken down horses that come out of those stables? They're suffering. We had to do something. And all the kids we asked agreed with us. Then we ran out of time. We would have—"

Cat was interrupted by a loud knock on the door and raised voices outside.

"I'm sorry, Dr. West," said Tom's secretary, Jo Wilson, opening the door and peering in. "The Countess von Konigsberg was knocking. She says it's an emergency."

Tom sighed in frustration. "Why don't we continue later?" he said softly to the students. "Sorry." Cat and her crew packed up.

As the student editors moved off to their classes, they met Dean Jane Levi in the corridor. The thirty-something school administrator was looking put-together as usual in a cream and red houndstooth suit and moderate black heels.

"That Hot Shit Countess Serenissima just kicked us out," Cat hissed to the dean and strode off. Jane's eyebrows lifted as she approached the head's office for her morning report. She gave Jo a warm smile, pausing at the secretary's desk.

"Tom left me a message that he was meeting with the *Chronicle* kids about a legal threat. But Cat said in the hall just now that they got booted out by the Hot Shit Countess. What's up?"

"Cat got it right," said the dignified Jo, nodding at the head's closed office door. "Oh, she's a handful."

Jane smiled. "Is that your opinion, or something Dr. West told you?"

"Now, now," said Jo, patting her perfectly coifed salt-and-pepper hair. "You know that's been over for months. But something has dear Serenissima on the warpath."

"I'll check back later," said the dean. "Call me if she emerges with Tom's scalp in her teeth."

Tom West was thinking along somewhat similar lines as he greeted the frighteningly attractive designer. His office always became sultry when Serena visited. Her frosted mane was perfect, her eyes lupine, her Italian tweed suit appeared to be balanced implausibly between executive and seductress, and her familiar scent came in waves. She appeared confident of her effect. And Tom was already deep in memories . . .

What happens when a woman who always gets her man doesn't? Last Thanksgiving, Tom thought he'd freed himself; yet he couldn't make it final until Christmas Eve. That was when the Countess had made her naked plea to reassert her control. It was her needy son Chris — a very decent boy who'd attended CC and was now at boarding school — who prevented the head from making a clean break; the kid was desperate for some household adult to provide a reliable presence, and now and then, Tom couldn't resist stepping in to do that.

"Jesus, Serena, you were outrageous just now — always the grand exception."

"Correction — I was insistent," she flared, then immediately cooled to a simmer that still looked dangerous. She looked him over, pink tongue flicking her top lip. "And I apologize abjectly. But Tom, I really had to see you before my flight to London this morning. Had to, had to." She moved to the sofa and settled next to his stack of stuffed animals, gifts from students. The pile fell toward her and Curious George landed muzzle first into her lap.

"Naughty boy," the Countess said.

Tom shook his head in disbelief as he said, "OK, shoot."

"Natasha wants fervently to transfer to Miss Jessups. And Tom, dear, her forever happiness is dependent on her getting in. I know it's late."

"Well, Natasha is a wonderful girl, and her community service work has been outstanding. So, we could emphasize that."

"Please, Tom, you know I'm talking about her grades. It's easier up there in Connecticut, so to be fair and honest, you could send grades out that have been translated into Miss Jessups' grades. That would be helpful to their admissions people."

After nearly five years as a Manhattan head, Tom thought he'd seen and heard it all. Apparently not. "Well, I do understand it would certainly be helpful to you, Serena. But I won't change the teachers' marks."

Serena's long slender fingers stroked Wuzzy Bear's frizzy head, fiddled with his little tartan scarf. She looked up with watery lids and said quietly, her lip trembling, "And I thought you appreciated the thousands of dollars in my own designer jewelry, bags, and perfume I donate every year to the Holiday Fair. I really did, Tommy. And I've never asked for anything since Chris and Natasha came here. Never. And now I'm treated like this."

Tom tried to contain himself. No wonder her acting career had lasted as long as a pre-theater dinner. Better come up with something tempered, something diplomatic.

"I'm sorry you feel that your donations were in vain, Serena. I know you got a whopping tax deduction at the Fair for that old inventory."

CHAPTER 2

Robert George Cattivo, the most influential property developer in New York City and Christ Church School's most powerful trustee, had risen at his usual five on the same foul winter morning with a surpassing confidence that never dimmed. With one exception.

"Puss, are you awake?" whispered Cattivo into the darkness of Babs' bedroom from the doorway.

Was there a rustle of 700-thread-count Egyptian cotton? He'd try again.

"Pussy, I have a meeting at the office before breakfast. Gotta run." Not a sound. "Gotta run, beautiful pussy lips."

He eased the door closed without a sound, then hesitated. That was no way to leave, not after getting in from Miami at two in the morning. He hadn't seen Babs for over a week. He'd try again. He stepped back to the thick white door with eighteen-karat gold bordering the panels and pushed down the European lever handle. "Babsie, Pussy, are you awake?"

"Oh, yeah." Babs' husky soprano came from the dark. "Oh, yeah, *now*, thanks to you; your Babsie is very much awake. But no, your Pussy isn't awake, if that's what you had in mind. Dahling."

Dahling. That was all the invitation Cattivo needed. He stepped into her bedroom and continued, now in full voice. "I knew you'd want to know, big deals brewing, could mean that forty acres in Bedford you've been dying for. You'll finally have your numero uno equestrian center. I got in late from Miami and I've got a meeting at the office before breakfast with some guys from Jacksonville. We're close to another big deal down there. Then, there's Hoboken—"

She cut him off. "Oh, the places you see and the people you meet!"

He had to pause. "They *do* make *our* world go around. And I wanted to remind you about the CC college meeting tonight for junior parents. It's at seven."

"Shit. Will that creep Dr. West be in charge, again?"

"He's still the headmaster."

"That guy makes me lie awake at night. I despise the thought that Georgie's college chances are in his moronic, over-educated hands. You know what a jerk he is, and yet you refuse to fix it. If you weren't such a pushover on that precious board of trustees with your nose up the ass of pathetic Wither Bramston. You know, his wife got me to put her on the Kips Bay benefit board? And she's gained a zillion pounds. She must crush the life out of that mouse when they fuck!" She chortled hoarsely and felt for her Pall Malls on the bedside table.

Cattivo joined her chuckle. "They've only done it once. And since their daughter's nearly fifty, Bramston may be getting horny."

"So, make damn sure you're next in line to lead the school trustees when she smothers that old fool. Maybe you'll take over about the same time I take the Costume Institute board chair." Babs turned on her light, lit up, inhaled with a smile, and blew a smudge pot's worth of smoke over her bed.

She was a new woman. "Why don't you have Henry bring you by and pick me up on the way to the school this evening?"

"I'll have to meet you there — meetings up my wazoo all day — Jersey at three."

He could see her more clearly now, sitting up — disheveled, susceptible. He moved nearer.

"Damn," she said, glancing at her clock. "You woke me three hours early."

"Sorry, but I wanted to touch base, Sweet Pussy." He was a step from her bed.

"Well, thank you and good night. Write when you amount to something." She snuggled into her pillow and turned to face the wall.

That was their old motto. Early on, when Bob was trying to bed and engage Babs, the Miss New York runner-up, he'd suspected that she was holding out for something beyond his Brooklyn apartment. That was the first time he'd told her, "Maybe I ought to just go away, honey. I'll write when I amount to something."

That evening, in the back of his Bentley on his drive to the school, Cattivo glowered at the letter from Hoboken that he'd just been given; they were threatening to hold up his building project unless he personally appeared at the variance hearing. He already had to be in Atlanta that day. He fidgeted with the Phi Beta Kappa key on his watch chain; he didn't have a watch on it, only the key at the end, tucked in, so it didn't show. That'd be vulgar, his father — whose key it was — had always said. Cattivo never told anyone that he had inherited the key — he didn't mind when people jumped to their own conclusions.

As he approached the four-storey school building, Cattivo brooded, once again, on why he had it in for the headmaster. It had started with Babs' humiliation at the welcoming reception for Tom. That was more than enough to establish a grudge. The new guy had deliberately scorched the evening at the expense of Cattivo's wife when she was trying so hard to fit in on the Upper East Side. But even worse, the bumbling new headmaster had also helped to ruin Cattivo's air rights development plans. He'd been inches away from nailing those two air rights projects — the August Belmont Museum and Christ Church parish towers — which would have made him the leading player in Manhattan, at least among the people he cared about. Why, he'd even sold his "greatest good for the greatest number" argument to that damned architecture critic at *The Times,* but then Tom had stuck his nose in and wrecked everything. All of Trump's flashy stuff was child's play compared to erecting monoliths against the Manhattan skyline *on behalf of greatly valued cultural institutions.* Bob almost had it all.

Since Babs would be coming tonight, Cattivo had cautioned her to play it safe with Tom. The headmaster appeared to be helpful when Monica had applied to college, but they couldn't risk any upset over Georgie's quest. Cattivo decided to bide his time, not to tip Tom off that he was gunning for him. He'd heard that one word from a headmaster to an admissions dean could easily doom a kid. Of course, Cattivo figured that by the time Georgie applied next December, Dr. Thomas West would be long gone, with a new headmaster in place. But that slippery son of a bitch was, well, slippery. Shit.

As the car pulled up, Bob Cattivo bounded out of his limo with his British trench coat flaring behind him. Away from home, his supreme confidence had returned — West had better watch it. He strode into Jo Wilson's office and fumbled with the coat hanger, already riled. His riling usually occurred within the head's study, so he was ahead of schedule. Jo sprang up and moved over in front of Tom's door. She often stayed late to ensure that Tom had everything he needed for his evening meetings. And to defend him against the barbarians.

"I'll go right in," Cattivo informed Jo as he brushed past her, rapped sharply, and opened the door.

The head was reviewing his speech notes for the evening ahead. Tom didn't look up to see who the intruder was because he already knew.

Cattivo, in a dark pinstripe Savile Row suit, was outraged by being ignored. "Goddammit, Headmaster, look at me!" He leaned over the ancient mahogany desk, black eyes boring in, punching home his message.

Tom dropped his pen and looked up at Cattivo. His was a face you could invade Poland with. "Bob, you know I've got Parents' Evening in fifteen minutes. I've got to tell them their kids can't all go to Harvard."

"Never mind that — right now I want you to get this straight: if you can't control this railroad, we'll get somebody else to run it."

Tom sat back, alarmed. Bob Cattivo, his least favorite trustee, was always jumpy, but right now he was out of his skin.

"We need leadership, *real* leadership. Let me tell you, it wasn't only about making the railroads run on time — Mussolini could sure as hell handle those lefty editors. Now your students have mired the school in Central Park horseshit — and *you're* only dealing with snot-nosed kids, for Christ's sake, who still have to have their asses wiped before they go to press. You're supposed to be the Big Kahuna, so take charge, West, get this place under control."

Tom knew about Cattivo's obsession with Mussolini. He had even gone so far as to design his office at the MetLife building after Mussolini's, making sure that it would take a visitor thirty seconds to walk from the door to his desk. Tom shuddered as he recalled one command performance. He had seen the short leader barking orders to acres of lesser folks below his aerie. Cattivo had made billions with apartment and shopping mall developments in New York, New Jersey, and the New South. And by now, he had heaped enough on Christ Church School to own the board president's ear and to charge into the head's study any time he wished.

"And strike two, the Countess called. In tears. You broke her heart today — you broke the heart of our richest mother! I tell you, Tom, all these ..." his hand swept over the bookshelves with a dismissive gesture, "these ... worn-out books, and you don't have the sense any good businessman needs to stay afloat. Babs was right five long years ago — you're out of your league here, 'East is east and West is west.' We're gonna get your overeducated ass!"

He turned and stormed out.

CHAPTER 3

Tom struggled to return to his evening talk. Maybe his sense of history would help. "The Society for the Propagation of the Gospel in Foreign Parts." Tom reminded himself again — that was what the London pioneers had called themselves when they founded Christ Church School as North America's oldest royally chartered institution. It was after Charles II and the Duke of York, the future James II, wrested New Amsterdam from its Dutch trading company in 1664. The royal English brothers were determined to make the Dutch outpost, renamed New York, an Anglican/royalist enclave in their new empire. Instead, they got a rambunctious, polyglot frontier settlement with a proper English school as the last bastion of their dream. That school had been under some kind of siege ever since.

Now Tom's mind moved to recent history — that morning's siege by the Countess. And he was proud of his response: "I know you got a whopping tax deduction at the Fair for that old inventory."

Tom had recoiled at Serena's explosive response and hoped that no students were in the vicinity to hear her cursing like a standup comic. He wasn't worried about Jo, who helped the curdled Countess into her coat and politely sent her on her way, turning back to her boss with a wink and civilized fist pump.

Tom glanced at his familiar surroundings. The Headmaster's Study — traditional sanctuary of twenty-five headmasters — featured walls of books, a creamy wooden mantel and fireplace, scarred leather wingbacks and a sturdy sofa. Yeah. A sense of history regarding that Society in Foreign

Parts was fine, but it couldn't compete with contemporary commerce and power. Tom tried to breathe deeply and concentrate on his notes. Shit.

Dean Jane Levi knew these junior parents were school veterans. Up until the moment Tom had mounted the marble steps and rung his antique school bell, the fathers had been wolfing the bite-sized pizzas while the mothers nibbled the cheese cubes arrayed on the tables beneath the double chandeliers in the Great Lobby. They turned dutifully to the youngest head in school history and saw an angular, rangy man with a prominent nose and cheekbones and sky blue eyes. Tom's blues were the only ones Jane had ever seen that were warm and understanding. And no doubt some New Yorkers saw that as a weakness.

"Welcome to your first College Admissions Evening," Tom began. "I know you feel some anxiety over this topic. Our objective this evening is to relieve you of your concerns . . . and perhaps provide some new ones."

Jane winced. Tom's sense of humor had once again been applied at the wrong time to the wrong people. The parents remained silent.

Tom seemed to sense that he had gotten off to a rocky start and talked too long, trying to regain his audience.

"Finally, let me emphasize that competitive excellence is not the full story of our vision for Christ Church School. We love the life of the mind *and* the spirit. We teachers constantly address the knowledge most worth having, but also the life most worth living, and our place in it as striving, decent, ethical human beings. We like to think those values are not merely a means to an end, but at our best, an end. Our school's ancient motto, 'To whom much is given, much is required,' reminds us of that responsibility."

In the silence that followed, one father called out, "Dr. West, we're here tonight to get our kids into Harvard, not into heaven."

Tom smiled as everyone else laughed.

Jane sought out the waggish father as the parents filtered into the library for their small group sessions. She knew the college counselor would be hard-pressed to place this guy's son; he was a kid who had never worked up to his capability and had been on probation for cheating. After greeting him, she said, "Mr. Pomerance, a word to the wise: you should know that Tom's faculty backs his concern about character one-hundred percent. I hope you do, too." A flustered papa assured her that he most certainly did. Several times.

Before the meeting, the head had told Jane of Bob Cattivo's declaration of war. On the surface, Tom looked pretty cool. But Jane knew better. She had seen Fast Bobby standing at the back with his usual smirk and his wife Babs — the original sequin in the rough — wincing over the speaker from her seat. So, they couldn't wait to get rid of the brainy, western interloper. And no doubt his closest ally, the dean. Shit.

CHAPTER 4

The February evening had turned crisp and clear and Tom decided to take a walk to simmer down after the parents' meeting. When he got to Sherry-Lehman Wines on Madison and Sixty-Fourth, he turned back uptown to stroll past the neighboring schools. Thirty minutes later he had passed P.S. 6 and the Dalton and Spence buildings, then moved up to the Hunter College High School and doubled back past the old Kahn mansion on Fifth and Ninety-First, which was now the Convent of the Sacred Heart School. Those sisters were his favorites. They were like the generous, slightly racy aunts every adolescent needed. It was Sister Jean who had planted a full mouth kiss on him during the last Heads' Guild meeting at the Cosmopolitan Club and vowed to keep checking the eligible mothers at her school for him, as he was the only single headmaster in the group. Tom told her he wished she'd get a move on and that she'd have to be a miracle worker to match his Betsy. How he missed her, especially tonight, facing the Cattivo onslaught.

Betsy Livingston Schuyler hadn't come from the other side of the tracks; in truth, there were several trunk lines between her lofty Cleveland suburb and Tom's tenuous hold in his hardscrabble downstate hometown. They had both made large accommodations for the other across that gulf because they shared an idealism and they were horny kids. They were united in their dream of making a difference in the world when they met as graduate students at the University of Chicago — he as a scholar-teacher, she as a social worker. With her degree fresh in hand, Betsy founded a free tutoring program for disadvantaged kids. It was going well, but she died in the effort — killed by an angry mugger out for an easy mark. She was Tom's sole family, and he'd had to make do without her for ten years. The desolation was always with him, but it came on stronger whenever he grappled with a setback.

Tom knew he was at a disadvantage with Cattivo. It wasn't his kind of game, despite the fact that he knew the philosophical origins of the man's thinking. Cattivo was his own embodiment of perhaps the first "modern thinker" — Niccolò Machiavelli, the Medici civil servant. Tom had covered him for years in his history classes, and lately he'd begun to realize that Cattivo had mastered the Machiavellian success story. Tom, however, found himself comparatively defenseless: *Because the world is mostly evil, a prince who fails to act because he is concerned about principle, sooner effects his ruin than his preservation.* Tom knew that the essential problem Machiavelli analyzed in *The Prince* was how *to make a new prince appear to be an established one.* Cattivo had already bragged to a *New York Magazine* reporter that Machiavelli was the only reading in college "worth a damn for a Manhattan developer!" He even supplied his own translation — "Swift action trumps palsied principle." So, it appeared that Prince Tommy could theorize about what was happening while Prince Bobby could make it happen. *Hence it is necessary for a prince who wishes to maintain his position to learn how not to be good.*

When Tom returned to his desk, Cattivo's evening threat came back in living color, buttressed by flashbacks of the junior parents' comments that night. He couldn't help but pull out an old pack of Marlboros from his center drawer. He had quit two years, a month, and two days ago. But the smell would be gone by morning. A deep pull and he felt a little less tense, but that wasn't enough to forget his evening. He looked down into his center drawer and read the two statements on paper strips he had glued inside: **Whose Problem is this?** and **Remember the Other 90%.** Yeah, *his* problem, and how could he remember the wonderful parents when ten percent were pounding on his door?

Tom forced his attention to the fifteen student essays from his senior European history class awaiting his review. He was soon happily engrossed in the work he loved, starting with a fine essay by Matt Ernst on the artist Tintoretto's devotion to personal capitalism, based on the new Venetian acquisitiveness. The students always stirred him with their promise.

An hour later, shouts drew Tom's attention to figures on the sidewalk beyond the black ironwork fence outside his windows. He saluted the *Chronicle* school newspaper staff on their way home after a late shift. Editor and film-nut Cat Balewe, in a faux-fur cap with bouncing earflaps, gave him a wave. Sports Editor Maury Davis and Features Editor Matt Ernst gestured on either side of her — they wanted in. Tom motioned them over and met them at his maisonette door. They came into the vestibule as Cat said, "My editors and I wanted to apologize again and restore a semblance of our honor by eating crow."

"Come on in," Tom said, and led them into his office. "I doubt we'll be interrupted this time. Sorry about this morning." He picked up the old *Chronicle* from his coffee table as they sat. "Now, back to the 'sickly bags of bones.' Did you or your reporters do any research at the stables — *anything* that resembled responsible journalism?"

"Of course," Cat replied, sitting forward. "Well, we tried to — I called the stables, but they refused to talk. The story was based on what we've seen in public. And there was this one guy we met at a party, you know, he used to work there. He's the one who really got us going on it, said they didn't even have a vet. I have his name and number."

"But Cat, why was it published as news rather than as opinion?"

"I understand, and I do know better. We had it set as opinion, but we needed a big bang headline, you know, to make a splash, push our circulation above Dalton's. And I know you told us not to worry about circulation, you just wanted a quality school paper. Guess we f—screwed that up.

I apologize. Won't happen again." She sighed and looked sideways at her associate editors, then back at Tom.

Matt and Maury looked sheepish and nodded.

Tom rose from his chair. "Well, that's it. The answer to my question is, 'No. No responsible journalism,' unless you have notes and files developed on the story. If so, get it all to me so I can give it to our lawyers."

"We'll keep searching for our notes, but we're a little disorganized in the office," said Cat.

Tom could believe it — he'd seen their office. He looked at the three editors who'd screwed up. Except they weren't editors who screwed up, they were kids — hardworking students — who excelled in their studies, his class included.

"Thanks for coming in. We'll get through this together."

Tom looked at them as they rose; the trio still looked tense and worried.

"Whoa! I don't want you to leave here tonight looking so downcast. Let's go upstairs and find something to eat besides crow. I was about to make cocoa and open a tin of Scottish shortbread."

They peeled off their parkas and followed him up the stairs to his darkened apartment.

Cat sniffed. "Smells like my mother's Marlboros. You don't smoke, though, do you, Dr. West?"

"I had guests in who do. Earlier."

Cat was a cool junior. She might not be the first CC student a visitor would notice, but she would be among the first the teachers nominated for best all-around kid. She had fresh, blonde good looks and brown eyes, but she wouldn't qualify as the girl next door — too serious and too sassy. That combination meant that her top two editors treated her as a precocious younger sister who deserved their respect and loyalty.

The two senior boys couldn't have been more different physically: thin, bespectacled Maury and tall, athletic Matt. Or more similar in interests — each notched straight '5s' on four AP exams as juniors, and they had been inseparable from their days at P.S. 6. Although they were keen sports fans,

Maury's "terminal klutzdom," as he called it, meant he played sports writer to Matt's starring role on the soccer and baseball fields.

In the kitchen, Tom threw plentiful scoops of Droste chocolate in with the heated milk. Then he put a cup of marshmallows into his giant blender, added the hot cocoa, and turned it on until the rich chocolate was suffused with foamy marshmallow. They all sat around the kitchen table, ate the shortbread out of the tin, didn't touch the napkins Tom put out, and discussed the NCAA Final Four and the Academy Award chances of "Capote" and "Brokeback Mountain." Cat hoped Kate Winslet's new movie, "Little Children," would be her career role. Maury and Matt had seconds on the cocoa, which they claimed was the best in Manhattan.

"Oh, Dr. West, before we go, I wanted to tell you that I googled Dr. Johnson on horses today — I love him," said Matt. "Something like, oats are fed to horses in England, but in Scotland oats're fed to Scots."

Tom laughed with everyone, then said, "Very good, but the Scots have their own answer to that observation. They ask, 'Then what do Scottish horses eat — English cooking?'"

As they left, all three thanked Tom and promised too easily they'd go home to study or sleep. Despite their Columbia journalism awards, the hard-working student editors had put Tom in the trustee line of fire. The legal threat was against Tom and the school trustees as putative publishers because the editors were minors.

CHAPTER 5

"I'll be in shortly with your coffee, Dr. West," said the elderly lady in black and white uniform as she handed him his favorite chocolate brioche on a snowy cloth napkin. She had adopted him on his weekly 7:00 A.M. breakfast appointments at his board president's office. And that coffee couldn't come fast enough — he'd finally gotten to sleep in the early A.M. with more than his usual Scotch and more stale Marlboros.

Tom would have been fascinated by his visits to the "Common Room" of

Bramston & Bramston if they were not job-related. The place was unique. It was an open triangle that occupied an entire floor of the Flatiron Building and contained thirty identical antique roll-top desks in dark wood with amber-shaded lamps. There were no partitions and no visible personal items, so while the effect was beautiful, Tom imagined that it was taxing to work in. More than once he had seen a parent pull out a drawer and check on the welfare of a glossy photo of a child within. There was one compensation: a wooden tea and coffee cart circulated among the desks with English biscuits during the day. No charge. The municipal plaque said that the firm was the city's oldest real estate management firm, circa 1820. Tom suspected that some of its current denizens had been on the original staff.

Wither Bramston, V, trim, tidy, and silvery round the rim, greeted Tom at the door of his suite overlooking Madison Square Park. "Good morning, Headmaster, I trust you slept well." The greeting was invariable, as if based on the assumption that the visitor had slept in the Common Room curled up on a desk with its sinuous ribbed top tucked under his chin. "Have you anything in mind this morning?" Bramston asked as they sat.

"I'd like to show you my plans for a real improvement in faculty salaries and minority faculty recruitment," said Tom.

"Well, yes, I trust you've got that well in hand . . . if you can raise the funds. But I do have more important concerns this morning." Wither paused at the sharp knock and the delivery of his tea and Tom's coffee, which were served in china cups on a Gadroon-edged silver tray with matching pots. Tom liked the panoply — if only the cups were mugs.

Bramston sipped and cleared his throat. It often needed clearing. "I shall try and put this as gently as I can: the sky is falling, not to put too fine a point on it."

"Really? Guess I got here just in time."

"Not a matter to joke about. *Your* sky is falling."

Tom put his cup down and leaned forward. Bramston was looking intently at something over Tom's shoulder.

"There was your snubbing of the Countess yesterday — 'whopping tax deduction,' indeed! And I'm afraid that *Chronicle* story really ripped it.

Members of our executive committee are indignant over the threatening letter the Reverend Dr. Philips received from the Central Park Stables lawyer. He was deeply aggrieved. We've never had this kind of unpleasantness at the school." Bramston sipped.

No, thought Tom, not since the American Revolution. Or when the Civil War riots closed the school. He set his cup down a bit too hard, but nothing shattered. "Wither, I'm meeting with the rector later today. I've already met with the editors. I think it can be an important learning experience for the students because—"

"Tom, please," Bramston broke in, "whatever you do, don't rile up the Rector Dr. Philips with your misplaced candor. That son of Dixie might pull the carpet out from under you when the school's lease contract comes up. Trust me, I know leasing contracts. And I know carpeting. And it wouldn't stop there. The entire structure could disappear. *Then* try to run your school on the sidewalk."

"The editors have apologized. It won't happen again."

Bramston nodded slightly and poured seconds. "Now, to be fair, we all know you've put the school on the map. Heck, before you came, we had to accept any kid from the one-zero-zero-two-one zip code if his name didn't end in a vowel. And I wish to assure you of the board's respect for you."

Tom was touched. Was this Bramston's attempt at leadership, or was it friendship?

"I don't think you are remotely aware of the stakes here, Tom. We're talking of your position at Christ Church. And I'd like to help; there's a real possibility that the rector and I can fix you up with the position at St. Paul's School. You see, I'm on that board as well as being Senior Warden at Christ Church parish, and a fourth-generation alumnus up there — I did a PG year. It all still swings some weight. You know we've got a leadership vacancy up there again. Huge endowment — you could disappear into your classroom and never come out."

Tom couldn't think of anything to say.

Bramston leaned across his desk and continued in a low voice. "Now, I think I can take the liberty of telling you that many of our trustees have told me for years that they share your desire for an endowment campaign. We all give you full credit for suggesting a capital campaign, so rest assured that you have changed people's thinking."

"So, what's their gripe with me, then?"

"Oh, Bob Cattivo has convinced *most* of them, and even me, that you'd not be any good at it. After all, I sent you Sam Spencer, one of my best young men, as your development associate. But you didn't get off square one. Guess we're leaning toward Bob's view that we should change horses before we start to cross that fund raising stream. You should be proud of your evangelism: you've told us and told us we need endowment. Now we're converted. Nothing personal, Tom, but we're *redefining* your job based on your vision about the future of our school. I'd put it this way — we've had our prophet, now we need our salesman."

And with that, the headmaster was dismissed from class. At least the brief meeting meant Tom would be back before school started. Bramston's interest in Christ Church School seldom went beyond the hope that school and headmaster would remain something the Manhattan Orderly Class could be proud of. And yet, as he left Bramston's office, Tom knew he had to come to grips with that "misplaced candor" that concerned Wither. But what else could he do, alone and scared to death as he was sometimes? He no longer had Betsy as soul mate and fellow skeptic. After her death, he had tried not to express his acerbic irony. It wasn't easy.

The anxiety continued to build as Tom caught the subway. Heat lodged beneath his diaphragm. He couldn't be fired for *not* altering a transcript or for viewing the school newspaper as a classroom, could he? But this fund-raising thing. He had tried to light a fire under Spencer to get cracking, but Spencer, a poster boy for nepotism, had insisted that he would handle the endowment, leaving the annual fund to Tom. And while Tom's fund was now near the top in New York, Spencer hadn't raised an endowment dime.

It was axiomatic that the best school boards always had a strong president to provide continuity and control. He'd seen it at other top schools, but not at Christ Church. Wither Bramston tended to many old clients his forebears had developed, but his venerable firm was also a favorite of the renegade property developers. "Bramston's" listed as the leasing agent bestowed a patina of old New York respectability on even the most ill-advised mid-block needle tower. An increasingly large slice of Wither's business was managing Bob Cattivo's Splendid Properties, Ltd. That would explain his recent appointment of Cattivo as chair of the board's powerful nominating committee. Now Tom's nemesis controlled the keys to the kingdom: board membership and officers.

CHAPTER 6

Tom's footsteps on the mosaic floor echoed off the ceramic brick walls of the Great Lobby with only the oil portraits of past headmasters to keep him company. Those stiff-collared worthies knew he was an imposter – born a non-Episcopalian west of the Hudson River, lacking an Ivy degree, without proper family background. He told himself again that he shouldn't give a rat's ass. He looked at the oldest portrait — late seventeenth century. The imported Oxford don didn't look all that well fed on the New York colonial diet. There was some comfort in that.

Before she died, Betsy had said to him, "I'm envious. Compared with my girls' school life in Cleveland, yours down in Kokosing was an odyssey — always on the edge."

She was being kind as usual. He'd been born beyond the edge — in an Ohio town of nervous old Protestant and striving new Catholic families with enough fatalistic Jews in the downtown commercial middle and a winning high school football team to buffer it all and make it work. Tom's father was an eighteen-year-old drugstore clerk who gave up his dream of becoming a pharmacist when Ethyl, the pretty cosmetics girl, became pregnant. His life was fixed at Tom's birth — he'd never make it beyond twelve-hour days as deputy assistant manager.

Ethylene Eberhard was a dreamboat from West Virginia. Her daddy always claimed that her name was special — it was her great-grandmother's — but the other kids teased that it came off a gas pump. There was a lot of that, growing up poor. She returned home only once to find that everything had changed, the men wiped out by black lung and the women gone to Charleston for work. When Ethyl and Thomas settled down, they thought it a wonderful fate that a Buckeye and a Mountaineer found each other and fell in love.

Thomas continued to believe it, but the idea soured for Ethyl when he was drafted into the Army. She was emotionally removed from her toddler Tommy from his birth. She seemed to view him as the fallout from a stupid moment of pleasure with a stiff-pricked kid who sold rubbers but couldn't keep one on. Private Thomas Sylvester West returned, in his khakis and bearing a purple heart, to the life he knew at the drugstore while Ethyl found a job as a receptionist at a car dealership.

It would never have occurred to Tom's students that their head grew up in a trailer. Nearly every spring the Kokosing River flooded their trailer court, and they tugged their portable house away from the greasy plague. That meant living light. And it meant that his mother, who dreamed of a house, made life difficult for the mild, dependable husband who couldn't get anywhere in a family-owned drugstore beyond opening and closing the shop six days a week with a brassy Kahiki key ring.

Tom lived light all through grade school. After his father's death, he had little time for grief. He helped keep things going, making money as a midnight stock boy at the new supermarket on the highway and sharing the cooking with his mother. She was adrift and hurting financially after her husband's death.

Tom guessed Ethyl simply couldn't take the pressure when she finally left her son and Kokosing. That son managed to keep his shame to himself and make the rent payments during the summer, but, on the first of September, Tom took his belongings in two shopping bags to a furnished room. The landlady kept quiet about her homeless minor because she needed a boarder of any age or condition. He managed to stay level through high school with his paper delivery, midnight grocery stocking, and summer golf club jobs.

Tom heard in his varsity locker room that somebody's uncle saw Ethyl "looking good" at the big Chevy dealership in Columbus. He never wanted to investigate. He was better off on his own. Hiding his shame and living light taught him a lot, something he used when he escaped to Ohio State. As soon as possible, he was off to Scotland on a Rotary overseas fellowship. St. Andrews and Chicago, in turn, provided a blessed anonymity and an academic meritocracy in which he excelled.

Tom was grateful for living the American Dream: poor boy from small Ohio town escaped to friendly universities. Good people and breaks helped him find what he loved doing — teaching kids — from a Chicago inner-city public school to a New York private school. He became the dean of a Washington, D.C. Episcopal girls' school enrolling South Carolina, Massachusetts, Montana, and California congressional and lobbyist daughters. His next move had brought him back to Manhattan and the original colonial school as head. He took a final look at his predecessors in the lobby and assured himself that it couldn't have happened if he hadn't mastered his role and lines.

Could it?

Tom paused in the barrel-vaulted entryway. Every morning, the sepulchral silence was obliterated by the voices and bodies of 600 pubescents and adolescents with a collective SAT verbal median in the ninety-seventh percentile and a hormonal index that was equally intimidating.

Tom went outside to help supervise the seventh and eighth graders waiting at their sidewalk entrance separate from the high school students. The lone teacher assigned to the daily rotation smiled broadly as the kids swarmed over Tom, flashing new sports equipment, dental work, and electronics.

"Put 'em away, please," called Tom. The click of cell phones and all manner of tech ware that he didn't even have a name for preceded the stowing of them in back packs, not to be touched until after school. Some parents and media had reviled Tom when he banned the use of such communications during the school day shortly after becoming head. He'd said, "If you're in our school community, you must be *in* our community." He also set up a dedicated telephone-messaging center for parents, dentists, and doctors to contact the students through the security desk. After a month of grumbling and "Dr. West's Breakfast Club" suspensions, CC's classrooms and hallways emerged safe from cell phone interruptions and the behind-the-back texting practiced in other schools. Several parents now suggested that Dr. West run an additional breakfast for their children who were prone to taking calls during dinner or in the family car.

Tom liked being with the middle-schoolers — they were only beginning to show the stains of the adult world, and they thought they could learn everything. A few thought they already had.

There had to be an adult presence to protect the vulnerable middle schoolers from their classmates. The slower readers and the playground wusses inevitably attracted the incipient bullies. It was like the old brooder in the utility shed where his grandfather had tended the chicks. If one pecked another's head and the wound yielded a trickle of blood, the other downy, lovable creatures were soon pecking the injured companion to death. It was red in tooth and claw in chicken house and middle school. And there was also a lot of that going around in adult Manhattan.

Tom had to remind himself later of that note inside his desk drawer, "**Remember the other 90%**," when two sets of seventh-grade parents bore down on him after the middle school assembly. All four brought up their students' grade reports and attacked the teachers' grading practices. In sum, their kids were the victims of an overly rigorous grading standard that would affect their college chances.

"I can assure you that Dean Levi and I monitor our grade distribution constantly."

"That's not good enough," said one of the fathers, shaking his head vigorously — it was always one of the fathers. "I want action. We didn't send Danny here only to see him get knocked out of the Harvard-Yale-Princeton box in his first year."

"And that goes for us, too," said papa two.

Tom took a hasty breath. He should simply tell these parents to be patient and that the children needed to realize that they were now in a more competitive place than their previous schools. Above all, something tempered, diplomatic. But these guys asked for it.

"Actually, our problem has always been one of grade *inflation*," said Tom, "like every other school or college since the seventies. I hope you didn't park your kids here only because the *Wall Street Journal* said we have the best Ivy acceptance record in the country; only about a third of our seniors get into H-Y-P anyway. Most have the good sense to go to excellent small liberal arts colleges where they can get a fine education from professors happy to be teaching undergrads."

The parents were speechless. Good. Both mothers pulled their husbands away, no doubt wondering if Dr. West would hold their opinions against them when push came to shove in five years with college admissions. It would be tempting.

When Tom arrived in Cat Balewe's basement office, she was editing on her large Mac screen. She turned to him immediately.

"Dr. West, all we've got on that Central Park Stables story is the date and time Matt called them for that interview, which they refused. We don't even have the names of the two current drivers who gave us the cold shoulder."

"I'll inform the lawyer, for what it's worth," Tom said.

"Well, it's diddly-squat — I can see that. Are we — am I — in big trouble?"

"Well, I *would* like to beat you and your editors black and blue. And it's hardly over."

She pulled her lips in between her teeth. "My mother won't like the sound of this," Cat sighed. "'There goes Harvard,' I can hear it now. You going to tell her?"

"No, Cat. You are."

She was startled. She looked down and shuffled her black Chinese sandals.

"Tell her that you're in no legal difficulty, the school is. And that we must keep it in perspective — if you and the other editors are trying your best to be responsible with every story, I'm satisfied. If she wants to talk to me, I'd be happy to take her call."

"Okay, I'll tell her, but she's not around much these days, she's got a new boyfriend up in Westchester. He's got two daughters . . . younger than me . . ."

He waited, as it seemed she wanted to go on, but she looked down at her desk and thumped the eraser end of her pencil on the surface. End of discussion.

He didn't have it in him to scold her further, not a kid who'd never had a real parent. What she needed was an adult in her life who loved her enough to draw the line. Outside of this recent episode, Cat had always been both ethical and reliable. If Christ Church was ever going to produce journalists and writers, they would have to encourage these kids and then take whatever lumps there might be. There were already too many Wall Street successes among the alumni, and Tom's prescription was more artists, professors, scientists, and do-gooders. He knew the investment bankers, arbitragers, and hedge funders among the trustees wouldn't share his view. And he suspected that they were already lined up with Cattivo to fire him for not running his school properly. But maybe he was too influenced by his own hostility to their privileged role in the capitalist system — the never-sweat, non-productive type Marx had described so well. Maybe he should have parked that opinion long ago. It did appear to be a luxury now that he was part of the system. When the school heads got together at their New York Guild meetings, they often matched their alumni: Horace Mann boasted Roy Cohn and Eliot Spitzer; Fieldston countered with J. Robert Oppenheimer; Collegiate named Ben Vereen and John-John Kennedy; Trinity had its unlikely trinity — Humphrey Bogart, Truman Capote, and John McEnroe. In those tongue-in-cheek competitions Tom could only note CC's own Wall Street hall of fame and a famous eighteenth century axe-murderer named Mercy Justice.

Tom crossed the courtyard between school and church to make his peace with Richardson Philips, the angry Episcopal priest who was his landlord.

"Only fifteen minutes, Mr. West," his secretary said. "The Reverend Doctor expected you to call yesterday."

That meant Tom had fifteen minutes to explain why the man had been threatened with legal action over the dodgy capers of a student newspaper he never read.

The black-suited divine sat back in his jumbo chair with a labored sigh when he saw Tom. That action pulled his pudgy legs off the floor, baring white shins to match the white clerical collar scaffolding his jowls. Tom thought him worthy of Whistler — a study in black and white.

"I don't want a smidgen of headlines about your student paper's gutter journalism. I don't want our church dragged through the mud. We could manage very well without your school's rental income. Your trustees know this, even though *you* seem to need a reminder." Philips sighed heavily, shaking his head. "I know what you really need over there — you need me to act as your Ethical Compass."

Ethical Compass? Tom hoped the Rector couldn't read his mind. No thanks, he'd forgo the privilege of having an obese personal Ethical Compass sitting on his shoulder, or wherever such compasses tended to perch.

Philips seemed to read his speechlessness as humble hesitation. "Well, think it over, Thomas," he said. "The Lord works in marvelous ways." The back-up position would be "mysterious" ways. Yet, mustn't be a Doubting Thomas.

Tom had endured ten hectoring minutes on running a school properly by a man who never had. He had reached his limit of abuse when nature lent a hand. Philips tired visibly and his demeanor became almost avuncular. He was sleepy after his daily lunch at the 21 Club, where *New York Magazine* reported he had a private wine locker.

"They could still apply the hand of experience to the seat of knowledge where I come from," the divine said. "Of course, up here the pointy-heads don't allow it. Must be tough running a school where you can't spank 'em when they need it."

"Oh, it's been done, Dr. Philips." And those who did are no longer with us, Tom added silently.

"Glad to hear it. Now go on back to your charges and sort it out. And remember, no broken bones or bruising!" He chuckled at his homegrown, Pomerol-nurtured wit.

"Thank you, Dr. Philips. For the advice. And the time to think over your offer." Hard work this "suffering gladly" thing. But only until the new ninety-nine-year lease was sealed.

CHAPTER 7

Cattivo wrote his order and handed it to the club waiter at his elbow. "The Balvenie for us," he said, indicating himself and Bramston. "And Wild Turkey Rare Breed for our Kentucky Colonel here." He smiled at the Reverend Dr. Richardson Philips across the aged-oak game table. A couple of those and the Colonel won't know if he fries chickens or sinners, thought Cattivo as he rolled the Phi Bete key in his fingers above the table.

The men occupied themselves with casual conversation about the NCAA basketball tournament until the drinks were served. Cattivo toasted his guests and took control.

"We won't have to transgress club rules about no visible business papers this time from the looks on your faces, gentlemen. So how did it go?"

Cattivo nodded at Bramston, who looked pleased with himself as usual. "Just call me 'Good Cop' — like you told me. I think it went well this morning." He sipped carefully.

"I softened him up last evening," chuckled Bob. "So, how was he?"

"Well, he was Tom. Confident, cynical, whatever you call it, but he hung on my every word. At least after I told him his 'sky was falling.'"

"Meaning?" asked Cattivo.

"It was my way of diplomatically telling him his jig was up." Bramston saw the puzzlement on two faces. "See, I told him that snubbing the Countess was bad enough, but that what really ripped it was our dear rector receiving a threat from the stables lawyer. That surely got his attention. He apologized several times. Then I mentioned my gift of Sam Spencer, Jr. to help him raise money and how disappointed we were with his record."

Bob wondered if Bramston believed his own spin. He had been at the end of his patience with young Spencer when he unloaded him on CC.

"Oh, and Dr. Philips," Bramston continued. "I floated that New England boarding school possibility."

The rector grinned and held up his glass appreciatively. "'Offload,' I think the computer geeks call it."

Cattivo saw that Bramston had shot his wad. "Well done. I'll get refills." He snapped his fingers at the waiter and turned to the Rev. "And how did it go in the vineyard?"

"Well, I wasn't the bad or good cop — I was just myself — in control from the get-go. Wish you'd been there, I gave him a real southern grilling. Pinned his ears back. Told him I was fixin' to cross that courtyard and spank a few of his brats, if he didn't!"

"He's the Rare Breed," Cattivo instructed the waiter by nodding at Philips, chuckled, and then said, "How did Tom handle that, Richie?"

The doctor took a quick, greedy sip of his fresh drink and coughed into an overweight, freckled fist. "I left him some time to reflect on what I'd said. He appreciated that very much. If you two hadn't tipped me off, I might not have taken advantage of this *Chronicle* thing."

"That's the way to go," said Wither Bramston. "We'll all come out ahead."

"Bob," said Philips, "I hadn't realized how weak Tom was with these kids. Oh, you'd harped on it, but it wasn't until you made that God-sent gift for the altar restoration project that I took notice." Philips took a long pull and smiled. A little too beatifically, Cattivo felt, and he wished Philips would stop referring to his six-figure altar gift in quite that way.

"So Bob, when did you become aware of these problems at the school?" the rector continued.

He can smile any damn way he wants, thought Bob, if he keeps pitching over the plate.

"Well, I have to go back a bit. Remember our headmaster screwed all three of us in his first year over the Belmont Museum air rights controversy. We'll never forget that, will we?"

Bramston frowned and shook his head. "No, never forget."

"Or forgive," the divine said. "If West hadn't got involved in fighting the Belmont air rights test case across the street, well, we could have repeated the same deal over our patch. We could have made a killing with the developer and, most important of course, our church mission would have been greatly expanded. It still makes me soppin' mad."

"Well, I have to defer to my Babs," said Cattivo. "She had him in her sights even before that — ever since our welcome reception in his honor. She had a couple of rooms redecorated for that evening — really, just for Tom West — and he spoiled her party. Classless lout."

Philips turned toward the bar. "Say, could I have a freshener-upper over here, waiter?" The others covered their tumblers when the waiter looked their way.

Bramston looked thoughtfully at Cattivo. "So, our first showdown regarding Tom will be at the Executive Committee meeting. That means Ms. Meredith Ross and the Bishop will join us. How do we proceed?"

"Well, we'll have to be diplomatic with Ms. Ross — she's always been a quiet trustee and a little mysterious to me. But the Bishop is a certifiable insane liberal, so I can imagine he encourages Tom's humanism. But they'll come around as they view Tom's behavior more clearly."

"'Certifiably insane liberal,'" said Philips. "I like that."

"Well, those two have said at meetings that he runs a strong school, that is, what they consider important — student and teacher quality and morale," said Cattivo. "But I've got to get them to look deeper, and to do that I need more evidence of Tom's malfeasance. Ross is brilliant and a tough boss, I hear, so we need to come up with dead wood on the faculty, student behavior gone to hell — which The *Chronicle* has already helped us with. Then I can link that with the budget — his nonexistent fundraising record." He paused. "Remember my motto: 'The dramatic appearance of reality is always stronger than the reality.' Those two trustees and the rest of the board'll come around."

A fresh tumbler of Rare Breed awaited Dr. Philips. He seemed to have no doubt as to whether it would yield as he dove in. Cattivo and Bramston traded smiles across the table.

CHAPTER 8

Tom found that since Cattivo's challenge in the office, it was somewhat helpful to recall instead the nice things that President Bramston said at their meeting: "You've put the school on the map," "assure you of the board's respect," "changed people's thinking," and "nothing personal," although the latter got him stirred up. Tom mostly sought refuge in his classroom with his students. And they were studying one of his favorite periods: the first Renaissance stirrings — when the European world began to become recognizably "modern." Always tricky, these labels for the past, for if the outward, material signs were various and difficult to pin down, how could an historian presume to get at how people in 1500 were thinking?

Tom's best answer was by reading what they read and what they wrote. He did use a textbook for context, but the core of his teaching was primary sources. His students had struggled earlier in the term when he insisted they read and attempt to understand, even try to empathize, with the religious mind of Thomas à Kempis. But when he assigned Machiavelli's *The Prince,* his young Manhattanites settled more comfortably into the mind of the past.

"So, what have you come up with during your weekend with *The Prince?*"

A forest of hands. Unusual on a Monday morning at 9:50. "Caroline?"

"For starters, it's written in an antique but modern way. I mean, it's graceful."

"Yes, a good point. And how about the substance of his argument?"

More hands. They obviously got into Machiavelli almost instinctively and soon agreed that Chapter XV was the heart of the book. Tom challenged them to write out that chapter's thesis. As they read their work aloud, he chose one to write on the board: "Because the world is mostly evil, he who fails to act because he is concerned about principle 'sooner effects his ruin than his preservation.'"

Another student added, "See, that is so different from the sappy stuff you made us read from the Middle Ages. I think Machiavelli must have been courageous to write this stuff, Dr. West — Florence was still a devout cathedral center."

"Leo Strauss couldn't have put it better." Questioning looks. "A Chicago political philosopher." They looked confused. "That's philosopher, at the University, not a Chicago politician."

The class laughed. Except for one girl.

"What's wrong with you guys?" interrupted Cat Balewe. "Machiavelli's basic appeal is that wickedness is okay if you have a worthy end. Are you saying that you agree that 'the end justifies the means,' Dr. West?"

"You tell me. It wasn't my assignment over the weekend."

Forty minutes later, Machiavelli was still being defended and attacked. Tom knew the Medici apologist never failed to get students' juices boiling. The majority of these seventeen- and eighteen-year-olds saw a basic honesty in Machiavelli's argument, but they still preferred the nonviolence of Jesus, Gandhi, and King.

Before the bell rang, Maury Davis summed it up: "Yeah, that's the way it is out there — dog eat dog."

Matt Ernst quickly added, "But don't try Machiavelli at home with mom." He got a punch on the shoulder from Cat and a smattering of applause.

Tom loved the classroom. And the kids. Here, he could forget about the sky falling. Guess he hadn't done what Cat might call "diddly-squat" in his own defense against Cattivo. He preferred not to think about it as there was nothing from Cattivo, Bramston, or Philips for over a week. Bramston had postponed their weekly meeting since the full board meeting was imminent. The thing would probably blow over anyway — they were all too busy to get worked up over a student newspaper, and he could always ask Serena von Konigsberg to cool it. She still owed him big time.

CHAPTER 9

The Executive Committee of the Board of Trustees of Christ Church School traditionally met an hour before the full board in order to set the agenda. Vice President Cattivo alternated as chair, sharing the honor with the other vice president, Meredith Ross. He had proposed her as his co-vice president because he figured a younger woman looked good in the position and wouldn't threaten his own accession when Bramston died of constipation. Cattivo picked up Bramston and Philips in his Bentley because he figured his troops could use a pep talk on the way up to the school.

"Where there is no vision, the people perish," said Bob Cattivo.

Philips grinned. "I didn't know you were a student of the gospels, Bob."

"I'm not, only the gospel of success. But I do remember how you used that, years ago, when you addressed our Belmont Museum trustees. You cleverly offered your support for our project if we'd support yours. You described what selling your air rights and building the high-rise apartments over the church would mean for your vision and mission."

"Ah, yes. I did get warmed up that night, didn't I?" Philips smiled. Then scowled. "But of course, it was all spoiled when our headmaster cast his lot with the other neighbors and complained about the loss of sunlight for his school. Moaning about perpetual darkness for his students and teachers."

"Bleeding heart crybaby," said Cattivo. "But those do-gooders won, even after I quoted Peter Drucker to bookend your point: 'The best way to predict the future is to create it.' And I threw in Robert Moses as well, but he doesn't fly as well today as he used to. Tom West gave the loony landmarks people exactly what they wanted. If that bunch had been in charge centuries ago, New York City would still be huddled south of Wall Street."

Philips and Bramston nodded vigorously.

"The decision not to permit the buildings to expand was a tragedy for us," said Philips.

"Truly," Bramston offered.

"You know, fellas," said Bob. "I spent more bucks on that feasibility study than I ever have. I had to remain *sub rosa*, as you remember, but those two fifty-storey towers — for a wonderful museum and an ancient church — would have netted our institutions hundreds of millions. To enlarge their good works. And, of course, I might have put a few shekels in my jeans as well."

Bramston and Philips guffawed as the driver stopped. Cattivo stepped onto the sidewalk and led the way into the school. They were soon settled in a small conference room off the library.

"We will have to be united this evening. We've never drawn the line on Tom before. I still don't know about Ms. Ross — she's a cool one. I'm only pleased that the Episcopal Church grants full liberty to its laity and clergy to disagree with their bishop — don't ever forget you don't have to obey your hierarchy. Remember, guys, the Bishop applauded Tom's stand against our museum and our parish church's best interests. And soon after, when the Bishop practically apologized to his muggers in Riverside Park from his hospital bed, we got a true view of the liberal mind."

Bramston looked uneasy. "May I remind you that he's still the Bishop of New York — our pastoral leader."

Cattivo tilted his head back and looked his ally over. No, it surely couldn't be that Wither Bramston would place ideology over his meal ticket. He'd have to reprogram the senior warden's knee-jerk obedience to his Bishop — rattle his cage more often. A simple reminder about the millions he raked in from Cattivo's properties ought to do the trick. Bob depended on the wallet trumping ideology. His thoughts were interrupted by Philips.

"But perhaps not for long." Philips read the astonishment on the others' faces. He loved secrets. "There are advantages to serving on the board at St. Luke's Episcopal Hospital. But, of course, I can't honorably say more."

"No, of course not. We understand," said a solemn Bramston. Spoil sport, thought Cattivo, Richie was going to spill before Bramston's ethical intervention.

"And, speaking of, here's our favorite Bishop," announced Cattivo, who was sitting facing the door. He stood.

The Bishop held the door open, tipped his tweed cap, then removed it with a sweeping motion to lead his companion, Meredith Ross, into the room. The Bishop liked what he knew of her and only wished he knew her better. She was an Apple senior-management alumna and now headed her own burgeoning software firm in Manhattan. The Bishop knew her husband as a charitable leader. Tom had said that she was a great mom and invaluable as chair of the trustees' faculty benefits committee. As the Bishop threw his coat and cap over a side chair, Cattivo pulled out a chair for Ross next to his.

The Executive Committee seldom took votes. Instead they tried for consensus. Thirty minutes was enough time, the Bishop soon saw, for Chairman Cattivo and his two loyalists to reach "consensus" over the Bishop's objections and the abstentions of Ross.

The Bishop mused that although he could be termed a "Trinity careerist," he was unprepared for the unified unholy Trinity that now faced him on the Committee. When Ms. Ross offered an optimistic opinion on faculty morale, Bob pursed his lips and tilted his head in puzzlement. Ross immediately qualified her comments with, "I am aware, Bob, that an outsider can never see the full picture."

"I couldn't agree more, Meredith," said Cattivo, patting her on the shoulder. "I only wish there was some way for us to check those teacher evaluations we hear so much about from the headmaster."

"Has anything come up that we should know about?" she asked.

"Well, I'm hesitant to get into this." He paused long enough for the Bishop to worry. And Cattivo did appear reluctant to continue. He chewed the corner of his lips, shook his head, and appeared to make up his mind.

"No, I must. I'm beginning to think there's considerable concern among the parents over Tom's personnel policies. I had another example this week: two couples, all four at Goldman or Lehman, who had what they insisted was a 'frightening encounter' with the headmaster at school this week when they merely inquired about the quality of a teacher's grading." Bob pulled out his Blackberry, fiddled, and read aloud. "'He practically threatened to jinx our kids' college chances if we didn't go along with whatever wisdom he imparted.' That's a quote, by the way. And they asked me not to use their names." The Blackberry was stowed. "I would suggest that our president review the faculty personnel files."

The Bishop was not convinced that "whatever wisdom he imparted" was in any Lehman or Goldman lexicon, but before he could respond, Bramston spoke.

"Now, I have plenty to do for the school already. I would suggest that our two vice-presidents take on the job."

"What do you say, partner?" asked Cattivo, turning to Ross. "I wouldn't want to take it on without a teammate."

"It seems an unusual expedient," said Ross. She surveyed the table of her elders. "But if you all think it absolutely necessary, well, yes."

Dr. Philips' immediate, effusive support meant another "consensus" victory for Cattivo.

The Bishop was determined to head this off at the pass. "I must protest this procedure. It is tantamount to a vote of no confidence in Tom. And it would mean we've moved from policy, which is our job, into operations, which is his." He saw that Ross looked confused, but he had to settle something with Cattivo. "Bob, I guess you're still unhappy after five years that we didn't select the other finalist — your Fortune Five-Hundred candidate — to run the school?"

Cattivo was unresponsive and the Bishop undeterred. "Surely you'll agree we must all pull for the man we've got?"

Cattivo peered innocently at the cleric and shrugged. "I'm simply unhappy that the man we've got isn't up to it. But I saw this week how clueless he was with the Countess von Konigsberg; he's tone-deaf — how could he alienate *her*? What a great mom. She recently gave a million to her son's academy in Massachusetts, for God's sake. And there's Tom's pathetic handling of the student rag. 'Pull for him?' He doesn't pull for himself. I'm afraid he's got to go. There, I've said it, and I'll make it my business to make it happen."

Cattivo checked his watch. "Now, as the others have no doubt arrived next door, meeting adjourned." Ross had started to raise her hand but was ignored.

The Bishop was the last to leave the little conference room. He had foolishly gone after Cattivo when he should have pursued his procedural complaint to get to Ross. And he was amazed that Tom had done the impossible — he had united two diametrically different people: old school Bramston and arriviste Cattivo.

The Bishop remembered hearing Bramston complaining about Donald Trump less than a year ago across the Brook Club's dining table. "Barbarians at the gate, always the barbarians."

As for Cattivo, he had sounded off at the enterprise luncheon they both attended at the Hilton. "Christ Church School is mired in the past, everything is tradition, no place or appreciation for New York's *real* movers and shakers, our 'creative entrepreneurs.'" He leaned and spoke in the Bishop's ear. "You know, I mentored Trump."

The Bishop determined to get more involved at the school; he hoped he hadn't waited too long. Holy shit.

CHAPTER 10

Tom greeted the trustees as they entered the school's Robert and Barbara Cattivo Seminar Room. Years before, Bob had paid for the remodeling of a classroom "fit for the trustees," including the Alex Katz pictures on the walls. Tom watched them mingle and settle around the expansive oak table. Most had arrived by the time the Executive Committee filed in. The Bishop patted his shoulder and Meredith Ross dropped her eyes as they shook hands. She must have a crisis at work, Tom thought, she was usually so effervescent and warm. She took a seat by the handsome Seventh Avenue fashion pioneer from Orchard Street who was now peddling cruise line and preppie nostalgia to every upper-income enclave in America. The trust-ees at the table were a mix of parents at the top of their game in the city. The dominant group were the plain-vanilla alumni investment bankers and brokers who graduated from Harvard, Yale, or Princeton and led the top male clubs there. Two highly respected corporate executives and one corporate lawyer constituted a quiet but influential trio. Finally, the two *ex officio* members required since the seventeenth century founding: the Episcopal Bishop of New York, whom Tom greatly admired, and his court-yard neighbor, The Reverend Dr. Philips, who always insisted on his title of "Doctor," even though it was honorary from a second tier Southern college that didn't even offer master's degrees. The twentieth century had added the Parents' Association president as *ex officio*, and Sally Ernst, Matt's mom, added much needed brains and beauty to the board landscape.

The most unfortunate thing for Tom was that these impressive men and women had never been allowed to be impressive as Christ Church School trustees. Sure, they were kings and queens of their own mountains, but, as school trustees, they were corporate cogs following President Bram-ston's lead when they could detect it. They were all enormously busy and had their own battles at work; hence, they didn't go looking for a board-room fight at their children's school. They were not the sum of their parts primarily because they didn't have a strong board president. And Wither Bramston simply endured the meeting at the head of the table in the family tradition — wan, fidgety, and increasingly parched.

Ross' uncertain greeting worried Tom, and as Bramston and Philips stole stealthy glances at him, he knew something was off-kilter. When President Bramston called the meeting to order, disposed of the reading of the minutes, and called on "our valuable and visionary vice president, Bob Cattivo," the head felt the heat of anxiety pummel his chest.

"Mr. President," Cattivo stood and read solemnly from his notes — he had never done this before, "I feel it is my duty under the laws of the State of New York as trustee of this ancient educational institution to place in the minutes a record of all the daily aggravations some of us trustees have had to get involved with."

There was an audible stir among the trustees, as if they had all decided to change their postures simultaneously. Cattivo paused to let them resettle, leaned into the table, thumped his papers into order, and looked directly into the faces of his colleagues. "And not simply 'get involved with' but, if truth be told, that we bailed the headmaster out on." He paused, returned to his text, and raised a finger for each indictment. "The libelous school newspaper, kids smoking pot in neighborhood apartment house lobbies, students falling victim to Marxist teachers who envy their parents' success, even to a steady alienation of those parents. Example: Dr. West recently bragged to veteran parents at college night and to new parents just this week that he was glad only a fifth of our seniors get into Ivy schools because they aren't worth a damn anyway. And a successful and most generous mother came away from a conference with the headmaster in tears."

Crack! A table full of trustees looked Tom's way, and only then did he feel and see it — the Bic pen in his writing hand was in two pieces, the plastic sleeves now held together only by the plastic refill. The sound seemed to echo in the room, matching the heat in his chest as it moved up and burnt his forehead. He took a hurried slug from the Saratoga water bottle and felt the cool dribble on his throat as he spilled it down his front.

Cattivo cleared his throat to regain attention, smiling thinly at Tom as if in sympathy. "Finally, he even refuses to get a Blackberry so that I, or you, can contact him when we need to." He looked up from his notes and glared at the detritus of plastic and ink on the pad in front of Tom. "My God, we've had a busy time saving this guy's skin." He sat down with a sigh.

The guy inside the skin was seething. Admittedly, negotiations with the stable remained a little shaky. But they'd had only a few smoking complaints recently from local residents. And, yes, there had been complaints from some parents two years before when a leftist teacher married an heiress and his sudden Park Avenue address prompted him to spout some guilt-ridden rhetoric in the classroom — otherwise it was a Marxist red herring. As to the parents and the Ivies, Cattivo's version of events was grossly exaggerated, though perhaps Tom had been goaded into losing his temper a bit. And the mother he'd brutalized, well, to defend himself discreetly he'd have to inform somebody on the Board, perhaps the Bishop, about the Countess's attempt at transcript fraud. And his little T-Mobile cell phone was fine — when he remembered to turn it on — but he'd be damned if he'd get hooked up in such a way that he'd never be away from his job and Cattivo. But what to do here and now, short of a punch to Cattivo's kisser? Such accusations, once floated, could never be contained, much less eradicated. He mustn't protest too much, but something had to be said to clear the Cattivo-generated miasma. And above all, he must not lose his temper.

Tom raised his inky hand and began to rise. "Wither, if I may respond to Bob's concerns?"

"No need, Headmaster." With both hands extended, President Bramston calmed the air with an insistent pumping motion. "This meeting is no place for such a debate. We're here to address next year's budget."

Tom sat. Orwell was right — some animals were still more equal than others.

Bramston picked up and studied his agenda, then smiled benignly at the glowing sconces beyond the trustees' heads. "Umm, which you are most welcome to do. Now, Headmaster."

Tom stood and began to walk them through the proposed budget for the next school year. The trick was to emphasize the major items while spending sufficient time on items with a notable increase to allay any suspicion that he was trying to slip something through. Tom wasn't really comfortable with corporate budgets, and it must have showed. At his first falter, the investment bankers were at his throat. It was as if Cattivo's attack had set them off. Time after time, they challenged Tom's assertions about the value of various budget expense lines.

"I see this exorbitant number for the online Readers' Guide to Periodical Literature and Oxford English Dictionary under the library line. Why can't the teachers and students just use Google?" asked an investment banker parent whose year-end bonus had made several top ten lists of banking excess.

"Because the internet offers a wealth of sources, some valid, some not. We want to provide them with current, reliable references."

"Well, why don't you use old print ones, get a huge discount." The trustee sat back with a grin, seemingly pleased with his opportunity to demonstrate how his world operated.

"I guess for the same reason you don't subscribe to last year's *Wall Street Journal*," Tom said.

The bankers saw Cattivo frown at that exchange and became quiet enough for Tom to finish.

"Given the budget we've discussed," he said, "I'm afraid I am the bearer of my usual message. We can't remain in our leading position unless we charge adequate tuition and launch an endowment campaign to alleviate those increases. Even though our annual parent fundraising is near the top in the city, we have been invading our dwindling endowment because our tuition levels are below our competitors'. Our staff morale remains remarkably good, but we can't continue to expect mediocre pay to maintain excellence in our people and programs. We're now twenty percent below Collegiate, Chapin, and Brearley at nearly every pay level."

The discussion of Tom's remarks made it clear that the trustees definitely wanted the head to maintain the school's *Wall Street Journal* standing as "Number One." They were too busy, however, to be much help with the actual fundraising. They wallowed in tales of past futility and Bramston couldn't find the rudder.

Finally Bob Cattivo rose, script in hand. "I think we have all seen that the old college presidential giants are a dying breed," he said. "You know, the famous ones like Hutchins at Chicago, Conant at Harvard, and Brewster at Yale." He put his script on the table. He would wing it. "They have been replaced by modern men, men who may be former generals, like Eisenhower was at Columbia, or Toro lawn mower manufacturers, like the man who saved Dartmouth. These are people who know how to raise the kind of big money we need to do the things we'd like to do here at Christ Church."

Bramston stirred. "Where is this leading, Bob?"

"I'll tell you. As long as we have this headmaster, we'll never make the big bucks we need." He looked over at this headmaster and readopted his sympathy for the wounded dog smile. "Nothing personal, Tom. But folks, you see, he's like most academics who get jumped up to this position without life experience winning wars or making lawn mowers — he knows how to spend it on teachers and free tuition rides, but he doesn't know how to make it. And that's why I strongly recommend a management review of the current administration."

Looking up at Cattivo, Tom said, "We should operate like other major schools in Manhattan. We should energize our trustees to get involved in raising an endowment that would allow us to have competitive salaries and scholarships."

"But, my friend," Cattivo said, his face showing some strain, "that's *your* job, as I've told you every fu-riggin' year."

Wither's chair squeaked.

Cattivo muttered, "Sorry," and continued. "Now I do agree on one thing — the need for endowment. You've made the point *ad nauseam* since you came. We need an endowment as much as this country needed to escape Al Gore's green apple environmental quickstep. But I'm a man of action, not words. Therefore . . ." He lifted his briefcase and poked his hand inside. "I'm going to jump start this endowment campaign and with a little bit of luck we'll have it humming like a Toro." He tossed a four-page document into the center of the table.

"That's an unsigned legal instrument. It gives the school a half interest in the new Splendid Plaza Mall in Sarasota, which has a current value of twenty million and is rising fast. The school will hold it for a minimum of three years to clear any IRS queries for me. All that remains is for me to sign it and we'll have that endowment."

A warm wave of approving comments greeted Cattivo's announcement. Wither Bramston rose to his full height. "Well, first, Bob, may I thank you on all our behalf for this generous gift—"

"Hold on, Wither." Cattivo, still standing, pushed Bramston gently to his seat, then picked up his papers and waved them aloft.

"Now, you need to hear the lynchpin of this. As chairman of the Nominating Committee, I will sign the twenty million over to CC only if this board votes to approve a management review and a new membership requirement. I so move: that President Bramston arrange for a performance review of Tom West by our next meeting and that henceforth we elect only new trustees who throw five million dollars on the endowment barrelhead. I know I can get five men to step up to the plate within six months. The result would be a war chest of forty-five to fifty mil that would put us in the top ten Manhattan schools. In another ten years, well, the sky's the limit. But my offer is only good for tonight — I want action now!"

The uproar that resulted from Cattivo's challenge ran well past the hour when Wither Bramston usually rapped his signet ring on the table and adjourned the meeting with, "The ice is melting, gentlemen." That was the way his father and grandfather had dealt with their imperative of 6:00 P.M. adjournment. Wither let the meeting run over for the first time in recorded history, and he barely managed to keep some semblance of order. Speaker after speaker weighed in with strong statements. A kind of consensus developed among the investment bankers, brokers, and hedgers: don't look a gift horse in the mouth. No such maxim encapsulated the assertions by Tom, the Bishop, the executives, the lawyers, and Sally, but all of them argued that selling board seats was wrong in principle. The first vote showed the trustees were split down the middle on the Cattivo motion, and Bramston hesitated to break the tie.

The Episcopal Bishop of New York now dominated the discussion. Tom always reckoned the Bishop had been recruited from Central Casting. He was tall, ruggedly handsome, and socially liberal in the way that only old, secure money could be. His civic and social weight was considerable as long as there were Astors and Vanderbilts around his Cathedral of St. John. The Bishop felt strongly that the reputation of the oldest Episcopal school in North America was at stake, not to mention its founding parent, the Church. Fingering the hammered silver cross prominently lodged on his rich purple shirtfront, he played the "unseemly" card, a move aimed directly at the board president. He knew Bramston well. As an Episcopalian, Wither had heard rumors of the unseemly and knew it couldn't be permitted within a hundred croquet court lengths of the Bramston family name. So he finally voted no when confronted with the necessity of breaking the tie on Cattivo's motion to sell trustee seats. Bramston barely had time to commend himself for fighting off mammon and bad taste when Bobby Cattivo rose to announce he would be taking his toys home.

He held his Sarasota mall gift aloft. "I'll give you all fifteen minutes to come up with an alternative that I can accept; otherwise, I'll tear this up. Twenty million bucks down the drain." He headed with his papers to the door, where he turned and pulled his left cuff back to expose a button-studded golden block of Rolex.

"Synchronize watches," he ordered. "Nineteen-thirty nine. See you in fifteen minutes." He pressed a button on his watch and was out the door.

"My, my," said President Bramston.

"Yes, in two words," said the Bishop rising. "If I may, Wither, I should like to be excused to find Bob and see if there's some way through this procedural maze."

Tom would have loved to be privy to that corridor conference. On one side, the Bishop — he could use the Cattivo millions to complete his own cathedral choir school project. On the other, Cattivo — he would dearly love to be elected to the St. John's Cathedral board of trustees and was a long-time supplicant. Only one factor was certain: Tom's school was the pawn.

The cleric returned in five minutes with a motion that mollified Cattivo. It was passed by the time Cattivo rejoined the group. The Bishop's motion instructed President Bramston to arrange the management review of the head that Cattivo had pressed for earlier, but it put his endowment offer and board membership requirement on hold until the fall meeting. In turn, Tom would be challenged to raise twenty million to take the place of Cattivo's twenty million. If the head was successful, the sale of trustee seats would be forgotten. For Tom, that meant that the school was no longer the pawn. He was.

Bramston had a final question. "Bob, if Tom is successful, would your gift still be available?"

Cattivo scanned the room from beneath his prominent brows.

"I would have to be persuaded. But why deal with long shots? Remember the sure thing." He grinned as sweetly as he could. "If Tom doesn't make it, my twenty million is yours. Along with my board election plan and a dynamic capital campaign led by a new headmaster."

After the meeting, Tom walked slowly down the hallway that opened onto the cloistered courtyard. The corridor light shone out through the arches and was suffused with horizontal snowflakes driven into the garden darkness. The wet flagstones indicated that it was near freezing. As the only twenty-four hour inhabitant, Tom liked to imagine the urban garden oasis was his own. He had planted bulbs every fall and added perennial beds. He stopped and pressed his forehead against the cool glass pane of a French door. The wind was strong, creating havoc with the snow, rain, and the whipping branches of the rhododendrons. It was dreary, wild, and beautiful out there. Inside, it was simply dreary and wild. Back in the boardroom, Tom's proposed budget had been passed after a brief discussion, but without his recommended tuition increase to cover the deficit. The board was already counting on Cattivo's twenty million dollar bailout.

CHAPTER 11

"Move over, Machiavelli," Tom told his secretary Jo Wilson the next morning. "Ask Sam Spencer to come in. After I'm finished with him, we'll run ads for a development director."

Spencer came in at 10:15 when he arrived at school.

"Sam, I'm going to do you a personal favor. Mr. Bramston 'loaned' you to us as our 'Development Associate.' And he generously paid your salary and that of the secretaries you brought along for three months. Then he insisted I put you all on my payroll."

"Gee, Tom, I didn't know about that."

You don't have a clue about more than that, you knothead, thought Tom.

"But it was sure generous of Mr. Bramston," Sam continued. "Did you know he and my dad were roommates at Harvard and that he's my godfather?"

The former, yes, the latter, no, but that explained a lot.

"Sam, I'm returning you and your crew to Bramston Real Estate today — we'll have to manage without you. I know it's been hard for you to fit in here — daily attendance, early hours — so you'll be happier back home with your godfather. Perhaps Mr. Bramston won't insist you come in as early as we require and you'll have more time for your squash matches and leisurely lunch every day. Tune up your game and you can probably reclaim that Racquet Club championship!"

Sam Spencer seemed mildly surprised. He should have been stunned. Tom figured Bramston's reaction would make up for his ward's subdued response.

"Oh, and Sam, Jo will give you a letter I've written to Mr. Bramston explaining everything. Just hand the sealed envelope to him."

Dear Wither,

Last night's meeting made a number of things clear to me. One, I need to begin immediately on my quest for twenty million bucks. Two, I must rid myself of any encumbrance that might get in my way to achieve that almost impossible goal.

Hence, I am returning the encumbrance you blessed me with two years ago.

I shall look forward to seeing Sam's name atop the New York squash rankings soon.

Sincerely,
Tom

Jo Wilson sat and watched Sam emerge from the head's office as though he didn't have a care in the world. Maybe he should. Maybe he would, later in the day. She liked what she saw in Tom that morning, even though two other school heads' secretaries had already told her that no head in New York had ever raised twenty million in six months from a standing start.

When Jo entered Tom's office, she found him staring into space. "Tom, what shall we call our fundraising position in *The Times* advertisement?"

Tom snapped to attention. "At the risk of alienating all those hired guns who invented their own comforting euphemism 'Vice President for Institutional Advancement,' let's go with that old-fashioned euphemism 'Director of Development.' It'll stick out like a sore thumb in *The Times* and the candidates will assume we're terribly out of it. Which I am."

"You don't want to try 'Chief Money Groveler'?"

"Wish we could, but now you're moving in on my dignity — I think that's what I'm supposed to do. Jo, I haven't forgotten what you taught me in my first year when all the other secretaries asked to be called 'administrative assistants.'"

"Oh, yes." Jo said. "I insisted on keeping the title I've had for thirty years. Now I'm proud to be the only 'secretary' on the payroll. Soon the linguistic police will rename the President's Secretary of State. I wonder how a visit from the 'President's Administrative Assistant of State' will play in London and Paris?"

CHAPTER 12

Jane Levi and her old Radcliffe roommate Sally Ernst, now a Metropolitan Museum curator, met for lunch at Sarabeth's once a week. Sally wore her usual gray suit with a black turtleneck and, after the board meeting, she was loaded for bear. They had to wait in line for ten minutes for a table and that was almost too much for her.

Jane noticed. "I've never seen you chew your nails before — tough day with the Vermeers?"

"Nothing to do with work. That's going well." Then silence from the nail biter, as Sally must have decided she couldn't spout in the line.

They were seated, ordered quickly without a menu, and Sally was off.

"It was my first CC board meeting and there are a lot of very heavy hitters on it who were very welcoming. I realized I have a lot to learn. Or not."

"Huh?" Jane leaned over the table.

"Well, I came away with the most god-awful feeling, Jane; I don't know what to say in my monthly report to the Parents' Association. Most parents read it to get some sense of school leadership and direction from it."

"Well, at least the mothers do," corrected Jane with a nod. "So, spill, I won't see Tom until late today."

"What I can't get over is that the school these men — I'm one of four women and none of us spoke — so it was only the men. Oh, and when this Wither Bramston finally ended the meeting he said, 'The ice is melting, *gentlemen*, adjourned.' I looked over at Meredith Ross and she said, 'Guess *we* aren't adjourned yet.' And I said, 'We'll simply have our own rump parliament — I certainly qualify!'" Sally looked flustered. "Where was I?"

"First, the nails, now confusion. What's next, old girl, hot flashes?"

Sally laughed.

"You were starting to say something about the school, the men . . ."

"Sorry, yes, the school these men described — that Robert Cattivo described — had no relationship to the school I have loved ever since Matt entered six years ago."

"Tell me more."

"The suits from Wall Street, led by Cattivo, looked determined, even organized, to bring Tom West down. Cattivo said the *Chronicle* was out of control, the students are hanging out in apartment lobbies smoking pot, Marxist teachers hate our parents' success. Oh, and that Tom made our most generous mommy cry — whoever that is — and that he thinks the Ivy League sucks."

"Well, I don't know about that other stuff, but how did Tom find out about our alma mater?"

"Please, Jane, I'm serious and damned angry. It was a nasty attack on his leadership. And I haven't heard anything from the parents or at the school about any of the charges Cattivo made. But then it transmogrified into an attack on Tom's fundraising and resulted in a motion based on a twenty million dollar bribe by Cattivo that we ought to sell places on the board for five million."

"Five million for a board seat? That's too cheap — Trump would double it."

"Jane, be serious."

"I can't be with this nonsense. Did you make this up?"

"And here's the real kicker: the only way the Episcopal Bishop of New York could blunt Cattivo's attack was to agree that Tom had to raise twenty million by the fall meeting."

"No way."

"Jane, if I and most of the other Jews on the board hadn't sided with the Bishop, Cattivo's motion to sell trustee seats would have passed. Believe me, everything was topsy-turvy. Just terrible."

"Sounds it." Jane took Sally's hand and squeezed. "And Jo told me before I came over that Tom fired Sam Spencer this morning."

"Barely know him. I did hear about two years ago that Spencer had been hired with a staff of two as the development officer to help Tom. But I've seldom seen anyone in that office."

"For good reason," Jane said. "He's usually at the Racquet Club with those other WASP stiffs on the board who don't lift a finger to help. Let's hope this means, against the odds, that Tom can get control of his predicament."

CHAPTER 13

Dean Levi arrived later at the head's office with a list of her student predicaments and her new laptop. "It's my Ultra Mobile Personal Computer, hasn't even been released officially, but Ben operated on a Samsung exec who hasn't forgotten."

"Will that thing put my laptop out on the street?"

"Maybe for five minutes. Until Apple strikes. Then this will be out there too."

Tom sighed. "I'll fill you in on my bloodletting at the board meeting when you finish. Sorry I couldn't get to you this morning."

"Jo told me you had a hectic morning. So I'll get right to my agenda." She checked her screen. "I've got the usual suspect teacher and a couple of other things. I'm going to the Student Court with that physics exam case this week; it looked airtight, but it's not."

"Dr. Lawlor again."

"Yes, our 'veteran' teacher continues to leave his exams out in the lab, or this time, as I found out, in the cafeteria, and then demands we find and punish any student who picks them up. Can you remind me why we keep him around?"

Tom smiled. "Two reasons: he is a good physics teacher."

"But not great. And that's only one reason."

"Two: it's impossible to find physics teachers."

"Too true."

Jane continued. "I'm watching a couple of new kids I mentioned at college night — Riccio and Cash. They're both suburban transfers with honors records, but they're having trouble with the work load."

Tom took notes on his laptop as she talked. "I liked their parents that evening."

"Good. Finally, I'm working on getting a spectator bus for the big game at Riverdale — our team will need all the help we can give them. And that's it from Sam." She tapped her screen.

"Why do you call that little thing, 'Sam'?"

"Because saying Samsung Ultra Mobile Personal Computer takes too long."

"I stand enlightened."

Their banter was important to both of them. Jane Morse Levi had been Tom's first hire and they really clicked. She was petite with black hair and sparkling, intelligent eyes. She was a striking woman, but had decided against "the nose job that would make me devastating." Tom agreed with her husband, surgeon Ben Levi, that she was perfect the way she was.

Most of the faculty trusted Jane, even though she was known to have the head's ear and, a few said, his heart. Jane was an unusual educator — a fine psychologist who had proven to be an excellent administrator. No Freudian overstuffed chaise covered with oriental carpet for Jane, but she did take a couple of cigar puffs with Tom and Ben after their dinners at home that sometimes followed the men's weekly squash match at the Harmonie Club.

Tom had one item for Jane. "Have you heard anything about Coach Worthington? In the girls' locker room?"

"Nope. And I try never to think ill of a winning coach. We only have one."

"That's the all-American approach — no questions asked unless there's a losing season."

"No, I really haven't heard anything. He runs a very tight ship. Who reported a concern?"

"Pam Pogrebin at the college evening. She said it was vague but she was unnerved by the tone of comments made by the girls in the back seat on the way up to the Rye tournament last weekend."

"Good mom, good judgment. I'll look into it." She tapped out a note and closed her notebook again. "That's it for Sam and me today. Except for that bloodletting you promised to fill me in on."

Tom told her about the board meeting.

"Boss, you've got to talk to Sally Ernst about this, bring her in, she could help. She's the elected head of the Parents' Association and she knows the parents."

"I've thought about it. I'm tempted. But should I be *using* the PTA president?

"Listen, buddy — nobody uses Sally Ernst."

CHAPTER 14

The bachelor Bishop lived simply on one floor of what was formerly the "Bishop's Palace" on the grounds of the Episcopal Cathedral near Columbia University. Twenty years before, he had given up three floors to found the St. John Choir School and the elementary school remained his greatest love. Tom knew it as the source of some of his faculty's favorite students. The Palace was situated in the Close with gigantic St. John the Divine rising alongside; it was very private and felt like a provincial English cathedral town. The Bishop knew he had to get involved down at Christ Church School, far beyond what he'd had time for previously. And since he loved showing off his cooking, he had invited his favorite headmaster up for dinner soon after the board meeting. He served Tom cottage pie in a small barrel vaulted dining room. The pie was perfect: ground sirloin and veggies in rich brown gravy that seeped through the crisp crust. Two Irish setters lay under the Tudor oak table and their weight settled gently against the men's feet.

Now as they moved from easy conversation about English rugby and American football, to the state of the school and the head's state in the school, Tom confessed, "I need your help, oh, do I need your advice."

"So, shoot."

Tom told the Bishop about Cattivo's threats in his office and the difficult meetings with Bramston and Philips.

"But there was more, Tom. What was all that about the school's 'most successful and generous mother' being reduced to tears by the mean headmaster'?"

As the Bishop heard the story of the Countess' visit, he asked questions and assembled his own picture of Cattivo's artful reordering of the facts. When Tom finished his narrative, the Bishop summed it up.

"Damnedest sin of omission I've ever heard — you won't alter a transcript!"

The stately Bishop chuckled and took a bite of Stilton and wheat biscuit followed by a sip of his 1994 Port. Heavenly.

Tom matched him.

"And what have you done since the board meeting?"

"Here's where I am: I returned Sam Spencer to sender and I have determined not to teach for the spring quarter."

The Bishop grinned approval.

"Oh, yes, I heard about the return of the Bramston prodigal well beyond his shelf life. I told his spluttering owner yesterday when he called that he'd have to deal with his own problem child and not shift it elsewhere." Another sip. Celestial. "As for not teaching — excellent — that should free you for planning and appointments at any time. Well done."

"Thanks. But I'm afraid I'm still afraid. Terrorized of failure."

"Good. You should be." The Bishop immediately decided that he could work with this man. "As a board member up at Yale, I had some experience with the kind of rash challenge Brother Cattivo laid before the CC trustees. I find it helpful to take an optimistic view of human nature at such times."

"Despite much evidence to the contrary?"

The Bishop smiled and nodded. "Precisely. But at Yale we could have worked it out. Instead, we swelled up with pride and horrification: 'Not on our sacred patch, parvenu.' In retrospect, we lost an opportunity to close the endowment gap with Harvard, which hasn't been guided by such Puritan scruples since the early eighteen hundreds."

"But at our meeting, you got Bramston to vote against selling trustee seats."

"Faint victory. And most likely temporary. Selling trustee seats *is* unseemly, but don't forget the excitement Cattivo generated among the Wall Streeters — all those rambunctious Ayn Rand disciples. He'll soon have the votes. Hence, to be kind to myself, I punted. More realistically, I bought time and put your neck on the block."

"Well, the boat was being swamped," Tom said.

"Yes, and as usual, we were without a captain, so Cruise Director Cattivo took charge."

They sipped slowly and watched the fire.

"Tom, I do want to defeat Cattivo's noxious plan," the Bishop continued. "I confess that I arranged a pact with the devil at that meeting. And it wasn't my first, truth be told. But I like to think it was my version of Jesus' advice to be 'wise as serpents and innocent as doves.' I promise I'll give you names for your campaign and help in any way I can." He paused and sipped. "I'd also like you to meet a CC alumna whom I've depended on for years — Lulu Thorndike Leonard. I've got ten years on her, but I still remember her as the smartest debutante in years. She had a meteoric career as a reporter with the old *Herald-Tribune* before she married Leonard and she's still dynamite. Knows everybody and their secrets, from the bartender at the Carlyle to the oldest Beekman Place socialite. I'll call her."

The Bishop recharged their glasses, then stirred the fire and himself. "It's a fine art — this lifting the purses of the impious — and it can't be a success if you follow St. Paul's warning to his young acolyte Timothy to avoid 'filthy lucre.' Money-grubbing is truly a jealous mistress, and more significantly, an addictive enterprise. My warning to you is that if you avoid a seared conscience *and* the money-grubbing addiction, you'll be a failure as a fundraiser and lose your job. So, you see my exhortation to you isn't uniformly cheery, except to remind you that both my battle-seared conscience and money-grubbing addiction have provided opportunities for thousands of Harlem kids to attend this choir school over the years and have a decent chance in life."

The Bishop saw Tom shift uneasily and drain his glass.

"Now let me help you gird your loins for your fund-raising mission." The Bishop placed a neatly-typed three-by-five index card in front of Tom. "For you. I keep a card like this at hand — remember, expiation *may* come later, but this will get you through the present sin-filled day."

Great ideas enter into reality with evil associates and with disgusting alliances. But the greatness remains, nerving the race in its slow ascent. Alfred North Whitehead

Tom reviewed the evening in the taxi home. He loved the crackling fire, the smell of beef and ale and dog, and the talk of rugby. He hadn't wanted the visit to end. It was the best part of Tom's brave new world, and he wished the other parts of the trustees' world could match it. And yet the Bishop's days were not spent in that cozy dining nook. In fact, Whitehead's world was Machiavelli's world. Could Tom ever make it *his* world?

At law school, he couldn't buy into the bromide that the Anglo-American adversarial justice system was properly balanced. It was obvious to him that justice depended on access to legal talent and that all lawyers were not created equal, or more precisely, the purses of their clients weren't. So, he had retreated into the groves of academe to pursue a cleaner career. He took a history doctorate and his research and teaching about the past kept him free from contemporary ethical stress. Then he moved into administration. Now, dreaming of actually offering excellence to both the disadvantaged and advantaged by raising lots of money, well, he'd finally have to take the dicey plunge. And the Bishop had sounded a lot like his least favorite trustee.

"Life is made up of these little compromises," the Great Cattivo had once lectured him. "We all have to do our part to keep the mortal ball rolling."

CHAPTER 15

Sally knew that Jane had practically pushed Tom into this jogging date, if that's what it was. When Tom couldn't find time to meet with her on Thursday or Friday at the office, Jane had prompted him to ask Sally if he could run with her on Sunday. Sally ran four or five times a week and had seen the head jogging on the weekends. She wasn't sure that this would be much of a workout for her.

"Oh, this feels good," Sally said as she moved into step with Tom and they headed south on the drive behind the Metropolitan Museum.

"Yeah," he said. "S'wonderful." His mouth sounded parched. Probably still coming to grips with how a woman five inches shorter could comfortably match his running stride.

"Good idea, Tom. And I'd do anything to get a free breakfast at Sarabeth's."

"Yeah, but the deal is," said Tom, already breathless, "you have to finish the run in the same county as me."

Sally slowed and checked him out. "Do you mind if I get down to business?"

Tom looked surprised. He probably couldn't believe the diplomatic CC mother-in-chief was being so blunt.

Before he could respond, she said, "I know Mr. Cattivo was cherry-picking his parents; his examples didn't represent the parent body I know."

"But the other trustees don't know that."

"No. And they showed their ignorance and passivity in so many ways I don't know where to begin. Did his charge that you alienated parents ring a bell?"

"Guess so, yes. Seventh-grade parents unhappy with their kids' grades. The conflict happened, but I offered the proper Ivy percentage and corrected their H-Y-P fixation. A little pointedly, I admit."

She chuckled. "I'll bet you did!"

They gained quickly on a black Central Park carriage, its tall back wheels edged in red and a manure bucket swinging at the back axle. The rig was plumed with red feathers and pulled by an aging white horse that Sally noticed wasn't very white. The animated young driver, sitting high on his bench seat and wearing an oversize top hat propped by turned-down ears, swung around frequently to relate the wonders of New York to two goggle-eyed, graying couples.

They passed it on either side and came back together.

"But you saw how far I got at the meeting. Bob made the charges, then Bramston shut me down."

"And I found it all a little too pat," said Sally. "No, really a conspiracy — Bramston's 'Where's this all leading, Bob?' sounded like a straight line for the righteous crusader. It also sounded like what I've heard about our Metropolitan Museum's trustees invading the director's office in the nineteen-eighties."

"Tell me about it."

"The way I heard it, the trustees took over management and finances from the professional director. And next thing you know, the trustees started questioning curators' artistic judgment. Well, it was a disaster, and the running of the museum was finally returned to the director, after some juicy news coverage."

"I'll google it."

They moved past the large green boathouse that housed an armada of rental rowboats and began their long curve south and west with the Plaza Hotel on their left. Soon they were running parallel to Central Park South, the sun glinting in sparkling asterisks off the new hotel at Columbus Circle. She was really pushing it.

"Sally, talk, so I can keep up," Tom said tightly. "Such as where'd you get that old St. Louis Browns cap."

Sally talked. She explained how her immigrant father believed that feigning interest in baseball would make him seem more American. But while he suffered with the sport, what he called "its indeterminate length and determinate boredom," his daughter got hooked. She wanted to be loyal to the old Brooklyn Bums. But that train had pulled out, so she switched to the old St. Louis Browns.

"Why them?"

"An interred team couldn't break my heart."

"I'm not sure of that proposition. Ask any Cubs fan."

Sally laughed with resonance, but felt herself pulling away from her son's favorite teacher. Slow down, idiot, she lectured herself, his tongue's hanging out.

"Jane filled me in on Sam Spencer. So, how goes your search?"

"I've already got fifty resumes — all experienced hot shots and we can't afford any of them. You don't happen to know a brilliant young fundraiser, do you?"

"Curators don't get involved very often with our fundraisers," she said, slowing her pace. "But hold on, there's a younger guy at the Met who impresses me a lot — Jay Erickson. Well down their totem pole but a comer, according to everyone. And probably more within your budget."

"Well, we paid Sam Spencer top dollar at his age and only got reports on his squash ranking. His prospects were all friends of his father and Wither Bramston from the Brook or Racquet Clubs."

"How did they turn out?"

"Worthless — I've spent two years finding out that they had little connection with CC. I think Sam 'developed' the list over a third martini at daddy's club."

By the time they turned north on West Drive and labored up the rise to the Tavern on the Green, Tom looked wet and strained. He appeared to recover his wind at the Bowling Green plateau; there, they saw a flotilla of senior ladies in white uniform — broad-brimmed hats, severe blouses, long skirts, and soft shoes — flow over the billiard-table turf, chatting intently as they played.

The wide stretch of asphalt at Seventy-Second Street was being invaded by daddies carrying a few *Times* sections and pushing their wriggling toddlers in strollers, by children on little pink and blue training bikes, and by an occasional rollerblader testing his technique, sometimes requiring a narrow escape through the moving mass. There was also a flow of tourists from Central Park West who gaped at the Dakota apartment house and stopped at Strawberry Fields, the John Lennon memorial. Sally slowed again and looked at Tom.

"I'll get you something on Jay Erickson. I know he studied art history at Princeton — we've talked. I like him very much. I think you will, too."

"Know anything more about his life?"

"Only that he grew up in Minneapolis and loves Scott Fitzgerald. That's why he went to Princeton. And his colleagues joke that despite working harder than anyone else in that office, he's still popular."

Sally regained her pace on the stretch along the boating lake and Tom did his best to hang with her. They worked their way up the long rise at Ninetieth near the bridle path by the reservoir. A few horsewomen dominated that chewed up surface, scattering city slickers frightened by the four-legged monsters.

They ran silently for a few minutes until Tom couldn't hide it any longer — she was running him into the ground. He gasped, held his chest, and she relented. He finally confessed he was proud that he hadn't barfed all over his sneakers.

"You mean that unless they ask for time to think about it, I haven't asked for enough?"

"Yes. At least at the Met."

Fueled up on Jo Wilson's espresso, Director of Development Jay Erickson was finishing the last of his tutorials for Tom. It had been ninety minutes a day for two weeks while Erickson was hiring a secretary and setting up his office. Tom was pleased to see that Jay was a fellow coffee addict and even more pleased with his intelligence and work ethic.

"I'd have thought that if I give a number that correlates closely with what they might have been thinking of giving, well, wouldn't they be impressed that we've done our homework?"

"Not 'impressed.' I'd say relieved, but hardly flattered. And here's why: the self-described New York mover and shaker doesn't mind that the guy asking has overestimated his worth or power, that is, his capacity to control the world with his bucks."

Tom shook his head. "I'm afraid I understand. Where do I start?"

"I'm working on that. You know that I've finished interviewing all the board members who were available the last two weeks. But, I've come across something that shocked me."

"Let's hear it." Tom turned to his laptop.

"First, the good news. As you know, most of your trustees are tops in their fields, very impressive. And they were all very gracious to me, all agreed endowment is long overdue and some gave me solid leads. Oddly, not a word about Spencer — two of them had never met him."

"I'm not surprised. But what shocked you?"

"That's under the 'bad news': Mr. Bramston and fully half of the trustees did not give a penny last year to the school. Not a sou."

"And I asked every one of them," said Tom. "I knew the trustee percentage was about fifty percent, but the parents were at ninety-five percent. I certainly didn't publicize the trustee figure — it would be deadly if the parents knew."

"It may be a world record. In Bramston's defense, he did seem vaguely concerned about that, and he assured me he *had* donated to the new residence hall at Harvard." Erickson made a face. "Pure Bramston," said Tom. "And that guy has served as an example for the others. When he welcomed several new trustees onto the board last year, I heard him assure them over drinks that no one would pester them for money."

"Well, his going AWOL has created a power vacuum on the board, it seems to me," said Erickson. "And Mr. Cattivo has moved in. Wow! That guy is carrying the whole board. He gave me the most graphic description of what he has done, or given, and what he expects in return. He seemed to like me, said he likes folks from St. Paul and that he didn't trust New Yorkers much. That I might see some Scott Fitzgerald in him. I guess I looked puzzled, so he said, 'You know, *The Great Gatsby*.'" Jay shook his head in puzzlement. "Tom, he is either the most brutally candid or most duplicitous man I've ever met."

Their eyes met and Tom spoke. "Would you settle for both?"

CHAPTER 16

The Great Gatsby himself invited Tom to what he termed a lunch "to celebrate your New England magic." Tom was mystified by that and, although reluctant to spend time with his attacker, his curiosity won out. Cattivo's hot and cold attitude seemed to be influenced more by the vagaries of his southern property developments than by his burning desire to bring Tom down. Or so the head preferred to think. And this "magic" business must be good news. At least he could hope that it meant that the entrepreneur wanted to bury the hatchet he had poised over the head's neck.

Cattivo welcomed him warmly at the Four Seasons. After the inevitable banter about the Yankees' prospects and the latest Splendid Properties' success in landing promising mall acreage in Jacksonville, Cattivo took control as the Dover sole was served. "I called it your 'New England magic' on the phone and I meant it, Tom. I wanted to thank you for fixing the Countess Serena's daughter up at boarding school. You finally got that right. So, you can continue to play your innocent little games, my friend, but never underestimate the wisdom of the finagle factor in human relations."

Tom had to admit the little dynamo cut quite a figure. Cattivo had remarkably black hair, blown dry and swept back from his retreating widow's peak; tiny, close-set pin-point eyes under bushy gray brows; a smoothly-shaven ferret face. And his usual expression reminded Tom of the snarling stuffed wolf he'd seen in Bob's office under his Louis XV gilt desk.

"Bob, I can tell you in all honesty, I didn't do anything for the Countess that I wouldn't do for any CC family." Tom saw instant doubt.

"Really. Still in denial, eh? You'll learn that life will be a lot easier when you grow up and take credit for your necessary shenanigans. You see, the Countess Serena told me that the headmistress up there was *ve-ry* helpful, said you'd called to introduce the family, and I know what that means."

Poor Cattivo couldn't allow for the possibility of integrity in humans — he made everything into an insincere power game featuring flying shit, where the winner had the biggest fan. CC seldom had kids transfer to boarding schools because, as Cat Balewe explained in the hallway one day when her mother was pressing her on the subject, "I'd much rather be in Manhattan on Saturday night than in East Earmuff, New England." In the rare cases he had such transfers, Tom always called the prospective school to ask if he could be helpful. The headmistress of Miss Jessups confessed she would kill to get a new gym because girls' schools had to compete with the former boys' schools, now coed, that were jock-heavy. "Tom, I would welcome the von Konigsberg daughter and the family generosity, no questions asked."

The headmistress followed up with a call to inform him that after Natasha's acceptance, the Countess had immediately pledged the first two million dollars toward the school's proposed field house. The school head admitted that her only concern was how they would fit the full Serenissima Leonhard von Konigsberg name over the entrance.

CHAPTER 17

The Bishop made good on his promise to bring Mrs. Lulu Leonard into Tom's fundraising scheme when he asked them both to dinner at the Union Club. Tom saw that she was the original bright-eyed, indefinably aged package of dynamite the Bishop had described. She launched in with little preamble as soon as her specified "Gordon's gin, up, please hold that dreadful vermouth and fruit — they muddy the juniper" was served. She and the Bishop sat together on the yellow and cream love seat and sipped their identical martinis in unison. Quite a pair.

"Ah, I'm revived. Only takes a sip."

"Really? A single sip?" said the Bishop.

"Oh, perhaps fifteen or so, Mr. Literal. But I never gulp . . . like you do."

A good time was had by all and when prompted by the Bishop, Tom told Mrs. Leonard of his challenges. She was particularly interested and questioned him at length about the *Chronicle's* legal threat. At the end of the three-cornered discussion, she turned to the headmaster. "Now, Tom, I do read your column in the alumni newsletter and I'm still in touch with many of my Christ Church classmates. But I confess I haven't done a blessed thing for CC since I graduated."

"Sinful," said the Bishop. "And why is that, Lu?"

"Because no one asked me."

"May I be the first to ask?" said Tom.

"You may. And you'll no doubt be the last, given my age." She looked him over. "I accept."

Later that week on a gusty, gray March afternoon Tom drove eighty miles to Dutchess County to have tea with Mrs. Leonard. The sudden invitation meant that he would miss two classroom observations, a faculty meeting, and the big baseball game with Collegiate. Lulu's estate on the Hudson contrasted greatly with its northerly neighbor, the Vanderbilt mimic of some European pile. Her native flagstone house had been built by her former husband, the creator of a weekly news magazine. Tom was reminded by her ex's memorabilia around the house of the twentieth-century Yale trinity: Leonard, who gave the world a quick news fix; Robert Hutchins, who promoted the Great Books culture fix; and William Benton, whose gift was Muzak, the first elevator fix. Tom reckoned they were Yale's answer to the earlier Harvard trio of Walter Lippman, John Dos Passos, and T.S. Eliot.

Mrs. Leonard lived a comfortable life "in the river boonies," as she put it, mixing her golfing and hiking along the Hudson with frequent trips into the city for music, art, and her considerable philanthropy. She had a thin nose with delicate, transparent nostrils, trusting gray-blue eyes, and a large mouth, primed for sardonic action. She wore her salt and pepper hair in a natural, curly frizz. Although she had worn a striking blue cashmere dress in the city, here she combined a smart Davidow gray heather wool suit with stout English walking shoes. They sat before a large native stone fireplace with snapping logs; a gray-garbed maid and two snoozing golden retrievers with worn leather collars completed the scene. She served Tom loose Fortnum & Mason tea from a gigantic silver service and was especially proud of her cook, Nellie, who could prepare rimless, tasteless watercress sandwiches with the best. She was also proud of her perennial borders, but she feared the accursed phlox mold would be back again. Thus prompted, he began to describe his courtyard city garden in detail. Perhaps too much detail, because she broke in.

"I'll look forward to seeing your garden, but as I have a late tee-time and think I can get in nine holes, let's get right to work, Tom."

The Bishop had warned him that nothing came between Lulu Leonard and her golf.

"Now, since I've already addressed you as 'Tom,' you must call me 'Lulu.' No exceptions; it's pure selfishness on my part, makes me feel younger."

"Do you mind if I take notes on my laptop?"

"Not a'tall, I must look into that myself. Now, I should fill you in that the Bishop 'saved' me when I was lost years ago after my divorce. He has been my pastor and friend for years now; as a result, I owe him mightily and I'd like to help you get on with your job. And that includes keeping it, if what he tells me is correct. That job seems to be 'lifting the purses of the impious,' as our dear Bishop likes to say. I prefer to call it 'social engineering,' a healthy redistribution of wealth, which, when you come down to it, is what the impious Buffet and Gates and the others are finally up to."

She rose easily and went to an antique secretary near a bay window looking out to her daffodil-laden lawn. She brought him a purple folder that she opened on the coffee table in front of him. It was stuffed with twenty or more sheets of closely written notes on prospects. Tom noted that the list was in alphabetical order and was buttressed with clippings. "I've been working on these prospects all week. I wanted your driving up here to be worth your time."

Tom was overwhelmed. "This is wonderful. So detailed. Thank you."

"This file alone should keep you busy for a month or so — you will note that I've called or written about twenty of the top prospects and have included their affirmative responses. By 'affirmative' I mean they will see you, mostly at their clubs, I suspect. Don't hesitate to call me and let me in on how it goes — I do much prefer that to these impersonal emails so much the rage. And a word to the wise: don't use email with any of these prospects unless they invite it. And then only sparingly. A handwritten note is always appreciated, I find."

"Thanks for the advice. I'll be in touch. Much of this is new to me, you understand."

"So, the Bishop told me, but that's really a point of honor — this modern money-grubbing world is too much with us sometimes. You'll understandably be a bit hesitant to barge into these lives. Don't be. Tell them I insisted you meet them. Every one of these people owes me or the Bishop for favors real and imagined. And don't forget, as the headmaster of the hottest school in town, *you* also have some favors people might like to try on."

Tom managed a weak grin.

"Now, let me tell you a bit about these Manhattan clubs where you'll be 'soliciting,' sometimes with me, if you'd like. You'll be at the Union, the Knickerbocker, and the River — there are others, not many — all with nuanced social foundings that have not survived economic changes. So, they're all meant, and thought, to be 'exclusive,' but 'exclusive' is a fungible concept, rather easily replaced at times in our fair city with *money*. But, mind you, because these are proper clubs," she raised her forefinger at him and finished by beating to every syllable, "only when there are heaps of it."

She saw that Tom tried to stifle his laughter, so she guffawed until she shook him loose.

"You'll have to keep in mind, Tom, that we all are insecure and need reinforcement — talent and diligence are never enough, even for those most gifted and successful. Much of New York's history has been written by those who have made it and then banded together in clubs, churches, synagogues, and political parties to protect their piles and social preserves."

Lulu paused for a tea break. Tom joined her and they both smiled over their cups. "I'm long-winded on this because I've tried to think clearly about what I do. Now, all of this protective banding together, you might say it has amounted to an abhorrence by third-generation parvenus of first-generation parvenus. It didn't take rich New York families who had already 'arrived' long to forget Cornelius Vanderbilt's ferryman's language and culture even as they recoiled from New York's even newer money — the kind realized from Rockefeller oil monopolies in Ohio and from Carnegie steel efficiencies in Pittsburgh. But the leading families met the richest enemies and included them — but only after the crucial generation or so had passed that allowed the newcomers to clean up their language, be very generous to widows, orphans, and museum directors, and stop spitting on the floor. And you, representing a school that tries to be pluralistic, much as the Bishop has, will be playing both sides of that divide. Good luck, you'll need it!"

Tom felt that he had sat at the feet of one of the wisest people he had ever met. No wonder Lulu and the Bishop were so close.

Within weeks, Tom saw that Lulu had nailed the clubs he visited when she had instructed, "You'll find that their interiors and patrons are all understated, with the exception of the martinis. All our clubs have excellent martinis — practice makes perfect." The drinks period before dinner lasted forever with outsize wedges of tasteless, chilly domestic cheese hacked at and put on treated grain that belonged in a cereal box, or as part of the box. But Tom finally figured out that the fluidal ritual was merciful — conversation came easily and one couldn't taste the overcooked meat and veggies later.

CHAPTER 18

Tom slipped into an English II class at the beginning of the period. He tried to visit several teachers a week — it was important for him to see every teacher in action at least twice a year. His visits were not universally welcomed, although he liked to believe they were. Those who viewed him as the invader were most adamant that he was Capital and Management, and they were the valued workers who were exploited. It remained a sore point with Tom — how to reconcile his fading Marxism with his living autocracy. After he made two more teacher observations, he headed for his own class. He'd better make the most of it, as he'd soon be out of the classroom with his full-time money raising.

For the next fifty minutes, Tom was in his favorite world teaching his

Western Civ class. He sometimes had grave doubts about whether he knew what he was doing as an administrator and what he was becoming. The conscience-sapping glad-handing of the good, the bad, and the ugly, the superficial relationships with thousands of parents, trustees, alumni, and far too often with students and teachers plus anxiety's bile because of Cattivo's attacks, well, it all left him questioning himself and his new world. But in Room 112 he was safe: fifteen students, Erasmus' *Praise of Folly*, and him. At the least, a retreat, at its best, a paradise.

Tom knew that teaching didn't consist of dramatic breakthroughs every day; no, it was one of daily integers of inquiry and learning, of mixed success and cumulative effect. "Be patient with yourself," he told younger teachers. "We teach for the ages."

As Tom left his classroom, he shook his head in wonder — what a great racket! He actually got paid to visit these teachers and teach these kids. But in the new term he wouldn't have time to do either.

Tom stepped carefully over the legs of students seated in front of their lockers, the boys and girls flirting while trying to give the appearance of studying. At one point, he was blockaded by the legs of several lanky juniors.

"None shall pass!" boomed a voice.

"I have no quarrel with you, good sir knight," Tom pleaded, "but I must cross this bridge."

"He's finally got it," said the Black Knight.

"Yeah, but it's taken him years for that one line," said another.

Laughter, derisive and approving, as the legs were pulled back. Tom had been challenged and passed by the Grand Vizier of the Monty Python Club, all six-two of him from size thirteens to gulping Adam's apple, red-tipped ears, and brown cowlick. Tom recognized his own spitting image at that age.

CHAPTER 19

That afternoon, Tom nearly dropped his cell phone when he remembered to turn it on and saw that he had a message from the Countess, Serena von Konigsberg. Foreign number. His mind raced.

Betsy's death in Chicago had been over ten years ago and no woman since had come close to inhabiting his heart. Not that he hadn't tried. He found the women of New York and Washington both interesting and willing. But nothing permanent developed, as none appeared to be a keeper or considered him one, although some remained friends. Then the English interloper slid into view — a powerful New York designer and Christ Church mother.

It was in August last year that the Countess "popped in" to meet Tom and ask him to thank the teachers for her son Chris's education at CC. She told him how happy Chris was at his new boarding school, but didn't even mention her daughter Natasha, who was still at CC. She wore a simple yellow summer frock with a pleated placket that swelled more than de la Renta likely intended. She had a flawless peaches-and-cream complexion, aquiline nose, and thick raven hair parted off-center and held with a thin blue band to accent her eyes. She appeared to be the typical English rosebud who took a degree at the Sorbonne.

She said, "I can't spend much time with Chris, but it's always quality family time."

"Yes," Tom wanted to say. "Just like Michelangelo's *Pieta* at St. Peter's — now, *that* was quality family time." He was sick to death of the buzzwords to cover absent parenting. "Parenting?" That was another word he'd had enough of.

"I'm afraid," Serena continued, "he's become too much a Mummy's boy, so I reckoned a boarding school would sort him out. His father says he was much like Chris at the same age. The Count is a superlative person and provider and would do anything for Chris and me. And yet, parenthood's not the most efficient way to sort out your gender preference, is it?"

The vulnerable Ms. Konigsberg definitely had Tom's sympathy. She had shipped Chris off to a New England boarding school — the richest school in America — renowned not for its academics as much as for its historical service to nineteenth century robber barons' progeny, helping them cover their fathers' tracks with artistic and charitable philanthropy.

Soon after her memorable appearance at his office, an embossed invitation to Serena's post-Labor Day dinner party arrived. She had scribbled on it, "Be my date, Dr. West. I've got uneven numbers. Please!"

Serena greeted him that evening with the perfect balance of warmth and distance. The previously well-wrapped, demure mother was stunning in her sheer black chiffon hostess pajamas, her tiny bare feet in mirror strapped and heeled sandals. He had arrived early, as requested, to set up the bar. She tied a Harvey Nichols apron around him and launched him with a gentle pat on the ass. She did her own cooking with the help of her housekeeper, and her chauffeur served the oysters, luscious fillet, Parma potatoes, and trifle.

Tom enjoyed the party immensely because nobody asked him about a pending admission to Christ Church, and that was a first. Serena was breathtaking — warm and funny and completely in control. She did hover over him a bit and took his hand several times as though they were on familiar terms.

It seemed natural when she asked him to stay for "a thank you nightcap." She handed him a snifter and motioned him to the Mies settee.

He sniffed. "What's this?"

"An old Armagnac. I think it's more rustic than cognac."

"Oh, very nice . . . I see what you mean. And that?" Tom pointed to a painting, figuring he might as well lay it on the line. He had no idea who the artist was.

"A Derain — my father gave it to me for my sixteenth birthday." Tom must have looked puzzled. "Derain's Fauvist period." Oh, that helped a lot.

"And the music? *The Lady Killers?*"

"*Exactement.* Cherubini's Quintet." She pronounced it Kayrubini.

He was on his second snifter when the chauffeur left and the house-keeper went to bed. Tom was fascinated by the conversation, but soon lost his concentration when Serena stroked the back of his hand as it rested on the caramel leather between them. It was one of the most erotic rubbings he'd ever received. He told her so. It seemed the honorable thing to do and his third brandy insisted.

"Ah, then I didn't spend my schoolgirl years doing those brass grave-stone rubbings in vain."

He took her hand and followed the tendons to the wrist with light kisses. He pushed her sleeve up. "Ah, a female bicep — one of my favorites!"

She sank against him and giggled.

"What's so funny?"

"I'm very ticklish. And I remembered one of my father's favorite jokes — my mother hated it. What's English foreplay?"

"I give. What *is* English foreplay?"

"Forty-five minutes of begging."

They both giggled. He whispered into her left ear, "But I can't wait that long and your mascara is running."

They soon decided that Mies' severe design had its limits for their in-tentions and moved to her bedroom, which featured melancholic and spare streetscapes. She didn't bother identifying them and he didn't bother ask-ing until breakfast. They were Utrillos.

As always, a Serena memory brought Tom consternation and confused longing.

He wiped his sweating hand on his corduroys and tried to stop gripping his cell phone so tightly as he returned her call. "Serena? What are you doing in Argentina?"

"Saving rain forests. What else?"

"It was polar bears at Christmas. Are you trying to succeed Eva Perón down there?"

"Funny boy. I made a gift to the Rainforest Council and they invited me down."

"Aren't the rain forests in Brazil?"

"A technicality. I'm staying with a friend outside Buenos Aires. He's a leader in the Rainforest Council and an international polo player."

"What does he do for a living when he's home?"

"Not does. Did. He chose his grandparents ve-ry carefully, as I did, silly Ohio Hoosier boy."

He couldn't bring himself to correct her. He just wanted off the phone.

"So, Tommy, I wanted to ring and tell you thanks for that transaction at Miss Jessups. Natasha is thrilled."

"You're welcome, but your Robert Cattivo already thanked me."

"Really? I didn't ask pops to do that. Guess he thinks he can buy anything."

Yes, and there's a lot of that going around, thought the Ohio Buckeye boy.

"Now let me get to why I really rang."

Yeah, let's. "Go ahead."

"Dear Tom, could you, *would* you, take care of Chris during his boarding school March holiday? See, I can't get loose from this rainforest conference."

Tom closed his eyes. Perhaps if he waited long enough he would think of something to say.

"Pretty please. My housekeeper rang — she has pneumonia. I simply must keep Chris away from that. Darling, he has nowhere else to go. Otherwise, he'll be out in the cold."

At last, he thought of something. "No, Serena, no. You come home and be mommy — he's a wonderful, witty boy." Crap, now I'm trying to sell her son to her.

"Tom, he worships you."

The worship-worthy headmaster didn't peep.

"OK, I give. I was going to tell you anyway and simply forgot — I've already played the generous mommy at Miss Jessups. And I'll match that for CC. Two million."

Oh, no. Now you've put a price on your son's head. And on mine. He couldn't think of a proper response.

"I said I was going to tell you anyway. You tell me when, Tommy."

"Thank you for telling me anyway — I'll send you a pledge form. Now, come home and be Chris' mommy. He'd love it."

He heard the muffled sobs, then, "You'll break his little heart, Tom, you will. He's counting on *you*. He said so, earlier today."

"God, Serena, you didn't promise him again before checking with me. Did you?"

CHAPTER 20

This was not going to be easy, thought Cattivo, as he and his deuce of conspirators settled around the club game table two days after the trustee meeting. He had already reamed Bramston out, asking him on the phone the day after the trustee meeting how he would feel if Cattivo canceled thirty percent of his total management income. He told him that's how he'd felt when Wither voted with the Bishop against him.

From Wither's hangdog face that afternoon, the message had been received. It was unclear from the Rev's expression what message, if any, he had received. So, Cattivo began his narrative of what had happened to him at school the day before. He gave a brief sketch of how Tom, the Bishop, and Meredith Ross had pulled the rug out from under his attempt to gain access to school personnel files the day before.

"So, gentlemen, I guess I have to announce a rare setback."

"A 'rare setback' announced over my Rare Breed, you might say," said the Reverend Dr. Philips, holding his tumbler aloft. He smiled proudly at his two companions.

Yes, *you* might. I certainly wouldn't, thought Cattivo. But he said, "Oh, that's good. And so true. You know, Wither, we really should join our witty colonel in his favorite Southern whiskey one of these days!"

"At my age, that Kentucky firewater would have me dozing off," said Wither Bramston.

"And I'd be drinking out of the spittoons," added Cattivo. They all had a belly laugh, and Cattivo was aware that Philips' effort lasted the longest. Okay boys, time for business.

Cattivo continued, "But we can't laugh off the cowardly way that the Bishop and Ms. Ross gave in to our illustrious headmaster when push came to my shove."

"You reckon Ross and the Bishop got together with Tom, or maybe the other way around, before the Bishop rang you to say that they agreed with Tom after all?" asked Philips through squinting, wary eyes.

"Maybe, Richie. No, probably," said Cattivo, trying to sort the grammar.

"Why, that's a damned conspiracy, Bob. At least where I come from. Where one's word still counts for something."

"They almost admitted it to me," said Bramston. "When he telephoned, the Bishop said that we had all gone too far in the Executive Committee, and that Ross never thought Bob meant to raid school offices unless Tom approved."

The two looked at Cattivo, who responded. "I may have been a little hasty, but based on that resolution, I had the right — remember, you all gave it to me — so I walked in there and told the assistant behind the counter, or whoever was guarding the central records, some kid, who I was and to please hand over the teacher evaluation files. Well, she refused. And that was that."

Philips drained his glass. Cattivo signaled. The barman got busy. But not soon enough. The Reverend Doctor had nothing to occupy him, so he looked more confused than usual and probed while he awaited his drink. "But I don't get how the Bishop and Ross got involved. What really happened during 'that was that'?" Christ. Cattivo hadn't wanted to go into all that. He pulled out his Phi Bete key and fiddled with it.

"Nothing much. The kid looked flustered, said she'd have to ask her boss.

I thought she meant Tom, but she called the 'Registrar.'" Cattivo gestured the word with crooked forefingers. "Then out from the lair came a coarse creature of the female variety, I think." He paused for Phillip's chortle and got it. "I had to repeat my spiel — hell, you'd think I was asking for a priceless piece of school property. And she said she'd have to call *her* boss, which she did, and came back to tell me that, 'Doctor West doesn't know anything about this business. And said no one should have access, even you, without the head's written authorization.'"

"'Of course he doesn't know,' I told her carefully, 'because he isn't on the highest policy-making body of the school — that's the Executive Committee of the Christ Church Episcopal School Board of Trustees chartered in the Province of New York under Royal Charter a hell of a long time ago.'"

"Bravo, well said," said Bramston.

"But the fat gal said, 'No way, José.'"

"Why, that's outrageous," said Bramston.

"No respect anymore," said Philips, shaking his sad head. "The very idea of calling you a wetback."

The Rev's remark puzzled Cattivo for a moment, but he recovered. "It did tick me off, so I moved right over to the file cabinets behind the counter and began to read the labels. There it was in the second row — 'Personnel. Faculty.' I tried to pull it open. Saw it had two locks on it. Fatty gloated. Until I saw that the assistant whatever had left the next cabinet ajar. I reached to pull it open further and Fatty slapped my hands!"

"So, whadya do, Bob, whadya do?" The Rev was on the edge of his chair and hadn't even started his drink.

"I looked around and there was a crowd of biddies gathering and that Dean Levi coming way down the hall. I said something diplomatic and escaped."

"Good for you," said Philips, enumerating on his fingers. "So, that's when Levi called West who called the Bishop who called Ross who agreed Wither here should be called to tell him they changed their minds and to call Bob off."

Jesus, thought Cattivo, he pulled off a riff that John Cleese would be proud of – four pudgy digits and a thumb's worth. More exercise than he's had all week. Explaining his minor setback to nosey Richie Philips and pansy Wither Bramston was putting him in a foul mood.

"So I had Meredith Ross to lunch yesterday. Ate so much crow she felt sorry for me, and then I hit her with the Cattivo-Ross Real World Summer Internships at CC. The kids we choose will get real-world experience in my firm or hers. If she goes along with me. Needs a week to check it out. But Meredith sounded very excited by the possibility of working with the students. Thinks the parents would love it, which is why I came up with it. I could use some parent allies against Tom West. Maybe you two could think about current parents you know and float this possibility with them — you can make it work."

CHAPTER 21

Tom knew that faculty meetings in late winter were the worst. The elements finally triumphed over the assertive, optimistic New York spirit. The wet and chill winter had taken its toll. On the streets, plows pushed a late snowfall to the curbs and the gutters brimmed with an icy mix of something that could have been artichoke margaritas. The snow remained in Central Park, but near the sidewalks it was shot through with trailings of dog urine so plentiful that Manhattan children assumed snow came in two flavors.

Tom expected the faculty to be fed up this time of year — with the weather, the students, parents' demands, their salaries, each other, and themselves. A late afternoon faculty meeting offered an opportunity to vent. Faculty meetings before March break were to be avoided, but this one was necessary — a number of juniors were going off the rails.

Jo came into his office. "Dennis Warren is outside again and would very much like to see you before the faculty meeting."

Tom looked up from dialing a return phone call to Bob Cattivo's office. No time for the call. Thank God. "How does he look today?"

"Worse than ever. No, I take that back. He's about as bad as October but better than December — though more like last spring when he disappeared." Jo paused to catch up with herself. "I think you'd better see him."

Dennis stepped pigeon-toed into the room in battered brown Weejuns, his face gray and lined. His willowy figure was hunched and listed to the left. He wore a limp sport jacket and a blue button-down shirt with the tie knotted a good inch below and off-center of the tightly buttoned top. This from a guy who had taken surprising pride in his Christmas job — clerking at Brooks Brothers.

Dennis Calvin Warren had grown up in Africa with Presbyterian missionary parents. He had taken Yale honors degrees in classics and had become a masterly teacher, even as the students privately and affectionately termed him "the African Queen." But during the past few years Dennis had been noteworthy for unexplained absences several times, and parents had reported he had been seen sitting unsteadily on a park bench off Central Park West. The previous administration had let the situation fester and passed the shell of a man on to Tom. Dennis had rallied under Tom's initial tending, but in the last year he had become increasingly irascible and threatening with his students. Early in the current academic year there were frequent rumors of his striking students who were slow with their conjugations. It was during Tom's investigation of a rash of hitting incidents in January that Dennis resigned, effective at the end of the year.

Dennis apologized in his high-pitched, plaintive voice about taking Tom's time. He settled into his familiar perch on the sofa.

"You know, I don't feel the same about teaching as I used to. Oh, yes, people used to respect Mr. Warren's profession." Tom watched to see if he realized his own little joke. Not a glimmer. "And I surely had my Camelot years at CC. Only had a few bumps in the road recently." Yes, Tom thought, but we do expect our teachers to give us more than the twelve days of teaching you managed last term. Especially when Dennis had refused treatment

— Tom and Jane had begged him repeatedly — for what she guessed was bipolar disorder exacerbated by alcohol.

"But the reason I stopped in," Dennis continued, adjusting trouser pleats that weren't there, "is that Mr. Cattivo — that's what I call him even though he tries to insist on 'Just Bob,' so typical of that nice man, an everyday billionaire, isn't he?" He looked for agreement and plunged on when he didn't get it. "Well, he told me the other evening over our *third* dinner at Le Bernadin — I'm practically a fixture there now, even met Eric Ripert twice. Well, Mr. Cattivo told me that I shouldn't retire. Just like that. And that he'd fix it with the board so I could stay as long as I wanted. I thought it only fair to let you know what he decided."

Dammit. When Dennis resigned, he told Tom that he was enthusiastic about the possibility of a trip to his birthplace in Africa. Some of his parents' old mission colleagues had written him an invitation and he had seemed energized by the prospect. Now Cattivo had confused him. But what was Bob's end game?

"Dennis, I will not allow any trustee, Mr. Cattivo included, to invade my job. And I was doing my job when you and I came to an agreement that you were happy with. That agreement stands, as far as I'm concerned."

Dennis furrowed his brow, plucked at his bottom lip, and steadied himself by leaning forward and placing his right palm on the coffee table. He looked over at Tom. "It's all so confusing. At least for me. Don't know whom to believe."

Tom waited.

Dennis sat back with a lingering sigh, placed his hands on his knees, and shook his head. "Well, frankly, Tom, I don't really know how I'm going to get through this term. I really don't. The students are so damned dilatory and I'm so tired all the time. Why, I could go to sleep on this sofa in a minute. Yes, I could." The man looked dazed.

Tom stood and held out a corduroy pillow from his wingback chair. "Here, Dennis, have yourself a snooze. You'll feel better for the faculty meeting. Come on over when you've had your nap." Dennis took the pillow and Tom caught his acrid alcohol breath. He'd brief Jane before the meeting.

The purpose of the faculty meetings was for the teachers to compare notes and figure out ways to aid struggling students. The discussions ranged from physics to athletics, from divorces to drugs. Tom knew it could be the teachers' finest hour as they talked earnestly about each student on the concern list and what they were seeing in the classroom and on the playing field; it could also degenerate into a slough of despond if not directed skillfully. The teachers were each teaching seventy to ninety students a day in four classes. Tom, who had attended and taught in public schools, thought that the lighter teaching load was the most telling difference between the public and private sectors. Other things being equal, the CC teaching schedule allowed more teacher time for personal student conferences and for prompt paper returns. At CC all the students were very bright and about a third came from the ranks of the Manhattan privileged — rich or powerful or both. The teachers were seldom rich or powerful, except in their relationship with these children of wealth and power. And when that relationship was spoiled, ugliness could result. Tom knew the dynamic well.

The meeting moved briskly for forty minutes — Tom always limited these meetings to one hour because he never forgot the dire feeling he had as a teacher when dim administrators chaired meetings that had little focus or no end. The discussion was disturbed at that point by the entry of Senior Master Teacher Dennis Warren. He looked remarkably refreshed from his nap despite the corduroy striations on one cheek; his tie was knotted neatly, his hair combed — Tom recognized Jo's ministrations. Dennis pulled a vacant chair at the table back to the wall, sat, and tried to stretch each of his nonexistent trouser pleats taut until the cuffs rested on his shoe tops. At that point, as if aware of the gathering silence and expectation, Dennis crossed his right leg delicately over his left and spoke.

"Tom, I'm sure you won't mind my simple query. We wouldn't be forced to engage in such tedious discussions of privileged scoundrels if the administration were to follow my advice." He paused.

There was a rustle around the table. A few teachers consulted their laptops, raised their eyebrows, shrugged, or sighed, but they were now fully attentive.

"If I may be so bold, I believe we should at every grade level ask ourselves the tough question that none of the five headmasters in my forty-five years here has had the wit or will to ask."

"And that, Dennis, would be?"

"Simply put, should little Tiffany and little Georgie, every one of these non-productive cretins, be allowed to stay on indefinitely at Christ Church? That's what we should ask, Tom. Yes, from grade seven to the end of their junior year. Yes."

"But we do that already, Dennis, when we grade our students for their year's work. Most students will have at least eighteen term grades posted by at least six teachers."

"Ah, but that doesn't address my point."

"Which is?"

"That we should improve our student body every year. They don't have to flunk out — we should trade them in for better models. We've heard you tell parents that you believe Christ Church teachers are 'not just good enough, but the best,' and you've traded in a number of teachers for better models. Admissions claims we have thirty applicants for every one we can accept. So, why don't we make space annually for the 'not just good enough, but the best' students, based on aptitude scores and nothing else, regardless of gender or color or income or which side of Central Park they live on or whether they are connected to trustees who have given you and CC oodles of money." Dennis was flushed and caught his breath. "And get rid of this toxic flotsam we have to discuss time after bloody time — *that's* my bloody point!" Dennis glared around the room, then sat back with a sigh.

Three rookie teachers were grinning and nodding at the end of the table. Mac Corutore, in a chambray worker's shirt, tie, and black jeans, pumped his fist. "Right on!" he said.

Tom reddened, squinted at the trio, and looked back to his Senior Master Teacher before adjourning the meeting.

Tom walked rapidly down the corridor. Thank you, Bob Cattivo, you interfering bastard, for trying to force me to keep our own Miniver Cheevy on the staff after he has refused help and was content to retire on his dreams and considerable family inheritance. We didn't let you get into our personnel records, so you attack by upsetting our balance with three-star Michelin cuisine.

CHAPTER 22

"You overstuffed asshole, it was your big-shot talk that made Maury go to pieces."

"Shut up, you siliconed bitch."

Tom's appointment with Maury and his family had gone a little downhill.

Although the Davises were among the handful of parents he didn't know, Tom had no need to look at Maury's file when they came in with their son. He had the honors student in his history class, and he knew the opinions of other teachers. None of the teachers could understand Maury's recent nosedive. The boy wouldn't talk. Even Jane couldn't root out the cause of his difficulties.

Maury was a slender reed with a narrow head and fine features, an epidemic dose of acne, and eyeglasses thick enough to justify his middle school moniker of "six-eyes." He had led his mother and father into the head's office — he knew the place well because he had been the *Chronicle* sports editor for years. Seated between his parents, he pulled all the animals close, placed a large chocolate bear on his knee, and looked up expectantly at his teacher and head.

Maury's father was fiftyish, short, and had coarse features unlike his son's. He wore a gray-green suit with a subtle sheen to it, white shirt, black string tie, and mid-calf brown boots, halfway to Laramie. Tom had seen his name associated with thoroughbreds at the New York and Florida tracks.

Maury's mother, the second Ms. Davis, was a tall thirtyish blonde with nice features pinched into a permanent frown and hair in lacquered swirls. She added heels that could never make it across a racetrack — they gave her an additional three inches on her husband, which she didn't need and he could have used twice. The parents hadn't looked at Tom or each other; they appeared to be appraising the furniture.

"Maury, Mr. and Ms. Davis, I'm glad we could get together."

Mr. Davis sat with hands clasped over his keg of a torso and breathed heavily through wide, dark nostrils. "Wish I could say the same. That ball-busting Dean Leviticus ordered us in here. Guess she makes the law around here." He'd forced a grin and Tom joined him in his little joke.

Tom opened the folder. "Let's see, Dr. Levi filled you in on the telephone. When you didn't respond to her letter." Tom tapped the file. "You have a fine son here, you should be proud." Ms. Davis beamed. "But Maury's other teachers and I are concerned over his recent work. We agree he's on top of the material in class, but he's still not getting his work in."

"Hell, I figured that if we were coming in, we'd talk to the Big Tamale, saves going through five or six teachers, the dog catcher, and that dean. I'm amazed at the bureaucracy around here." He paused, looked sideways at Maury, nudged him, and grinned. The boy grimaced.

Maury's mother cleared her throat, looked at Tom and back to her husband. "We ought to be more diplomatic, darling."

"Don't count on it," he'd said and turned to Tom. "You see, I don't understand you people. Maury has been one of your stars here. He's straight A, eight hundred scores on that SAT, musta got the wrong teachers or something."

"Actually, Mr. Davis, he has some of our veteran teachers. I have your son in history again this year and he always was a superior student until recently. For all of us."

"Yeah, Sam," said Ms. Davis. "Looking for excuses won't get us anywhere."

"I don't think I was talking to you," he said. He added, with a wink and mock whisper to Tom, "This is a little complicated for a former Vegas showgirl."

Tom wondered how he could get anywhere with this guy. Maury had now stiffened with shame and his mother reddened and closed her eyes. Her husband ignored her and addressed the head.

"What I want to know is what you're going to do for us after these huge tuitions. See, I want him in Harvard, or at least Penn. I know a couple of trustees at Brandeis—"

"Lay off the big talk, Sam, we've all heard it too many times."

"What? You gonna talk to me like that?" He was spitting across his son. "If Maury had a real mother all these years, he wouldn't have fallen apart this year!" He looked triumphant. Maury spilled his bear as he moved away to a neutral chair, his head down while he gripped the arms. Ms. Davis closed her eyes and breathed heavily, opened them, and unloaded on her over-stuffed asshole, who in turn questioned her cantilevered construction.

That was when Tom had leaned forward and hit the couple with what the students called "the Chapel Glare."

"All right, I've had enough. Either you two conduct yourselves with some dignity and remember the purpose of our meeting or you can haul ass outta here. Is that clear?"

Both parents mumbled some kind of assent, snarling like corrected curs. That was progress. Tom took the opportunity to make a few points.

"Maury is a wonderful young man — I know you're really very proud of him. But he's been a mystery to us recently. Maybe now I understand the pressure Maury lives with. I don't presume to be a counselor, but I can work with you both on giving Maury the opportunity to realize his best future. Why don't we start right now?"

Silence. Except for the father's labored breathing.

"Okay, Doc, you're the boss," Mr. Davis said finally. "You got all the college cards anyway. Go on." He couldn't resist shooting his cuffs and checking his watch.

Tom laid out his plan. "We'll rewrite our confidential school profile of Maury and explain the pressure he's been facing, then ask for a revised submission. It can do nothing but help. If that meets with your approval, I'll spend some time with Maury right now to get started."

"Do we have a choice?" Mr. Davis said, hands raised off his tummy and spread

wide. Then he looked at his wife. "Okay?"

Ms. Davis had better things to do. Like pick at an errant cuticle. Finally, face contorted with the effort, she bit at it, looked up, and saw three people peering at her. "Sh-ure, guess so," she said through a mouthful of nail and skin. "Let's go, Sam."

She needn't have bothered, as he was already moving. They were content to leave their son and didn't look back. God, Tom thought, if I desperately wanted that woman to say goodbye to her son, or even look back at him, what must Maury be thinking?

Tom followed them to the outer office and got a tepid handshake from Mr. Davis and a glance from his wife as she adjusted her transparent Gucci cashmere shawl and escaped into the New York winter. Well, it wouldn't be far to the car, but that would be quite a chilly ride unless they had come in separate limos. Tom returned to his office and squeezed Maury's shoulder as he passed his chair. Maury had reclaimed his chocolate bear and cradled it.

"They're pretty hard on each other. Mom says they stay together just for me." The boy blew his lips out. "And I don't want that responsibility. Mom's not home much now — she's got family in California. Dad promised we'd do some things together, like we used to, but he's busy with his horses and he was down at Gulfstream Park for most of December and January. Pretty rank, guess I've been a little bummed."

"Home alone, then?"

"Cat says it was almost like the movie," Maury said. "I couldn't tell my teachers, or anyone, about what you just saw." He sighed and tried to smile. "Tell the teachers I'm sorry. Wasn't their fault."

"Maury, you haven't anything to be sorry about. But we do have some work to do. And since you're doing four AP courses and the exams aren't until May, well, there's hope. Let's review each course." He placed the file on the coffee table and opened it.

Tom restacked his bears on the sofa after Maury left. How could parents

like that have such a sterling son? Over the past year or so, the boy and
Cat had spent more time at school. It occurred to Tom that there was no
reason for either of them to go home since there was no home there. He
recognized the feeling.

Maury went directly to the *Chronicle* office. He sat down to work alongside
Cat and Matt and several other writers. When the others trickled out thirty
minutes later, Maury saw Matt sit back and look over at him.

"How'd it go?"

"Disaster."

Matt moved his captain's chair toward Maury's desk. Cat shut the door
and joined them. The three formed a triangle in the back corner of the
office. They had used the formation before.

"A disaster, except," Maury said, "Doc saved it. Grotesque, but I know
Mom and Dad, and maybe . . . no, won't happen, too many cheapass insults.
They're fucked — you've seen what they're like around each other. Yeah,
Doc saved it, he says I need to overlook them, get my own ass in gear."

The three sat in silence — Maury could hear Cat's gentle thumping of
her pencil eraser on her knee. He raised his eyes to her and asked, "Can I
finish the coffee?"

"Yep," Cat said, viewing her knee, not missing her silent beat.

Maury sat back down with a sigh and drank. "Ugh," he shuddered. Put
the cup down.

"Did Doctor West look alright?" Matt asked.

"What?" Cat blinked in surprise.

"Sure, why not?" said Maury. "Maybe tired. Nothing new."

Cat turned to Matt. "Where did *that* come from?"

Matt dropped his chin into his chest. Scowled. Slid down. Hands in
pockets. Not like Matt, so Maury waited. Cat bounced her eraser.

"Okay. Got home last night after practice. Mom was on the phone in the
kitchen. It was Aunt Jane; they always talk on the phone as they're making
dinner. Mom was so intense. Big trouble."

More silence. "Go on," said Cat. "Don't leave us hanging — is your mom in trouble at work?"

"No, but Doctor West is. I couldn't get the whole gist of it, but Mom and Aunt Jane are angry as hell with Mr. Cattivo. Something about his interfering with Doc's running the school. And about our *Chronicle* — Mr. Cattivo attacked Doc because of our story. And also with his raising money, I guess. Mom said Cattivo was a 'barking egomaniac' at the trustee meeting. Then she said, 'Oh, Mr. Warren!' listened to Aunt Jane, and hung up."

"Did you ask her what was going — no, you couldn't, could you?" said Cat.

"No, she didn't know I was listening in, but I did ask how Aunt Jane was doing, something like that. Mom sorta blew me off, like, 'Well, you see her more than I do.' And I couldn't push her, could I?"

"No," said Cat. "But you could keep your eyes open. We fucked Doc royally — we should try to get him out of it."

Maury could only think of one out. "Matt, remember those old Holmes films we used to watch?"

"Basil Rathbone and what's his name."

Maury looked blank. "Yeah, the dummy sidekick." He said to Cat, "You'll know."

"Yep. Nigel Bruce as Dr. Watson. Equal billing. Not bad for a dummy."

"And those kids running around hunting for clues?"

"Baker Street Irregulars."

"Well, that could be us. Irregulars," Maury said. "I mean, it sounds like Doc is close to being fired, maybe because of us."

"But Doc hasn't asked for our help," Matt said. "He doesn't even know we know he's in deep shit."

"So we're like, 'irregular Irregulars,'" said Maury. "We don't have to play by adult rules. As if they had any."

"Count me in," said Cat. "How well do you guys know Georgie Cattivo?"

CHAPTER 23

Jane Levi could see that Tom had had a bad night. He looked fuzzy — eyes blinking, guzzling Jo's coffee, and stretching his neck more often than necessary. She hated to add to the weight of his night. But she had to. She came in after receiving Dennis Warren's call.

"Tom, I wanted to report that Dennis called me five minutes before his first class this morning. It was that whiney voice: 'I had dinner with the Cattivos last night. And I'm somewhat indisposed. Too much *foie gras* and bubbly. Won't be in today, Levi.'"

"He still calling you 'Levi'?"

"Yes. He likes to treat me like a ten-year-old calling to someone on the playground. Oh, he knows what he's doing alright."

"Yeah. Dennis does. Damn. He seemed more stable, with his retirement plans all set — until Cattivo got into it and told him he'd rescind his resignation. I think that's what led to his reckless diatribe at the faculty meeting. Dennis is terribly conflicted and unbalanced now. And it's contagious. Cattivo's messing with our teachers."

"Well, it's hard to read how those rookie teachers were affected," said Jane. "Or the rest of them, because Dennis has been telling them that Cattivo saved his job after we tried to fire him. It's unsettling for any teacher, even though they're well aware that the guy should go."

Tom made to get up with his cup. Jane hopped up and took it from him. "Let me. You look like hell, not to put too fine a point on it." He sank back into his wingback.

Jane returned with his coffee. "I was thinking of Monique Weber fighting us last year over tutoring Georgie Cattivo in French for big bucks from

Babs. Even though they both knew our rule: no private tutoring of your own students. Do you remember?"

"I finally had to tell her I would be happy to approve her tutoring . . . the day after she gave me her resignation."

"No, boss. I was there. You said, 'Five minutes after I fire you.' It worked."

"And Babs Cattivo stormed in here fussing and cussing."

"Listen Tom, I know Dr. Ben Levi would prescribe a night at the Levis for you. I'm making chicken curry and he picked up my favorite Scotch last weekend — Dalwhinnie."

"Nope. Thanks, but I promised myself I had to get to bed early tonight — up all night with Cattivo's wolf. My trusty Dewar's and Marlboros helped, but even they have their limits. Which I reached."

"You look it. Well, we three will be left to conspire on our own, then."

"Three?"

"Oh, yeah. Sally is coming over. She's never heard of that wolf under Cattivo's desk." Jane saw his sudden indecision. What a poor actor. Like all men.

"Actually, if you think I'd like your scotch — hair of the wolf that bit me. I did pass the Dalwhinnie distillery in the highlands years ago on a student trip from St. Andrews."

"Really? What was it like? Pretty, I hope?"

"Oh, yes, very. The hills were covered with purple. And small streams glinted down through the heather."

"Perfect. Highland water for my Dalwhinnie."

"Among other ingredients. Those hills are also covered with sheep."

"Dr. West, could a penguin *really* wear a 'Waiian shirt?"

Anthony Levi, who had been saying he was "almost five, that's when you go to school," since he was three, sat on Tom's lap, his head snuggled into Tom's right shoulder. Tom always read Tony's bedtime story when he stopped in at the Levis'. *Tacky the Penguin* was the current favorite and Tony had it down cold, so Tom couldn't skip pages.

The little guy wore Oscar the Grouch pajamas and fuzzy red Elmo slippers. Tom loved holding the boy after bath time, when his damp hair smelled of shampoo. There was something in the boy that was ineffably innocent and vulnerable, something too good for this world, something that might be soiled or crushed in New York or anywhere. When Tom looked into this child's deep brown eyes framed by enormous coal black lashes, he knew Original Sin didn't work, no matter how well Eden was rendered on medieval plaster.

"Dr. West?"

Back to business. "Hmm, well, Tacky *does* wear a Hawaiian shirt, so the question is why."

"Yeah, *why*," said Tony. "Mom always says that's the tough one."

The boy pushed away a bit to look directly up at Tom and blinked. "But I'm too sleepy for *that*." The boy paused, still thinking overtime. "Now could you tell me a real story, please, with no why at the end, like when you were little? Daddy does that."

Tom agreed, but only if Tony would get into bed. Tom needed the time to imagine what he could pull up from his Ohio small-town world that the Manhattan boy might like. There were the spring flooding of the trailer house, the meatless weeks, the used clothes, the absent mother. Maybe not those things.

Tom followed the boy across the room. Tony adjusted the night light and hung over the side of his bunk bed, his dark eyes luminous with expectation.

"Don't make it too scary, but a little scary's okay."

Tom sat in the bedside rocker and waited a minute for the silence to have its effect. Only a faint taxi horn from the street below got through the double-glazed window plastered with Cookie Monster decals.

"I lived in a very small Ohio town about five-hundred miles west of Manhattan. Most of the time we played ball or rode our bikes—"

"That's what Daddy did up in Watertown. They played ball all day, they never stopped, they just played ball all day."

Tom remembered the glorious summer when he was ten most of all. It had been a continual pitched marital battle in the small trailer house that

May, and his parents decided that Tommy should leave for a while so they could try and get it back together. It turned out that the only thing that was different when he returned on Labor Day was that Ethyl was even more unhappy with her life.

"But there was one summer that was special, Tony. When I was ten I took the bus down to West Virginia to live with my only grandparents. They didn't seem to have anything — no electricity or running water, but they did have home-grown corn, tomatoes, melons, fresh butter, wild strawberries, squirrels, chicken fryers, and hand-cranked ice cream on the Fourth of July."

"They ate squirrels?"

Oops. At least he hadn't mentioned the coons. "Yes, Tony. They were poor. But I loved the life down there. And I was never bored — we read library books every evening by the kerosene lamp. But not for long, because I was sore and tired from fixing the fence and weeding the two-acre garden and milking their cows."

"What was your favorite thing to do?" That was a surprise — Tony had been nodding off.

"My favorite was following my grandad everywhere. Especially tagging behind his plow, I'd meet him at the end of the row. 'Tommy, stay cleara the blade!' he always shouted, 'it could kill ya.'" Tony was wide awake now.

"I'd spring into action — hitching up my jeans, taking off my leather work shoes and socks and racing after Granddad and his plow. I had a clear path — the newly-sliced furrow the plow had made" — Tom used his hands to demonstrate — "its flat bottom carved out of brown earth gave me a cool surface that I could run or walk on. I loved making footprints in the furrow, only to have them wiped out with Granddad's next trip and a fresh soil path laid out for me."

"That sounds fun," said Tony, trying to sit up.

"Well, when I tired of chasing the plow I'd sit and look closely at the furrow bottom and side of the blade's last trip to find the little pink worms remaining. See, Tony, I had been told that worms could remake themselves after being cut in two, but I never saw it happen. Even though I waited and waited and even nudged their glistening little bodies with my finger. But not for long, because that plow would soon be back, providing new opportunities for my white feet and the robins that hopped down the moist furrow and read it like a menu."

Tony smiled weakly, lay back, and those lush lashes closed the curtain on his day. Tom pulled the blanket up, tucked him in, and watched his little chest rise and fall in peace.

Tom's summer in West Virginia had never been repeated even though he begged — he was so intrigued by his hillbilly Granddad who made do and lived for his evening reading. He wondered if his mother hadn't spent a lifetime trying to put that rustic innocence behind her. She shouldn't have bothered — her son had spent half his lifetime trying to forget her Kokosing and coveting her old West Virginia. Now it was his representative childhood memory, the only one he treasured.

Down the hall from Tony's bedroom, Sally Ernst and Ben awaited in golden corduroy sectional comfort. Jane sat in a black leather Eames chair. The room glowed with crimson Orientals, gold and black upholstery, and Federal period furniture from Jane's family.

Ben handed Tom a snifter. "Your reward."

Jane couldn't wait. "So, how'd my little fellow do?"

"He was wonderful. Just dropped off. He insisted on a Buckeye yarn."

"Tough audience?" Sally asked. Her French twist had the added attraction tonight of having single ringlets at the side.

"A wonderful audience, but my story was wobbly. Like Ben says, it's tough dredging up this stuff."

"I know what you guys are talking about," Sally said. "At first it seemed hopeless to tell Matt about my childhood in Morocco, because he's exposed to so much more than I was. Then I realized it was the simple things he loved hearing about — the earthen ovens at the market, a tiny spring in the woods."

Tom nodded and labored not to stare at Sally. She noticed. So did Ben, who came to the rescue.

"Jane and I haven't caught up with each other this week. Is there any news on the 'Barbarian at the School Gate'?"

His wife looked at Tom and Sally, shrugged her shoulders, and shook her head. Before she could speak, Ben said, "That bad, eh? You'll all forgive me, but I lead such a humdrum life in six A.M. scrubs that 'Tom and Jane go to School' stories enthrall me."

"It is getting very annoying, darling," said Jane, sitting up. "Not your enthrallment, just the crap this guy Cattivo is vomiting our way." She immediately pounded her head with her fists. "See?"

"Yes, dear, I do see." He turned to Sally and Tom. "That is the first time in history that Jane Morse Levi has committed a mixed metaphor. Robert Cattivo must be one inspiring dude."

"Go ahead, you two," said Sally. "Enthrall Ben with the bastard's latest caper."

Ben raised his eyebrows at Sally and turned to Tom.

"Well, this week we witnessed Dennis Warren go to pieces, thanks to Cattivo," Tom said. "And today Jo Wilson heard in the faculty lunchroom that Babs Cattivo had invited some senior teachers to dinner."

"Did that Joan Rivers lookalike invite them as a group?" Ben wondered.

"No. As individuals."

"Well, isn't that what you have promoted since you came to CC, Tom? Getting the trustees to have increased contact with the teachers? And if brittle Babs — I was on the hospital charities ball committee with her last year — wants to entertain teachers at home, well, it surprises me, but perhaps it's a breakthrough."

"Perhaps," said Tom.

"Perhaps not," said Sally, sitting forward. "Don't forget that this was the hostess of Tom's welcome reception, where she shunted the teachers into that safari room at the back and they had to serve themselves Budweiser, sausages, and pretzels. Babs put the trustees and us Parents' Association officers into the Mies parlor where we were attended by male waiters serving canapés, premium Scotches, gins, and Krug champagne."

"I missed the delightful occasion — running late on my rounds," said Ben.

"It was a horrible evening, you idiot," said Jane, having recovered her ability to speak. "Their huge gothic town house on East Sixty-Fourth looked like a decorator show house rental. Every room looked as if a different show-off designer had done it — a modernist parlor in metal and glass, Babs' precious Laura Ashley 'morning room,' a minimal Op Art dining room — and the teachers and I were stuck in that hideous tent of leopard print linen. Until we were rescued by the only person who caught on to what was going on."

"Yeah, we saw Tom gather up an armload of bottles from the trustees' bar and head for the back of the house," said Sally. "On the way out, he said something to the Bishop, who also took a load back to the teachers."

"We safari-goers cheered in the tent. It was the perfect reception after all," said Jane. "It meant the teachers had a leader who wouldn't take any crap."

"Babs sang her own opinion of me as I left," said Tom. "Nice voice."

"What was that?" asked Ben.

"'East is east and West is west. And the wrong one we have chose.'" "Holy shit, that explains a lot," said Ben. "I've never heard that story."

"Ditto — I didn't know about that last part," said Sally.

"Triple shit — why didn't you tell me, Tom?" said Jane. "I wondered why that woman looked daggers at you on college night last month. She's still apeshit after four years."

"Yes, to use a precise diagnostic term that fits," said Ben. "But are the Cattivos entertaining the teachers in the tent again?"

"No, Jo said everyone was treated to Le Bernardin's tasting menu," said Tom.

"What? Wow, that's a cozy little three-hundred dollar tasting for each." Ben smiled, then looked baffled. "But why?"

"We think he's fucking with our faculty, but we don't really know and I hate to think about it on a Friday night," said Jane. "Darling, I see four empties. And I so hate to hate on an empty snifter."

CHAPTER 24

"Sheena MacKay is her name," said Lulu Leonard on the phone. "She still visits her dad up here almost every weekend. She's done very well — started at the *Chicago Tribune*, nominated for the Pulitzer twice. Then, back to New York and the *Daily News* for the last five years, now as metro editor. I'm very proud of her — she's a real tiger. She'll have some ideas about your student paper. When you told me at the Union Club how you'd like to protect those kids, despite their mistake, well, I thought of Sheena. Good luck."

Sheena was Lulu's Scottish gardener's daughter who had grown up "under my feet," as Lulu put it. Tom was hesitant, but he made the call and Ms. MacKay talked with him about the *Chronicle* story Lulu had sent on to her. The first thing she emphasized was her debt to Lulu: "I'd do anything for Mrs. Leonard — she sent me to college and graduate school so that I could have the career that she never completed when she married that tyrant." And before she finished, Mackay said, "So, you still think there's something in this half-cocked story your kids wrote, but you admit they didn't investigate much, or follow due care whatsoever. Even a lousy ambulance chaser will probably clean your plow in court."

She had precisely summed up their first talk. It looked bleak.

That weekend Tom took some photographs on Central Park South. He picked out five horses, the real losers among the three-block queue of carriages across from the Plaza. He sent the photos by email to editor Mackay with, "Please take a look at these. I went down on Saturday and Sunday and these are representative horses."

Sheena was on the phone Monday morning.

"'Representative,' hell, headmaster, five bad 'uns out of thirty? You must have flunked journalism one-oh-one. And remedial logic!"

"Guess you've nailed me. But at least a third looked pretty ragged."

"Aw, I was having a little joust with you. And I agree on that."

"Point taken. But how did you know there were thirty horses?"

"I had a reporter on the loose after covering another Trump non-event press conference at the Plaza earlier today. She checked out the horses herself. Off the record, she's up at the stable right now applying for a job."

"If she gets it, she won't last a week shoveling horse manure."

"Gee, I didn't know there was another word for that. She's one of my best — it may take her less than a week to clean it out."

"Fingers crossed. Let me buy you a drink at the Plaza. We can check the nags out the window."

"You certainly know journalists. But Lulu warned me about you — that you could be very persuasive. Let's leave it at 'fingers crossed.'"

CHAPTER 25

Bob Cattivo emerged from the Christ Church portal into a perfect New York spring day. Sunlight flooded the mellow scene. Even his Babs would be sweetened by a day like this, he thought. But maybe he was the one who could use a dash of nature. Daffodils inside the wrought iron fence, cherry blossoms bursting, or maybe that's apple. Whatever. Pineapple for all he knew. All this bloom in the city and he hadn't noticed. He really should learn what the hell he'd planted up in Bedford — Babs handled that every weekend, she was very faithful to their garden and friends when he couldn't get loose, which was always. He thought, I've got a hundred thousand bucks worth of shrubs and stuff up there and I can't name a single one for sure.

He might have lost at least that much by coming to church today, instead of being on the phone to Sarasota. Damn. Still, the music was first rate, thanks to the Cattivo Music Fund that hired the choirmaster away from St.

Paul's, London. But must Philips' sermons always be about his benighted childhood or acned adolescence, or his first pet's death, or first year in seminary, or not hitting the curve ball — when would that guy run out of his crises of faith?

Bob was the last in line along with Senior Warden Wither Wellington-Cortelyou Bramston, V as listed in the church bulletin. No wonder he never used his middle name.

"Dr. Philips, another fine sermon. Very moving about your almost leaving the seminary." For the zillionth time. "We're very happy, you didn't; right, Wither?" Bob handed the moist paw of the Reverend Doctor off to Bramston to pat dry. Or lick.

The doctored divine grasped Bramston's hand but leaned back to Cattivo. "Why not join me and the Senior Warden for something rare in my study?"

Ouch.

Cattivo wondered why it was called a "study" since it was devoid of anything resembling a book. Correction: one day he had seen a thin volume entitled "Snappy Sermon Starters." Too bad Richie hadn't also bought the companion volume. There was an expensive collection of framed reproductions of ancient manuscripts on the walls. He'd once asked Philips if he could read them. The preacher said, "Oh, no. No one can. They're in Greek and Hebrew." Cattivo was surprised that didn't bring on a regret, followed by a remembered soul crisis, or at least a failed seminary language exam and a quick dash to his desk because he felt a sermon coming on. Still, the firewater from a spring somewhere in Hardscrabble, Kentucky was undiluted and comforting. It even led Cattivo to a somewhat rash summary of his crusade to unhorse Tom West.

"So, we've got the faculty in an uproar over Dennis Warren's future. And Babs and I are finding what's on their minds by entertaining them. I don't think they're appreciated enough by their headmaster."

"That's good of you, Bob," said Bramston.

"Very good of you. But I hate being sued. Anything on that?" said the Rev.

"I can tell you two something in strictest confidence: I have made contact with the Central Park Stables lawyer. Turns out he's a litigator with Craven and Caddisher and I've seen him in action — he's a real junkyard dog, and he was more than eager to sit down with me. I wanted to ask if we could come to an early settlement—"

"What would that mean for me?" interrupted Philips.

"Well, for you, and all of us, it would get us out from under this disaster. He's taking my offer under consideration. That's all I can reveal."

Of course Bob wasn't rash enough to tell them the real substance of his Stables lawyer session — that he made sure to put a bee in the guy's bonnet about the circumstances of the libel. He explained that the *Chronicle* was without any faculty supervision for that first issue because Tom hadn't appointed a replacement for the retired teacher-sponsor. Voilà! The school lawyer would no longer be able to continue to argue that the school's leader exercised due care in supervising the student publication.

Cattivo concluded. "So, you can see I've been trying to keep that leaky school afloat."

"That's good of you, Bob," said Bramston. "But from Tom's weekly reports to me, I gather he's doing quite well with his fundraising. The Bishop and his old philanthropic ally, Mrs. Leonard, seem to be nudging things along."

"Yes, I get the same impression," Bob granted. "But I aim to keep Tom so busy trying to dampen our love and generosity to teachers and students that he'll be chasing his own tail by summer, instead of the almighty dollar. Plus, he'll soon have to deal with that damn student newspaper. And I think he's already on the ropes — it was something the Countess Serena von Konigsberg said at the Costume Institute party last night . . ." He paused to let it sink in.

"The Countess? Whooee — what'd the Countess say?" The Rare Colonel just couldn't wait, could he?

"She asked if we'd been working CC's headmaster a little hard." Make him wait.

"That all?"

"Serena thought he looked tired and not as responsive as usual."

"So, you know the Countess pretty well, do you?" persisted Philips.

"Not as well as I'd like; I just heard that she's a weakness of Tom's." That seemed to satisfy and cheer them both. Not a bad Sunday morning's work after all. Much better than pruning Babs' pineapples in the country. And she hadn't had melons for years.

CHAPTER 26

The Bishop had found himself in need of an afternoon nap since early April. He'd ignored other unsettling symptoms. It didn't amount to much anyway. And Tom West's appearance always heartened him. Still, he decided to remain seated and asked Tom to pull up a chair alongside his desk.

"Tom, I've very much enjoyed meeting some of your allies over the past few months. I even discovered that your Parents' Association president is one sharp cookie." The Bishop looked at his guest directly to see the effect of that. Tom blushed, grasped the arms of his chair and squirmed a bit.

"Sally was telling me about her new assignment: preparing an exhibit on the Dutch School. There are some New York pictures in private hands that might be pried loose."

"We haven't talked much about her project, I guess," said Tom, "because I've been so driven by my own predicament. Sally knows the other parents so well that she's been invaluable to Jay Erickson and me in suggesting possible donors."

"Well, she's a keeper, I can tell you." The Bishop was rewarded with another blush from the headmaster. Better not push anymore, he thought. "And that new development director Jay Erickson you've hired is also impressive, Tom. When you brought me Jay's new CC alumni CD files, I asked our techie to correlate them with our diocesan computer parish files, and here they are — upwards of three hundred."

The Bishop winced involuntarily as he leaned and handed the folders over the desk. Ridiculous, showing that pain, he thought. His young visitor obviously tried not to notice, which made the whole thing worse. Discipline, you old fool, discipline.

"Tom, I know many of these folks because they are parish leaders and they might prove helpful. Lulu recognized at least half of them and some are already on her list."

"Wow, and to think we've never thought of using a church connection with our alumni."

"The price of secularism. And several of these folks have told me over the years of their pride in being CC alumni, even if they haven't any long-term affiliation."

"Like Lulu."

"Well, something like Lulu. She has her own category." The Bishop sat back. "Sure you don't want me to tackle Bob Cattivo over his unwarranted interference at school? I could beard him at our interim Trustees Exec Committee meeting in May if you'd like."

"No, thanks. You've done enough for me. Plus, it's my battle." No doubt Tom was sensing that the old man in front of him wasn't quite up to it.

"There's no way he can weasel his way out of this," Tom continued. "He overplayed his hand and I'll nail him. He's got no possible defense this time."

"Well, good luck. I remember seeing my grandmother try to chase a weasel around her precious henhouse with a hoe. Remember, Tom, a cornered weasel might prove to be a pretty fierce customer."

Tom soon discovered he should have listened to the Bishop's advice on handling weasels. He met with Cattivo face to face with only the wolf under the desk between the two of them. The ferret narrowed his eyes.

"So, Dr. Headcase, what's all this 'serious business' you wanted to discuss with me?" As Tom shifted in his chair and began to speak, Cattivo added, "Are you here to announce your resignation?"

"Hardly. And I said '*very* serious business.' I came down here to tell you that I'm onto you and your machinations with my teachers. First, you poisoned Dennis Warren's thinking by guaranteeing him his job even though I had already arranged for him to retire with some dignity."

"But I barely know the little fellow."

"What, 'little'? He's got a good four inches on you, Bob!"

"You mean the Greek and Latin teacher, don't you? As I said, I barely know him."

"Yes, *that* Dennis Warren. The one who claims you had him to dinner three times at Bernardin."

"*Le* Bernardin, please. Four times, but who's counting? Delightful fellow. Bet you didn't know he was born in Africa. Yale man."

"Well, barely-know-him-delightful-African-born-Yalie Dennis quoted your promise to 'fix it with the board' so he can stay as long as he wants."

"Really, is that the best shot you've got? Haven't you noticed that dear old Dennis, who may be a shade taller than me, doesn't always get things straight? Haven't you found him losing it at times?"

"I have found, since you got to him, a man who is confused about his future and about who is running the school. What you've done to him is very sad and very wrong, Bob."

"Don't get so dramatic. That Presbyterian was born confused. Probably grew up among the Pygmies." Cattivo looked bored with his company as he fiddled with a pre-Columbian figure on his desk.

"I'll try hard to ignore those insults to a man who has given his life for the young." Tom hadn't expected such outrageous comments from Bob. He paused to regain balance. "And back to your meddling, you must be ignorant of the fact that several parents threatened lawsuits over Dennis' slugging their kids in the classroom. Wither Bramston and our school lawyer knew about it and agreed with my action in helping him 'retire' at the end of the year. And now you've messed with Dennis and tried to unravel my plans. And his. He actually was looking forward to his retirement and a trip to see his parents' graves in Liberia at the mission school. You've spoiled that for him."

"Don't get excited. I've done nothing I'm ashamed of. Unlike you, who has let the prisoners take over the goddamn school."

"The prisoners?"

"Don't think you'll get me off track with word play, Mr. Head in the Clouds, and I don't mean Socrates."

Oh, yes, Tom remembered, Cattivo and Babs were the noisy patrons of a Greek revival theater company down at NYU.

Tom returned to the attack. "And recently you've also been taking other teachers out to dinner regularly. I can only imagine what your intentions are, especially in light of your promises to Dennis Warren. Perhaps the other members of the Executive Committee would like to know of your meddling in my running of the school."

"Oh, please," said Cattivo. "They wouldn't be concerned, they would commend our entertaining teachers, as the headmaster has nauseatingly suggested over the years."

"I do know from what six teachers have told me or Dean Levi that you have got them stirred up by asking them what I should be doing to help them do their best. Plus, you confuse them by asking immediately about their 'dream trips.'"

"Well, that's really Babs' doing, but anyway, we simply wanted to thank Georgie's teachers for what they've done for our son."

"We'll see what the exec committee thinks, because Georgie hasn't even had Ruth Soros in English or Pat Osborne in math. And yet you took them to Le Bernardin."

"Babs must have got mixed up. She isn't perfect. And I still like the idea of trustees letting all the teachers know how much we appreciate them."

Neither man spoke for a full minute. Only the occasional brush of the granular pre-Columbian figure Cattivo rotated between his fingers against the leather pad on his desk broke the silence.

"Now why would you want to protect your precious teachers from being appreciated, eh? Guess I hadn't realized how insecure CC's headmaster really is."

"Is that *your* best shot? Pathetic."

"Enough. My friend, if you bring any of this shit up to the trustees I'll deny it, not the teachers part — that happened, and I'll get Babs to take it easy, she was maybe a little mixed up. In fact, we'll stop taking the teachers to dinner, since you insist. But if you bring up Dennis, your beloved dipso classicist, I'll ask why the hell you haven't cleaned house long ago. You've tolerated, even encouraged him by calling him a 'Master Teacher,' despite his loutish behavior to Babs at the holiday fair a few years ago. Why, he even told her CC should trade in our kids for smarter ones."

Cattivo seemed moved by the memory and when he looked up from the rotating piece he held, his eyes were glassy.

"So, don't try to hang that meddling charge around my neck. I was just trying to protect my Babs and my kids."

CHAPTER 27

When Whitey Case, the father of two CC graduates and long-time school attorney with Debenham and Plimsoll, came into Tom's office, he looked more grave than usual. And that was gravitas squared.

"Tom, I'm sorry to be the bearer of a serious setback for our defense of the Central Park Stables' threat. I was banking on the fact that the courts have been reticent to step into the operation of private schools when the school has been conducted with reasonable care. But their attorney now claims that the CC school administration was derelict in taking due care with the *Chronicle* last September."

Tom looked at the man in the dark serge suit. "What in the world is that about?"

"He claims that the *Chronicle* was without any supervision last September after the retirement of the English teacher who had done it for years. And that the first issue containing the stables exposé came out without any adult supervision. Ipso facto, negligence."

Tom tried to remember the usual mad rush at the start of school in September. The bile rose in his gullet; he swallowed and swallowed again. "Let me make a call."

As he dialed Jane's extension, he tried to look dutiful and responsible himself. Whereupon Jane admitted haltingly the bad news that yes, she got Ruth's acceptance to take it on *after* the paper's first issue of the school year because the teacher had been away at ninth grade orientation camp. Tom turned back to his lawyer.

"My watch, Whitey, and I screwed up. Their lawyer is right. We didn't have it covered."

"I'm sorry to hear that."

"But, how could their lawyer have discovered it?"

"He'll never tell."

"What are the damages?"

"More than you can afford. Probably. I'll have to reassess our position, but it means we don't have a strong case, or any case, to defend. We might have squeezed by before, but this breach of due care blows our defense." Whitey stood and zipped his briefcase.

It was heaven-sent for Robert Cattivo when board president Wither Bramston appeared at his office unannounced and informed him of the school attorney's call. This Bramston was jumpy and at his wit's end. No, that was his usual status; today he was edging toward ballistic.

"I don't know what we'll do. It'll be all over the papers: 'Top Prep School Libels Stable!' They'll love the story of the rich prep school being brought to earth by one of the last surviving stables in the city — the very institution that cares for beloved horses and provides the carriage rides of romantic tourist memories."

"Due to the negligence of the school's fuckup headmaster," Cattivo finished. "I warned you and everyone that this guy was a disaster!"

"He did own up to it, I'll give him that much. So, what'll we do, Bob?"

"I'll have to think this over, Wither. But I may be able to talk to that damned junkyard dog again. Maybe he and the stable owners will be open to an extortionate . . . but discreet settlement."

"But that will be ruinous for the school budget, won't it? And we'll have to discuss it at the May Executive Committee meeting, won't we?"

"I'm afraid so, but it's time they all know about Tom's incompetence, especially Ross and the Bishop. The stable will definitely play hard ball with us now."

"I'd give anything to get out of Tom's mess."

"Well, if you hadn't kowtowed to the Bishop at the last board meeting, I could have brought in several new trustees at five million a pop and we'd have bounced Tom out on his ass already."

"I said it already, Bob — I'll do anything to get out of Tom's mess. Really."

"You may have to. Has Tom said anything to you about the agenda for the Executive Committee meeting?"

"No, but the Bishop has. He is to present something about trustee interference with Tom's running the school. He wouldn't say more."

"And he won't, I imagine."

"What do you mean?"

"I mean that I'd be prepared to step up to the plate and cover the damages the stable insists on. But only if you cover my tail in the event that the Bishop tries to bring up anything about that damned 'interference' business. You're still in charge of the committee agenda, so don't allow your Bishop to put it on the agenda and get Ms. Ross all stirred up. Please forget, for once, that he's your pastor or shepherd or dance instructor, whatever. And be careful with Ross — she's still an unknown — she decided not to participate in my summer student internships because she may be in China. I don't know whether to believe her. You'll have to be strong, Wither, this could get ugly."

"Anything. I said it. And I'll do it. You can count on me. But he is *our* bishop, not only mine, Bob."

Cattivo hoped he could count on Bramston, despite that extra "but." That dinner with young wide-eyed Ruth Soros was worth every penny. Babs, take a bow, she was the one who probed about that Central Park Stables story. "Oh, no," said tipsy Miss Ruth Muffet, sitting on her Bernardin tuffet, "the editors ran that stables story two days before I was put in charge, so no one was in charge." Now he could take proper steps to deal with Mr. Headcase.

CHAPTER 28

Cattivo had been looking forward to this meeting, especially as he planned to do all the talking. He had his own maxim for such occasions, which he'd like to have someone like Alex Katz do up in a golden frame. It'd be tiny, succinct, and a killer:

It's a Dirty Job and I love doing it.

"Tom, come right in and sit yourself down."

Cattivo motioned over his male assistant. "Would you like a drink? I recommend it, even if it's only ten. After all, as I told you on the phone, we have, to borrow your phrase, '*very* serious business.'"

"Just coffee, please," said Tom. He looked pretty cool. Far too cool.

The assistant stepped into an alcove and the espresso machine hummed. He served both men and disappeared. Not a word was spoken. Cattivo noticed that Tom stirred his cup far too long. Good.

"So. Mr. Headcase Tommy, I'm going to ask you a question this morning that I'm sure you'll recognize from the last time I had the pleasure of your company in this room." Cattivo took a leisurely sip of his coffee, patted his lips dry on a small Tuscan napkin, assumed a languid angle in his chair, and said, "Are you here to announce your resignation?"

"No, Bob, I'm not. What you did to Dennis and my teachers was, as I said before, sad and wrong." That was unexpected. Doesn't this guy know when to fold? Don't lose it, Bob, enjoy the moment.

"My, you're still capable of being indignant and of making ill-considered comments. How must our headmaster have handled the news from the CC lawyer that his world was falling in about his ears?"

"I took responsibility immediately. It was on my watch. No excuses."

"*It was on my watch,*" Cattivo mimicked in a tinny voice. "No, it was on your incompetent, fucked up, arrogant, overeducated watch! That's what it really was. And you're here because I'm calling the shots from now on — which may include your firing — but, for the moment, I'd like to make you an offer. Very much an offer that you can't refuse. No, I take that back, I merely want to tell you what we'll both do in the next forty-eight hours until the Executive Committee meeting is over. First, I shall have a meeting with the Craven & Caddish lawyer representing the stables. In that meeting, I shall try to recover the school's reputation from the disaster that you've brought down on us, by buying off the lawyer and the stables from any more legal action. I figure that'll cost me somewhere north of two or three million. But I love and respect CC School as much as I don't think you do, so I'll pay it. In return, you will keep your mouth shut about your trumped-up stuff about my interfering up there at school. Not a word from you or the Bishop must be heard before, during, or after the exec committee meeting. Got it?"

Tom got it, said so, rose, and walked out.

Cattivo hadn't enjoyed it as much as he expected. Next time.

CHAPTER 29

As Tom drove north on the Taconic Parkway toward Lulu Leonard's that Saturday morning he had to smile despite his hangover. She had embarked on a "two-way crusade" to confer weekly with Tom over his fundraising and to improve his golf game. He hadn't played since high school when he'd caddied at the local Ohio public course and the pro would allow the kids an occasional twilight "bash," which was well-named because he had no instruction and merely tried to emulate the better local golfers' swings.

"For a former caddy and college athlete, your game is scandalous," Lulu stated after their first round. "We'll start over." Each Saturday morning Tom found himself increasingly enjoying his weekly walk and talk and rigorous shot instruction — Lulu had reigned as club champion for twenty of her younger years and was a keen student of the game.

As he drove he tried to shake his triple whammy of the day before: Cattivo's command performance and gag order, a ragged evening conversation with his biggest donor prospect so far, and his retreat into late night oblivion with a bottle of Dewar's and a pack of Marlboros. He had told himself at the time that he needed them both, but it left him worse off when he woke at eight with barely enough time to make it to Lulu's usual ten Saturday tee time.

He wasn't proud of himself. But yesterday he had escaped Cattivo's oppressive office with some pride and knew he had been honest, if unsuccessful, in his quest for millions in the evening. But where did honesty get him last night? And he dreaded facing Lulu and the Bishop over lunch because they expected a complete fundraising report, including last night's foray. He couldn't shake the Oyster Bay defeat of the night before. The Bishop and Lulu had set up the call with retired Fortune 500 CEO Ted Stevens. He'd graduated from Christ Church School in 1938 and been noteworthy for his generosity to the Bishop's cathedral building and to the New York Botanical Garden, one of Lulu's favorites.

The Stevens family patriarch, a widower with a housekeeper/cook and an Old Masters collection, couldn't have been more gracious to "Headmaster West" from drinks to steak and potatoes and whiskey bread pudding.

Tom thought his pitch was going well during decaf coffee when the Harvard grad interrupted, "Well, this is all most interesting, sounds as if the old school is in good hands, especially that Ivy record I read about in the *Journal*; and, of course, I know your Wither Bramston — well, not this Bramston, perhaps, but his grandfather and father. Used to see them up at Vinalhaven every summer. Where was I? Oh, so tell me about your school's chapel. I loved chapel. Every morning at eight-thirty. Quite the thing to start the day. I'm the senior warden here at Christ Episcopal, Teddy Roosevelt's old parish. I think he was also senior warden here. I owe it all to daily chapel as a CC schoolboy."

This won't be easy, thought Tom. "We now have chapel once a week. And you'd be interested to hear that the Harvard Chaplain, Peter Gomes, is one of our regulars every year. The kids love him."

"Well, Gomes is all well and good for a Baptist, but 'once a week chapel'? Might as well abolish it kit and caboodle."

Tom didn't think it the right moment to reveal that a majority of the faculty had voted to do just that. The old boy was too polite to say it, but the absence of both daily chapel *and a student body that appreciated chapel* put the kibosh on any gift from him. A sizeable gift, if the Bishop and Lulu were correct, that would have put his campaign total well on the way to his target twenty million. But after "kit and caboodle," the conversation veered increasingly out of Tom's reach.

Was there a way he could have sold Mr. Stevens on the 2006 Christ Church School? Yes, he could have lied through his teeth. The old boy would probably never ask to attend a daily chapel where he would have expected to follow his old Book of Common Prayer throughout. Tom had considered fudging all that during their conversation because he figured eighty-eight-year-old Stevens would never live to check up on his old school. Despite that possibility, Tom had told him the truth. That there was nothing he could do about the current weekly chapel and nothing he wished to do; it was more religion and philosophy than most kids could stomach anyway, but he believed in combating religious illiteracy. In fact, he explained, every time he found widespread classroom ignorance over Biblical allusions in history and literature, he knew it really was an important part of the curriculum.

And there was nothing he could do about Peter Gomes' Baptist affiliation. And no doubt Stevens paid a rare Anglican compliment to the Harvard Baptist chaplain, however backhand it was. Still, the parting was amicable and he sent warmest wishes to the Bishop and Mrs. Leonard.

Later that morning, his golf hadn't gone well. For the first time, Lulu insisted he try her sidesaddle tall putter and gave him all kinds of physics "laws" as to why it made sense. It was uncomfortable at first, and he had visions of himself putting like a sissy, but he had remarkably good luck with it. By the eighteenth hole, Lulu considered him converted and promptly bought him his own at the pro shop for their future forays.

The Bishop, who was spending the weekend, joined Lulu on the sunny terrace overlooking the Hudson after Tom left for a school track meet at Randall's Island. They had to bundle up.

"I'd rather shiver a little and stay out here if at all possible," she said.

"Same here. Much prefer it." The Bishop involuntarily shivered in sympathy.

"I saw that. You are a dear. Even with your 'thorn in the flesh,' you're game for my nonsense."

"I've never witnessed 'nonsense' from Lulu Leonard. Mischief, yes, countless times, but never nonsense."

"I can also be serious. And I shall try for a few minutes. What did you make of Tom today?"

"Hmn. Let me stall. And you?"

"I saw a hassled head of school. From start to bloody finish, Robert Cattivo has been a step ahead and driving him bats. And last night, an honest teacher and headmaster who came afoul of today's student body reality. And Ted Stevens' lack of reality. And what did you see?"

"Yes. Hassled. And hungover. Tom went through goblets of Pellegrino."

"I shouldn't doubt it after his black Friday."

"No. And what did you make of his request that I not press my plan to charge Cattivo at the Exec Committee for his malicious interference at school?"

"Curious. And so unlike Tom not to explain his about-face."

"Still," the Bishop said, "Cattivo must have pulled something to scare him off."

"Doubtless. How do you feel about it?"

"Tom's silence hurt me a bit, I'll confess."

"I'm sorry. You deserve better."

"I deserve what I get, Lulu." He looked at her carefully. "I do get the impression at times that you might have some plans for our Tom. Is that possible?"

"You've caught me. I have had him outfitted with a top NY editor."

"And I continue to have an inkling about what a Met curator could do for him."

"Would a wager be in order, your grace?"

"Why, yes, a graceful one might be."

"You Episcopal bishops are certainly more tentative than the Catholic ones, aren't you?"

"Perhaps. Guess so."

CHAPTER 30

Cattivo knew his "orientation meeting" with Wither Bramston and Richardson Philips was at least as important as tomorrow's trustee executive committee meeting at the school. Hence, he asked Bramston to host it at his office, knowing that even Philips knew Bramston & Bramston was a strict alcohol-free operation. Wouldn't do for the cleric to forget his lines or plot at the trustee meeting. Cattivo knew that Wither wouldn't over-indulge in anything, except perhaps his patented groveling to the Bishop.

Bramston's dutiful tea lady left her boss content behind his accustomed cup of afternoon Darjeeling and his two guests nursing mild coffee and holding plates ringed with small medallions of white bread topped with either salmon paste number one or white paste number two. Cattivo discovered quickly that the taste was similar, but the salmon one might be slightly off so he dispatched only number two, perhaps a bleached salmon, something from a Norwegian cookbook. He thought that Philips appeared disoriented, no doubt adrift without his traditional 5:30 P.M. Kentucky fried orientation.

"How goes the battle, Bob?"

"Moderately well, thank you, Richie," said Cattivo. "Perhaps a bit slow for my Babs, who has wanted to see the back of Dr. West for years, as you both know."

"Your Babs surely gets to the heart of things, I will say that," said Philips, studying Cattivo's face. "But what's this 'moderately well,' talk? Doesn't sound like you."

Our divine is certainly sharper today, thought Cattivo, who might have preferred one drink in him. "Merely that I fear Tom and probably the Bishop are gunning for me again."

"If it'll make you feel better, spill it. It's what I do all day as pastor," said Philips between mouthfuls of salmon mush. Cattivo had heard the preacher "spill" most of what he thought he knew but had never seen him assume a pastoral role. Maybe he could give him some rehearsal time.

"Thanks, Richie. It's only a feeling I have. I think Tom has convinced the Right Reverend Bish that his precious preserve Christ Church School in the Province of New York has been invaded by a barbarian called the Most Un-Revered Robert Cattivo. The High and Mighty Headmaster Doctor West calls it 'arrant interference.'"

"Bull roar," said Philips. "'Pretentious authority always resists false irreverence,' I read that somewhere, though it might be just 'irreverence' without the false, though it could also read, 'resists interference.' But I'm sure about 'Pretentious authority.'"

Yes, you've got that down pat, Cattivo mused. "I'm afraid Tom has been very persuasive, even though I've been trying to save the school's *and his* reputation."

Bramston shook his head. "Well, then, the Bishop is sadly misled. Because if you hadn't interfered, stepped up to the plate, to bail us out of that stables business, we'd have been in a proper state."

"Yeah," Philips added, "if your 'interfering' in Tom's school gets out to the other trustees, why fudge, they'll agree with me — that 'ole Bob should have got himself involved sooner, maybe then we wouldn't be threatened with an embarrassing lawsuit.' Now that shouldn't be interpreted as my criticism of you, Bob, anything but. Anyways, what other burdens are you carrying?"

"Well, it does get worse, I must confess," said Cattivo. "And this goes back to my foiled attempt to investigate Tom's so-called faculty evaluations. You see, I've been researching Dennis Warren, getting to know him. And in an attempt to be fair to him, I even had him to dinner. And Babs had some other teachers to dinner, but only to thank them for what they did for our Georgie. And she let me tag along."

"That Babs, getting to the heart of things!" said Philips.

"And what a nice thing you two have done for the teachers — having them to dinner," said Bramston. "So, Bob, what was your conclusion about our Latin Master, Mr. Warren?"

"Just this: Tom calls him 'Master Teacher,' and that's worth ten thousand dollars per year more, but what I've discovered is that he's been a drunken schizophrenic all during Tom's watch. And now he doesn't even like going in to teach, he told me. His world has been turned upside down."

"Well, Tom did arrange his retirement at the end of the year," said Bramston.

"All I know is that Tom has really confused the poor guy. Dennis doesn't know whether he's coming or going now."

"How long has this been going on?" asked Philips.

"Babs pointed it out to me years ago when Dennis insulted her at the holiday fair, when she chaired it. You both remember she ran it until she lost heart after Tom arrived. Why didn't Tom get rid of that drunken fool years ago like we do in the real world? I can't imagine an alcoholic goldbricker lasting at Bramston and Company." He looked at Bramston, who ate it up.

"Absolutely not."

"Or at the Christ Church Parish office, right?"

Philips bowed in modesty.

"You see," Cattivo pressed, "the mind boggles at how many more weirdoes Tom has nursed along at the kids' expense."

"Well done, Bob, all this research and the dinners," said Bramston. "And I think I speak for the entire board of trustees when I say 'Well done.'"

"Thank you both, your approval means everything to me." Cattivo let it all sink in as he finished his coffee, while Philips, on the edge of his chair and by stretching toward Cattivo's plate of uneaten salmon, ensured that Wither's maid's feelings wouldn't be hurt. "He licked the platter clean," came into Cattivo's mind.

"So, where does this leave us in regards to tomorrow's meeting?" said Bramston.

"Yeah, how do we stop this conspiracy against us? What do you want us to do?" added Philips.

"Let me think a moment. I guess I wasn't sure about all this until you fellas led the way." Cattivo looked into his empty cup — wished it was larger — and became as pensive as he could before he replied.

CHAPTER 31

The Bishop had to admit Robert Cattivo ran the devil's own efficient show at the CC Board of Trustees Executive Committee meeting. Since it might be the only meeting until the fall board meeting, Committee Chair and Vice President Cattivo said he would provide "a fair and balanced" review of the February resolutions and the current financials. And he did. After Bramston chimed in with a note that Tom's fundraising seemed to be going well, the Bishop's guard was down. Everything had appeared hunky-dory until Cattivo became grave and hesitant.

"I'd like to say that is all our business for today. Alas, as a trustee with responsibilities that outweigh my personal desires, I simply cannot."

There was an immediate stir from committee members. Vice President Meredith Ross looked wide-eyed, President Wither Bramston matched Cattivo's gravity, and Rector Richardson Philips looked like the proverbial cat just as the canary stepped out of the cage. The Bishop wondered what the detour was about.

It was about two items, Cattivo said, as he began slowly. The first was Tom West's malfeasance in not appointing a faculty sponsor of the *Chronicle* before the first issue appeared in September. The dilatory action had spelled doom to the school attorney's defensive strategy.

"No!" interrupted Dr. Philips. "What does this mean for us, Bob?"

"About three million dollars in settlement costs. Plus attorney fees. That's my best guess after meeting again with the Central Park Stables' lawyer, Joe Samuels, from Craven & Caddish."

The Bishop awoke and interrupted. "'Again'? You met with their lawyer *before* this came to light?"

"Ah, well, yes," said Cattivo. The Bishop moved in.

"But surely that's not something our own attorney would welcome. And what did you *tell* their lawyer in that first meeting?" Two strikes.

"Wither here had no objections to my meeting. And I was simply—"

The Bishop broke in: "Did our attorney know about and authorize your meeting with the stables' attorney?"

"Please let me finish, Right Reverend. I was simply getting the lay of the land — I thought I might gain valuable information for our side." Cattivo appeared a tad flustered.

"Hmn, and which of you gained the most valuable information, would you say —you or the experienced litigator?"

"I resent the inference," Bob huffed.

"I'm sorry you took offense, but the Craven man is well-known as a skilled litigator. Did you not feel overmatched?"

"Not especially. I deal with his type every day; don't forget I'm in real estate. And I think you'll find that since our defense is shot and we haven't a prayer according to our attorney, that I'm the only man with an answer."

"Go ahead, Bob, tell him," said Dr. Philips with a self-righteous smirk.

"I have told President Bramston and our headmaster that I would be willing to arrange a discreet payment to end the Stables' impregnable position in this legal action. And by the way, it would mean that I would have to move funds to liquidity at a probable loss to me of a considerable amount."

"Well, I for one can only thank Bob Cattivo for pulling the fat out of the legal fire our headmaster got us into," said Philips. "It's hardly the time to question the man who saved our sacred reputation. I move that our president send a strong reprimand over the *Chronicle* scandal to the headmaster."

"Second." For once, Bramston sounded decisive.

The Bishop's "no" vote was joined by Ross' abstention. Passed.

"I'm pleased that could be agreed on," said Bramston. "Now that you have our full confidence, Bob, what was the second topic you wanted to discuss?"

Cattivo looked daggers across the table at the Bishop, who maintained his usual calm manner but inwardly steeled himself not to give an inch. Cattivo fondled his Phi Bete key for a moment and seemed to gather strength from it.

"Now, if I may, I merely wanted to say that I have had dinner with our Senior Master Teacher Dennis Warren. I learned that he is a confused, perhaps depressed, man on the eve of his retirement. I did what I could to support him at this difficult time. I only hope that he receives proper support from Dean Levi and his headmaster."

The Bishop saw the picture now. The wily Cattivo silenced Tom's legitimate charge that he was interfering with the operation of the school with his teacher dinners and promises by now saving the headmaster's skin in the *Chronicle* case. The Bishop suspected that the trustees would never fully know what went on at Cattivo's first unauthorized meeting with the stables' lawyer.

Meredith Ross was both puzzled and frustrated. She had loved her older son's teachers, especially his favorite history teacher, Tom West. So, even though the launch of her five-year-old firm's IPO demanded impossible hours seven days a week, she had accepted a seat on the CC board of trustees as her younger son entered high school. And she had liked the job, enough so that she was talked into the newly-created token female vice presidency alongside the dominant trustee, Bob Cattivo. Year by year they alternated in chairing the executive committee; except this year her co-vice-president had been unusually busy either invading the school personnel records or saving the school from legal action. And all she knew came from what little she was told after the event. It reminded her of what her husband said used to occur on his Brown University board of trustees when he was elected years ago — most were kept in the dark while the real business was conducted by a select few. But the Old Boys and New Boys CC School network hadn't included her, and she found herself caught in a cycle of being kept in the dark and never having enough information to vote intelligently. Oh, if her Princeton classmates could see her now — first woman to breach the male university eating clubs bastion, and now meekly abstaining because she was too goddamn ignorant to vote!

As the executive meeting adjourned, Meredith determined once again to get close to the one person she trusted on the whole board, the Episcopal Bishop. Unaccustomed as she was to confronting a large, hammered sterling silver cross on a manly chest, nonetheless she had to find out what was actually going on from him. The patrician Bishop had always been approachable, even warm toward her. She was always reminded when she saw him in action of the most ridiculous thing she had ever heard from the Christian scriptures, that first century rabbi preaching on the mount: "Blessed are the meek, for they shall inherit the earth." The Bishop was actually like that, even if her business world was worlds away.

Meredith followed the Bishop to the sidewalk. Before he sensed her beside him, he winced and groaned as he turned to hail a taxi. A yellow car swerved toward the curb.

"May I offer you this cab, Meredith?"

She accepted his gallantry, even though she had seen the old man wracked with pain — she did have an important R&D meeting back at the office in twenty minutes. Damn. She was becoming like all the men in Manhattan except for one gentleman from Morningside Heights who had already inherited the Promised Land.

CHAPTER 32

When school attorney Whitey Case told him the news that morning, Tom asked him to come up and meet with the *Chronicle* staff and Ruth Soros, their sponsor. Standing before the assembled editors, Whitey looked like a pinstriped sore thumb when he announced, "The Central Park Stables withdrew their suit this morning."

The students erupted in applause and laughter.

Whitey continued, "Before we get carried away, here's the bad news: they had a credible case against your paper, so we had to adopt a defensive position. My best tactic was in negotiating for an extended period." Only Tom knew how expensive that "extended period" was.

"What do you mean, 'credible case'?" asked Maury, who was seated next to Cat in the middle of the group.

"I mean that they may well have won at trial if they, as a beloved horsey New York institution, appealed for relief from the vicious attack published as news by a privileged prep school newspaper without faculty oversight, that is, lacking what we refer to as due care."

There was a collective intake of oxygen at this point.

"Why, you might well ask, if our position was so weak, did they drop their case against us? Well, if you had read the *Daily News* yesterday, you would have seen that two of their reporters lowered the boom on the Central Park Stables." He pulled a copy of the tabloid from his briefcase and opened it. "Here, and I quote, 'The horses are ill-kept, poorly fed, un- loved, and even lacking the services of a veterinarian.' That was the tip of the iceberg. Their report was based on an extensive investigation, includ- ing undercover drivers and groomsmen, and it was more than enough for the stables' lawyers. So, please remember, we didn't 'win' this case, we got bailed out by the *Daily News*."

The student editors were stunned and chagrined, but mostly relieved. Tom wondered if he had ever witnessed a more "teachable moment"— the buzzword when he started teaching. And he was sure he was even more relieved than the editors; now Cattivo would not be called upon to pay a settlement and use it to bludgeon Tom.

Case said, "You should know that *The New York Times* always has putative legal review of their copy before publication. That might not be a bad idea here."

"Dr. West, is that going to happen?" asked Cat.

"Hardly," Tom said. "We are not assigning a lawyer to you, Cat" — the kids looked uncertain — "but mostly because the school budget can't handle it." He smiled and the editors chuckled along with Case.

After the meeting, the Irregular Irregulars assembled without preamble in the corner of the *Chronicle* office around Maury's desk. Cat inspected Maury's pencil horde, finally choosing one.

"Dammit, we've been asleep at the switch," said Matt. "Doc has had to deal with all this legal crap we caused while we were reviewing for our APs. I've done nothing since we decided to lure Georgie in so we could get some shit on his dad."

"We've hardly seen Doc since he gave up teaching," Maury said. He looked at Matt. "Have you picked up anything more from your mom about Mr. Cattivo trying to nail him?"

"I know she still talks to Aunt Jane about it all the time. That guy is after Doc, that's for sure, but what can we do?"

"Georgie is in his own world, I've found," said Cat. "Matt, maybe you'd better start being nicer to him. You're his hero, after all, being a jock."

Maury snickered, Matt blushed, and Cat grinned and drummed her pencil on the desk.

"Listen," she continued. "We've always had too many people on staff who only want it for their college applications, so we have to beg them to get their copy in. But Georgie has delivered."

"Yeah, I agree, and I'll tell you what turns Georgie on — besides Matt, that is," said Maury, watching the jock grit his teeth. "He's a techie geek. And he's good enough that he helped field test Firefox and knows a helluva lot about some kind of new browser that Google is working on. He told me he does all his dad's apps. If you had a tech editor, he'd be perfect."

"What do you mean, 'if'?" asked Cat. "As of right now, I do have a tech editor for next year. And his initials are GC."

"Sheena MacKay of the *Daily News* is on the phone, Tom," said Jo.

Tom was figuring out how to afford an additional English teacher to staff the new Writing Workshop the department had proposed for all ninth-graders in addition to their regular English curriculum. He'd forgotten to send Sheena an email of appreciation after Whitey's meeting yesterday. And the story came out two days ago. Ingrate.

"Sheena. Tom here."

"You'll forgive me calling — I've learned that putting anything on email risks the damn thing being made public in the future."

"Too true. And I apologize for not calling you first with my thanks. Sorry."

"No apologies necessary. In this business, no one expects thanks."

"Well, thank you for a fabulous exposé – our editors were thrilled!"

"How about your lawyer?"

"He was so thrilled he 'took it under advisement' as to whether he should celebrate."

"I know these guys, we have a few creeping around us down here, but I doubt any litigator would be pleased when a case is dropped without a settlement being hammered out, complete with commissions."

"His girls graduated CC, so he really is on our side. And yesterday he engineered a way to make the stables pay his, or our legal expenses."

"Super, and Lulu told me you had already rung her to tell her the news. Our story really hit home with her because she loves her horses almost as much as she does her golf!"

"She is a delight."

"And she suggested that I should take you up on that drink at the Plaza."

This could get complicated. "Why sure, I was wondering if I could broach that now that my fingers are uncrossed."

"You name the day. I suspect you're busier, hate to admit that, but Lulu says you are."

"I'll email you some possibilities. And you should know that one of our parents on the Humane Society board told me that the mayor's office ordered an investigation of the Central Park Stables. They've been ignored for years, but your story forced the issue!"

"You've made our day down here — I'll tell my crew!"

CHAPTER 33

Tom was torn between what he had to do — get out and talk people into giving him money — and what he felt he wanted to do, which was find out how the Stables' lawyer discovered the late appointment of the faculty paper sponsor. He had already asked Cat and her staff if anyone had inquired about the chronology of the story and sponsor. No, not anyone, they agreed. Tom had been careful not to intimidate Ruth Soros — a shy, thirtyish woman who was an excellent teacher — with questions about the stables story because she hadn't been in charge. He knew her well, as she was also the sponsor of the Lesbian, Gay, Bisexual, Transgender chapter at CC and he had gone to bat for her when needed. Now, after the session with Whitey Case, Tom met with her and asked as casually as he could if she had fielded any criticism from other teachers or parents about how she handled the kids' desire to do "exposés" on the *Chronicle*.

"No, not really, the teachers all know that Cat and her staff are always wanting to do something about the school lunches, city government, or about the academic pressure here. And they do, but carefully enough not to go beyond their evidence. They know they've gotten a lot of leeway from us and don't want to abuse that trust. They really do. I'm proud of them."

"Thank goodness that Central Park Stables threat is behind us. I was worried that you might have been getting tough questions."

Ruth Soros shook her head. "Nope." And then she frowned in concentration. "Well, not unless you count Mr. and Mrs. Cattivo. And their questions were quite roundabout, probably not even relevant. See, I was so excited to be eating at Le Bernardin, it was all a blur of super food and service, exactly like I've read about in *The Times* and *New Yorker* but never experienced." Tom thought she still had stars in her eyes. Then, she came down to earth. "Funny enough," she continued, "they did ask me about how it was being the sponsor of the *Chronicle* — imagine that they'd be interested in that! I have to admit I was flattered. And Mrs. Cattivo kept asking me about the *Chronicle* horse story, how it was researched, said she'd studied journalism at Adelphi. I had to admit my ignorance because I was in charge only from the second issue on. Well, that's about it, I guess." She looked at Tom directly. "I didn't do anything wrong, did I?"

"No, of course not. Jane and I couldn't be more pleased with your guidance of the paper, and with your evangelism for George Eliot!" Ruth left with a smile on her face.

Tom sat in his chair and marveled over Cattivo's craft. So now he knew. Cattivo was the traitor in their midst. Yes, he'd lay it out for the Bishop. And then they'd lay it out for President Bramston who would clear his throat and say, with a look at the Bishop, that such behavior assuredly wasn't Christian, was it? And Cattivo would most likely demand that they question Ruth Soros. Not good. No, the only result of Tom's righteous inquiry would be that Soros would be terribly torn up and blame herself forever — she'd be the prime casualty. After all, it was too late — his own trustee reprimand was already history and would no doubt be used in his official evaluation due at the next board meeting. Cattivo had escaped. Even his bank account hadn't been touched after his showboat move. It was done and dusted, as Tom's St. Andrews history professor liked to say. If only he had time to investigate Cattivo — there had to be something the guy could be nailed on. But that kind of quest would inevitably divert him from his main job, his only job: saving his own skin by raising money.

And Jo, coming in to commiserate, had read him properly as usual.

"I haven't heard any more quotes from your beloved Machiavelli, Tom, not since you sent Sam Spencer packing."

"Yeah, you're right. I forgot that part about, '*It is necessary for a prince who wishes to maintain his position to learn how not to be good.*' And that's been fatal in dealing with Bob Cattivo."

"Don't blame yourself — Mr. Cattivo has been schooled for years at the post-graduate level of property speculators!"

CHAPTER 34

Tom's fundraising had been going very well before Whitey Case's earlier bombshell about the collapse of their defense to the stables threat. And there had been the constant backwash interference over Cattivo's finagling with Dennis Warren and his teachers. He had banked on the trustees' Executive Committee to discipline the out-of-control trustee. That went out the window over the possible *Chronicle* payoff deal he'd struck with Cattivo. He had to honor that, despite the fact that after Sheena Mackay struck, he didn't need it. Well, the Bishop would be intrigued by the ethics of it all — were there any?

Tom did the only practical thing he could think of: he put his focus back on the prospect list. His fundraising operation — almost at the five million mark — wasn't a military exercise, but it ran along similar lines, simple and direct. The Bishop and Lulu helped unearth prospects among the alumni, while Jay Erickson and sometimes Sally Ernst found more among the parents and grandparents. Jay also prepared the financial background for every lunch and dinner with prospective donors. In fact, the reservoir of prospects was deep and wide, and there was a daily revelation to Tom about his constituencies and himself.

"You've seen the article in *Crain's* about me, I'm sure, so you know that I built the business from nothing. Here it is, the 'King of Felt' — I brought you a reprint." Tom's luncheon guest rustled in an inside pocket, handed it over.

"Dad left me a quarter-million-a-year carpet pad operation in a basement off Queens Boulevard. Now I got nearly a whole block, *on* Queens, only two blocks down from LeFrak City. So, like I say, I was thinking of a simple reminder to the kids for my ten thousand, say a plaque on the door of the library, just a simple reminder the King of Felt passed that way."

Tom swallowed his response – "Sorry, KingahFelt, but ten thousand won't buy that much — would you be happy with a sticker inside the computer closet door in the science lab?" Why didn't Tom say it? Definitely not because his temperament and manners had improved much since his February challenge; no, he simply needed the money to keep his job. Somehow his personal development wasn't as exalted as the Bishop's 'seared conscience,' but it was starting to land some loot. And he discovered that every parent prospect was aware that the head knew his kid. That was the easy part for Tom and perhaps the best part for the parents — in Manhattan's frenetic, stressful, impersonal urban world, the head of Christ Church School was watching over their child. So, before the King of Felt finished his coffee, he had agreed to fifty thousand dollars.

The school year was wearing Tom down. He wasn't teaching, so he was raising endowment money full-time rather than being a real schoolmaster. Much was off-kilter for him at school because he was off campus nearly every day from eleven to three and often in the evening as he entertained parents, alumni, trustees, and "friends of the school" at the club. Teaching had always been his *raison d'etre*, with the kids and other teachers as his colleagues in learning. Now, he was losing touch with his reality. He only hoped it didn't show at school.

And gradually it was drawing him in — there was something fascinating about the work when it wasn't about carpet padding, or waste disposal, or aluminum remanufacture, all of which brought in over a quarter of a million. It was a pleasure to be in the handsome Stanford White-designed University Club almost every day. The immense dining room windows overlooked both Fifth Avenue and the Modern's sculpture garden — he could make out Picasso's goat through the trees. Still, he was uneasy sitting at a table with multi-millionaires discussing how to memorialize them and their families. Tom figured his ignorance was glaring as he tried to engage a succession of successful New Yorkers, but they didn't seem to mind as long as he was looking out for their sons and daughters at school.

CHAPTER 35

Cattivo started his intimate pep rally by cheering Wither Bramston and the Rev. Philips. He raised his glass of Perrier to them both. "Thanks for the leadership and downright 'common sense' you both showed under fire at our committee meeting." Bramston seemed a little uncertain about it all, but Philips was quick to respond with a sweeping motion of his own supply of something stronger.

"We were more than honored to be there, and to be part of your team. Right, Wither?"

"Oh, yes, exactly. I was a little nervous when the Bishop started asking questions. But only a little."

"No need to be — I'd say he was just doing Tom's work. Or trying to," said Cattivo.

"Attempting to gain his scriptural 'pound of flesh,' I'd say," said Philips.

Cattivo wondered if this was a biblical reference or something to do with Shakespeare. He chuckled appreciatively. "Yes, and you'd say right. They'd really like to take it out of my hide, wouldn't they?"

"Yeah, and I can only say to them what Senator McCarthy said to his Commie critics when I was only a pup, 'Have you no sense of decency?'"

Having a drink with the Reverend was always an adventure. "Who would like a freshener-up?" he asked, as if he didn't know already.

"Count me in," said Philips.

Cattivo snapped his fingers and eyed the club waiter. "You're counted."

Cattivo and Wither sipped slowly as their companion received his drink. Better lay some groundwork now.

"Babs tells me that she saw Tom and Sally Ernst jogging together one Sunday while she was up on the reservoir track. They looked pretty serious, especially Tom, tongue hanging out and struggling, so maybe not much in the way of a romantic relationship has developed, I don't know. She thought they probably just ran into each other — Sally's a regular with a group of Road Runner guys — they're pretty fast and according to Babs, Tom certainly doesn't fit into that category."

"Isn't Sally Ernst Dutch, or was it Moroccan Jewish?" Bramston asked.

"One of those Shepherdic types maybe; I think they come from shepherd stock like our Good Shepherd," said Philips.

"Yeah, probably," Cattivo said. "But who cares? We've got a bigger fish to fry, and," he drew it out, "I've got an angry wife to satisfy." That got their attention.

"Babs is very unhappy with me these days, thinks I've let her down. She says I'm 'behind schedule on the *outing* of Tom West.'"

"That settles it, if she's right, we ought to fire him yesterday!" said Philips.

"She meant 'ousting,' of course," said Cattivo. "She wants him gone before Georgie applies to college this fall. She's sure he'll sabotage Georgie's chances." Better not mention any more of his plans for Tom's demise — easiest if that remained a mystery. Cattivo could have told Bramston, but he knew Philips loved mysteries like *the Da Vinci Code* and couldn't keep secrets. Hell, he's spent his life in the pulpit blabbing about mysteries.

"I can believe that," said Philips. "Somebody ought to investigate that kind of behavior. I mean our headmaster's, of course, not Babs.'"

"Well, that's right on topic for me," said Bramston. "Bob, I'd like to move on the board resolution that I am to conduct a full evaluation of our school's management."

"Have you got somebody in mind to do it, Wither?" said Cattivo.

"I do, indeed. Somebody who has real Wall Street experience and who has taught at business schools. I'm not ready to announce yet — our deal isn't done — and he's pretty expensive. Not out of line for a consultancy like this, of course, but plenty expensive for a school budget. No need to alarm the other trustees."

"No, we can't have that," said Bob. He knew it was important for Wither to feel that he was in charge of something. "Listen, Wither, you should have the man you want, the best you can get. So, I'll spring for his fee no matter how much. After all, I saved a few shekels when that *Daily News* exposé on the Central Park Stables came out. Just keep it to yourself, please."

Bramston broke into the best smile he could manage, along the lines of Calvin Coolidge.

CHAPTER 36

English teacher Ruth Soros canceled her appointment to see Tom on a Tuesday. On Wednesday, she came in to tell Jo that she had changed her mind again and needed to see him ASAP. She was soon settled on Tom's sofa greeting the bears that fell toward her from their stack.

"Ruth, your kids knocked the top off those English Lit APs again this year!"

"Oh, you know how it is, with the brilliant and motivated students we have, any doofus could compile a great record. You've proved that yourself in European AP."

"Thanks. I think." Tom grinned.

Ruth threw up her hands. "There I go again — I get a little mixed up in here, well, everywhere, as you have learned recently — I didn't mean that *you* were a doofus when I said that." Making her blush was not difficult, but the eternally innocent teacher also had a razor-sharp intellect and her students appreciated her for both qualities. The combination was dynamite and raised her from being a respected teacher to a beloved one.

"Well, Jo tells me that you probably have something else on your mind this week." Tom prayed that it wasn't a follow-up to the "double your money" offer she had rejected from St. Mark's in Dallas last year.

Ruth was uncertain how to proceed, but visibly gathered herself. "I got a check here in the mail for thirteen thousand dollars. Only a check with the note '#1 of 7 Teachers of Excellence.' Mailed in our school's postal zone the day before. A cashier's check in a plain envelope. Nothing else. I think it's supposed to be a secret."

First, relief. Then, concern. But don't show it, Tom. "Well, nobody deserves it more than you do."

"So, did you and Jane know about it, maybe arrange it?"

"Oh, no, I wish we could do that for you, but we wouldn't, not a secret check."

"I haven't cashed it. I was concerned about it. Is it legal?"

"It must be. Would you like me to look at it?"

"Yes, I'd like somebody to investigate. It's so unexpected." She extracted a neatly slit envelope from her shoulder bag and handed it over.

The check inside was drawn on the Farmers and Merchants Associates Bank, Grand Cayman. Bad news.

"May I have Jo make a copy? You should keep the check."

"Yes, please do. Then should I cash it, or at least try to?"

"That should be your decision. But if you were my sister, I'd advise yes. And let me know if the sky falls in!"

Although Tom was out of the office raising money when Ruth rang later in the day, she reported to Jo that the check was good. And Jay Erickson met him when he returned to the office after school. Bad news hunch confirmed — Jay couldn't get beyond the Cayman Monetary Authority firewall to trace the account. And neither could the IRS because the little island nation was a "secrecy jurisdiction" where the world's wealthy parked their piles beyond taxation's reach.

On Thursday the faculty lounge got an unexpected record workout. Right after a morning assembly that let out early, many teachers grabbed a cup of coffee in the lounge. They checked the day's mail and their watches as they drank. Pat Osborne, veteran math instructor, held up an envelope she had just opened with, "Holy Mackerel Snapper!" and quickly amended, "Sorry — I meant no offense to the religious fanatics in here." There was a round of laughter, as she frequently poked fun at her own Catholicism. As people moved over to join her, she waved a half sheet. "Has anyone else received . . ." she checked the check ". . . an anonymous cashier's check for thirteen thousand dollars this morning?"

Now people's laughter became mixed with a babble of questions.

"I don't have a blessed clue, it must be *my* divine visitation," Pat answered time after time. "It reads '#2 *of 7 Teachers of Excellence.*' See? I'm still not number one!" The laughter was more muted as they gathered around her and passed her check around — it was from a bank in the Cayman Islands. The tag line of numbers and "Excellence" set everybody off.

Every class change that day saw a train of teachers checking their mail slots to see if a similar plain envelope had arrived. Since Tom had already departed for a luncheon date, teachers with a free period descended on Jane Levi's office.

Later, Jane stayed at school until six to fill Tom in on the wild day. She sat back on his sofa looking exhausted. When she ran out of breath, Tom spoke.

"Those numbers 'two of seven' on Pat's check must have been dynamite — who else will get lucky!"

"Yes, and they pressed me for an explanation — who sent the money and why? I told them it was news to us, and exactly what you told Ruth without mentioning her: that we would never do something secret like that. They seemed to accept that, but only for ten minutes; then they demanded to know who else got one. No one else had admitted any knowledge. It was edging toward suspicion of all their colleagues — the missing six. I'd call the teachers' condition by lunchtime as 'general dismay' to put it mildly. Or, more realistically, 'unfocused anger.'"

"I haven't heard anything," said Tom. "My emails are all piled up because I was at the Downtown Association for lunch, picking up twenty-five thousand dollars when it should have been a hundred and striking out in New Haven this afternoon. Was there a round two?"

"During our after-lunch coffee we had a full house in the lounge because everyone wanted to be there when the second shoe dropped. Ruth Soros had taken her students up to a Columbia Victorian seminar this morning, but when she returned and heard of the brouhaha, she announced that she received check number one and that the check was good. Then, they all asked Pat what she would do with her check. 'Cash it,' she said. 'My husband says we'd be crazy to look a gift horse in the mouth — it's a year of mortgage payments, even after taxes.'"

Jane described how Pat and Ruth were forced into an edgy discussion on why they were chosen for the windfall and who could have sent it. "People like them both, of course, and no one questions their excellence, so everybody soon began to bore in on the missing five checks.

"The atmosphere crackled. And it got worse when your new Junior Class Dean Mac Corutore jumped in. 'We're a learning *community*, aren't we?' he said. Then, something about doing the 'right thing' and 'sharing as a community.' That really set people back on their heels. See how tangled the whole damn thing has become? We've now got teachers looking in each other's boxes to see if anyone else received a check. All of our nice, gentle, civilized teachers are simmering, and a few seem to suspect you of some underhanded move. The only sane person was dear old Sam Rogers who sat quietly reading his *Nation*."

Tom chuckled, "Yeah, but only because he always turns his hearing aid off to concentrate!" They both smiled in agreement, but Jane was quickly serious.

"After school, Ruth and Pat came in very disturbed — the very two who should be over the moon! A few other teachers seemed to coalesce around Mac Corutore's approach that the two should come forward and share their dough.

"Pat took it pretty well but Ruth was weak in the knees. They said Pat asked everyone why they should share, especially if the other unnamed recipients didn't share their's? Apparently, the place became a tinderbox as the Corutore group speculated on the five other 'obvious' star teachers to 'fess up. Ruth said there were 'strong feelings' but Pat was more blunt. She said it was the nasty comments that compelled them to come to us."

Jane sat back in the sofa. "There, boss, it's all yours." She grabbed Paddington. "But this bastard Cattivo is mine," she added as she pinned the bear to the couch and throttled him.

"You think he's behind this?"

"Definitely," said the Dean.

They both sat silently. Their subsequent discussion was so intense that it was nearly dinnertime when Jane remembered that Ben was on late Thursday rounds at the hospital and that she and Sally had planned their weekly meal around that. At 6:50, it was too late — Sally would already be on her way to their seven dinner.

"We haven't finished — you'll just have to come to dinner with Sally and me."

"That's the only good news I've had all day. I accept."

Tom meant it — he had grown more dependent on the president of the CC Parents' Association than he'd admitted to himself. He wasn't surprised that Sally's entrance into the discussion of the day's issue at dinner was seamless.

Jane and Tom had tried to piece it together: the two check recipients had been Cattivo guests at Le Bernardin, *except* that even seven checks did not account for the ten teachers who reported their fancy dinners, and there could have been more. So far, they only had evidence of two checks.

"In short, there's not enough evidence for any 'pattern,' is there?" Sally said.

The three agreed the culprit had to be Cattivo, although none of the teachers had made that point yet. And the trio didn't think they could prove Cattivo's part, not with the untraceable Cayman checks. And even if they could prove it, what would that get them? Board action? Of what nature?

"And can we even properly use the term 'culprit'?" Sally asked. "Is giving underpaid, excellent teachers a nice check for 'excellence' something that deserves censure?"

"Well, if it is Cattivo," said Tom, "that is a conflict of interest as Georgie may have one of the seven teachers now or in the future."

"Okay, that's a valid point, but we're back to the difficulty of proving he's behind it," said Sally. "And we don't even know all the recipients, do we?"

"Or even if there are seven in total — that cute little numbering system, '1 of 7' could be a ruse to stir things up, mess with us; so the teachers will think some of their colleagues are holding out," said Tom. "I can see Cattivo doing that."

"Hell," said Jane, "I can see *me* doing that. I'd get the impact of seven gifts and only pay out two — what a bargain!" When she saw their reaction, she added, "Just kidding. Kinda."

Sally gave her old roommate a mock karate chop. Tom shook his head and said, "Nail her for me, too!" Sally complied with a laugh.

"And if you can't trace the donor or donees, what's left?" said Sally. "Only absurd actions. Force the teachers to give it back? To whom? Force them to share, so the taint is shared?"

"I'd like to do something," said Jane. "My superb faculty is imploding!"

"Technically, it isn't any of your business," offered Sally, tucking up a corner of her mouth. Don't stare at her lovely mouth, Tom reminded himself.

"Yeah, all of our alternatives are impossible, if not fatuous," said Tom. "And I can't help thinking that these thirteen thousand dollar checks are a way of trumping our usual summer merit fellowships of ten thousand dollars — it's ten thou plus taxes. Trumping and second-guessing, really. So, the real threat is to faculty morale. Jane and I will have to spend a great deal of time on that. I'll cancel my promising Friday donor appointments, stay at school, and we'll try to get control of this thing."

Jane nodded. "I'm with you; it's all we can do."

Tom looked at Sally. "And, unfortunately, two of my calls tomorrow were with parents you identified — the Higgins and Sanborns. Jay and I didn't even know about their family foundations."

By 4:00 P.M. on Friday, it looked as if he might lose the whole next week of fundraising to the burgeoning controversy over the anonymous checks. Teachers had flooded into his office and some sounded like wounded middle schoolers: "It isn't fair!" And he couldn't improve on the answer that they, as teachers, told the students every day when pressed: "Life isn't fair."

Then Ruth stopped in late in the day with an idea. "I remembered only today that at the dinner Mrs. Cattivo led us into that make-believe talk about our 'dream trips.' But she told us about hers as well, so that probably doesn't relate to my check. But she did say something at that dinner to the effect that 'excellent teachers' should receive 'special treatment.'"

Even though the wonderful teacher was bubbling with her remembrance, Tom knew that Babs' comment was what he and thousands of other educators and critics of American salary scales had also said — it was hardly self-incriminating, at least in court under the rules of evidence. But Ruth's recollection certainly could be helpful.

"Now that is interesting, Ruth. And it might jog some other memories. You should try it in the faculty lounge."

CHAPTER 37

Tom canceled his Sunday exercise to drive the Bishop to a preaching and confirmation engagement in Dobbs Ferry. The Bishop wasn't up to driving himself, although he claimed he was feeling better. Many years before, he had cut the expense to the diocese of the full-time driver and limo he inherited from his predecessor — "The savings paid for five full scholarships at our choir school!" he explained on the way.

Tom was deeply impressed with the reception the Bishop received at the Zion Episcopal Church, which had been founded by Washington Irving in the 1830s. Perhaps even more impressive was the dynamic presence of the ailing eighty-year-old Bishop. Although he was clearly exhausted when he climbed into Tom's car after the service, he soon began asking questions about the school. After a report on his fundraising, Tom laid the whole Cayman check business out for him and gave him the bank codes on a sheet of paper. The cleric said he'd see what he could do and be back to Tom later in the week.

First thing Monday morning, the Bishop emailed Meredith Ross details of the Cayman check mystery at CC School and Tom's concern about faculty morale. She replied that she agreed with the concern and would conduct her own investigation. She unleashed her considerable company resources by turning two of her Young Turks loose on the mystery after telling them in clear language that she didn't want to know their methods, only the account source in Grand Cayman. Although Ross' life was devoted to the Internet, she readily admitted to using the phone for confidential matters, so she phoned the Bishop later with the findings.

"My team met with the same result as Tom's guy: the usual Cayman banking silence. I'm sorry to let you down, Bishop, especially as I appreciate the trust you extended to me."

"And I, in turn, appreciate your time and trouble with this."

"Don't mention it. I have been wanting to be used more on the trustees and this was one of the first times I've been asked. I can see why Tom is trying to dampen the understandable anxiety the teachers must feel. My parents were both teachers and I can only imagine the furor those checks have caused. Anonymous checks with a secret agenda to a few teachers seem to me to be more than mischievous. And expensive. Correct me if I'm misguided, but wouldn't you agree that there's more here than is visible to Tom and the teachers?"

"I admit I've been baffled and frustrated and even at times, as you know, angered by the proceedings. But I'd be reluctant to charge any connection," he said.

"Hmm, you'll pardon my thinking, then, if I ask if the checks are an attempt to undercut Tom? As you know, I chair the subcommittee to award seven merit summer fellowships of almost identical amounts. It can't be a coincidence. What do you think?"

"I can't say for sure, but I'm open to future persuasion, Meredith."

This left them both pleased with themselves, she because he had trusted her and used her given name for the first time, and he because the seeds of proper concern and suspicion were planted in her noggin.

The Bishop immediately reported to Tom that Ross' crew could not breach the Cayman barrier either. He rang off with, "Have fun."

Sally Ernst sensed that her running companion would have done better if she had brought along a Vespa scooter for him. On the hottest and most humid spring day so far, they had agreed to do a Central Park loop after work since Tom had missed his Sunday jog.

"I slow you down," Tom said. "You shouldn't have to give up your most important workout of the week just to limp around the park with me."

"I really don't mind. It's a good time to talk. About your campaign. And I don't 'limp,' it's slower, sure, but we don't 'limp' — it's more like slow race-walking. No, that's not right, it's more like, oh, I don't know, but I don't mind." Zip it, she told herself.

Tom obviously didn't know how to respond. She knew he was thinking about how fast a slow race-walker was.

She plunged on. "As I said, we can talk about your fundraising cru—, uh, campaign. It's the only time we can."

"And your exhibit planning," he said. "On your Dutch exhibit."

"Yes."

She checked his white on white legs — OK, maybe not as bad as she originally thought, not bad, a certain angular stride, could be improved if he'd ask, not helped by his tacky canvas camp shorts. He ran like a male jock who had never tried distance running before, short, choppy steps that ran out of oxygen fast, still his old football wind sprints. Gasp, gasp.

Silence for three or four minutes. They jogged another quarter mile.

Tom checked his running companion. A glow from the moistened hair tendrils following the curve of her neck to the fragile thrust of the shoulders outward. Fragile — hardly, especially the silky stride that easily exceeded his. No wonder the Road Runner guys gathered around her like an escort flight. And always that placid, bemused face.

"Sally, we both know that the only way this will work is if you do the talking. I can't talk and get my breath at the same time at this pace." She turned to watch him and easily kept up with him as she sidestepped alongside. "So, talk," he ordered.

She grinned and talked. "Well, I'm making progress with the exhibit loans — we've got our targets planned — which ones we'd like, which ones we must have. Now, I have to contact the owners, mostly museums, based on our mutual balance sheets."

"Explain?"

"See, the Met has a history with dozens of museums worldwide. Most owe us for past loans. My exhibit has top priority to use up some of that debt and good will to press for valued Old Masters. There's a limit, of course, especially as such paintings are always rare and no museum willingly depletes its most attractive holdings."

The explanation and explainer engrossed Tom for several miles. At least until the explainer changed the subject.

"That's enough of my dream exhibit. We've only got another mile. I really wanted to bring up something else."

"Sure, shoot."

"It's about my Matt and Maury and Cat. I need your advice on two things. First, those three have gathered at our apartment on Saturdays for brunch for over a year. So, I'm used to them and vice versa. They talk as if I'm not in the room, and recently they've been calling themselves the 'Irregulars.'"

"I - r - r?"

"Yes. But they haven't volunteered what that is. And I haven't asked. You know them as well as anybody — ring any alarm bells?"

"Not at all. 'Irregulars' is a stretch for them. Cat is the closest, but no, nothing alarming."

"And they've also become more secretive around me — this is number two — several times in the last couple of weeks, they've fallen silent when I came into the living room when they were talking intensely."

"Arguing?"

"Not exactly. But maybe. And they soon adjourn to Matt's room. That was a first. It bothers me because it's so unusual."

"And because mom wants to know if Matt has a problem. Right?"

"Right. But last Saturday, guess what. Georgie Cattivo came over with Maury."

"What? You're pulling my leg."

"Yes. 'Georgie Porgie,' as Matt used to call him, our favorite trustee's pride and joy."

"I don't get the connection to our trio."

"They say Georgie is 'shadowing' Maury in order to learn the ropes of how to be a columnist on the *Chronicle*. He's going to be the new tech editor, covering computers to cell phones."

"That's certainly his fixation," said Tom, "to the detriment of his grades; but look at Bill Gates and Steve Jobs. He's quiet, and I used to think of him as mommy's boy, but he may be daddy's now. Bob is nuts about him. It'll be hell to pay if Georgie doesn't get into the Ivies, even though it's a long shot."

"Well, imagine my surprise after having him around. I like Georgie. He's almost an angel with that chubby choirboy face. He's polite and I'd even call him gentle, if a little unctuous around me: 'Oh, you look so nice today, Mrs. Ernst!'"

"Well, 'unctuous' is better than daddy's naked bellicosity. Do you think these 'Irregulars' are aware of trustee politics and Cattivo's vendetta?"

"Not a chance. How could they? Unless Bob and Babs have poisoned the boy against you." She shook her head, "But those three would set Georgie right in a hurry."

Tom loved being placed in Sally's confidence. She sounded like a friend now. Could it be more? Don't push it, smart guy. Just start running more than once a week.

CHAPTER 38

Tom thought the aura of faculty confusion and distrust was overwhelming at the four P.M. meeting to air their concerns about the anonymous checks. It was a short meeting with no real news — still only two of the "seven" checks were accounted for, so he could only reiterate his ignorance of the source.

"So, Tom, you say you and Jane know nothing of these checks. Right?"

The interlocutor was young Mac Corutore, whom Tom had appointed Junior Class Dean over the objections of Jane last week. She'd said he was too young and inexperienced. Tom had argued that the other class deans were getting long in the tooth and that the students deserved the rookie pied piper as their mini-dean of students to provide fresh ideas and approaches. Mac had certainly provided that with his repeated claims that all the teachers should share in the unexpected largesse of the teachers' checks.

"Right. We were as surprised as Ruth and Pat when the checks arrived. Jay Erickson and one of our trustees have been unable to trace them beyond the Grand Caymans Monetary Authority's firewall that protects the secrecy of their banks' accounts. Something like one-point-five trillion is lodged there, according to various U.S. and European authorities. That's all we know."

"That doesn't do much for the rest of us, does it?" That whine came from a haggard and tense Dennis Warren, who had showed up for the meeting even though he had missed his classes earlier in the day.

"Dennis, I would simply caution everyone not to harass Pat and Ruth over this," said Tom. "We all know they are among the finest teachers in creation and I, for one, am pleased that they received an unexpected boon."

The murmur of the group encouraged him to press another point, one he had avoided because it might trigger a touch of paranoia as to why anyone would want to cause confusion in their midst.

"This is not a matter of Pat and Ruth versus 'the rest of us.' For example, we can't assume that the 'missing' five checks actually existed and were received by colleagues. To be precise, I don't know if the other five checks ever existed because anyone, even you or I, can label a cashier's check with whatever we wish — '1 of 7,' or '1 of 70.'"

The murmuring increased as the new possibilities were apparent. There were no more questions, but confusion and suspicion still reigned as he closed the meeting. The lingering feeling he had was that much of the trust he and Jane had created over the years in their dealings with the teachers had been seriously eroded since those dreadful checks had arrived.

CHAPTER 39

Sally was way overdue in setting up next year's Parents' Association program, which had to be approved by the headmaster. She hoped Tom didn't mind when she insisted on the office meeting, one he had postponed since early May because of everything he was trying to juggle. Their infrequent runs followed by Tom rushing off to catch up at his office had hardly been the place for substantive discussion or getting acquainted. She could talk freely and did on their runs, but she'd be damned if she'd virtually walk so he could catch his breath to answer. Tom West often seemed harried, not always in control, and increasingly vulnerable; but she had begun to wonder if she didn't prefer that to the Masters of the Wall Street Universe she met through the Met and had dated for years.

Sally arrived at Tom's office laden with the treasurer's records and her own plans for teachers they'd like to invite to the Parents' Association monthly meetings. Thirty minutes later they had finished, and he seemed to enjoy hearing about her invitation from the Bishop to accompany him to a confirmation service in Millbrook in two weeks.

"At first, I thought it was outlandish," she explained. "Then his seriousness *and* sense of humor kicked in. The Bishop said he would love to hear about my Dutch exhibit at the Met and compare notes on your fundraising prospects. And that maybe he could talk Lulu Leonard into some lunch before we returned to the city so we could have our first 'Money Raising Summit.' Oh, and he assured me that he now had 'a reliable, if over-qualified, chauffeur,' so I needn't worry on that score!"

"If you're still uneasy, you can take it from the chauffeur that the drive will take longer than the service itself."

She was thinking the invitation over, big time. A Sephardic Jew going with the Episcopal bishop to a church service? It didn't scare her — she'd gone a few times with friends as a girl in Amsterdam — but hardly with the Bishop, if the Dutch Protestants even had one. She did like and respect this Bishop after seeing him in meetings and reading about him in the papers. Tom had already claimed that she was now an important part of his fundraising team, like Lulu Leonard. And Lulu! She'd heard intriguing stories about Lulu's love of Vermeer from curator friends at the Frick Collection, where she served on the board. She might be useful.

"Thanks again for steering me to gold last week," Tom said. "I contacted the van Vorsts on Central Park West. Wow, I had no idea — six figures — we're now over ten million, halfway! How did you figure they might be generous?"

"I didn't figure," said Sally, "but I always liked her when she was a class rep. And I hoped they might be descendants of the original New Jersey Dutch founding family van Vorsts. Who knows how many Old Masters might be floating around in such a family. That's really why I steered you in that direction — I admit it, self-interest. But how did you do it?"

"I told Mrs. van Vorst of our endowment campaign and waited. She didn't miss a beat, invited me to dinner and said they'd always wanted to have me — her daughter's favorite history teacher three years ago — for dinner. That made it easy. Corny's back for the summer and we talked about Gordon Wood — her senior thesis adviser at Brown."

"So you sneaked in as a teacher and emerged as a flush head."

"That's about it. The apartment was very impressive in a restrained way."

"So, scout, did you see any Dutch School paintings for my exhibit?"

"You're asking the wrong scout. There were many pictures in every room, mostly prints, engravings or lithos maybe, I wouldn't know. He's proud of his map collection in the library, showed me that and, in the dining room, several seascapes by . . . 'van de' something. I simply don't remember. It had battling sailing ships."

"Van de Velde? Was it Willem van de Velde?" Sally was beside herself.

"Sorry, it sounds a little familiar, but that whole wall was filled with pictures. But there was something I did notice — the most impressive thing in the whole place."

Sally was hanging on his every word.

"The dining room walls were covered, floor to ceiling, with gold-embossed russet leather. Unbelievable!"

Tom couldn't help but notice that her deflated sigh indicated she was disappointed in his report. He hadn't made any points that day with Assistant Curator Ernst.

Tom remained baffled by the Parents' Association president. He tried to compartmentalize his job and his personal life. He had learned the hard way when the Countess had rushed him off his feet last fall. Even when he managed to extricate himself from her seductive tentacles, he was left with the sometime 'foster care' of her neglected son. Serena always drove a hard bargain. Like now, when she seemed to be stalling on her two million pledge. That made him more than gun-shy with divorcees and maybe even with widowed mommies at CC.

Sally had been invaluable with his fundraising. The families she had identified as possibilities were already in for over two million. But he'd have to tread warily with her regarding the nitty-gritty of how he made his appeals and deals with the donors. He remembered her response at the Levis' second dinner when Tom supplied the wine.

"Wow, Tom, Petrus! Any more bottles at home?" asked Ben.

"The rest of the case. An admirer sent it over." Tom smiled to himself. The others looked at him with interest. Tom couldn't help feeling pleased with his secret.

"Merely 'an admirer'? That's all we get? It may be my curatorial training, but might we ask you to be more specific of its provenance?" said Sally with mock formality.

"Uh, well, Bob Cattivo. It was in appreciation for a favor for his friend even though I told him I hadn't done the favor."

"Sure, that makes a lot of sense," said Sally. "Even beyond the lack of credibility, it means that you're consorting with your own enemy after what

I saw at the trustee meeting. You can't descend to Cattivo's cunning brute level, Tom."

"That's horribly naïve, Sal," said Jane. "He's got to get close enough to him to hit below Cattivo's belt. Tom, I say get your ass in gear, run over the bastard."

"I can't believe you really believe that, Jane Warburg Morse Levi."

Jane shot a look at Sally, cleared her throat but didn't say anything. Tom busied himself with his meal.

"Moving right along," Ben said and topped up their wine glasses.

Tom could have related the story of Cattivo's mix-up over Serena's daughter's unexpected acceptance at boarding school to Ben and Jane, but never to Sally, who had already noted in passing, "The Countess's maternal instincts are nonexistent."

But now, watching Sally gather up her Parents' Association files, he determined to begin his assault, or rather, quest of Ms. Ernst after Matt's graduation when the deck cleared. Maybe Jane could even help out a bit.

Sally's aura remained after she left his office, prompting Tom to take quick stock of himself and his campaign. His early revulsion about asking for money was dissipating as he had begun to haul in one-hundred thousand and five-hundred thousand dollar gifts. It now went beyond what the gifts could mean at the school; his pride at reeling in the donors and returning home with the pelts was becoming addictive. Damned if he hadn't reverted to a primitive hunter-gatherer. But given Sally's feelings about that Cattivo wine gift, he couldn't count on that woman at the mouth of the cave to applaud the hoard he dropped at her feet. And beyond the pelts, he couldn't admit to her the erosive effect it was having on his own values. The Bishop and Lulu seemed to understand and cheer his efforts, but Sally Ernst was something else. He was coming to grips with the realization that, more than anything, he wanted to impress her with his performance as fundraiser, as a guy who could take charge and "win." But he'd soon have to face a reality: he'd risk losing any chance with her if he ever came clean on his methods.

CHAPTER 40

After Sally left his office, Tom attempted to get through to Bob Cattivo, but his secretary said he didn't wish to be disturbed. The young man was studiously cool to the CC head. Maybe Tom should have told the young snit to inform Herr Cattivo that the head rang to say that he had just thrown Georgie out for drug dealing.

Tom steadied himself by walking the halls, sampling the Sloppy Joes in the kitchen — delectably fatty with who knew what cheap cuts — and returning to his desk. Cooled down, he tried another call to Cattivo's office. All the other trustees had provided their private numbers to him, but not Robert Cattivo.

Cattivo burst onto the line with his patented, "Whosit?" as if he had been too busy to be given the multi-syllabic, complicated, "Tom West."

"Tom."

"Fuck do you want?"

Then a telephonic wrestling match followed about whether anything Tom wanted to see him about was remotely as important as Bob's latest office/residential tower development in Hoboken. "That's on the Hudson," he explained. "Got in a little late, after LeFrak, Rose, and the others, but it's all gold over there! With a piece of the ferry service, I'll get my residents over faster than if they lived in Brooklyn."

"Bob, we need to talk about the health of the school."

"I know. It hasn't been good for nearly five years. Right? Since you came."

Tom didn't bite.

"OK, if you swear it'll be worth my time, we'll have a quick lunch at eleven-thirty down at that greasy spoon, Café Centro, at their bar thing

— don't come up, I'll meet you there. Thirty minutes, tops, I've got a noon lunch at the club."

Bob had the lobster soup, Tom the fish burger. No preliminaries necessary, it was clear Cattivo didn't want to be there.

"Bob, do you have any knowledge of untraceable cashier checks for thirteen thousand dollars each from a bank in the Cayman Islands, seven of them, sent to our teachers?"

"My defense, as if I need to offer one, is simple: prove it. And have you seen all seven checks?"

"No. We only have two checks."

"No? Then you'd better say 'two checks.'"

Why am I always on my back foot with this guy? "Okay, try this on: so far, the *two* checks have gone to teachers you and Babs entertained."

"And I'll bet they use the same toothpaste, too," he snarled. "Golly gee. So, now we've established a pattern, have we, that whenever something blows up in your school your immediate response is, 'Cattivo's behind this.' And I guess given our recent history, I shall have to keep fielding your tiresome charges until the trustees catch on and you get yours at the fall board meeting."

"Given 'our recent history,' Bob, the showering of our teachers who were your guests at Bernardin with fat checks from nowhere that just happen to be three thousand more than our summer fellowship checks, well, surely you can see my logical conclusion as to the source."

"*Le* Bernardin. Well, perhaps. Given our immediate history." Bob sighed with boredom. "And both of us keeping in mind that that history is sealed. Yes, I can grant you that."

Tom had to go for the jugular now.

"It would appear to me to be a clear trumping, if you will, of the seven fellowships we award every summer. We've tried to trace the checks into the Cayman bank and got nowhere."

"Which bank? And which one of your yahoos checked?"

"Merchants Associates. And my yahoo was Ms. Ross, who used her top people."

"Touché."

"You remember that Ms. Ross chairs the committee that awards our merit checks after interested teachers make fellowship applications for summer travel and study."

"I didn't remember that she was involved. Tell me more." Tom could see that the mention of Board Vice-President Ross hit home — Cattivo considered her his creation.

"Our procedure allows the department heads and me to reward merit, as expressed in the teacher's willingness to do extra study and travel. President Bramston and many other trustees have expressed their support in the past and as they know, I had planned to increase the number every year until we reach twenty. This year's increase was axed in my budget."

Bob ceased his desultory attack on his soup and sat. Was his lower lip out slightly?

"Bob, I honestly don't know why you are being so difficult. Think of your own self-interest: whether or not I'm still at CC, you want Georgie to have a good senior year ... but if the faculty continues to be upset about these anonymous checks, they simply won't teach as well. If you work with me to clear this up, the teachers' morale will be where it should be in September. Please."

Tom hadn't much hope with this appeal. Bob sat rearranging his stainless knife and fork and ignoring his food. He finally took a sip of iced tea, viewing Tom over the rim of his glass. Tom matched him. Real High Noon stuff.

"Hey, when you insisted on coming down here this morning, you took me by surprise. I've been busy, too busy, and sometimes I get a little short with people." He looked intently at Tom and continued.

"When I made that deal with you, over what you and the Bishop seemed to think was interference in the school, I stuck to my word. All that was, and is, over for me. Just as you did — you kept to your word, even though it had to hurt after the *Daily News* bailed us both out. I appreciate that integrity; it's not something I'm used to. But this business, this takes me by surprise. And I hate surprises. I'm sure you do, too. And yes, ensuring that Georgie has a great senior year and goes to college where he wants to go, yes, that's number one for me."

"We'll do our best to make that happen."

"We'll see about that. But this I can say: I had nothing to do with sending any checks to your teachers. Nothing."

CHAPTER 41

"I've still got nothing on that basketball dressing room rumor. Zilch. The girls seem to have made a vow of silence. I'm afraid it's one of those damn things we can't ferret out and yet if it blows up in our faces later, we'll be blamed for not doing anything about a scandal we knew all about."

Jane Levi had been waiting for him after school with news and fresh coffee. Tom typed notes on his laptop as she talked.

"Another area I'm worried about is our kids' involvement with social spaces on their computers. After we warned them about MySpace, they moved on to Facebook thanks to college friends. We've warned them, of course, that nothing is truly private, but I heard from two other deans this week that their kids have been the near-victims of sexual predators over the past few months. One girl even met the boy, who turned out to be a man, at the Roosevelt Hotel lobby before she got wise. It's scary stuff."

Tom shook his head. "And some still trust the technology to protect them. Add to that, our kids think they're so sophisticated that they can see through those internet come-ons. Some are sitting ducks; like that time the Moonies challenged a couple of our kids at LaGuardia to continue the debate at their place in the Catskills. And that Internet stuff on the students' own computers is not even something we can legally get into."

She nodded. "I'll preach some more in assembly, but you know they've already tuned us out on this. And by the way, speaking of things we can't get into, Cattivo's evil was very much present at the faculty meeting today. Susan Marcus asked, 'What has Tom done about those seven fat checks two weeks ago?' I told her that because we could not find the source, the matter was nυ a school issue anymore, if ever."

"That's all we *can* say to them, Jane."

"Well, no one was happy about that, but when I asked, no one had any advice. Except Dennis Warren, who said, 'That really means that five people in this room are holding out.' That led to quite a brouhaha, including some nasty comments flying, and they didn't forget to include you, Road Warrior."

"I'm pleased. Hate to be left out." Tom shook his head and looked over his screen.

"I called time out by quoting you to the effect that we didn't even know there ever were seven checks, as opposed to only two. Things quieted down, but Mac Corutore had the last word: 'Dennis is right, that doesn't mean shit for the rest of us.'"

"They're still angry and confused," said Tom. "How did you handle Mac's eloquence?"

"I ignored his comment and we moved on."

"Good work. And you're right — Cattivo somehow was in that room, but I can't prove it or do anything about it. And he categorically denies it."

Jane shrugged, poured him another cup, and looked him over. "About time for another dinner, Tom?"

He didn't answer — he was replaying his misstep with a donor at the Knickerbocker Club earlier — he'd probably asked for too much, so he came away empty. He'd have to follow that up, somehow. He started, looked at Jane. "Sorry, woolgathering. I screwed up another one today."

"Woolgathering, *again*. Good cause, my friend, but you could use a distraction. Are you game for a celebratory dinner at our place the evening of graduation? Ben would love to see you, and I'm sure the most eligible widow in Manhattan will be free."

"Tell Ben I'm sorry about missing our squash week after week. And as for that widow, what chance have I got?"

"Probably none, given your post-Countess scruple about school mothers." Jane shook her head. "Less than none, after you made today's *Post*."

She pulled it out of her desk. "Can't have this rag in plain sight around the school. Here, Page Six. 'Our favorite designing Countess has returned to Gotham from Argentinian polo fields. Perhaps to re-woo the mercurial beauty's Favorite Headmaster?'"

Shit. Probably planted by Serena's flack — it had happened before. "But our CC people won't put it together, Jane. Or even see it."

"To hell with 'our CC people,' Tom, your piece is in the same paragraph with a bit here about a new Met trustee, it's probably up on the curators' bulletin board over there already. This may be enough to drive Sally toward good old Jerry Stone, who's now on the Met's Visiting Committee."

"Yeah, but it isn't like that at all with Serena — we're finished. Not exactly amicable, but well, I haven't seen her since Christmas, even though I've left messages for her about the two million she's pledged." Jane appeared unconvinced. "Really. It's over."

"Then why does her son sometimes stay with you when he's in town?"

"I guess because Chris considers me a kind of surrogate parent. When she leaves him by himself, he knows he's always welcome at my apartment, and not because there's anything between his mother and me. Sure, Jane, she uses me, but he's a very lonely kid. You remember what he was like around here."

"Oh yes, I do remember, he was very alone."

"And remains so. I think he might be a pariah up at boarding school."

"Then don't hesitate to call on me if I can help. Poor kid." She checked her watch. "I'm running late. Sorry to have waylaid you on this, but you needed to know about that article."

CHAPTER 42

Tom hadn't considered his affair with Serena, the Countess, a success, except for the unexpected development of his relationship with Chris. It was only when Tom had been roped into visiting Chris on parents' weekend last fall with Serena that he woke up. The boy had written to Tom about his excitement over Tom's upcoming visit before Serena had even invited him. Tom gave Serena an expletive-charged scolding, but he couldn't wound Chris, so he went up for the visit. He discovered that the boy was having more social difficulties up there than he'd had at CC.

Tom was familiar with parents who were too self-centered to do much for their children, but his affection for Serena at the time had made it difficult for him to see her lack of concern for Chris. He did remember that the previous week she had called her son "soft in the slippers" when Tom demurred at her using her usual "light in the loafers" line. Could that be a loving mother's term for a son who was very sensitive and vulnerable, or was it her way of distancing herself from a son who might remind her of his gay father?

In the weeks after they returned to the city, she never mentioned her son unless Tom asked. At the same time, she tried to lavish cufflinks and clothing on him and seemed hurt when Tom refused them.

"No more presents," he'd told her. And at Thanksgiving, he'd broken it off.

Or so he'd thought.

Serena had been the latest of his star-crossed "romances," all of which, in hindsight, were more like casual flings. Tom continued his track record of being lonely and horny; and even when he met someone to alleviate the horny, he was still lonely. He worried as to whether he could throw himself wholly into a relationship, as he had with Betsy. But if Tom had major doubts about any long-term alliance with Serena, she didn't seem to have any such reservations. She seemed to have no reservations except at Jean Georges. And she summed up her own impossible view — "I'll bide my time, darling. I suspect you've noticed that whatever Serena wants, Serena gets."

Her fixation with that little motto came due at Christmas.

Tom's breakup with Serena at Thanksgiving brought him some relief. And yet, he felt a continued responsibility for a lonely boy who was trying to fit in at a provincial boarding school in New England. When Chris phoned to tell him that he had quit the rugby club because a few of the other players had called him a "fuckin' fag," Tom talked with him for an hour and wrote him a warm letter of encouragement. Since then the boy had continued to keep in touch, calling or writing once in a while and stopping in at Tom's office for a talk and dinner when he was in the city.

Serena didn't make any contact until the weekend before Christmas. In the meantime he heard that she had no shortage of male escorts at holiday charity bashes. He had once told her that he loved walking Manhattan streets and inhaling the pine aroma from the trees stacked for sale in front of the shops. She announced on the phone that because of everything Tom had meant to her son she had planned a "no strings attached" evening purely for him: they'd walk and inhale the trees, attend the Messiah at Carnegie Hall and have supper at Jean Georges.

It was a most thoughtful gesture. He melted until she amended it.

"And of course you'll come and stay the night. I'd love that. I admit it. So, there, heartbreaker."

God, she made it difficult. He waited several counts, but she couldn't wait.

"I've told you I don't care that you don't have much money because I have enough for us both! But I won't beg, Tommy." Her voice rose. "Oh, forget it—"

"Now, Serena, don't hang up, please!" he interrupted. "Here's an even better plan — I'll help you with Chris. But our hitting the sack again would only complicate it all." He spoke rapidly before she hung up. And also before he changed his mind.

On Christmas Eve morning around 10:30, she tapped on his office window and explained that she had a Christmas package for him. She was holding a hamper.

When he let her in, she was wearing her mink-lined trench coat, which she kept on because she was still chilly. She opened her hamper loaded with all his weaknesses — buttery croissants lined with dark Belgian chocolate and a thermos of espresso she'd brewed herself.

Tom almost enjoyed their time together. They talked about Chris' social problems at school — it was news to her — and his plans for summer theater internships. She mentioned she'd been working on polar bear protection. The conversation flagged as the coffee and pastry disappeared. Serena brightened and rose.

"And now, I think it's time you got your Christmas present. An offer that you can't refuse."

She stood with her back to the windows and opened her coat — she was wearing her trademark diamond choker, her black croc knee-high boots, and a red and green Christmas ribbon around her waist with bow above her black pubic thatch trimmed in the shape of a Christmas tree.

Tom was blown away and oddly touched. And he surprised himself with his response.

"Oh, Tannenbaum, you are a truly beautiful sight, but you're inviting a big mistake to happen here. And I tell you that it's nuts — we'd destroy each other. I'm sorry."

Serena broke into tears, then tucked and buttoned herself in.

"You're a brutal fag son of a bitch, Tom West."

It wasn't much of a memory to raise two million on, thought Tom.

In late May, after a quarter-million dollar meeting with a Westchester County McDonalds' multi-franchise multimillionaire whose granddaughter was a CC junior, Tom was ecstatic. Never underestimate the power of a quarter-pounder, he said to himself as he chomped one in a White Plains McDonalds' — he felt it was the least he could do.

He opened his laptop. His first email was from Serena.

"Tommy, dear,

I'm using email because you never seem to be on your cell or in the office when I call. Guess you seldom answer your cell when out meeting donors. You've got to learn to do that, Tommy, people understand if you have it glued to your ear; don't worry, it heightens your value, they're honored to have some of your time. Tip: keep it at your ear even when there's no call. That's how I handle that.

Now to your two questions on my voice mail. Number one, I did not have my publicist plant that Page Six item. I learned my lesson the first time we did that last fall when you pinned my ears back! I knew nothing about it but I have to admit, I rather liked it!

So, back to your number two question. Yes, I have held up my gift, and yes, even though I promised you last month, or was it two months ago? Well, anyway, I admit I did promise that you'd get the same two million I gave Miss Jessups (only not the 'same' millions, a different batch). But I can't just yet. My financial team is getting me ready to break out three boutiques in Europe next year and we're already behind schedule because money is so tight for that kind of gamble. Although it isn't much of one for me because my designs are flying off the shelves at Saks and Nieman and in our Rodeo Drive flagship! How about that? Anywho, that's why I can't help out right this minute.

Chris sends his love (or would, if he were here with me).

Love & dirty kisses, Serena"

The Countess' excuse rang hollow for Tom — Fast Bobby must have moved in. Less than four months to go and his twenty million dollar mountain had just gotten bigger.

CHAPTER 43

Tom sat between the Reverend Dr. Philips and the less reverent, if priestly, Dr. Levi and presided over the 322nd graduation exercises of the Christ Church School in the 1500-seat Christ Church sanctuary. Tom liked this rite, particularly in a secular society that generally considered itself liberated from fanciful sacerdotal ceremonies, but, at the same time, was hungry for some break in the monotonous profane calendar. That was his official line, anyway, but deep down he also loved the opportunity to wear his hard-earned maroon Chicago doctoral gown in public. At his elbow, "Doctor" Philips was decked out in his unearned mauve doctor of divinity gown. The surrounding raft of trustee lawyers wore doctoral gowns that signified their bachelor of law degrees had been transmogrified into *Juris Doctors* by a dictum of the leading law school deans. Tom wondered when the MBAs would receive a similar anointing.

Fortunately, the occasion's basic good cheer from the happy seniors, the relieved and grateful families, and the fatigued faculty generally overwhelmed Tom's baser musings about his own vanities and those of his fellow denizens of the academic swamp. And Tom had another pleasant prospect lodged in his mind: Matt Ernst's imminent graduation meant Tom could begin his quest of Sally Ernst at the Levis' that evening.

The head concluded his welcome: "Our school has witnessed the Manhattan Island colonial riots, a national revolution and war, more local riots during the Civil War, twentieth-century wars, social ferment, and twenty-first century terrorist attacks and wars. Our school's own values have changed considerably during that historical experience. One example is in the way our graduating seniors have been organized. In the eighteenth century, Christ Church School ranked its graduates by their family's social position — it was a custom shared at the time with Harvard College, the only American college that predated our school's founding. And while African-American students have had a place at this school predating the Civil War, our black graduates were placed at the end of the academic procession until the nineteen-fifties. Such reminders are indeed sobering and we shall leave for future, wiser generations the burden of exorcising our current method of presenting the graduating class alphabetically."

Seventy-five minutes later, graduates in gowns and mortarboards clutched their diplomas and spilled out through the cloisters into the sunny courtyard, their families in hot pursuit. By the time they reached the silver plates of cookies and the giant bowls of punch, teachers and parents had caught up with them. Everyone mingled and congratulated one another for accomplishments real and illusory. Maury Davis hugged Tom and held on for a while. The boy's parents had already left separately. Matt Ernst shook Tom's hand and patted his shoulder, but drew back when he realized his mother and Dean Levi were watching.

Junior Student Marshal Cat Balewe joined the group, accompanied by her mother, Abby "Easy" Collis Huntington Balewe. She was a lean, deeply tanned, handsome woman with fly-away salt and pepper hair and wire-rimmed specs. She had been quoted in *New York* magazine as saying that her daughter's father had been "lost in the miasma of a Grateful Dead park concert." Easy added that didn't matter much to her because she could "do without a *man*, but not without *men*." Tom knew that Easy's fast life was made possible by her having chosen her California ancestors well — they had speculated on the first transcontinental railroad based on generous federal land grants. She also owned a fortune in art and a slot on the Modern's board. A spendthrift at the museum and a miser when it came to spending time with her daughter, she had been quoted on Page Six as saying, "What the young need most is freedom and a trust account."

Cat appeared uncomfortable with her mellow mother until she parked her with the head and quickly joined Maury and Matt at the punch table. Had there been a mischievous tightening of the corner of the editor's mouth when she shucked her mom? For his part Tom welcomed the opportunity to talk to the elusive "Easy."

"Nice to see you here, today, Ms. Balewe," Tom said.

"Please, Easy'll do — Ms. Balewe was my grandmother."

"Easy it is. I must tell you how much I respect your daughter. I hope she told you that her classmates elected her Junior Class Marshal for today. She's also done a fine job as editor of the school paper. Setting up that inter-school literary review this year was pure genius."

"Such a genius she got you into deep do-do with that tight-arsed stable."

"But it turns out the *Chronicle*'s charges were correct," Tom said. He could see Easy wasn't following. "Didn't Cat tell you the legal threat was dropped?"

"Oh, she never tells me anything. I was surprised she told me about that business at all. Guess it was because you said you would beat her if she didn't."

"Well, not quite," Tom said.

"It was a new vocabulary for her and she seemed to enjoy thinking that, anyway. At my end, I did my duty — I warned her that losing her editorship would imperil her Harvard chances, even if Stanford was a family cinch." So, it was for America's frontier aristocracy.

Easy looked at her Spiro Agnew watch. "Now, if you'll excuse me, I'll take my knockout genius down to the museum for lunch. Wanna show her off."

Jane edged into Tom at the punch bowl as the crowd thinned.

"My God, did you see poor Dennis?" she whispered. "He seemed both hungover and drunk. We all helped him make it up the steps."

Tom winced. "Yes, I did. He came in yesterday. I begged him to get medical attention."

Wither Bramston, in his faded crimson Harvard gown, cornered Tom between the punch bowl and Jane. Tom remembered that, in a nostalgic school moment, Wither had revealed he hadn't sat the SATs to get into college — his fourth-generation inherited Harvard gown insured the exemption. So, it was for America's East Coast aristocracy.

Wither was as excited as he ever got. "Bob Cattivo has agreed to pay the consultant to do the trustees' management report on you. That man has such endless love for our school — he always comes through. It'll save thousands for your budget!"

Tom couldn't muster much enthusiasm over the project, so the best he could do was a wan smile as he picked at the scattered cookie remains on a silver tray. Wither, disappointed at the headmaster's response, drew himself up and looked up at Tom.

"Well, I for one think that's a capital thing for Bob to do, Tom, a capital thing!"

Tom rallied with specious enthusiasm. "Indeed, it is, Wither. Indeed it is!"

Jane leaned away from Tom as if he had something that might rub off, while Wither wandered happily away with his brimming cup of warm punch. Tom could hardly wait until he could tell Ben and Sally that evening how Jane avoided the plague.

Sally wasn't there.

"Don't ask, Boss, I don't know what it means," Jane said that evening when Tom arrived. Jane had expressed Sally's regrets; she was accompanying Jerry Stone to his annual dinner at the World Explorers' Club, where he was to receive an award.

The two dozen Dutch tulips Tom had brought — a dozen each for Jane and Sally — stood on the liquor cart, the yellow and red a stark contrast against the black of the window. He broke protocol by having his second Scotch before dinner rather than after.

Sally had been a little reserved toward him after the recent Page Six gossip. It didn't seem entirely unwarranted, although Jane promised she'd help sort it out. It was turning out that the Sally campaign was more complicated than raising twenty million bucks. Damn Page Six and Jerry Stone.

Tom realized that it was about time he came to life — Ben and Jane had been doing their best since he arrived, but were also clearly frustrated by Sally's absence.

Ben couldn't contain his curiosity. "Tom, it's been so long since I've seen you that I'm out of touch with your trustee from Hell — Whatshisname Cattivo!"

"Thanks for ruining our evening, darling," said Jane.

"Well, since Sally isn't here," said Tom, "I can tell you about Cattivo's latest move. It involves a person I was counting on for a two million dollar gift, a former parent, and an old fri—"

"Oh, yes, and with whom you were linked by the ever-reliable *NY Post*," interrupted Jane. "Now I see why you wouldn't have told us this with Sally sitting here."

"C'mon, I'm all ears," said Ben. "I never get to hear about this kind of thing at the hospital."

"Okay, Ben," said Tom. "So, I asked Serena this week for the gift she promised me when her daughter got into boarding school. She informed me that she is cash poor and won't be able to honor her pledge as she has to raise serious money to expand her boutiques."

"But what does that have to do with the Evil One?" asked Jane.

"Merely this. Cattivo made a point of telling me several weeks ago that the Countess Serena had asked him to be her financial adviser.'"

"So, he axed her gift," said Ben.

Jane agreed. "But Tom, with this guy you have no recourse — it's her money and her adviser. This is the slickest one he's pulled. Let's eat to get the taste of Cattivo out of the way."

They ate the soft shell crabs Ben cooked to perfection. No one could rise to anything beyond the most prosaic comments on weather or politics. And Tom made it a point to assure them that the Vouvray he brought for the crabs came directly from Sherry-Lehmann.

"Dammit!" said Jane as they finished. "Cattivo always manages to crash our evenings together. Ben, sweetheart, you're relieved of kitchen duties while Tom and I do the dishes." She went to the kitchen, turned the water on, and set to work. Tom grabbed a towel.

"And I'll be in the living room pouring large Scotches for us all, especially me," said Ben.

Jane and Tom joined him within ten minutes.

"Can anyone think of anything inspirational to talk about or shall we fall back on Jane's Dalwhinnie?" said Ben as he passed out the snifters.

"I can try," said Tom looking to Jane. "How about the lowdown on our absent curator? You've never told me how you met at Radcliffe."

Jane waved her Scotch at Tom. "So sorry about our no-show." He appreciated the sympathy vote. She settled at the end of Tom's sofa and tucked her legs up. "To be fair," Jane continued, "Sally only said she'd try to come, but that her life was 'getting complicated.'"

Jane became nostalgic over her early days with Sally. Her assigned Harvard roommate was born Estrella Malka in Fez, Morocco. And her first college weeks were hard. "Sally's socks were rolled the wrong way, her

wardrobe was limited, and she told me she felt out of place being surrounded by talk of places and schools she'd never heard of."

"And you didn't mind giving her lessons on social assimilation," Ben said
as he passed some nuts.

"Yes, I was force-feeding her on makeup, cigarettes, and boys, and I felt
pretty smug. But she soon indicated that she didn't want to follow my social
lead — that she'd rather go to the Boston art museums than to a Harvard
mixer with me. Since I'd led my class at Trinity, I wondered who this Mo-
roccan/Dutch/Brooklyn immigrant kid from Tech High was, to challenge
Manhattan's sophisticated Jane Warburg Morse."

"Go on, sweetheart, get to the punch line," said Ben.

"The answer came after the first term: Sally blitzed me in every class of
the core curriculum — high honors work from the get go. The come-down
was probably exactly what I needed — quiet, understated Sally, apprecia-
tive and loyal to her roommate to a fault, had beaten the crap out of me."

"Is that when you decided to kill her?" asked Tom.

"She'd never turn her back to me, so I gave that up. Just as well, because
we settled in as roommates for four years."

Jane explained that Sally had not permitted herself to get very involved
with any other man since John Ernst's death. "Other than Jerry Stone. It
turns out that one of the Met trustees introduced them because Stone's
mother owns several Old Master paintings, including one that may be by
Frans Hals. It would be a real coup to get it for Sally's exhibit."

Jane finished her scotch, placed the glass carefully on a coaster, and
shrugged. "Stone's family art must present an unusual attraction to Sally.
Manhattan hunks and heirs have tried to get at her for years and she was
barely civil to them. So, I'm surprised about tonight — going with him to
that dinner makes it so *public* — I wish I could do something, Tom. And
when Matt leaves for college, well, who knows?"

Ben and Jane escorted Tom into a taxi at midnight. Jane hugged him at
the open cab door. He burrowed into the cab's sagging springs and watched
Jane push the door closed and step back into Ben's embrace at the curb.
He waved as the taxi pulled away. They lifted their faces in the lingering

evening mist and he saw Ben pull Jane close and kiss the top of her head. They grew smaller in the halo of a street lamp. He dozed in the back of the cab, blinked awake when the car hit the curb, and over-tipped the driver. Soon he tucked himself into bed with his malted medicine from Perth.

Tom tried to reconstruct his current Simenon. He reviewed several pages and couldn't remember a thing. He closed his eyes. That wolf under Cattivo's desk was now watching his every move. He'd prefer to recall Sally Ernst's quiet beauty, but Serena's flashing eyes and thighs intruded — she'd left her tracks all over Tom. Tracks for Sally to see. Or perhaps he only flattered himself to think this was relevant for Sally — after all, his interest was initially in getting all she knew about the parent body so he could save his job. She knew it and so did he. She was wonderful as a member of his team. A fine colleague. And that's clearly how she still viewed it. Live with it, Tom.

SUMMER, 2006

CHAPTER 44

On the Monday following graduation, Tom had been wrapping up an afternoon session with the faculty to plan the following school year when Jo Wilson pulled him out into the corridor. At 1:47 that afternoon, a St. Vincent's Emergency physician had pronounced Dennis Warren dead. Cause not determined. At the close of their session ten minutes later, Tom made the announcement and cancelled the Tuesday and Wednesday workshop.

Tom sat beside Jane at First Presbyterian Church in Greenwich Village on Thursday morning. He was pleased to see almost all the teachers and several dozen alumni in attendance. There was only a scattering of current students. The service began and the minister extended his homily-eulogy past the typical twenty minutes because Dennis' parents were well-known African mission founders. Tom had re-read Dennis' school file and now had his own version of the man's biography. His first twenty years were very strong, the next ten distinguished, and his last eight an unsteady record of decline, depression, and sickness. His death carried a sting. Tom hunched his shoulders and bridged his eyes between thumb and middle finger. Jane noticed and leaned gently into him.

Later in the taxi, they sat unmoving, the bright sun reflecting into their eyes as they pulled through the intersections in Lower Manhattan.

They had already compared notes on the way down about the effects of Dennis Warren's suicide on the faculty. The news crackled through the community when the suicide verdict was delivered the day before. There was both shock and sadness, and perhaps a kind of *sub rosa* guilt permeated the faculty consciousness as well. Dennis' arrant ways were well known to teachers. Many had given up on him long ago. Still, the memories of the sporadic hopefulness in Dennis' eyes, his witty riffs on Oscar Wilde, the temporary lift in his pace combined with his colleagues' amnesia about the students left with an absent teacher, all argued that maybe he could have pulled it together; perhaps he could have become the fine teacher most had only heard about from alumni but had never seen. Generally, the teachers were left afloat; they had already lost much of their cohesion after the two big checks had arrived and now they were terribly anxious about a senior colleague taking his own life. That left a divided faculty, but one that seemed to develop a ragged consensus that Jane and Tom probably hounded Dennis to death while Mr. Cattivo was only trying to make him feel better about himself. That consensus gained considerable force when forty or so teachers received letters from "Bob and Babs Cattivo" that week. Bob wrote, "I am saddened that Mrs. Cattivo and I cannot continue holding the dinners we have so enjoyed with Christ Church teachers. We were planning on inviting the entire faculty to join us seriatim in order to let you know how valued you are in our estimation and that of the trustees. Unfortunately for our plan, Dr. West asked me not to continue the wonderful evenings. I shall, of course, honor his request as we always endeavor to preserve constructive board/head relations."

The day before, Tom had acknowledged to Jane, Sally, and the Bishop that the Cattivo letter was a master stroke — Bob had told some of the truth, and then bundled the faculty and trustees together against the tyrannical West — thereby screening the Cattivo manipulation of Dennis Warren, Ruth Soros, and others at the earlier dinners.

Tom was sure he knew what Jane was thinking. He'd filled her in on the way down about Dennis' visit to him the day before graduation, two days before his suicide. Tom had released Dennis two weeks early so he could prepare for his trip to Africa. But when he came in to see Tom he'd seemed uncertain, confused, and confessed that he didn't understand why Cattivo hadn't returned his dozens of calls.

Tom looked over at Jane in the cab. She was holding her upper arms close, as if enduring a cold draft. He broke the silence. "It's a terrible thing to have happened. Dennis was so relieved and at peace with himself and the school during our long talks after he resigned. He became depressed only after Cattivo fiddled with him during those dinners with false promises. Dennis told me later that he was ready to grasp at straws when Cattivo and his wife took such avid interest in him; after all, he'd never lived like that and loved eating and drinking next to celebrities."

Jane spoke into the bulletproof plastic divider in front of them. "I know he didn't like me, Tom, he felt I persecuted him. God, I tried to keep it all about his health and not about his atrocious attendance record. But he wouldn't budge on seeing a doctor."

"No, he wouldn't, but he did offer a reason to me early on," said Tom, "And it was chilling to hear from such a brilliant scholar and teacher. He said, 'Save your breath, missionaries' sons shouldn't be diagnosed as dipsos.'"

Jane must have been aware of the involuntary shudder of Tom's body. She took his hand and held it. The taxi moved northward along the FDR Drive and didn't stop until the two silent, unmoving passengers saw the familiar range of rusticated limestone meet the cement sidewalk through the side window.

CHAPTER 45

The Bishop's call was perfectly timed.

"Tom, I got your mailing to the CC community about Dennis' death. I also know what you went through in trying to save that mixed-up fellow after Cattivo got to him."

"Well, thanks," said Tom. "But I'm still mixed-up myself, I guess."

"Please, my son, remember that you did all you could for him and that you couldn't control what the Cattivos did to him. The relevant part of Niebuhr's prayer fits: 'God grant me the serenity to accept the things I cannot change.' You're in my thoughts and prayers, Tom. And I look forward to Sunday."

The man's profound passion did help and Tom was most moved by his use of "my son." It had been twenty-five years since he'd heard his father say that. But he did wish the Bishop would level about his own physical condition. Tom's worry intensified; might he lose his surrogate father?

The Bishop's voice settled him, so much so that he was completely unprepared for the surprise Jo brought in. She knew it was important enough to interrupt his office calm. It was a pale blue unopened envelope she centered on his brown blotter. Written in bold script was "*DR. TOMMY WEST, PERSONAL,*" and the address. A Phoenix postmark. Inside, a postcard with cactus dominating the desert sunset and the message, "*PLEASE, DARLING, I SIMPLY MUST HAVE MORE $.*" Enclosed was a Walgreen's receipt — an indecipherable prescription item at three-hundred and forty-seven dollars. "*Please, son, it's life or death!!!!*"

Tom pulled out his center desk drawer, felt into the back right corner past the Countess' personal card, and slid out his "Johnny Bench Crosley Field souvenir" — a round plastic photo disk of Johnny. The disk was attached to a bead chain that held other childhood treasures: a chipped green metal Matchbox Jeep, a 1968 Disabled American Veterans "Postage Guaranteed-Finder-Deposit Any Mailbox" Ohio miniature license plate, a one-inch plastic football labeled "Buckeyes 1970," and a three-inch brass cross with aspirin-sized blue "jewels" and milky inserts that used to glow in the dark above his bed. The bead chain collection all came from his dad except for the cross — that was his mother's contribution. Like this letter.

Where was that number? Dialing. Ringing.

He sensed this call would cost him. His skin tingled from handling the tiny cross and making this call. Now he began to sweat. Back came the dread, the anxiety he always felt over his family background. He was ashamed. What part had his own success in climbing the greasy pole played in his shame? He had tried to get as far away as possible from Kokosing, Ohio — no, not really the town, it was his mother he tried to escape. But she beat him to it — she had escaped from him years before.

And a stranger's voice came over the line. "It's only right, Tommy, my being your mother and all. Everything's so high now, I have to take the bus to Vegas to see my friends, wish I still lived there. I enjoy a good time in the city and I'd sure like to see you in New York."

That was unexpected — she'd always been content with his sending money and never showed the least interest in seeing him. Maybe age had changed her, now that she was in her sixties.

Her warm but unfamiliar laughter reminded him that he couldn't even picture this stranger. Then she coughed. And again. Rough rasps with no bottom until a final effort that sounded like the phlegmy depths were being emptied into the mouthpiece. That provided a reference point to the old days. "Sorry. You're not ashamed of your own mother, are you, son?"

He already was, or had been, deeply ashamed when she left and never looked back. And yet she *had* called him "son" just now.

"Tommy, are you there?"

"Yes, mother. But as I told you before, I can't do any more for you financially."

Silence. Yes, that was what this call was about.

"Well then, son, I guess it's time I come clean. Should have told you before. I'd been tired for months, sometimes it's a headache, real bad, puts me out for days. So, I got a full physical exam the other day."

"What did they say?"

"It's my liver, son. Hadn't had a physical for years. So I got this check-up down in Phoenix. Ricky insisted. Worst news there is."

"They found a malignancy?"

"I can't even say it. The C word, but I guess I'll get some practice saying it. Now I've been thinking of going on to Baylor in Texas, or somewhere. Should I get another test or something?"

"That's a second opinion. Always a good idea."

"Yeah, that's it. That's just what Ricky said. 'Now, you get a second opinion, honey, back there in New York where Tommy lives. The best of everything — the Yankees, skyscrapers, the doctors. *Caveat emptor*, you're one expensive woman.' That's just what he said."

"I don't know what I can do." Tom stalled.

She didn't say a word. It was a test of something. Did she sniffle a bit?

Looking down at the keychain cross he'd pulled out of his desk he said, "I can probably arrange something for you, Mother. I'll go to work on this; there may be a wait. I'll get you in, don't worry."

But, thinking about their history, how ludicrous to be affected like this. Ricky? Never met him — must be that used car salesman she's lived with for years — *caveat emptor*, indeed. He couldn't recall everything she said just now — it seemed vague and then concrete — he should have taken notes on his laptop. She must be shaken up by the diagnosis.

He was a little shamed by his hesitation about it all. But he had discovered an oddity in himself long ago: he had never been homesick, and he simply couldn't identify with college classmates who were. What made him think he could restore something that was never there? Anyway, what should it feel like? He had never felt for her what others seemed to feel for their mothers. *Never*. He guessed he was still trying.

CHAPTER 46

Bob Cattivo sat in his club's library under gilded, coffered frescoes and studied an early survey of Hoboken architecture. He wanted to make the right historical reference to carry his building proposal beyond the city zoning committee. "Jobs over Aesthetics" would do it for those birds, but he'd have to come up with something lofty and historically grounded for the regional press to chew on.

Bob liked his club, but he didn't love it. How could he? They let in people like him — Groucho was right. But there was a club he could love, one that was like the Knickerbocker, the Metropolitan, or the Union was, or wanted to be, back in 1900. How he would love to stride into that hall just off Park and sit at the long central table with the oldest, most powerful elite in the city. But he'd heard that "never a speculator" was the byword there. Obviously, they had forgotten that their forebears speculated to build the eighteenth century Manhattan family portfolios on Roosevelt real estate and Astor furs. And the only possible entree he had was the Bishop, who chaired the membership committee — someone he'd have to make peace with sooner or later. Meredith Ross' banker husband Ned was also on the Bishop's committee, but that was a long shot. And the last he'd heard from Ross, she'd set up shop temporarily in Shanghai to oversee her firm's expansion. Her message said she wouldn't be back until the fall board meeting.

Bob Cattivo felt high this afternoon. And without the alcohol, coke, and pills that had buoyed him for years, once he'd left his father and brother in the dust. In more ways than one — both those privileged SOBs were in their graves before his kids were born. Only Babs knew the story, if she even remembered after all these years.

He'd better get down to the bar to meet his "allies." He could still remember his favorite reading in Western Civ at Whittier, actually, his only favorite reading. He'd instinctively known the main premise, "the end justifies the means," but he'd had to digest more slowly Machiavelli's relevant part for him just now: if you win, your allies will insist on sharing; if you lose, you will have created enemies who know you too well. *Watch it, Bob.*

As soon as his guests were fueled in the bar, Cattivo took command. "Gentlemen, I know you share my sadness at the death of CC's great classics teacher, Dennis Warren."

"Oh, great loss," said Wither Bramston. "One of the Old School. Yale man."

"Yes, yes," said the Reverend Philips, "excellent Christian mission stock I heard. I knew him only by sight, but he was a fine fellow, one of the true originals—"

"Then, please," Cattivo cut them off before they nominated Dennis to replace Judas as one of the Twelve, "you remember I did my best to buck him up last spring when he was under attack from the headmaster; I took him to dinner, grew to love him. Now, I'm afraid Tom will try to get the inside track on this, force me out of the picture, by blaming me for encouraging Dennis to stay on. As you both know, I sent letters to a bunch of teachers telling them that Babs and I would not be able to entertain them to dinner as we had with their colleagues because the headmaster forbade it. I think that put Tom behind the eight ball with the teachers, but I'd like to do something more. I'd like to nail him cleanly on this Warren suicide, which fortunately happened just after my letters went out. Babs tells me that her sources say the teachers are reeling from the suicide — trying to figure it out." His hand felt for his Phi Bete key. "Would you fellas have any ideas?"

Cattivo had little hope with his query when Philips got his nose out of his whiskey long enough to stir. "Bob, I think I got it. At this stage, those teachers would love to blame someone or something for that suicide. Why don't you get up a big fund dedicated to Warren's memory, but in reality, a fat fund to pay them off? Just short of outright fibbin', and say it's a teacher reward kinda thing — how you think they oughta be treated! You'd get credit for caring about the teachers more than Tom, even on top of the fact that he won't let you feed them at Bernardin. Then they'd have to blame him for the suicide so they can clear themselves from any guilt. I see that a lot with suicides." He returned to his rare liquid.

Bob sat up straight and thought, St. Jude, club me! And I thought this coonskin ally was hopeless. What a devious, crafty mind — what a fine priest and ally. "That's genius, Richie!"

"But make it something that doesn't highlight Warren's Calvinism," said Philips. "Lots of folks who've been to college love to hate 'Calvinism.' Or 'Puritanism.'"

Cattivo bit his tongue. "Well, that's interesting," he managed.

Bramston was happily working on a gin martini — he'd finally got the nerve to ask for one, reckoned Cattivo. The poor guy had been forced into drinking Cattivo's Balvenie for years. And his favorite drink seemed to energize him.

"Yes, a juicy fund that they can tap every year and remember Warren when they get the check," said Bramston. He looked at Cattivo. "Wouldn't it?"

"Oh, yes, I think you two have got something," said Cattivo. "We can do something quite noble *and* meaningful for Dennis' colleagues — so they can see I've established *their* pot at the end of the rainbow, one that they can dip into every year." The allies sat back to think and drink while Cattivo replaced his key and pulled out his Blackberry. He tapped as he spoke:

"The Dennis Calvin Warren Memorial Faculty Fund. I'll kick it off with ninety-eight thousand and you two can top it off to an even one hundred. I'm sure my usual investors will see the wisdom of this whole deal — a real chance to take control of this powerful but renegade school corporation by forcing out its secret Marxist CEO *through his employees* — it's never been done! We can announce the fund to faculty and parents after our next Executive Committee meeting makes it official in two weeks."

"Perfect," Bramston said. "All that bottom up proletariat rising stuff I heard at college. Professor Brinton, I remember."

"Yep, whatever," said Philips.

Cattivo saw that there was agreement and joy in Mudville.

"Just one thing, Bob," said the Rev. "Don't forget to drop Dennis' middle name."

Cattivo returned to the library to finish the last of his Hoboken presentation — for a change he'd use no PowerPoint, no razzmatazz. The planning board was already aware that he'd paid for hundreds of local kids to visit Yankee and Giants stadiums to see A-Rod and Eli for the last two years. He'd pose as a simple fan of Hoboken residents Rodriguez and Manning when he made his formal request that evening for a simple planning variance that would put thousands to work today and house thousands of affluent taxpayers tomorrow on the shores of the Hudson — it would have made Sinatra proud.

When he finished, Bob sat back and looked up at the frescoes. Good thing Babs had never seen them; she'd want to do over her dressing closet. He'd lost some contact with her since the summer started. As usual, she had abandoned him and Georgie full time once she went to the country, where she stayed until Labor Day. She did promise last week to keep him current about the Tom and Sally Ernst gossip — he didn't know where she heard it all — and gave him an earful about being damn fed up with how long it was taking him "to boot that son of a bitch from Georgie's school." She sounded more threatening than ever. He still wondered, at least a little, about that Cayman retirement account he opened for them both years ago.

He had kept it growing with annual deposits, but when he secretly tried to check on it, Babs had changed the password. Bob couldn't say anything to her because they had agreed not to look at the total until his retirement. He figured she had obeyed Georgie's frequent instruction for them to change passwords on all their accounts. He vowed not to think disloyal thoughts and replaced them with Sinatra thoughts.

CHAPTER 47

It had been a week and a day since Dennis' funeral. Jane Levi, in shorts and a sleeveless blouse, leaned against Tom's open door after lunch on Friday and watched for a few minutes as he bent over his desk in concentration. She had left Tony in the middle school library. Finally, she walked in.

He looked up. "Hey, pardner. I was just thinking about Ben. He emailed that he's arranged an appointment for my mother to be checked next month. Full two-day diagnostics. You've got to keep that guy."

"At least through the weekend. He'll be coming by soon to take us out to the Hamptons — he's off duty and his chief gave us his house for the weekend."

"Good for you three — Tony will love the beach!"

"It'll be wonderful." Jane stepped behind his desk, patted his shoulder, and sat on the desk corner looking down at him. "But the real reason I stopped was to check on you. How are you doing?"

"Thanks for stopping — you're supposed to be off. It's going to be beautiful this weekend. By the way, we've topped eleven million, but it's slowing down — I may be desperate in a month, because I'll be running out of top prospects."

Jane inched forward from her corner and frowned down at him. "Tom, I'm not leaving until you level: how - are - you - doing?"

He looked down at his hands spread flat on his desk and flexed them. Then, he leaned back and relaxed. "At first, amid the confusion I guess I began to believe what the teachers seem to believe — that I was responsible for Dennis' death by fighting Cattivo's plan to keep him on."

"No, Tom. Never."

"I think I'm beginning to see it more clearly. I guess the call this morning from Dennis' attorney made all the difference. Dennis named me as his executor two weeks before his death. The lawyer said Dennis termed me his 'most valued friend' in the will. The attorney and I'll meet on Monday — he had no survivors."

Jane was speechless.

"Then I remembered how close we really were. Dennis used to stop by my office regularly to touch base. We talked about the old days, and Jo would help comb his hair, fix his tie — she always had him purring before he left. And how at peace Dennis was two months ago when he knew he was retiring. He said the old mission school his parents founded was planning a special memorial for them that they wanted him to dedicate, so I slipped him a little something to cover his expenses. He apologized to me for his teaching nosedive and was fighting back tears. He said he had never been happier than anticipating his retirement journey to Africa where he grew up."

Silence.

Tom finished his thought. "And then Cattivo entered the picture. Wining and dining the bipolar-alcoholic and promising him the moon."

"Good, Tom, you're thinking clearly. I think Cattivo killed that sick man during his crusade to kill you."

After Jane left his office, Tom made a phone call.

"Bob, you make it so difficult for me to get in to see you that I decided to use the phone for a very important message."

"Oh, I know, you're unhappy about the late Dennis Warren," said Cattivo. "I can't believe that little weakling snuffed himself. He wasn't the type — how could he have the nerve — musta been soaked in booze. And now, you'll accuse me of putting him up to it."

"Odd that you would bring that up without prompting, Bob. I'd settle for your admission that you pushed him into a fantasy that you'd fix it so that he'd be able to stay even though he couldn't manage to get to his classes more than a dozen times during the last term. How does that fit? It was your hounding him with promises that turned the trick."

"I swear I didn't say another word to Mr. Warren after you and I made our deal. Babs kept it up for a while until I learned of it and called her off."

"Simple, Bob. You and Babs so upset him he couldn't regain his balance, the serenity he had when he talked of his retirement and African trip. That's on your head. You'll have to live with it."

Now Cattivo sounded ever so slightly abashed. "Look, maybe we can do a deal on this. Like the understanding we reached last spring on my alleged invasion of your game preserve of a school up there."

"No, Bob, I learned from that 'understanding' with you not to deal with you again. I'm going after you on this — you wined and dined an alcoholic, depressed man. He ended up confused and unable to cope."

"Wait a minute. Maybe I've got something you need real bad."

"I swear I won't deal with you again, Bob. You're poison to me and my school."

"Not even for two million bucks, unrestricted, for your lagging campaign?"

"What are you talking about? Are you offering a gift?"

"Indirectly, yes. I'm the Countess' financial guru now. I put together a little investment group for her — along with three other trustees, if you must know, although others want in. So, well, maybe that two million she pledged could be freed up. If you behave yourself."

"I figured all along you got to her."

"Only in her best interest. She can't be giving like a banshee to every school that comes along if she's going to have the cash to create boutiques in London, Paris, and Rome."

"Forget all that. The record should stand: you killed Dennis Warren."

"Do you realize how absurd that will sound? A manic-depressive schiz-oid with an ancient drinking problem puts his head in a gas oven and you claim a trustee who generously took the aging queen to dinner is his killer."

Tom was staggered at Cattivo's language and momentarily adrift. He switched topics to gain recovery time.

"Well, then, do you happen to know who placed that ridiculous item on Page Six about Serena and me?"

"Oh, that. One of my people came up with it. Most eligible bachelors would welcome being the romantic object of the Countess von Konigsberg."

"Not this object. And you know it cheapens the school and me."

"Touchy, touchy. Guess you haven't heard the Manhattan maxim: 'You can print anything as long as you spell my name right.'"

"Of course I've heard that comic-strip line."

"Well, it works, my naïve friend. Remember, I know that I can't do anything unless other people want me to do it. And I also know that you don't know how to play in the major league. Now hear this, minor leaguer: while you try to engineer your libel regarding my part in the demise of the late Dennis Warren, I just may decide to come up with a civilized tribute to Dennis Warren to get the teachers' attention. Or maybe I'll redecorate a classroom with pricey African art spawned on some pygmy reservation and name it the 'Dennis Warren Memorial Seminar Room.' That on top of the news that you banned Babs and me from taking faculty to dinner and you're fucked royally with your teachers. I hope you know that you're already being blamed for his death."

Tom hung up. And five minutes ago, he'd thought he had Cattivo by the balls.

CHAPTER 48

Tom thought Sally looked dazzling that Sunday morning in a plum suit with black hose and pumps. He jumped out to open the passenger door, but she pointed to the back seat where she'd join the Bishop. As she got settled, the cleric patted her hand and called out, "To Millbrook, James!"

And Sally was pleased with the substantive talk she had with the Bishop about her Dutch exhibit. He asked intelligent questions about the artists and the canvasses she was after in North America. She even pulled out her Blackberry to make notes on the nuggets he provided regarding some of the owner-families.

When they had finished, Sally asked him where his love of seventeenth century Dutch art had come from.

"It comes from disappointing my father terribly in nineteen-forty-six when, upon graduating Yale, I forsook my place at Yale Law to travel in Europe and study art in Florence and Amsterdam. He felt that might be worthy of a daughter, but surely not of his eldest son."

"Bravo," came from the driver's seat.

"Thank you, James, for your unsolicited view. Please mind the carriageway!"

"But how did that lead to theology?" said Sally through a chuckle.

"Because I have a medieval mind, and that meant the art led me inevitably to theology — if it was good enough for Tintoretto, it was good enough for me!"

"Yes. That makes perfect sense," said Sally. "To the medieval mind."

"Admittedly, it was also the best retreat from meeting my father's insistence that I become a titan of the American bar."

Sally decided then and there that this Bishop was a treasure.

"I couldn't figure out any other time that all three of us could meet and discuss Tom's campaign," said the Bishop. "And since Lulu has invited us over for what she calls her 'Fundraising Summit' after the service, perhaps we should steer clear of that topic until we make it a foursome."

"Agreed," said Tom, viewing them both in his rearview mirror. Sally was so taken with her backseat companion that she had been only vaguely aware that the driver was stealing a look at her now and again. Mostly again.

Lulu greeted her "golfing buddy" Tom, the Bishop, and Sally with delight as they piled out of Tom's car. "Sorry I didn't make it to your service over there. But at least today I had the perfect All-American excuse: 'We were frying the preacher's chicken!'"

After the four finished a lunch of fried chicken, mashed potatoes, and local asparagus, Tom brought out his laptop and showed them his summer plan of attack. He'd printed copies for everyone and they all joined in, offering comments on the names and families.

"Ah, Neddy Sewell — I didn't know that old boy was still alive — Asheville, North Carolina, eh? Is worth it, Lulu?" asked the Bishop.

"Well, that'd be at least two days used up. Better to drive out to Short Hills to see Horace Taft and Charlie Tillinghast the first day and spend the next day with the Clarks and Jim Morton in Philadelphia."

"And don't forget Andy Solomon over in Princeton on the way back," said Sally. "He's not on any of our hit lists but he recently gave us a long-term loan of his Del Sarto Madonna. And he told me at the installation that he'd seen my parents' association report in the CC alumni bulletin — so, he may be a good candidate."

After well over two hours of intense prospect and schedule discussion, Lulu and the Bishop looked weary. Lulu sighed and asked for a summary of how Tom was doing with Cattivo.

"He has been counting on my values to shake or beat me at every point. For example, my attempt to stop Dennis Warren's ruinous teaching but get him out with what dignity he had left. He turned that into my persecution of the most senior teacher."

Lulu nodded. "From what I've seen of that man Cattivo at the Kips Bay Decorator Showhouse when I was chair, he *and his wife* — shudder — are expert at taking advantage of anyone with decent values. Welcome to the club, Tom."

"Well, I've tried to get control, but that man has the faculty in an uproar, the Countess' two million may be out the window thanks to his influence, and he is buying the consultant who will rule on my leadership."

"And he hasn't given us anything we can nail him on with the other trustees," said the Bishop. "His letter to the teachers about no more free dinners and his threat to you about funding a Warren memorial are mean and clever, although I doubt that you've lost your faculty quite yet. I'm sure they'd love to have you, and themselves — especially themselves — absolved of any shadow around Warren's death."

"I'd like to believe that. But any advice would be welcome."

"Well, I do have advice on dealing with Mr. Cattivo, which I've already discussed with Lulu. She's dealt with power-hungry, rapacious trustees for years and encouraged me to come clean with you."

Lulu drew back and smiled over at the Bishop. In turn, he pushed out his lower lip and nodded, then leaned toward the headmaster. "Tom, we have seven words: 'When action defers to principle, ruin follows.'"

"Sounds like Machiavelli."

"It is. My translation. And we have used that more often than you can imagine."

There was a noticeable pause in the conversation. Then the Bishop looked at his watch, noted it was five, announced that he didn't feel up to the drive home with the heavy Sunday traffic, and would stay the night at his favorite country house. He viewed Sally and Tom. "So, you two will have to manage getting home with your GPS and without my ITG."

"I'll bite — and that is?" asked Tom.

"My Invaluable Theological Guidance."

"I wish you well, pilgrims," said Lulu.

Tom and Sally were soon off, and the septuagenarian woman and octogenarian man moved to the wicker furniture on her grassy terrace overlooking the blue-hazed Hudson. Lulu turned to her companion with pointed interest.

"Yes, you'll expect a report," the Bishop said, placidly gazing out over the trees. "Did you know FDR registered to vote in Hyde Park as a tree farmer? Looking at your property that almost adjoins his down there, I can see why." He looked back at Lulu, who gestured frantically with both hands, speechlessly imploring him for the report. He grinned and nodded.

"Oh, yes, there were some awkward moments early this morning when we picked up Sally, I don't know quite what it was. They clearly hadn't seen each other for some time. They hid that well, or so they thought, and soon forced me to hold forth on the minor matters of sealing wax, cabbages, life and death. Now, how about your report?"

"I've done less well — I couldn't get Sheena and Tom beyond a drink at the Plaza's Oak Bar, even though my girl was willing."

"Well, I couldn't get Sally and Tom off the Central Park track!"

"You wily old fox — you just put them unchaperoned on the Taconic Parkway."

"But only in bucket seats, my dear. Think of the mischief if bench seats were still in."

"Such mischief is years beyond my ken."

"I haven't heard that word used in fifty years."

"That's about right for me, more's the pity. But as for our wager, I'll have to yield. Sally is truly right for that bright, idealistic man, and some-time-golfing galoot."

"Maybe, Lulu, but they don't seem that well acquainted." Seeing her surprise, he added, "Merely a sense I had — a kind of mutual reserve."

"Phooey. I predict it'll soon be 'Katie, bar the door,' so I concede our wager. What'll you have, Scotch or Scotch?"

CHAPTER 49

Sally wondered why the Bishop decided to stay overnight at Lulu's house, but Tom explained that he often stayed for the whole weekend when he wasn't tending to his flocks. She pressed about hidden agendas. Tom told her it was brother-sister and that Lulu had hinted her long-distance beau was a golfing entrepreneur in Scotland.

"Aren't they divine?" said Sally.

"Well, yes, but the Bishop isn't so divine that he stumbles over his halo, is he?"

"No, and he seems to view other tainted humans clearly."

"Amen to that. And not a word about his health all day, even though I swear I saw him wince several times as he was working the crowd in Millbrook."

"I noticed it, too, after you mentioned it at the reception."

They noted the cars tearing past them in the passing lane and agreed that the parkway's 1930s design was hardly appropriate for Manhattan's tense speed demons returning to the island after a weekend of relaxation.

"What did you think of the Bishop's advice to me earlier?"

"You already know what I think. I would hate to see you lower yourself to Bob Cattivo's level. That's all." She wanted to avoid taking the Bishop on. She had seen Tom's respect and affection for the man all day. Or was it reverence?

Tom pulled off the Taconic at the Poughkeepsie-Pawling exit.

"There's a station very close. I wouldn't want to run out of gas with the Parents' Association president's reputation at stake."

When Tom finished refueling and started toward the parkway, a gray Acura sedan followed with two cars for separation.

After they regained the Taconic, Tom and Sally spent the next hour comparing their backgrounds: how the boy from a small Ohio town and the Moroccan Jewish girl from Fez found their way to New York. She insisted he go first.

"Aw, you've seen my biography and heard me go on at parent evenings. Football jock goes to college and gets infected with ideas. From Ohio State to St. Andrews, then law school dropout, history doctorate, and teaching for love. Widowed in Chicago, escaped to New York boys' school, Washington girls' school, and back to Manhattan's Christ Church. Love the school, but the last chapter is likely to read 'fired for fundraising incompetence.'"

"Never. Not if our team can help it."

"I hope. Now, your turn. I really don't know your Moroccan and Dutch biography, and I want to hear it all."

"You'll be sorry you got me started." She leaned against her door so she was almost facing him and could more easily check his response. "My father's Sephardic forebears had lived among the Muslims of Fez for over five hundred years, but he feared for our safety after the Six-Day War stirred things up. He finally sent my mother and me to Amsterdam because of the increasing chaos around us. He stayed on because he was an honored senior accountant to the royal family."

Tom and Sally now took only passing notice of the lush serpentine parkway. She felt they were in a cocoon and that it was important to both of them that she got her story right. That might mean leaving out a portion.

"My years in Amsterdam were wonderful. I loved the streets, canals, and the distinctive Dutch houses somehow enlarging their cramped dimensions by their reflections on the waters."

"That must be fascinating to see," Tom said, with a sideways glance.

"Yes, but the city was far more than that for me. It was a refuge that nourished hope after being forced out of Fez."

She saw that he was listening closely and nodding.

"Near our Portuguese Synagogue, Rembrandt had had dealings and friendships with his Jewish neighbors every day. And when I saw in the Rijksmuseum that he painted Jews among his other outsiders, I was hooked. I was an outsider too, and yet I was beginning to feel Dutch — I needed to feel Dutch. That's why I dreaded my father's imminent order that we move to New York to join him. My mother and I didn't want to go. We hoped that Father might come to Amsterdam, as he was having difficulty getting his business off the ground over here. He tried hard, but that was not to be."

Sally stopped abruptly. I can't go on, she thought, and then realized that he didn't press her to continue because he caught her glistening eyes. They settled into a calming silence.

Later, as they entered the city along the Hudson, shimmering with twilight vermilion, Tom said, "I'm still wound up from our long day. Especially the plotting to defeat Cattivo. And I know that if I go home and try to relax I'll have too much Scotch. Got any ideas?"

"I was thinking along the same lines. I would invite you in for a nightcap, but Matt's having a couple of teammates for a sleep-over so they can get an early start tomorrow for their soccer clinic at New Haven. But if you're game, I'll spring for some of that fabulous rhubarb pie over at Herb's cafe on Lex."

CHAPTER 50

They were soon seated and served at Herb's. The cafe was sparsely popu-
lated — Tom saw that the graying sweater-set ladies and spiffy gentlemen
of the day had been replaced by a mix of the young and the slightly inebri-
ated. He didn't want the day to end.

"Okay, I know you'll have many favorites, but what is your favoritest
Rembrandt in the whole wide world?" he asked.

"Well, I already warned you not to get me started. My choice goes back
to my Amsterdam days. I think that the most beautiful Rembrandt, the one
that overwhelms with its revolutionary technique, is 'The Jewish Bride' at
the Rijksmuseum. Do you know it?"

"Just a reproduction in Schama's *Rembrandt's Eyes*."

"Oh, yes, and I should confess that the real reason I love it is that it was
my mother's favorite — we used to stand together and study it — she said
it legitimated our existence in Holland. It's full of mystery — the title was
added much later so we don't know for sure who the subjects were or anything about them. But I love that bride. She's plain, she's unsure of herself.
She wonders like all brides, is he Mr. Right? Yet she's already answered that
because she encourages his touch with a bold move — she holds his hand
to her breast. Jerry Stone said his mother claims that that proves they're not
Jewish! But this gal has nailed him and she knows it's for keeps. And he's
not bad, either. Oh, you should see it; I know you'd love it!" Sally hesitated
and colored with self-consciousness.

"That's quite a recommendation." He smiled — this was a new Sally.

"Have you gone back to Europe much?" Neat sidestep. Your turn,
schoolmaster.

"Quick trips to London to recruit science teachers," he said. "One real trip — Scotland on my honeymoon. Gift from my parents-in-law," said Tom. "Guess I've been a little overwhelmed by my school life. But I've wanted it that way ever since my wife died . . . was murdered." He got it out, barely. Why did he bring that up?

Sally caught her breath. "Oh, I'm sorry, Tom, I had no idea. Murdered. Does anyone at CC know? Sorry, I shouldn't have asked."

"No, it's alright. It's my problem; I should have been more open or something. But it never comes up anymore."

"I know the feeling — once we've adjusted and might not mind talking about it with a friend, it's ancient history for everyone else. I do understand."

"Exactly."

They ate the rhubarb pie silently and then turned to tending their mugs of coffee and looking at the Formica tabletop.

Tom took a chance. "Sally, we knew at school that John Ernst's death had taken a terrible toll on you and Matt."

"I hope it didn't show too much," she said. "It was four-hundred and thirteen days from diagnosis to death. Pancreatic. Rapid degeneration, then agonizing death, seemingly slowed by the radiation and chemo. Into the Valley of Death rode the little family. Fourteen-year old son, brave. Father, transparently brave. Mother, not brave but busy, always. I had my son and Jane and Ben and life to keep me busy. Then, after an eternity, it was over. And Matt and I picked up the pieces. The school was our anchor, and it was his scholarship at CC that made all the difference. It allowed us both to remain in our community." Sally looked up and into his eyes. "First draft. I know it needs work." Tom choked back a sigh.

She appeared relieved. She nodded at him, asked, "And you?"

Here goes. "Betsy Livingston Schuyler-West, always too good for this world. She used family money to set up a children's tutoring center near the University of Chicago on the South Side. She worked late with the kids and their mommies, missed her bus, walked. She probably tried to reason with the mugger, I know she would have, but when the police described the scene — with Betsy's dying body being dragged into the bushes and

raped — I stopped my ears." Tom gripped his mug. "It was a double murder — she was five months pregnant. And the killer murdered her forever
in my mind — I was left with the fixed mortuary memory of a slain and
suffering person, not of a wonderful, dynamic woman. And that'll do for a
first and final draft." Tom glanced quickly at her but he couldn't look into
her eyes — he knew he'd lose it if he did. She was teary.

My God. Tom couldn't believe it. They had crossed some Rubicon.

After Sally paid for their forty-minute snack, they set off on the mile and
a half walk to her building on upper Park.

They headed up the wide Park Avenue canyon: concrete, granite, limestone, and brick apartment houses with a break now and then for Roman-
esque church towers, the utilitarian Hunter College, and the castle-like
Armory. The boulevard was divided by the begonia-filled median and
edged by drifts of flowering shrubs along the sidewalks. Their colors were
darkened now and looked glazed under the streetlights.

Tom felt slightly dizzy from the soft June evening, the sepia lights from
the entrance awnings, and the woman at his side. He wanted more of her
Dutch world and asked for it. But after five minutes of the animated life
story of her mother's favorite Dutchman — Spinoza — Sally looked over at
Tom, tightened one corner of her mouth and was silent. Finally, she spoke.
"Goodness! I've rabbited on all afternoon and evening. You'll find it hard
to believe that I haven't talked about all this for years."

"But I've loved hearing—"

"To be continued," she interrupted. "And to think I counted on the drive
back to hear more about my son's head — the guy who can whip up a meal
that meets with teenagers' approval!"

"Aw, the *Chronicle* staff puts up with it every year because they like the
do-it-yourself, all-you-can-eat sundaes at the end! That and marshmallow
cocoa are my sole culinary triumphs, so we've already exhausted that topic."

Their walk up Park had become a dawdle. Neither seemed in a hurry to
get to Sally's building. And the other walkers, including a Dalmatian and
terrier duo, kept things comfortable for a while.

"So, I was wondering, did you also grow up with art?" Sally said. "What was your cultural childhood like?"

Tom waited for a border collie to give up circling them and move on. It was awkward enough having to reveal anything about his childhood to Sally, much less his "cultural childhood."

"You would have been near the Cleveland Museum, wouldn't you?" Sally prompted.

Well here goes, it had to happen sooner or later. "About sixty miles, but it was a huge cultural distance from my world. I visited the Cleveland Museum once as a boy by accident. The Indians were rained out and our baseball coach was desperate. I only remember long, quiet, parquet halls, and the walls dripping with gold-framed pictures. Years later I began to enjoy art and architecture, mostly in Germany and Italy during my working summers in Europe."

"Working?"

"I sold encyclopedias every summer at U.S. military bases to work my way through St. Andrews. I could earn enough during summer holiday to scrape through the college year."

"I've never heard of such an arrangement. Pretty enterprising."

"Pretty desperate!"

"And the Met, do you get over to our museum, or do you only come when the Yankees are rained out?"

Tom smiled with her. "I do get over once in a while, mostly to chase Tony Levi around the armor room and mummy corridor. I walk over to the Frick once or twice a week for therapy. But I certainly don't talk about the pictures to anyone."

"Why not?"

"I'm interested in the historical context, but I don't know anything about painting, really — the aesthetics, or even how art is made. When I stand in front of a picture and hear people go on and on about what the artist was doing, I usually haven't a clue what they're talking about."

"Don't be intimidated. Believe me, there's a lot of bullshit flying in the galleries. Do you have a favorite?"

"I do like that Rembrandt self-portrait at the Frick. After his bankruptcy. That's the interesting part for me, I guess, how the painting shows the man's utter humanity. It moves me — there's such hurt in his eyes and yet a glorious, fatalistic majesty in his bearing." Tom caught himself — he was talking to a Met curator. "Now *I* sound like a bullshitter."

"No, that is a lovely, moving painting, and for the reasons you gave."

Was she teasing him? She was nodding her head, seriously it seemed.

The flickering of light and shadow as they passed under the plane trees seemed to emphasize her cheekbones and vulnerability. No, not vulnerability, only her cheekbones. He was fascinated by her odyssey from Morocco to New York, but he was much more fascinated by her. She was mesmerizing tonight, even if he was confused about what to do about it.

They came to a stop at her 1185 Park entrance.

"Thank you for the favoritest day I've had in a very long time," she said.

"And thank you for being on my team," he said and caught himself. "I mean on the fundraising team." He was trying too hard. She smiled and chuckled.

He held his arms wide. She moved inside. They came together in an awkward hug. They separated and she was gone.

Tom was strangely relieved and even buoyant. But as he wandered home he tempered his hopes when he remembered how easily Jerry Stone had slipped into her conversation.

CHAPTER 51

"How's the tennis up there in horse country?"

"Mr. Gallosh, I don't pay you to make conversation. Rest assured that everything is fine up here — my serve and my saddle have never been better. What have you done for me lately?"

"Sorry, ma'am. Subject drove his cream two-thousand-and-two Volvo four-door sedan to the Cathedral of St. John Sunday morning, and emerged five minutes later with a passenger in the back seat, whom I assumed to be the Bishop of New York, as in the previous observation three weeks ago. My surmise was subsequently proven correct—"

"Please, get on with it; I already know you're a world class surmiser."

"Yes. Sorry. Subject then drove across town to one-one-eight-five Park Avenue where a thirtyish female, well-dressed and very attractive, joined the Bishop in the back seat. Subject then drove to Millbrook, New York via the Henry Hudson, Sawmill, and Taconic parkways at eight hundred hours as a kind of chauffeur, bowing and opening the rear doors almost like he was play-acting. They went to Grace Episcopal Church up there. Two hours later, subject drove the two earlier noted persons to an estate on the Hudson on Route Nine in Hyde Park, New York. Subject stayed there at the house for three and three-quarters hours and left only with the one-one-eight-five Park attractive female in the passenger seat."

"Yes, you've already said she was attractive. Don't belabor it."

"Sorry. Subject drove directly to the Upper East Side, parked, and accompanied the, a, female to Herb's Café on Lexington Avenue, north of Sixtieth. After forty-five minutes of intense talk separated by a booth table, the couple walked slowly over to Park and up to the aforementioned one-one-eight-five address. Where he left her and returned to his maisonette in the Christ Church School building."

"Did the couple have physical contact at any point in the day?"

"I did not observe any physical contact. No hand holding, no."

"How about in front of one-one-eight-five Park?"

"No. Except for a final hug."

"Well, why in hell doesn't that qualify as 'physical contact'?"

"All I can say is that it was closer to a handshake than a kissy-hug. It was weird the way subject held out his arms; he's pretty big and awkward and she disappeared in his bear hug, very briefly. That's why. More like a big brother and little sister. Trust me, I know the difference, I've got a sister."

"It's not much to go on. I expected more. If I give you his private school office line, can you record his conversations? Or get into his email?"

"I would prefer to discuss all business arrangements with you personally as before. I don't consider this telephone connection or any email secure. I'm sure you understand my caution for all concerned."

"Yes, I'm sure you're wise to be careful. No need to return to Otisville, eh?"

"You can say that again, ma'am. I will say that technical experts are expensive. The best handle no more than four clients, each a retainer, for around thirty-thousand dollars every six months, plus expenses."

"That's nothing. I spent that much on two teachers last month. I want you to return to Bedford on Wednesday, maintaining full whatever. I'll have your check ready. I'll meet you at the A&P parking lot again. Usual time. What will you be driving?"

"I've got a two-thousand-and-five Acura now. Gray."

"Good. That's settled." Babs Cattivo hung up. She sat for a while worrying a little about Gallosh. She knew he was faithful in his attendance at AA; she knew he paid his rent and kept up his credit payments. Still, he edged toward the personal more and more — nothing he said, more his hungry big browns and his convict's smirk. She had more on him than he knew, far beyond his federal drug sentence. She'd bring in the younger PI, Robert Chandler, to watch Gallosh for another week. The one with blue eyes. Robert had only one weakness. Miss New York had discovered long ago that all sexy men had one weakness. Except that damned, insulting Tom West when she cornered him in the Plaza corridor. Pushed him back into the men's room, smothered him, but he wouldn't play. First and last man who had ever refused her offer.

CHAPTER 52

Cattivo ushered the Reverend Doctor Richardson Philips and Wither Bramston into his spacious office and seated them in front of his desk. "Gentlemen, I appreciate your coming to my office for our executive committee meeting on such short notice, but we've moved along more quickly than I could have hoped on our project. I called in a few chips from our fellow trustees." His guests were hanging on his every word.

Cattivo always insisted on facing people from behind his antique Louis XV desk — he liked the combination of authority and class the desk conveyed and the warmth and coziness the open legs implied. He wasn't as sure of the snarling taxidermic wolf under the desk that also sat between him and his respectful, cozied guests. Babs had given it to him to celebrate his first coup — he'd taken the Rosen partners out of a lucrative Times Square hotel deal that placed him front and center as the "Commercial Comer of the Year" in Crain's realty ranking. She'd also framed the page from the magazine, which he liked to explain to visitors as his first award from the Hollywood porn industry. But not to these two; Bramston would be offended and Philips might not get it. Check that: Bramston might not get it, either.

"My god, Bob, how long you had this wolf-thing here?"

He's starting in early. "For twenty-seven years, Richie, this September tenth."

"Oh."

"Beautiful desk, Bob. Aaron's shop?"

"Yes, Wither." And before the Rev could butt in, "Now let my man get you thirsty fellows anything your liver desires." One of Bob's trim and fettled male secretaries emerged from nowhere.

"Thanks, Bob," said Philips. "My liver would like a hit of Kentucky's most important contribution to western civilization, not counting all us Kentucky colonels runnin' the country."

"I got in some Eagle Rare for my rare drinker. Would that suit?"

"Lordy, lordy, only the very best at Chez Bob!" Philips turned to the secretary. "Yes, and make it a rich 'un, boy!"

"And I'll have a Pellegrino, thanks," said Bramston. "With a splash of gin." The secretary, after a knowing glance at his boss, disappeared.

"Why do you have a couple of guys around here, Bob, instead of a couple of," Philips paused for some kind of effect, "chicks?"

That was unexpected. Still, mustn't disappoint his public, thought Cattivo. "Well, Richie, I guess I don't entirely trust my visitors, especially the doctors of divinity!"

"Especially us!" The divine was flattered.

Now to business as the drinks were delivered on a silver tray.

Cattivo handed papers across his desk and explained. "Here are the particulars of our 'Dennis Warren Memorial Fund.' I've been pushing my accountants and lawyers to get this wrapped up quickly. All contributors have provided written pledges — I don't want to get left holding the bag. We'll name them, of course, but should we list their amounts?" He knew the answer already.

"No, not necessary a'tall," said Bramston.

"Nix," said Philips.

Cattivo viewed his two allies, who had turned their attention back to his Edinburgh Crystal tumblers. Yep, these terminal tightwads wanted full credit as big givers alongside the authentic big givers.

"Fine, that's settled," said Cattivo, making notes. "I would like to wait until after our fall board meeting to call in all the Dennis Warren fund pledges — that keeps it out of the hands of Tom — we certainly don't want this to count toward his goal."

"That's wise. Would you like a motion to put this all on the rails?" said Bramston.

Cattivo looked to a second young man seated in front of a computer and nodded. "As chair of the June twenty-fifth meeting of the Christ Church School Board of Trustees Executive Committee, in Vice-President Ross' absence in China, I opened the meeting at five-seventeen with the required three-fifths quorum present, only the ill Bishop and the aforementioned Ross absent. The minutes of the last meeting were read and approved, and we adopted unanimously the resolution to accept five-hundred thousand dollars to establish 'The Dennis Warren Memorial Fund,' to be used for a minimum of fifty-thousand dollars annual teacher enrichment."

"Count me in," said Philips.

"Yes," Cattivo added with a look to the secretary, "moved by President

Bramston, seconded by Dr. Philips, and adopted unanimously, and so on. But don't close the minutes, we may have truly important news to add for our trustee mailing."

"This is a significant step in our history, Bob," said Bramston. "Or it will be, if it has the desired effect we planned."

"Yeah, it means we won!" said Philips.

"Richie, let's not count our chicks until they're sitting on our laps," said Cattivo.

The now well-doctored divine shook with giggles. Cattivo and Bramston looked at each other. A third assistant came in and nodded to Cattivo.

"Now the big moment. I'll ring the headmaster. I know he's in, my assistant just checked." He began to tap at the console on his desk.

"Tom, I've got us on the speaker phone here in my office."

"Oh, hello, Bob. What's up?" Lamb to the slaughter.

"Simply that our trustees' executive committee has been meeting today."

"I'm sorry, I didn't know — did you want a progress report on my fundraising?"

"No, that won't be necessary. We can wait until the next full board meeting."

"Well, is there something else? A problem?"

Silence. Cattivo turned to his allies and winked.

"No, I wouldn't say that, Tom, at least no problems at this end. But perhaps soon at your end."

"I don't like the sound of that, Bob."

"We didn't think you would."

"'We'?"

"Oh, yes — Dr. Philips and Wither Bramston are here with me in the office. We haven't adjourned quite yet. Thought a talk with you might be in order first. The Executive Committee has just now officially accepted my investment group's gift providing for a Dennis Warren Memorial Fund to spend fifty-thousand dollars every year on teacher enrichment. The whole to be administered by the First Vice-President of the Board of Trustees. I think you'll quickly see how it will play out with your beloved faculty."

"But you only told me that you *might* do something like that."

"Well, I hardly needed your okay, did I, so it's done. I think it will excite the teachers, don't you?"

"Yes, no question, Bob. And although I know it's meant as an attack on me, I have to admit it's a wonderful gift for the right cause. All official now?"

"Signed and sealed in our minutes that will go out today for the trustees. We'll be sending out the announcement to the teachers, parents, alumni, and the press as soon as special paper I'm importing from Belgium arrives with the CC school crest to do it up right. As far as 'official' goes, not until the day after our fall meeting, so you can't get your mitts on our Warren Memorial Fund. What'dya think of that?"

"I guess I can see what you're hinting at — it isn't a very pleasant thought."

"Sorry, I never hint, I put it plain. We think this is the time for you to throw in the towel, Tom. There's no future at CC for you now. The teachers will revolt when they see that you refused to save Dennis' life by keeping him on and that I, based on this gift, had the right idea all along, to save the poor bastard's life. Your resignation'll keep it clean, neat, and nobody gets hurt. You can resign gracefully and not have to wait for the inevitable firing at the fall trustee meeting based on your management record. Never mind the twenty million. You've given it a good try, I will give you that."

There was silence from Tom.

Cattivo tried not to show his emotion, but he couldn't wait all day.

"What say you? I won't even insist on planting my foot on your neck in the traditional manner. Why, I'll even send you another case of Petrus so we both can celebrate!" Once again, a wink at his audience. Bramston looked a bit grave. Philips was doubled over in mirth, his hand covering his mouth. Or as near double as he could manage.

"I think I'll give it a few days. Wouldn't want to do anything rash." Tom hung up.

"Damn," Cattivo said as he turned to his allies and pounded his desk so hard his pre-Columbian trophy bounced. "I promised Babs his head this afternoon."

"Don't worry, Bob, you've got it on a platter, you just haven't taken possession," said Philips.

"Oh, yes, he's on the run; he's shaken, nearly speechless," said Bramston. The first secretary brought in a tray of filled champagne flutes to toast their victory. Cattivo raised his glass: "To Babs and a new head of Christ Church School!"

They all drank to that and settled into a minute of companionable quiet. Until Richie stirred.

"Did'ja really give that peckerwood West a case of Petrus?" he asked. "I've always wanted one."

Bramston ignored that and said, "And Bob, I look forward to finalizing our contract with your new Jacksonville marina project."

"All in good time, gentlemen," said Cattivo with a smile. But he was newly wary of his allies and remembered the apropos sentiment from Brother Machiavelli: *When the prince sees that the adviser is more intent on furthering his own interest than that of the prince.* No problem, thought Cattivo, as long as I keep them both on the payroll.

CHAPTER 53

Within ten minutes of hanging up on Cattivo, Tom walked into Central Park. The Dene, one of his favorite places in the park, was shady and cool. He was still seething from Cattivo's cruel conference call. He had refused the trinity's demand that he resign because he had been blindsided. Now he decided that this July day in New York was too lovely and promising to allow Cattivo to ruin it. The tanned women with bare legs in light skirts and dresses played their part and he enjoyed his role as a spectator, along with legions of other men, toiling in seersucker and poplin suits and trying to appear blasé with the seasonal delights. He shed his jacket and felt the tension ease, even though he was late.

Tom approached the model boat pond and walked around it on the west side. Three boats with snow-white sails and russet hulls leaned into their efforts, mocking the gymnastics of their owners on the shore with radio controls. He paused for a moment to watch a boy of about four sitting regally on Hans Christian Andersen's bronze lap. The boy ignored his tiny sister's attempts to join him. She finally settled on a polished duck. The park squirrels twitched their tails and played finders-keepers around them.

Tom took the path toward the Metropolitan Museum. He saw a bench tucked into a sunny cul-de-sac that didn't see much foot traffic, although the few men passing by were checking out the sleek professional woman as she smiled into the sun. And no wonder, she was sitting easily, stripped to a sleeveless cream silk blouse with a yellow linen skirt pulled to her bare mid-thighs, and facing the sun with eyes closed. He stood nearly in front of her and saw the line where she shaved her legs to mid-thigh, a tiny mole at one demarcation. Tom felt the stirrings of jealousy, of wanting to claim or protect her from these strangers.

He whispered, "Sally?" so that she wouldn't be awakened. Was she really asleep?

With no shift in posture and barely a smidgen of change in expression, she replied. "You've interrupted my worship. Damn."

"I'm sorry to disturb your beauty sleep."

She smiled broadly and didn't hastily pull down her skirt and go into the mock concern of making herself presentable; she simply invited him into her comfortable lair and laid out the prosciutto and baguettes she had packed. He handed over the chilled diet soda and fresh cherries he had brought. Her ease prompted him to toss his jacket casually onto her bench. It slid off onto cigarette butts and an indescribable mélange on the ground. He picked it up, shook it, and parked it neatly, then sat alongside her picnic, trying to look comfortable and in possession of his wits. She watched his actions and smiled enough for both of them.

They ate while watching the toddlers pointing and stumbling toward the Central Park squirrels.

"I'd like to have one of each," said Tom.

"A boy and a girl?"

"No, gender isn't important — one child and one squirrel." He dodged her chop.

Tom finished her sandwich for her; she didn't need help with her soda.

"And how goes your planning for the Dutch exhibit?"

"Slowly," she said. "We're homing in on top seventeenth century paintings owned in America but never shown. My job is to obtain pictures that would serve as grace notes to possible Dutch museum loans, especially the Frans Hals Museum in Haarlem, near Amsterdam. Guess I'm too impatient to get the show on the road. My boss has already cautioned me because I'm about to start what he calls the 'discreet wrestle' with private owners next week. Now, tell me about your week."

"Same old, same old — Cattivo called," Tom checked his watch, "thirty minutes ago. He was on his speakerphone with Bramston and Philips in the room. He told me of his latest marvel, a half-million fund he's raised with those two and some other trustees in honor of Dennis Warren. The Sly One's of the opinion that the result will be my excoriation among the faculty for hounding Dennis to death. So, why not resign now — 'keep it clean, neat, and nobody gets hurt—'"

"Well, the teachers *are* stirred up. But, no, even he wouldn't say that," Sally broke in.

"He did. And I did." He looked down at the cherries, then up to her. "Hung up, that is." Did her face flash with the anxiety of his resignation just then?

"And lest you think my week has been wasted, a quarter-million here and there, and Lulu told me yesterday that she's on to something in Scotland and that it involves golf and money."

"That dear, intrepid lady. Any details?"

"She said her long-time correspondence with her favorite CC classmate has become more frequent, and has led to several phone conversations. We have no alumni record of him since nineteen-fifty-six. His name is Roderick McBain — the inventor of that famous McBain golf club. His factory is in St. Andrews. She says he was pleased that her golfing student was the CC head and a St. Andrews man, but she wouldn't tell me more. Only, 'it'll be your mystery for the moment, but you should concentrate more on your golf.'"

They were soon down to the last two cherries.

"Ever spit pits as a kid?" she asked.

"Sure," he said, lining up a pit in front of his teeth and blowing hard back over the bench into the undergrowth, "pwhoosh!" The pit arced two yards and buried itself in a bush. "You mean like that?"

"Yeah, sorta," she said then worked a pit in her mouth and let fly with a discreet "putt." She gave the pit a ride so hard into the trunk of a plane tree five yards behind them that it clicked and ricocheted a further two. She sat with her elbow over the back of the bench, eyeing him.

"Aw, you didn't really want to share our childhoods," he said. "You simply wanted to show off. Where'd you learn that?" A momentary gap in her sleeveless blouse exposed a sheer cream bra with dark areole.

"Sign of a misspent childhood. In the souk. In Fez. I loved hanging out in fruit and nuts." She cleared the picnic rubble. They both moved closer, leaned back, and turned to the sun.

Tom closed his eyes and inhaled deeply. "You smell of toasted almonds and honey. I could stay here all afternoon."

"Of course, we Moroccans all do." She also was speaking into the sun with her eyes closed. "But you won't stay, will you? For you have promises to keep."

"And miles to go before we . . ." He sat up. "Thanks for the rigged cherry pit spit."

Sally sat up and ran her fingers through her hair. "Listen, idiot, if you do go to Scotland, you must check out the Rembrandts at the Scottish National Gallery in Edinburgh. They have a fine self-portrait he did when he was fifty-one. I've heard it's superb."

"I promise. I just finished Schwartz's Rembrandt study you loaned me. But my ignorance of technique leaves me confused."

"What about?"

"'Impasto'— I'd like to see more of that. And I can barely pronounce chi-a-ros-curo. It seems to come up pretty often."

"Yes, I understand. Well, your favorite self-portrait at the Frick is loaded with both. Listen, if you've got the time, why don't you come back to the museum with me for coffee and I'll show you a painting or two with my magnifier. That'll make it easier to understand Rembrandt's technique."

CHAPTER 54

Sally led Tom through the large rooms devoted to Rembrandt.

"I should note in passing that there are several candidates for your look at impasto here. There, next to the door, is the portrait of Rembrandt's almost-neighbor — a bachelor with my favorite Dutch name — Floris Soop. And here is the fetching 'Toilet of Bathsheba,' which shows his early mastery on a smaller scale, although people don't notice the impasto jug and necklace any more than King David probably would have."

Tom found his own attention to the impastoed objects wandering easily to the mostly bare body of Bathsheba alongside. Sally smiled at his divided attention. "You can always come back to check out Bathsheba's unimpastoed jugs, Dr. West," she said, steering him on. "We'll just focus on one picture today. Over here. 'Aristotle with a Bust of Homer.'"

"Some of Rembrandt's early classical Leiden education surfacing?"

"That, and more likely the wishes of his hard-to-please Sicilian patron. Now if you want to experience impasto, look closely at this lovely gold chain with my glass."

The world as seen through the magnifier was fascinating. Sally talked softly in his ear as he gazed at the impasto. Their heads brushed slightly as they shared the glass. Her toasted almonds and honey fragrance was intoxicating.

"Hi, Sal. Tête-a-têteing with a brilliant art student?"

The interloper greeted Sally with a robust kiss on both cheeks. She pushed away and managed, "Not really," and blushed.

"I'm the not really-brilliant, not really-art student," Tom said as Sally introduced them.

Jerry Stone laughed and said, "And I share your interests — in both Sally and Rembrandt, Tom."

Jerry Stone was a distinguished-looking gray-haired man, glossy and tanned, in an English-tailored suit with lapels on the vest. The cloth was the kind Tom lusted after: a medium gray wool with open-weave texture and just the hint of a maroon check.

A guard who knew Sally approached her with an older couple's question about the total number of Rembrandts in the museum, and Stone joined her in answering. Tom took the opportunity to move back to the Aristotle painting. With her glass, he could see the layers upon layers of lustrous paint, even perhaps where a blister of air had burst to improve the viscous, tactile effect — unbelievable! He sneaked a look over his shoulder at Sally and Stone, who had resumed their discussion. He was at least four inches shorter than Sally. That was heartening until he watched them in animated conversation. Like very good friends. Stone was a charming man and wouldn't look out of place anywhere with anyone. Tom turned back to Aristotle's golden chain, his mind elsewhere, and he was soon interrupted.

"Tom, I read somewhere that you know my favorite designer, Serena von Konigsberg. I bet you are acquainted with those Utrillos of hers. My, I wanted those myself, but that gal had them locked up at the auction before I woke up." He looked carefully at Tom, who tried to give nothing away. "However," Stone continued, "I get to check 'em out from time to time." Thank God Sally was still talking to the guard across the room.

"You've probably known her longer than I, Jerry. Her son was at Christ Church until last year."

"Ah, and her daughter is about to go to Jessups. So, dating the customers. Well, I don't blame you, she's a real pistol." Stone winked as he moved toward the Vermeers.

Tom was relieved when Sally returned and took him up for coffee in the Trustees Dining Room. She ordered two espressos as they were seated.

"I'm sorry I didn't get back to you on the families you asked about, I'm under the gun here. And I should tell you that Georgie Cattivo is very much a part of the Irregulars now. He's been at loose ends — his mom is gone all summer, he says, but he wants to stay in town and 'batch' with his dad, except his dad is in Florida much of the time. He's around my place all the time with the other orphans. He's grown on me, but he's very lonely."

"What are they all up to?"

"Well, Georgie and Maury are very busy with their big laptops, which they bring over to work with Cat and Matt. They're both whizzes, Matt tells me, but I haven't a clue what they're up to. And with my work schedule, that won't change. Maybe I'll be put in charge of the Dutch exhibit if I can deliver during my trip next week." She sipped her coffee and frowned.

"Want to talk about it" Tom asked.

"Oh, I guess I'm a bundle of nerves these days because my travels have been preliminary so far. I'm just getting into it."

A pleasant-looking, somewhat bowed couple in their seventies hovered near the table.

"Dr. Ernst, I'm sorry to interrupt, but I wanted you to meet my wife, Gwen." Sally introduced the speaker to Tom as Oliver Chase. After some warm words, he said, "I hope you and the director can sort out the Dutch exhibit soon, because I'll be in the Netherlands in two weeks and I could provide a personal introduction to Meneer Champers at the Hals museum and a few others. I'm sure they would be pleased to work with the Met." The couple moved on and Tom reseated himself.

"The Chase galleries, New York and London?" Tom asked, quite impressed with the affection Sally inspired in the old gentleman and his wife.

"Yes. And now, Tokyo. Only five blocks away in his town house is a very private Old Masters collection, and he's already promised two pictures for the exhibit. Mr. Chase has the contacts in the Netherlands to really help us. He's also on the Met board, and he's a man of impeccable ethical standards. And, truth be told, there's a CC connection here."

"Oh? Doesn't ring a bell."

"His only grandchild is applying to CC. His daughter's son from London. I only hope that his grandson is one brilliant, well-balanced twelve-year-old!"

Tom chuckled with her, then said with relish, "I somehow think he will be, Sally."

She looked at him severely. She ordered another round of coffee and Tom studied her. When the coffee arrived he spoke.

"I saw your immediate concern that I might engineer something to pry the Chase grandson into CC."

"It was nothing, I just—"

"No, please tell me what you were thinking, if not saying."

She stirred her coffee. Again.

"Tom, it's only because I respect you so much. I've already told you what I think of Cattivo's bribery — that case of wine. It's difficult for me to see you compromising yourself with your campaign. I persist in thinking of you as a fine teacher and head — I've seen what you've done for many students, including a shy boy named Matt."

"Thank you. That means a great deal to me," said Tom. "But." He looked at her intently. "I'm afraid you may be betting on the wrong horse here. My fundraising campaign has changed my spots and maybe my soul. Right on schedule, as the good Bishop prophesied."

"I think I'd like to hear more."

"Well, Mother Confessor, it started with making the smallest integers of 'adjustment' in what I thought were my firm standards. Let me give you a couple of examples: college counseling and admissions."

Now Tom stirred his coffee needlessly.

"Most parents seem to think school heads have some 'in' with the universities; in fact, one head shared the college job with his wife, which definitely muffled student and parent criticism of his dodgy administration. I haven't gone that far, because I've found that merely not protesting when parents suggest that I have some magical Ivy potion does the trick. I let them jump to their own erroneous conclusions, especially the smooth operators who have H-Y-P on the brain. That really opens their wallets."

"Right, parents all feel that the head of school is someone we don't want to alienate over colleges, so we flatter the hell out of them," said Sally with a grin.

"Example two: a California head hired his wife to head admissions while he did college counseling — double jeopardy for the parents and kids! But upstanding me, I merely began to 'tip off' the admissions office to financial marks applying: 'Please look Heather Hedgerow over carefully.' Now, they ask me for suggestions. We may not be at Admissions Gate yet, but give me a couple more finagle factor months."

"But Tom, I've heard nothing from parents about CC making exceptions for people with money."

"No, perhaps you haven't, but the people who need the exceptions seem to have sniffed me out and they bring their checkbooks to lunch. It reminds me of what Warren G. Harding's adviser said when that presidential administration hit its stride: 'My God, how the money rolls in!' I've closed so many deals for family names on the library entrance doors that we'll have to break out four or five more."

Sally laughed despite herself. Then, sobering, she asked, "But what is the effect of all this materialistic groveling on you, Tom?"

"Like I said, it's nothing the good Bishop didn't warn me about — he warned me that this would happen, but only if I were 'successful'!" Tom outlined the word in the air. "Look, I embrace it now, I'm not a victim of anything other than my single-minded desire to make my goal and keep my job. In all honesty, I covet the deals I make and the money I raise even as I see my earlier idealism take a beating. Dare I call it the chiaroscuro of fund raising?"

"Light and dark. Yes, I guess you can." She looked down into her coffee, then directly at him. "But Tom, can't you see? That only provides a kind of sophisticated patina to what you're doing. And you know damned well what you're doing."

"There you go again, and I'm too far gone to care much about your censure, Sally." She looked bewildered. And he felt bewildered.

"But you'll be pleased to know that I have sworn off the Cattivo booze gifts. It's all part of his familiar 'You scratch my back, I'll scratch yours' world."

"Yes, but I can't imagine why anyone would knowingly allow him to get close enough to scratch their back."

Tom breathed deeply. "I don't find him any more attractive than you do, Sally, but he does sort of go along with my goals of faculty pay and diversity — he just doesn't think I can pull it off."

"You certainly don't sound like the man you were in February when the board laid down your challenge — you're turning into something else."

He sat back, more than a little confused and angry. No, Tom, not here. He toyed with the lemon rind in his espresso. He had to say something. "Is my 'development' any different from your consorting with an art lover who likes to collect art and curators?"

Sally rose out of her chair partially, then sat, flushed. She said, "What the hell is going on around me? First, it's Jane and now you — accusations that I'm putting out for the Met and the collectors. And she may have the smidgen of a right to suggest that as an old friend, but I certainly didn't give you the license to attack." Sally glared at him and over at the waitress, who looked away. She regained her composure and said softly, "I welcome being on the road for the next week — around here I seem to be surrounded by gratuitous, sleazy critics."

CHAPTER 55

Tom needed to be sure. He asked Jo to dial Cattivo and make sure he was on the line before he'd pick up. Jo soon buzzed. It was almost comical how quickly Bob got on the line when he figured the head might be submitting his resignation.

Bob Cattivo had been engaged in some delicate negotiations with the Hoboken planning commissioner. He'd left word in New York that he wasn't to be bothered except by his wife Babs, his son Georgie, and Dr. West up at Christ Church School. His secretary buzzed him. "Dr. West. His secretary says it's urgent."

Cattivo made a thousand apologies to the Hoboken official and went into the acid-green hall with his Blackberry. What a dreadful color he thought, mustn't let Babs see it. Could this be Tom's capitulation?

"Whosit?" said Tom.

"Whadya mean, who is it? You called me, Headcase. Fuck do you want?"

"Oh, sorry, a bit distracted these days. It is Bob, isn't it? This is Tom. Up at school."

"I know that. Maybe you ought to call back when you can tell me something I don't already know. I'm in a damned important meeting."

"Okay, Bob, I simply wanted to know if your Dennis Warren Memorial Fund is about to be announced, that's all."

"You can bet your sweet ass it is — the trustees will get my letter tomorrow, and the special shipment from Antwerp of embossed paper, already printed by the finest Flemish stationer, has been promised for early next week. It'll go out immediately. And thanks for asking — are you ready to make your decision?"

"Almost. You'll hear after your trustee mailing arrives. I need to see it to believe it."

"Okay. Different strokes, I guess. Well, it's damned impressive, I'll tell you, and next week when the teachers and parents see it, well, I don't want to belabor the point. Now, don't waver, Tom, man-to-man, I urge you, after you read it, to go ahead and resign. You'll feel better when it's all over, believe me. And I meant it about that Petrus. I'll even throw in a two-week luxury spa retreat for two at my new resort in Grand Cayman. Hell, I'll make it a month — just do it."

CHAPTER 56

Tom did feel better after he'd done it the next day. He waited until Jo Wilson brought in the one-page letter from Robert George Cattivo to "My Fellow Trustees." It announced the creation, effective the first of November, of the Dennis Warren Memorial Faculty Fund of five-hundred thousand dollars and it included an "Honor List of Donors," headed by Bramston and

Philips. No surprises — all except those two were shareholders in Cattivo's investment group. The listing would simplify Tom's work.

"Now, Tom?" said Jo after he read the sheet.

"Yes, Jo. Machiavelli time."

Tom's letter to the faculty, parents, trustees, and alumni was set to be printed that night and would go out the next day. The letter announced Dennis Calvin Warren's appointment of Tom as executor of his estate, and in fulfillment of the will's stipulations, the establishment of an endowment in the sum of one million and two-hundred thousand dollars named the Dennis Calvin Warren Faculty Fellowships. The fellowships would provide more summer travel and study opportunities for CC's teachers.

A courier service hand-delivered the letter to the trustees that morning. Tom spent the rest of the day following up in person with the seven trustee contributors to Cattivo's fund. He asked them if they didn't want to transfer their allegiance to the school's official Warren memorial, established by Dennis himself, so as "not to appear discordant and sowing division in our school community." They all were surprised, shocked, and disbelieving, but all finally accepted Tom's proposition. He promised he would add their generosity to his letter before it went out to the total CC community the next day. There was only one trustee exception.

The holdout was a very angry Bob Cattivo, but Bramston and the Bishop finally prevailed on him to move his own gift to the official Warren category after a few days of sulking. His reluctant action was noted by the faculty. The rout was complete when the head of the Faculty Association came into Tom's office a week later to reveal that he had emailed all teachers about the long-time friendship Dennis had with their head as the background to the estate gift. He also reported to his colleagues that a trustee's wife had told him, "Tom West is engaged in an impossible twenty million dollar campaign to keep his job." The faculty leader concluded that it would be helpful for Tom's drive if the faculty would pitch in with donations, as a high percentage of their participation could be a selling point to prospective donors. The man reported that, although many were on vacations or otherwise unreachable, over half of the faculty had already made donations; and a department head had referred to Cattivo's reluctant joining of Dennis' endowment as "blood money." For the first time since the February trustee meeting, Tom felt he had won a battle.

Jane was so ecstatic with Tom's victory over Cattivo that she stayed up until one A.M. to catch Sally in her Los Angeles hotel after the curator's workday and dinner.

"Was it dirty, Jane?"

"Still the Victorian, eh? Absolutely not dirty — not on Tom's part — he just gave Cattivo plenty of rope."

Sally emailed Tom her congratulations and an invitation to a celebratory luncheon early the next week after she returned from Chicago. She finished with, "I'm exhausted, but learning a lot and may also have some news."

CHAPTER 57

Cattivo had a mini-rebellion on his hands. He'd already postponed a crucial trip to Jacksonville and Sarasota in order to spend a couple of days mollifying the trustee donors to his Warren fund after Tom West had stolen them as partners in his own creation. They'd been forced by Tom to make their gifts effective immediately in order to join Dennis' estate bequest, and the result was that one million, seven-hundred and fifty thousand dollars had gone into the head's goal total. Cattivo's final humbling was paying for the special Belgian bond paper and printing bill of twenty-five thousand dollars and then having to junk the entire mailing. After he got his trustee investors settled down by tarting up the Countess' European boutique expansion prospects enough to change the subject, he turned to his base camp. But he found that even his most trusted allies needed to be sorted out. He had to agree to meet them both at Bramston's office when they insisted.

Cattivo looked around the Bramston head office. He couldn't imagine working there — ancient property, ancient realtors, and ancient ceremony

— as Bramston poured the afternoon tea into delicate cups and passed the English biscuits. What Cattivo would give for a mug of coffee.

"No hard feelings, I trust," said Bramston, "over the escalating events of the past few days?" He tossed a furtive glance at Dr. Philips.

Cattivo smiled. "No, of course, I don't hold anything against either of you. In fact, you were both wise to go along with Tom's high-handed proposition when you did. I held out on principle, of course, but the faculty heard of it and Babs' spies said that my reputation has taken a beating among some of the ingrates we entertained last spring."

"Biting the hand that fed them," said Philips. "That kind of madness happens over suicide, believe me, Bob, I know."

"Yes, I'm sure that's right. Madness," echoed Bramston. "Madness all around." They may be ripe for another push, thought Cattivo, as he sipped some kind of sissy, spicy, Indian concoction Bramston swooned over. He noted that Bramston seemed more in control of his environment here than anywhere else.

"So, gentlemen," Cattivo began, "when you look carefully at this whole deal, we actually did well with our headmaster over the past month or so. We produced, solely in the month of June, an optimistic headmaster, a depressed headmaster, an angry headmaster, and now a chesty, smug headmaster. He's right where I want him, jerking around like a yoyo. Remember the scripture: 'Pride goeth before a fall.'"

"Amen, brother," threw in the Rev. "And a haughty spirit before deconstruction."

"And yet we can't sit back and let his nature take its course," Bob continued. "The bad news for us is that now, without a distraction, he'll be single-mindedly beating the bushes to get to his goal. What have you got, Wither, do you know how much he's raised?"

Wither held the silver teapot aloft and nodded to each of his guests. There were no takers, so he helped himself and the other two waited for his reply. "During the summer we only meet every two weeks. I detect he's been reticent to tell me much, thinking I'd fill you in. I did get a call from

Ted Stevens the other day. He's an old friend of my father's from way back in the twenties when they both entered CC. Tom had been to see him—"

"Ted Stevens?" interrupted Philips. "I remember him from when his company sponsored Alistair Cooke on television. Gosh, I loved that show."

"You were saying, Wither?" said Cattivo.

"He wanted to know why we only have chapel once a week. He was planning to follow up with the Bishop. That's all."

"The Bishop again," Bob said. "Please don't forget that guy is lined up with Tom. Never forget it. And I'm done dealing with that CC bunch of teachers. At this point, they're not much use to me. There's even a rumor they blame me for Warren snuffing himself. But we don't need them, we've still got the trustees, and what we say, goes. So that leaves Tom West. I think it's time for something more direct. And sophisticated. Something you two can help with, probably handle better than me. You heard anything, Richie?"

"Only that the Bishop is still pushing that multicultural stuff up at the Cathedral — high-wire acts, Jewish reparations, peacocks in the garden — it ain't the Gospel I grew up with. But he's got that Cathedral board in the crook of his crosier."

"Really?" said Cattivo, unsure what the hell *that* was about. "Well, keep an eye on him."

"So, what's next for me?" asked Bramston. "I'm going up to Vinalhaven in a couple of weeks. I'd like to clean my plate before going. Want to do my part for you, Bob."

"Where are you with that head-search outfit?"

"I talked to the CEO. Otis Fish Wicksnuffer is an old colonial New York name, of course. We're probably related on the Fish side. He did say he was the best in the business because he's not part of the old boys — the old headmasters — so he can do what's best for the school, not serving two masters. I liked him, old Harvard man when it meant something, Fly Club, crew." He poured another refill for himself, elegantly performing the two lumps, early stir, Jersey cream addition, and final stir liturgy.

Bob was losing confidence fast. "But how can he not be part of the old school heads if he has to recruit them?"

"I think because he's never been one."

Bob might have to revisit that logic later. That would certainly keep Wicksnuffer mercifully ignorant of what heads actually do. But Bramston was still shaky from taking on the Bishop. Better to give him his lead on this, along with choosing the consultant who would review Tom's management. "When can he start?"

"He's ready to go when I give the word. But isn't it a bit early to move on that?"

"Generally, I'd say yes," said Cattivo. "But really, what harm can he do? Merlin told me what they learned at Dalton, after three searches in five years — in a head of school search you have to get in early so that the top prospects don't get snatched up before you start. Why don't you crank it up, Wither? Hell, it might even put Tom on the ropes."

CHAPTER 58

Sally looked gorgeous in a plum shirt with pleated placket and tailored black suit. Her French twist was faultless, her earrings tiny gold nuggets, and, as usual, he couldn't tell whether she was wearing makeup or not. There was, however, something a little different about her; for the first time, he could detect some fatigue around her eyes.

She toasted him with the sherry she ordered as soon as they were seated in the Trustees Dining Room.

"To the Good Guys. And your brilliant victory over the forces of darkness. When Jane told me last week, I was thrilled!"

"Well, thanks for inviting me to celebrate today."

"Tom, it's more than a celebration. It's an opportunity for me to apologize and confess."

"Please, comrade, there's no need." He paused and grinned. "But if you insist."

"Thanks for your comradely commiseration. First, I apologize for my holier-than-thou attitude."

"No, I appreciated your honesty. I take it you've had a nasty blooding."

"Oh, yes. I told you I'd be negotiating the details of the loans, having cultivated the best targets. My bosses were impressed with the groundwork I'd done, but that was where the cheering ceased."

"Why?"

"Because I thought that the collectors would be pleased to share their art treasures with the world." Sally paused and shook her head. "After initially agreeing to the altruistic motives I ascribed to them, they soon became 'gnarly,' as Matt would say. And then they unveiled their demands for their piece of three-hundred-and-fifty-year-old canvas. Hell, they wanted to be bought — they might as well have asked for half interest in the Metropolitan Museum Dutch collection and a lifetime of free chow here in the Trustees Dining Room." She looked down at the napkin she clutched beside her plate. She unclenched and they both smiled.

"And what was their back-up position when you refused?"

"I couldn't even get to those back-up positions," she said. "I was struggling to hide my horror at their egomaniacal sense of cultural entitlement. It's like working in an ethics meat grinder to pry those pictures away."

Sally's favorite waitress appeared, exchanged her badly mauled napkin for a fresh one, and took their order.

"It wasn't until I was in danger of losing the loans that my realistic boss arrived and whipped me into shape. Remember when you asked at our last lunch if you could call your fundraising chiaroscuro?" she said. "Well, I have a confession to make. I believe that word is perfect for describing the world I've discovered. I am now a believer in the bottomless depths of human self-interest and the necessity of basing art loans on that motivation. I guess I learned quickly because we nailed five out of six pictures!"

Tom toasted her with his sherry. "Well done!"

She returned the gesture. "Yes, even if we resembled ethical pretzels at times, we got the loans. Now I understand your precarious position at CC — with no swat team for backing — they all want a piece of you." She fastened those luminous eyes on him. Don't get weak in the knees, Tom told himself.

"It's the price of being an anachronism," Tom said. "Called 'the Headmaster,' now, 'the Head,' based on a seventeenth century model and my ruling a tiny kingdom at the beginning of the education rainbow." He tried to smile deferentially. "So, your bosses came through for you, did they?"

"Yes, as my department head put it, 'when you're up to your ass in alligators, it isn't easy to remember your goal was to drain the swamp.'"

"That deserves a needlepoint cushion."

"I'll save that for what he said this morning: 'if you can be in Amsterdam next week the same time as Oliver Chase, the director and I want you to take on our two-thousand-and-ten Dutch exhibit.'"

"Hey, that's wonderful news! Congratulations! Have you told Matt and Jane?"

"Not yet. I wanted to tell you first."

Tom liked the sound of that. Very, very much. He was rescued from an inadequate response when Sally's waitress delivered their plates, glanced at Tom, and winked at Sally.

"I promise you a proper evening to celebrate," he said. "I'm sure you'll be free about midnight when the World Explorers' Club winds down."

She narrowed her eyes at him. "Oh, yes, I will have several midnights free, but I wouldn't want to ruin your heavy midnight polo schedule with a titled beauty."

They both seemed to think they had taken that far enough and concentrated on eating. Tom was the first to emerge.

"Sally, I'm sorry I started that."

"So am I. But we should have a little talk sometime about our explorer and globetrotting friends; it always hovers over us. At least you've met my explorer; I've never met your globetrotter Serenissima — she was a non-starter in the parents' category at CC."

Tom smiled to himself and then at Sally. "Yes, sadly, Serena hasn't a clue in that category, and that's why I try to help with Chris, as Jane told you.

He's a good and very courageous boy. Would it be amiss for me to comment on your explorer?"

"Fire away."

"Only that one might wonder, oh hell, I wonder, if the gentleman is found attractive for his artfulness or for his art."

"The latter, my friend. And only the latter."

"I think we've already had our little talk, Sally."

"Agreed. Never again."

CHAPTER 59

Tom returned from half of a day spent in mid-town clubs — the Princeton and the Harvard — and informed Jo Wilson that he had little to show for his pitches to a drug company executive with two daughters at CC and an alumnus and former journalist who had just sold the movie rights to his best-selling novel for three million. The former pled hardship, the latter worried that he wouldn't be able to guard his pile in the future.

Jo had her own concern: she didn't know where the plain manila envelope left on his desk sometime that morning came from. She had gone up to the Business Office for ten minutes when classes were changing, but hadn't seen anyone in the office vicinity. He saw that her pride in running a tight ship had been bruised as he slit the envelope open.

He pulled out a single sheet of computer paper and read:

"You're not alone, Dr. West. Don't give up.

Sincerely,
Students United to Defend Our Head."

Both Tom and Jo chuckled nervously.

CHAPTER 60

"Wow. What a f-fine outfit." Tom stumbled a bit as he crossed the threshold, but managed to kiss her cheek with some cool when Sally greeted him at her door.

"Funny. This dress had a similar effect on Matt when I got it earlier this summer. Except he said, 'You're not going out in that, are you, Mom?' So I haven't, but I thought you'd like it. And I'll take a sweater this evening for cover. Is it too revealing?"

"Not in the least, you shameless slut. I love it."

Sally wore a simple black wrap-around von Furstenberg silk jersey dress, a childhood locket nestled in her cleavage, and went without hose, her tan legs sleek in the heeled sandals. Very sexy — he couldn't have imagined this Parents' Association president and elegant curator wearing it before, but he was already a believer. After their Met lunch, she had agreed to his invitation for a celebration evening on Saturday night. She loved the idea of a surprise and said she'd be flying to Amsterdam Sunday night but would already be packed. She also noted that the Irregulars were having a *Chronicle* working weekend to plan the fall issues at Cat's country house at Quogue, so Matt would be gone with Cat, Maury, and Georgie. Her son had even admitted the old trio had been routinely amazed at Georgie's computer skills.

Tom sat and watched Sally bring in glasses and a bottle of Bollinger. "The flutes are new — I've never had any — I wanted this to be memorable."

"The way you look in that dress has already made it memorable for me."

Sally blushed, then pulled up one corner of her mouth. "We seem to unload to each other when we're under the influence of coffee — what'll we be like after finishing this bottle?"

"Haven't a clue, but I'm willing to find out." She poured and he toasted her promotion and landing the first paintings.

Sally turned it his way. "And I toast a man who halted the barbarians at the school gates and made them pay half a million for the privilege."

They sipped and seemed happy merely to be. She poured again and resettled beside him.

"May I be the first to launch a Champagne confession?"

"Yes," she said, "please spill," and reached for his hand to help out.

"Thanks." He hesitated. "I . . . do you realize this's the first time we've held hands?"

She shook her head in wonder. "I know."

"Now that I've discovered that you live in the same gray world as I seem to have created for myself, for the first time I feel almost equal to you."

"I was too slow in realizing that I had created the same gray world, Tom, but you've always been more than worthy, my friend. I just didn't want to be a pushover."

She poured again.

"Tom, do you really want your awful, crazy job?"

"I'll fight for it." He held his hand up in swearing position. "Because it's a kickass job." He drank. "But how about you — do you still want your classy, sometimes sleazy job?"

"Try to pry me loose, buster."

They laughed and sat entwined. He checked his watch and whispered in her ear. "Now that we've settled on a sleazy summer, let's pry ourselves loose and into a taxi."

She lifted his hand off her thigh and placed it on his enlarged lap, saying, "And just when I was beginning to decide sleaze was good and I wasn't hungry anyway."

As they sat over their coffee at 10:30, Tom revealed to Sally that he had been aroused all night. "Ever since I saw you at six-thirty this evening. To the point of suppressed agony, completely unrelated to those oysters we had."

She returned his smile. "You know, we curators are always interested in the condition of our holdings; so tell me, what should we call your condition?"

"How about locket envy?"

Sally lifted her necklace chain from behind her neck and released the locket to slide slowly down to its resting places. Tom wanted to bark. Instead, he shook his head and chuckled to himself.

"Let me in on it," she said.

"Do you know there was only one time my dad sat me down for a talk, the only bit of formal advice he ever offered. 'Remember, Tommy, there's no logic in a stiff cock.'"

"Wonderful! How did that 'come up'?"

"Ouch. I think he was explaining the universe. Or maybe simply why a bright kid who wanted to be a pharmacist could get himself into a dead-end at a very young age and never recover. No dreams past twenty." Tom hesitated. Maybe he had said too much. And yet what he saw in her glistening eyes made it all right.

He said softly, "I would love to lie all night betwixt your breasts."

"Is that Tom West?" Sally said.

"Yes, but three thousand years ago it was Song of Songs."

"I should have remembered — it's a Friday night Sephardic staple. So I'm being wooed with words from King David's era. Don't forget, David's brain's limited blood supply got him into a heap of trouble."

"But this isn't simply a drained brain talking. I'm in love with you. Or better yet, I simply love you."

Sally paused before she answered. "That is better yet, especially the 'simple' part. And, Tom, I love you. I've been ravenous for you tonight." She held his hands resting on the table. "This wanting, this desiring, I'm like an uncertain teenager again. Only it's not 'again' for me. I've never felt this way before."

Only then did they become aware that the waiter had been standing at their side with a tray. Tom arched his brows, and fumbled with his wallet. After the waiter left for good, Sally looked at Tom. "Lord, I'm heated up.

Maybe a Washington Square walk before we get a cab?" She pulled her sweater from the chair and began to put it over her shoulders.

"Without the sweater. Please?" he said. "I want to prolong my agony."

"Sounds serious." She checked her watch. 'For erections lasting more than four hours, consult your physician.'"

"Yeah, but this is an Act of God, abetted by Scripture."

As they walked in Washington Square, she announced that she had picked up some Scottish smoked salmon and eggs for brunch after their run the next day.

"Hmn," said Tom. "I think we can improve our weekend plot this time. Let's stop at my place to pick up my PJs."

"Now you're talking . . . but unless you want to run in your PJs, why not pick up your running stuff, too?"

"Do you think I'll let you out of the house tomorrow morning?" he asked.

"Think I'll let you into your PJs tonight? Let's go straight to my place."

They laughed later over what passed between them during their first coupling. It was intense and wonderful, but not so intense as to prevent some of the wonder being suffused with humor. It was so voluntary and overdue that it verged close to laughter — if they hadn't been so horny that first night, they might well have broken up with giggles and laughter.

Sally challenged, "Lay on, MacWest!"

"Purely a labor of love."

Afterwards, she inquired, "Now, what do you have to say for yourself, Sylvester Tomcat?"

"Love's Labor's Lost."

They emerged from sleep at 8:00 A.M., their usual Sunday running time.

Sally was very vocal when she made love. Her only explanation was that she'd been storing it up for years. He loved it, and with that encouragement she really let go. During post-coital snuggling that morning, he asked, "Tell me, Babe, was it as good for me as it was for you?"

CHAPTER 61

Cat's weekend *Chronicle* planning session at her mom's Quogue weekend house had gone well — her mother left them alone in their own wing, complete with kitchen. Maury got to cook for everyone, which they all loved, and they had several breakthroughs.

Having Georgie Cattivo on the staff meant they could electronically edit the "new look" paper that Cat had only dreamed about. The staff had never had the computer smarts to do it properly. But Georgie made it look easy.

When Cat talked about doing the traditional interview with the head for the first issue, it became clear that Georgie hadn't a clue about his father's vendetta against Tom West. And from his comments about hoping to be allowed into the head's honors history seminar and joining Cat, it was clear that he could be Dr. West's champion. The other two left it to Cat to broach the subject of Tom's possible dismissal.

She didn't know quite how to do it, so she just did it. "We should do the interview just before Labor Day, but Georgie, you should know that some of the trustees have been trying to get rid of Dr. West."

"No way — why would they try that?"

"Well, some of them think Doc was too liberal with us on the paper, for one thing," said Matt.

"And some of them think he's not a very good fundraiser," added Maury.

Maury then explained to Georgie the original trio's frustration when they tried to come up with something that might compromise the anti-West board members. His scheme to hack some of their accounts had fizzled. And none of them had the cash to pay a private investigator to follow any of the target trustees.

"God, you guys are really something," said Georgie, grinning.

"But nothing worked. Oh, wait until you hear what Cat tried," said a proud Maury. He detailed her plan for Georgie.

Cat had grown accustomed to the president of the Alumni Association passing the *Chronicle's* open door and popping in before his weekly visits to the alumni office. Howie Baker, at thirty-five, was a leading member of Cattivo's investment group; hence, she figured he would know something that the Irregulars could use. He wasn't downright ugly and he made a habit of chatting her up with double entendres and winks when he dropped in. So, when he pulled up alongside in his vintage Austin-Healey 3000 with an invitation for a ride as she walked on the sidewalk near Seventy-Second and Madison, she steeled herself, leaned in, and smiled. He immediately suggested, "I'll whisk you across the George Washington Bridge to the rest area overlooking the Hudson at Alpine, New Jersey. It's fabulous. And secluded. You'll love my baby here." He patted the dash. And recited his car's pedigree. Any spark she might have imagined back at the *Chronicle* office cooled during his stick shift, torque, and horsepower bluster, so his invitation got him, and her, nowhere. Cat remembered a dental appointment.

"So, she still hasn't seen the Alpine view or the inside of that Healey Three-Thousand!" said Maury.

Georgie loved being put in the picture, having real friends. "Mr. Baker and dad are pretty close alright. But, shit, they don't have a clue about our school," he said. "*We* know how good the school is and how the teachers work hard with us all the time. And everyone says Doc's a great teacher. So, maybe *we* should use the paper openly to support him. Like an OpEd. I'll help write it and sign my name. We'll show those assholes that the students are backing Doc a hundred percent." Georgie was so flushed Cat got him a can of Coke Zero to cool him down.

When Maury, Matt, and Cat compared notes after arriving home, they still wished that Doc West would give some indication that he had gotten their manila envelope and their supportive message. On the whole, however, they agreed that the weekend had exceeded their expectations.

CHAPTER 62

Tom hung up the phone, fuming. The only thing on his mind that did anything to calm him down was Sally. And she'd been gone for three days.

Jo Wilson had trouble getting Wither Bramston on the telephone up at the family compound on Vinalhaven, an island off the coast of Maine. His daughter finally got him to pick up the extension down at his boathouse.

"I'm sorry but I only have a minute or so — it's such a fine day for sailing — I always tell my secretary not to give my number out." There was a clatter from his end and an impatient girl's voice, "Come o-n, Grandfather!"

"Wither, Wither? Are you still there? Okay. I've just heard this morning from the heads of Milton Academy, Penn Charter, and Exeter that they got notices from a headhunter that he was inviting applications for the Christ Church head's job. Do you know anything about that?"

"Oh, really?" There was an interminable silence from Maine. "Tom, yes, maybe they misunderstood somehow. You see, I knew I couldn't get to it until September when I return to the city so I thought it would be best to tidy it up before I left in June."

"Wither, that means that all the school heads and trustees in America will soon hear that Christ Church School is without a head. Not only is that unfair to me, it's ruinous to our school's reputation. And when it gets out among our own constituency, that'll kill my attempts at raising money — they'll all put off giving until the new head arrives. Wither, do you understand?"

"Well, guess they jumped the gun. But not by much."

Tom hung up on his board president. He had to, or he would have lapsed into profanity.

A furious Tom typed out a letter and sent it to Jo for final prep. Afterwards, he rang the Bishop because he thought his mentor should be put in the picture before his letter went out. The cleric agreed that Bramston's hiring a search consultant to announce the firing was beyond the pale.

"I'm glad you agree," Tom said. "Because I've written a letter to Bramston. I've reamed him out with the full story, copies to all trustees, and also threatened my resignation unless he is replaced as board president immediately. His sheer incompetence or duplicity will make him the laughing-stock of the trustees — he'll have to resign."

The Bishop paused before responding. "Tom, listen carefully. You can't fit all the trustees into the corner you think you've built with that letter. If you send it, the only result will be board consternation and . . . *your* departure. I'm coming down there right now."

He did. In twenty minutes, Tom heard the Bishop greet Jo followed by the soft murmur of their conversation. In his first year, Jo had told him that the Bishop was her favorite trustee. By the time the cleric came into Tom's office, he was sipping her coffee.

"Good afternoon, Tom. Where's your letter?"

Tom handed him the signed document. The Bishop sat and read it carefully. Tom sat chomping at the bit.

The Bishop looked up. "Tom, there is no question of the impropriety of Wither's action. The sheer stupidity of the man, if predictable, is overwhelming. All of which you summarized rather well."

"Thanks."

"However, I advise strongly against sending this out."

"But I have to. He deserves it. And so do I."

"You do deserve far better. Yes. And in this case, he is also very deserving — he's lucky to have survived so long without getting what he deserves."

Tom smiled.

The Bishop sat back, steepled his fingers, and looked with affection at Tom.

"'Revenge is a dish which people of taste prefer to eat cold,' Tom. And I think I have a better plan."

"I'm all ears."

"Now, first, you need a break — you need to get away — Jo told me that you haven't had a vacation in three years. Not even a long weekend. That's pitiful."

"I know. But it seems that whenever I get something planned, a school emergency comes up."

"'Emergencies you will always have with you,' as my favorite first century rabbi would have put it. As a member of the trustee executive committee, I hereby order you to take a long weekend out of the city. Pronto."

"But I can't. I'm pretty stretched as it is. I may have to take a loan to cover my mother's upcoming medical visit. Maybe next year."

"You misunderstand me. Not next year — *within days,* so that I can go to work in redressing Wither's mistake without you or your letter making it worse. I'll provide the money."

"You mean—"

"Yes. Not another word about it. You plan the trip. Jo will be given the means." Tom was dumbfounded. "A final suggestion," said the cleric. "You told me about wanting to see Amsterdam and its art when you came over for dinner. At the time, I wondered if the accession to the board of a Met curator of Old Master paintings and your growing interest in Dutch art were a mere coincidence. Since then, I have received intelligence that coincidence has no place in your lexicon. So, while you're at it, join that lovely curator in Amsterdam. I know about her trip because Lulu's best friend is Gwen Chase, and she and Oliver are right now squiring Sally to Dutch canvases and curators. Sally will be free on Saturday and Sunday — Lulu just checked."

Tom was truly "slobber-knocked," as his old Ohio high school football coach would have put it.

CHAPTER 63

Early Saturday morning, a train whisked Tom from the Schiphol airport to Amsterdam in twenty minutes. Sally was waiting with an endless hug in the hotel dining room.

The hotel, five brick storeys in the heart of the city, proved to be the perfect place for the pair from New York, or "Nieuw Amsterdam" as Sally put it, working on her rusty Dutch. Their room overlooked a canal, the red light area, and the Old Church on one side and the Amstel River on the other.

Sally had been very busy for five weekdays, three of them with Oliver Chase. His contacts were old and trusted friends, so she was welcomed warmly by the curators at the Rijks and the Frans Hals Museum in Haarlem. Her exhibit, featuring a rich Dutch life of dogs, people, and pubs, was now virtually complete, pending approval by the Met director. She even had an old Dutch maxim for her seventeenth century exhibit: "The nuzzle of dogs, the affection of whores, and the hospitality of innkeepers: none of it comes without cost."

Sally took Tom to the Rijksmuseum first thing. On their walk, they saw whacked-out hippies fresh from marijuana cafés strolling next to plump elderly Dutchmen puffing on cigars lodged dead center in their lips, as prosperous and self-satisfied as any of Frans Hals' or Rembrandt's burghers. Sally was proud to show Tom her girlhood city. She was rapidly recovering her command of the language, but after she reeled off several Dutch sentences Tom suggested she had contracted a rare throat disease, the sound of which no one else could possibly replicate. Only later did he recognize that the gifted affliction was widespread among the Dutch.

ROBIN LESTER

They went right to the Dutch Masters. Tom was fascinated with Sally's comments on artists and pictures, in part retaining the awe of childhood memory and partly the appraisal of an adult curator. After two hours and a short lunch break they moved to Rembrandt. Tom was mesmerized with the Rembrandt galleries.

Finally, they turned to Sally's favorite. She insisted he read what van Gogh had said when he visited the new Rijksmuseum in 1885 and saw "The Jewish Bride" for the first time: "Would you believe it, and I honestly mean what I say — I should be happy to give ten years of my life if I could go on sitting here in front of this picture for a fortnight, with only a crust of dry bread for food."

Sally and Tom stood together in front of "The Jewish Bride." He felt it was simply overwhelming. The ebony and golden frame and the hefty size of the canvas all contributed to the power of the moment. The story the artist told and his ability to make the personal universal drew the observer in and made the past into a timeless present tense. Van Gogh had said, "What an intimate, what an infinitely sympathetic picture." Two glowing figures, a man and a woman, stand against a dark background with indistinct potted plant and faux column. Her rich red dress with silver and gold picked up the simpler, but more golden, garment he wore. Groom and bride are in their own world as they gaze directly and thoughtfully ahead, not at each other and not at the artist — they are in their shared place. There is something from Ur of the Chaldees, from Sinai, from Temple Mount, uniting them, something so real and present that to speak of it would trespass the very Holy of Holies. The man encircles her with his left arm, holding her shoulder gently toward him as he places his right hand full across her heart. She now raises her left hand to cradle his palm against herself.

It was magnificent.

Tom and Sally were silent as they leaned together and stood before the oil and pigment altar. Twice the guard shot his sleeve and checked the time. Once he shifted his weight and the wooden floor gave a slight groan. They were oblivious.

Tom put his left arm around Sally and moved his right hand to her front

— she instinctively cradled his hand against herself. She felt resistance in his hand and looked down: he held a sparkling ring in front of her.

"Would you be my Jewish Bride?"

They rang Matt first. "About time," was the gist of his response. Jane and Ben Levi were full of congratulations, both claimed a marriage commission, and agreed to witness the vows when the couple returned. The Bishop was overjoyed, and when Sally asked, promptly agreed to marry them when and wherever. The New Amsterdam twosome walked the misty streets and canals arm in arm for hours deep in conversation about the future until they felt tired enough to return to their hotel.

Sally stood in a lacy half-slip, her side to him on the bed, brushing her hair out after its usual French Twist day. Tom was fixed on her breasts shaking and recovering with each full stroke of the brush. He loved watching her determined brushing and how her toned rump made the short silk covering flare and flutter with each stroke and ripple down to those long, perfect legs that could outrun a former jock.

"Let's kiss and make out," he said.

"How old-fashioned!" she said. "I'll have to play hard-to-get."

Sally stepped out of the slip, stood in her bikini pants by the bed and toppled over like a ten-pin into her fiancé's arms.

CHAPTER 64

The next morning Sally stretched, yawned, and luxuriated on the sunshine-stippled bed under the duvet. A foot, a flank, and a large nipple on dark areola were visible to Tom who imitated her stretch, quieted, and grabbed her.

They lay entwined, resting from a night of excess. He had called her voracious and she said he was insatiable. He knew better, said so, and she had proved him right by 3 A.M.

That day they retraced Estrella Malka's schoolgirl world on rented bikes.

They found her old apartment house — a beehive of the working class. Tom imagined what a comedown that was for the wife and child of a favored Moroccan accountant who lived near the palace, but Sally had never commented on that aspect of their life in Amsterdam.

On their bike journey along the Prince's Canal toward their primary destination Sally talked nonstop about her most significant girlhood experience. "After my mother gave me a copy of Anne Frank's diary in Dutch, I spent every afternoon after school engrossed in it, along with my French/Dutch dictionary."

Sally had never seen the Anne Frank House as a fully realized museum. She squeezed his hand as they waited for admission. Then they were in. They walked up the stairs. The bookcase swung away from the landing, revealing the hideout. They entered what for Sally was the sanctuary — the place where Anne slept and wrote and worried and hoped and dreamed. And affixed to the wall above her bed was a virtual tapestry of longing and escape: fading post cards and clippings of the Dutch Royal Family in faraway Canada, the princesses Elizabeth and Margaret from a free Britain across the Channel, and all the others, movie stars from an American fairyland and a picture cut from a German magazine of a shining, curly blonde little girl with fluttery lashes in a long organza dress. Sally didn't want to leave the room. She wanted to stay and feel the space — the bare chestnut tree outside "on whose branches little raindrops shone" and the strong tolling of the Westerkerk's bells. Anne Frank had been torn away and murdered by the Nazis, but the girl's room and some of what she saw and heard remained.

They wanted to spend the afternoon tracing Sally's schoolgirl explorations of the area. At the top of the Westerkerk bell tower they peered down toward the side and back of the Frank House almost as intently as the refugee Moroccan Jewish girl had years before.

The New Yorkers returned to street level and entered the Westerkerk, where Rembrandt had buried his twenty-eight-year-old son Titus and joined him beneath the floor tiles eleven months later. Tom and Sally sat in the cavernous church, his arm encircling her shoulders.

"Now that I'm here again," she said, "I can see why the original lack of graven images combined with clear ground floor windows served as a model for our Portuguese Synagogue fifty years later."

She pointed to the lighting. "I was so proud to see that my synagogue had gigantic brass and pewter hanging light fixtures like the ones I saw here in Rembrandt's Westerkerk."

"Lit by candles," said Tom. "It must have been beautiful on Friday evenings. You and your mother must have loved it."

"I did go early to see the old caretaker do the lighting, but we were seldom there for the services. I guess the aesthetics of the space and glowing candles was more our theology. We always inclined toward the God of the excommunicated Sephardic, Bento Spinoza."

Tom finished her thought. "Just as Einstein did."

"Yes. When Matt asked me recently, I admitted that his dad and I decided not to give him any training in either of our traditions."

"There is such a thing as religious literacy," said Tom.

"Okay, so I shouldn't ignore my family culture. But honestly, I'm so ambivalent about it. It's mostly that I hate an exclusivist heritage of any stripe — of the Elect, the Chosen, the Brotherhood, or of sacred soil including Jerusalem and Plymouth Rock."

"Amen, sister."

They sat silently as the sun escaped the gray and white clouds, streamed through the tall clear windows, and set polished wood and stone aglow. Just as suddenly, the sun was gone, falling prey to the moving clouds.

On their last day, they walked for miles in the city of canals and narrow dark brick houses with white-rimmed sparkling windows and fanciful but functional gables reflected in the water. Several times they crossed halfway over canal bridges and then paused to let the city settle around them. The sturdy black bicycles with high-set handlebars ridden by perpendicular Dutchwomen and men moved fast and silently over the cobblestones; the experienced water traffic from the mammoth glassy envelopes of gaping tourists; the workman's skiff that boasted fresh posies on a polished mahogany dash — it was loaded with cobbles and trailed a red-white-blue line with an indefatigable orange rubber ducky that cleaved a tiny ribbed wake in the dark steel-mirrored water; those and all manner of other floating objects providing a gentle rock-a-bye for the moored houseboats with Technicolor coats and stringy vines.

They were silent. Sally shivered and put her arm around his waist as they stood and watched the ducks swirling for the bread emerging and finally dropping from a toddler's sticky hand.

During their last evening, they concluded that Amsterdam was a moist but very romantic place — the pointillist moon glowed through a crystal mist as the weather warmed and provided a further intimacy. They stood entwined on a bridge.

"Darling, I was a goner from the time I saw you help save Maury last winter and spring. And when I saw how my son watched and emulated you."

"I was a goner in June. I think it was that mole on your thigh in Central Park that pushed me over the edge."

Later they lay together talking against the encroaching drowsiness they welcomed. The misty moon was stuck in the upper-left corner of the tall hotel window and shone into the room intermittently, while dark clouds with pewter edges moved across its face.

Into the suffused, grainy darkness they talked of their new life and of their hopes for Matt. They had loved hearing his eager anticipation of living in the head's house and having access to Tom's history library when they had talked with him earlier.

CHAPTER 65

My God, Cattivo thought when Wither Wellington-Cortelyou Bramston, V called in his inimitable quaver.

"Please come over to my club for an emergency meeting," then paused, as if waiting to be smacked for speaking up. When Cattivo remained silent, he finished, "Oh yes, Bob, that's what I'd call it — an 'emergency.'" Wither sounded full of suppressed anger, the only type he allowed himself. Still, Cattivo figured, any excuse to enter the Brook Club. But why, he wondered, was Bramston back in town?

"You no doubt wonder why I've called you here," said Bramston, at the head of the handsome mahogany table in a private dining room at the Brook Club.

"Why, yes," said Cattivo, "and why our ally Richie isn't here."

Bramston looked at him over his half-specs and almost whispered, "The Reverend Doctor might not fully understand the delicacy of our conversation today."

Cattivo whispered back, "I see," although he didn't.

"In a word, Bob, I've been humiliated beyond words this weekend. I can't remember such humiliation and I'd like not to have to undergo this Gethsemane again, if you please."

"I am sorry, Wither, truly sorry," said Cattivo. "But am I in some way to blame?" He felt for his Phi Bete key.

"Well, you did suggest something to the effect, at our last meeting, of 'Why don't you crank it up'?" He hesitated. "I even believe you said, 'Hell, it might even put Tom on the ropes.'"

"Why, yes, Wither, I guess I did. I meant, of course, that we should be ready to pounce once he resigns. Or when he's fired at our next meeting."

"But the context was this head search business, Bob. And you indicated we should get in before the top candidates were all taken. Like at Dalton. That was the context. Really. Yes. I rather think it was." This guy can't even make a declarative sentence stick, thought Cattivo.

"Oh, then I'm sorry, again. Wither, I've been in Florida for five days. What has happened in the meantime — this, a, *your* 'Gethsemane'?"

"The Bishop prevailed upon me to return to the city. Well, some other unimpeachable trustees also; and like the Bishop, they are giants here at the Brook. Very old, valued friends. They were quite upset because the Bishop had showed them Wicksnuffer's head search letter that went out to about fifteen-hundred schools and heads nationwide. It got their attention because it was a bit florid."

God, when Wither Bramston judges something 'florid,' it must have been in neon purple. "And those gentlemen objected to the prose style, Wither?"

"Well, there was also the matter of the announcement, the strong suggestion, maybe even the assertion, that the trustees had fired Tom West."

"Given the complete absence of fact in that," Cattivo said, "one can understand why, eh, Wither?"

Wither slurped his tea. And promptly spilled it on his peaked lapel with a tremble. Yes, Gethsemane would have that effect, reasoned Cattivo.

"Wither, nothing is lost, save honor. And that will prove temporary, I assure you, especially among your old, valued, unimpeachable friends."

"I'd like to believe that, Bob. Really, I would."

Cattivo stood. Bramston rose with him. Cattivo moved to the end of the table and embraced him. Very briefly. Shook his hand. "Thank you, my friend and business partner, you've done well, you've taken one for the cause. And I'm sure that after the dust has settled here at the Club, Tom West will still be on the ropes. And you put him there!"

Bramston responded with a twitchy, tentative smile that became a weak grin.

CHAPTER 66

The Bishop's two-page report on how he handled Bramston's published search for a new head awaited Tom on his blotter. Jo also laid out the actual mailing from headhunter Wicksnuffer. The Bishop had seen that the letter was erroneous in almost every detail and was couched in such pretentious language — *"The Christ Church trustees have duly considered the alternatives to what was widely considered to be dated, unsuitable leadership and wish now to embark into more spatially extensive waters entirely more appropriate to their amplified needs"* — that it was perfect for his purposes. He had three influential CC trustees to lunch and gave each a copy of the Bramston-inspired mailing. They were outraged by its facts and style. The one corporate lawyer and the two executives determined to join the Bishop in demanding that their board president immediately withdraw the letter and send out an apology for its contents and inconvenience at his own expense. Wither was forced to return to New York to meet with the four trustees. He stubbornly denied he had ordered the search and talked darkly of Wicksnuffer's "miscommunication." "*It was difficult to talk him down from that kindergarten intractability,*" wrote the Bishop. "*Not once did he admit to the three others what he told me privately: 'Bob told me to do it.' Finally, he called off the dodgy headhunter.*"

The Bishop finished his report: "*You may be disappointed, Tom — don't be — our humiliating Bramston and/or Cattivo now would not be as valuable to us at the fall meeting as the three allies we gained in our defense of school decency.*"

"The Bishop knows human nature," said Sally, after reading it with Tom.

"He certainly knows *my* nature," concluded Tom.

Jo also told them of the Bishop's invitation for them to visit at their convenience when they returned. They found it convenient in the late afternoon after they had made their peace with school and museum. When they arrived at the Bishop's Palace, a nurse in a white smock greeted them at the door and took them into his study. His face lit up immediately, but his warm greeting was delivered with a weak voice. He asked them to pull up side chairs to either side of his large club chair so they could hear him.

"Well, you'll have to recover from this setback by the middle of September when you marry us," said Tom. "Sally has been talking of nothing else since we rang from Amsterdam."

The Bishop revealed that his chemo would start soon. "I may be a little under the weather for a while and I can't, for the life of me, determine whether the oncologist's promise of 'at least a few more months' matches my occupational clerical projections of 'eternal life.' It shouldn't, not to a rational man, but then I'm beginning to suspect that a dying man is no more rational than a living Bishop." He looked from Sally to Tom. "Is he?"

Tom shook his head and said, "That's too weighty for me."

Sally silently reached across and lifted the Bishop's hand from the arm of his chair, then enveloped it in both of hers and kissed it.

The Bishop was clearly moved, as was Sally. They both closed their eyes and raised their faces upward. They gathered themselves, opened their eyes, and smiled a little self-consciously.

"I can see it now — a *Times* headline," said Tom. "'*Bishop Caught in Sephardic Séance!*'"

The Bishop gathered Sally in a hug and held an arm out for Tom to join them. He did.

As their taxi moved east on Cathedral Parkway, Tom broke the silence. "I didn't realize we were *both* searching for a lost father."

"Me neither, darling."

"Why don't we take a walk when we get over to Fifth?"

"I'm game. Then I'll have to get home to get a late dinner for the Irregulars."

CHAPTER 67

They settled on a bench at Fifth and Eighty-Fourth in the Ancient Playground built in honor of the Metropolitan's Egyptian wing across the drive. The slanting sun elongated the toddlers' figures as they darted over the pyramid and into the sandy surround. There were a few hurried rescues by mommies and daddies and nannies when the children tumbled.

Sally sat back, crossed her legs, and looked at Tom. Her face was tinged with the setting sun. She looked beautiful.

"What I've told you about my émigré life — Fez to Amsterdam to New York — is true, but it's not the whole truth, it's only the part I like to remember. Or really only the part I wanted a handsome, intelligent head to hear. Now, to *my* pentimento, which is really about my father." She reached out, intertwined her fingers with his and began her story.

"I guess, in reality, my father lost it all in his escape from Fez. The result was that he arrived in New York with champagne taste and a beer budget."

Sally explained that when she and her mother moved from Amsterdam to join him, they had to watch him struggle.

"Father loved the 'New World' term and used it often. He said it was the right place for a new start on an old life. He started working out of our walk-up in Brooklyn — Moroccan imports. You've seen the Flatbush studio photograph he had taken of himself to record who he was when he arrived in America. It's how I try to remember him."

Two years later, her father was barely hanging on: frayed collars, old, shiny three-piece suits, the works. It was devastating for him — such a precise, formal Frenchman, such a proud Moroccan, set adrift in brawling, casual America.

"His lonely futility ended when he fell in front of a subway train at rush hour. It was May of my senior year — he didn't even see me graduate. I guess I've kept the accident fuzzy in my mind — mercifully speculative." Sally stopped, drained, her chin quivering. Tom raised the back of her hand to his cheek. They settled in together on the bench.

"Merciful, yes," said Tom. "Count your blessings — my dad left me nothing to speculate about. And my mother left me far too much to specu-late about. Now, with her coming here next week, the truth is, I don't really know or understand the woman, even after years of therapy."

"Bosh. It'll all come back to you. She's your mother, after all. Sure, you haven't seen her for a while, but it'll come back."

"Yeah, that's what I'm afraid of — that it'll come back. It was the cancer diagnosis in Phoenix that precipitated her trip to New York, not our desire to see each other after nearly twenty-five years."

Sally said nothing, but shifted to look at him. It was dusk now, and the children began their exodus from the playground.

"I can remember very few conversations between my parents, but I knew one by heart. It was her invariable comment when he missed out on a pro-motion or when he didn't get a raise: 'You're such a pushover, Tom, so weak. We'll never escape this dump.'

"And, I guess he was weak. From the army, early 'Nam, and his asthma. Weak, except for one thing — he bought a life insurance policy against her advice. 'Like the ones in the *Saturday Evening Post*,' he told me. He explained it was for my education — to guarantee that, no matter what.

"'But that sure as hell won't get us a real house, will it?' That's how she put it. I guess she had a point, but all I remember is a gentle, war-wounded man, dreaming dreams, not of his future, he'd given that up, but of mine."

Tom related that the crisis came later, during his sophomore year. His father's health was always poor — severe asthma — and he had several episodes at the emergency room and missed work. And for the first time, they'd sent him home from work that Friday — they couldn't have a sick man hacking around a drugstore, and the boss had threatened his job. Ethylene had tried to get extra hours at the car dealer but was turned down.

"I finished my paper route that fall Saturday and found Dad outside the trailer wheezing and coughing. He didn't want to wake Mother. He was standing with his hands on his knees looking toward the sun flooding the carpet of autumn leaves and morning dew. 'Our trailer park is sure no Shangri-la, son, but I think it's beautiful,' he said. Oddly, I remember everything from that morning: the joy of working with Dad, even the warming sun on our backs as we did our weekly ritual with the old Ford before he left for work at the drugstore. But he wouldn't be going that day, he finally revealed, or any day. And yet, that didn't matter — we were a team — we added oil and I pumped air into the tires. The usual." Tom paused when he felt her hand gently stroking his shoulder.

"Dad chatted away about me — how I had pulled off the unthinkable at Kokosing High — I'd made the honor roll as usual, but I'd also made the starting football team as a sophomore. Dad was so proud; he said, 'You can't miss now! And of course you've got your education set up. Maybe next summer you can go to that summer school at Ohio State. Believe me, it's fixed with insurance.' Then he made me go in and study before I went over for the game.

"I studied inside at the little dinette table, and later I was in a rush because I was due to suit up. I heard the car running, but ignored it so that I could finish a paper. I didn't suspect anything and charged out the door on the other side of the trailer to my game. Well, he had hosed the exhaust into his car and sat in the driver's seat. Right there on the concrete apron outside our trailer. I was within ten feet of him in that car and I did nothing. All I had to do was stand up and look out the window."

Only a few stubborn stragglers remained in the playground. The lights of the city were coming on. Tom felt Sally's fingers resting gently at his shoulder. Then a squeeze as she spoke.

"Oh, Tom, you're being much too tough on yourself. An adolescent isn't responsible for an adult man's suicide. How did your mother take it?"

"She was virtually mute the week of the funeral and she seemed devastated. Then the insurance check arrived. Big surprise for her: it was made out to me, the sole beneficiary. She spent days trying to talk me out of that twenty-five thousand dollar insurance check. Even after I got another part-time job and figured we could make it, she said there was no way we'd survive without that college money.

"She finally threatened to leave me if I didn't sign. Some terrible scenes. Even though the banker warned me not to, I endorsed it to her down at the bank. I couldn't bear it. Neither could she, I guess."

"Jesus, Tom. She blackmailed her own son for the money. Is that it?"

"Yes. Oh, no. See, she felt she needed it right away to get by. More than I did for college three years off."

Tom looked away at the darkened, empty playground. "Then one evening after I got home from football practice, I found that she'd left a note for me on the dinette table: '*LOVE YOU BUT I HAVE TO MOVE ON —YOU UNDERSTAND*' — I'll never forget it. I never told anyone about it. Until now."

He looked into her eyes and she buried her face in his chest and neck, but she didn't lose it. He gently rocked her and said, "Oh, Sally. Maybe we should both write a new life story. And we both have a father now."

"Yes, darling." She paused. "For how long?"

CHAPTER 68

Cattivo was trying to keep too many balls in the air at once. He realized he was losing time and temper day after day. Besides his New York main stage, he had the three projects in Sarasota, five in Jacksonville, a couple in Birmingham, one big one in Atlanta, and always that old monstrosity in Miami — the Open Sesame building. The Cubans nearly cut him off at the crotch on that one, and he thought that being the leading Manhattan developer in the "Manhattanization" of Miami should have been enough to keep them at bay. No way, José. Their piece of that action cost him. The Cubans were organized – he'd give them that – from the building trade unions to anchormen.

That José line, where did he hear that recently? Oh, yes, that mouthy fatty in the CC registrar's office and that clueless Philips' "wetback" comment. Richie may have made it big at St. Whatever in Atlanta, but Cattivo would not bet on him in Miami. Well, he couldn't say Machiavelli hadn't warned him about how much it takes to recruit and keep one's allies. He'd have to do something for Philips — maybe goose up his Ponzi takings in his Cattivo hedge account. Bob sighed. Philips really thought the market fund was miraculous, not so surprising for someone who believed in the parting of the Red Sea, raising Lazarus, and changing water into wine. Which reminded him, some Petrus might do it for Philips. Cattivo made a mental note to have Morrells send him his last cellared case of '77. He was going to send it to Tom West when he resigned, but there would be other lousy vintages for him.

So, Petrus for the Rev, but what for the Pilgrim? Nothing that went in Bramston's eyes, ears, nose, or mouth got the poor man's juices going. He kept himself busy keeping that old firm old. Bob had almost lost him over that Wicksnuffer Gate business — it would pay to remember that Bramston was a WASP for the ages — his ethics calibrated by, "What would my club colleagues say?" He surrounded himself with them exclusively, except for Cattivo, who, in turn, kept Bramston's business humming.

Cattivo didn't have time to worry about this garbage — he had more important matters to orchestrate. Like Hoboken, whose logo was "Where's mine?" He had his building plans almost approved, and then it got complicated. The Jersey logo meant the more touches, the merrier, but that widened the criminal exposure because the inspectors, council, and mayors all ran their own Tony Soprano locals. He should have cut his losses and let it die. But shit, he couldn't walk away from his signature forty floors on the Hudson that everyone could see from Manhattan because he'd already named it "The George." The English patron saint would keep everyone buzzing with the requisite Anglo-Saxon imprimatur, but he and his son would know what it really meant. That should have been enough to get Georgie interested in what Dad does all day. But the kid was a little strange, still hadn't realized that he could hire the geeks to do all that tech stuff he loved, and that he didn't need to get his own hands dirty. But he'd be all right once he got his teeth into the idea that it wasn't only Mommy who could spend Dad's money.

Babs had never really understood Georgie. He suspected she was even ashamed of him, not up to her image. He was a little overweight, not good at sports, very different from her friends' kids who were all up there as free-loading summer assistants at the Pound Ridge club. Georgie found himself a job in the city — tutoring little kids in math for peanuts — he went early and stayed late, until the public school custodians locked up, and he didn't say where he went until his curfew at eleven, only "hanging out." So, okay, he was different, Cattivo would have to come to grips with that even if Babs wouldn't even try. And Georgie still knew his dad would do anything for him.

Babs was on the warpath again and she was right, of course — Tom was still the only East Side headmaster who refused to attend the Knickerbocker

Greys annual head's review because he claimed it had a history of racism. She was spitting nails over it, asked what's holding Cattivo up on "that dreadful man"? Her email said, "Every way I turn, I'm reminded and embarrassed by that man — last week he was the keynote speaker at the ACLU conference on student newspaper censorship, according to *The Times*. He's become a hero to those fools. When you get rid of him, you've got to promise to tighten the screws on that *Chronicle* bunch until they scream. Why, oh why, don't you act?"

CHAPTER 69

Ethyl West would be staying in the head's apartment while she had her examination. Tom was relieved that he had a separate entrance from the school because his mother's imminent presence somehow brought his shame home in the place where he had hidden his background pretty well. As an adult, he seemed always to have to play a role foreign to his origins — scholar, teacher, dean, and for five years, his toughest role. Now he was a serious, dignified, soon to be graying head of the oldest English school in New York. He hoped he could handle his mother and his role at the same time.

When Tom felt his diaphragm tighten in the LaGuardia arrivals area, he popped a couple of Rolaids — it made six for the day — the Dewar's and Marlboros had left their mark last night, and now his whole body was truly crapulous. He checked the flight number and suddenly realized they'd never exchanged photos, so he didn't even know what his mother looked like now.

At baggage claim, he watched the passengers from the Phoenix/Houston flight emerge down their stairway. He might as well "choose" his mother from among the possibles. A rather rotund lady of the right age in a flowered dress bulging at the edges of a self-belt looked away from his direct gaze and was claimed by a squealing little girl and her parents. A tall, rather majestic white-haired lady in a gray seersucker suit stalked past his questioning look. He watched her purposeful progress toward the luggage conveyor until he heard a tell-tale cough from behind. It started thin, ended heavy and loose. A gravelly "Tommy?" followed.

His mother was an arresting blonde of above-average height. She wore a powder-blue top with a scoop neckline, Gloria Vanderbilt jeans, lilac high-heeled sandals with an ankle bracelet, and a deep tan — she remained a knockout. And seemed uncertain how to proceed.

Tom gave her no help. He did recognize his own nose and cheekbones, refined considerably in her, and the sky blue eyes. She may have read his take, as she looked at him searchingly, then dropped her eyes. As he moved toward her, he noted the obvious cleavage but hints of crinkly parchment at the throat.

"Mother?" He was reluctant to embrace a woman he didn't know, and they both settled for her pushing a square red cosmetics case toward him. He took it and asked about her flight and received a short answer so that she could escape to the street. Outside, she lit and puffed an unfiltered Pall Mall down to the nub.

The renewed Ethyl returned to her son at the carousel. She stood with confident wide stance, feet at right angles, one long leg forward. She caught lingering glances from a guitar-bearing youth sitting on the floor and a but-toned-down fiftyish businessman chewing gum so tightly his jaw muscles bulged when he stared at her.

The Russian émigré driver watched Ethylene with interest as Tom hefted her cases — the larger one seemingly almost empty — into the trunk of the yellow cab. Tom tried to hand her into the back seat, but she ignored his hand and climbed in. He wasn't sure what that meant, probably simply that she wasn't used to such treatment, but it occurred to him that they hadn't touched yet.

As the cab merged onto the parkway, his mother turned to him, patted his leg, and said, "Now, Tommy, there's something I have to say. I want to make up for all the years we've lost. Maybe we can forget the past."

"And I only hope your visit gets some good results." The driver kept his eye on as much of her as he could manage in his mirror.

Ethyl was soon settled in the head's apartment. Tom gave her a tour. She looked politely at his first-edition Henry Adams histories, and then zeroed in on the autographed football in his office.

"So, you were on that championship team, Tommy. I remember hearing of that in Columbus. Something about the smallest school doing very well in the playoffs. Taking on the big boys."

"And I saw most of it from the bench, Mother—because of work, I missed practice."

She turned the ball in her hands after she blew the dust off the laces. "Here's the Prideaux boy. And Akers. This'un must be Byron's son. Dated Byron. Must be out by now."

She tried to replace the ball on the bookshelf, but it kept rolling. Finally, she got it. "Has to be right, just right, so's my star boy's name will show. Wished I could have seen you play. You oughta be proud of that, Tommy. That's a free ticket in Ohio for lots of things. Bet they even know about Ohio football here in New York. But there were no free tickets in my family. Never has been, I'll tell you that right now."

He thought maybe her voice broke a little.

He didn't know what to expect later when he introduced Sally to his mother at a Met lunch. Sally had staked out a nice table at the park window. They sat and Ethylene ordered a salad, a slice of chocolate cake, one chocolate mousse, and a white wine.

Ethyl seemed initially ill at ease with the conversation, especially about their engagement, but she soon settled comfortably into her wine and watched them both with a smile.

"I must get back to the salt mines. So nice to meet you, Mrs. West," Sally said after thirty minutes.

When she was barely out of earshot, his mother said, "She's pretty, Tommy, very pretty. Like that Penelope Cruz. Nose a little long, crowds her lip." Ethyl was thinking overtime. "She Italian?"

"Nope. She's Sephardic. From Morocco."

"That African, or A-rab?"

"Jewish. From Spain. They were driven out by Christians about the time of Columbus. The Muslims let them settle in Morocco."

"Sounds complicated."

"It was."

"She's sure dark. Very dark."

Ethyl had exacted a promise from her son to take her for an afternoon of shopping before she began the two-day series of medical tests. He suggested Macy's. She countered with Saks and Bloomingdale's. She shopped; he paid and carried.

Late that afternoon, they went to a steakhouse that she'd seen on some reality show.

"Well, this is very nice, son, just what I always thought New York would be like. I hope you don't mind if I have another Seven and Seven with my meal. Never was much for wine."

Ethyl ate with enjoyment and opted for a double cheesecake.

On the way upstairs at home, she talked nonstop. "Sure wish I could have seen you play. Bet you were the star. Little rascal. You were always like that, a little rascal around the house. Ran me ragged. But you were also my Sunday School boy — Mom's little Christian Soldier." She hugged him goodnight. "I'll never forget."

As soon as he got into the hall, he tried to rub the scent and greasy layer off his cheek as he moved to his bathroom.

He delivered her to the hospital at 8:00 A.M. When he picked her up at 4:00 P.M., she looked strained and tired.

"That was one hell of a workout," she said. "I just want to get back to bed."

She was up at 7:30 P.M. for the seafood lasagna he had heated up. Again she tucked in with enthusiasm, well-fortified by Seagram's, and she loved the New York cheesecake he had picked up for her.

The next morning, he found the cap from the cooking sherry on the counter, the bottle in the trash bin. It had been drained. He set out a selection of cereals and a bowl, and he put the sherry bottle next to it.

When she entered the kitchen, she said, "Don't think I'm up for cereal this morning, son, but I could go for some of that super cheesecake I had last night."

When she saw the sherry bottle, she added, "Well, when I saw you didn't trust me — you locked your liquor cabinet in the living room, didn't you? Well, when I saw that, what was I to do in the middle of the night? Couldn't sleep — still on Mountain. Didn't want to wake you, so I did the next best thing. And it wasn't great sherry, I'll tell you that right now." She shivered with the memory and grinned at him.

"I know I drink a little too much, Tommy," she said as she tucked into the cheesecake. "But I don't think it makes any difference now."

He wasn't sure he would ever see her at her best. Dr. Johnson was right again: impending execution had concentrated Ethyl's mind wonderfully. On the bottle.

CHAPTER 70

Tom delivered her for her second clinic go-round. She was to have her diagnosis conference at the end of the day, but she rejected Tom's offer to come over and be with her for that. She said she would prefer the taxi money.

She returned late in the afternoon. She'd been crying.

He held her hand and walked her up to the living room, sat her down in the deepest wingback, took her pumps, and got her fuzzy slippers installed.

"Thank you, Tommy. My, you're such a good son. And to think you used to be such a rascal. You ran me ragged!"

"I've got some fresh ravioli I think you'll like, Mother. We'll stay here and be together tonight. Do you want to talk about what the doctors said?"

She sighed mightily. She pulled herself into a corner of her chair and was silent. He waited.

"No, I don't want to talk about that. I must say they were all rather business as usual. You'd think they'd soften up, wouldn't you, think of the patient?" She lapsed into silence again.

Tom sat on the hassock in front of her chair and waited.

"It's liver cancer, Tommy. They wanted me to stay for treatment, but I'd rather just go home tomorrow as planned. Anyways, I can die better in my own bed. I won't be lonely, I've got lots of memories. I'll be all right. And Ricky will take care of me; he's only selling his Jap cars three days a week these days. Now, you wouldn't deny your own mother her little drink, would you?" Her eyes brightened.

She rallied under the influence of a gin and tonic. She insisted on mixing her next one. Tom confined himself to one Scotch — he figured the cook should remain sober. He needn't have bothered.

"And by the way, even though your mother was proud of your cooking last night, I didn't come all this way to eat at home, did I? I hear a lot about that Tavern on the Green. Do you think you could get me in there for my last night in New York?" He could and they did. She seemed to enjoy everything about the joint; or, at least she toasted everything in sight with a series of fresh drinks.

Tom was undone as they got out of the taxi in front of his door. Ethyl staggered out and before he could finish paying the cabbie and follow her, she'd fallen. He tried to lift her, but she wouldn't help. She lay back on her side on the sidewalk, tucked two hands under her right temple, and murmured that she'd see him in the morning. He prepared to pick the dead weight up, but he didn't need to do it by himself because help arrived. More help than he wanted. Georgie Cattivo and Matt Ernst dropped their backpacks and lifted, while Tom got his key in the door.

"What cute boys," the woozy Ethyl said, far more clearly than she had spoken in the taxi. She collapsed on a chair in the entry hall. Tom walked out with the concerned and embarrassed boys, thanked them, and saw Maury and Cat waiting on the sidewalk. No doubt all four had just left the *Chronicle* office. He felt he had to say something as the four coalesced on the sidewalk — God! One of them had just met his step-grandmother.

"Thanks so much for your help. I didn't think introductions would be in order, but that was my mother. She hasn't been well. Actually, been fighting it for years. She has been here at the hospital for tests and diagnosis. Didn't go well. She's depressed." Well, it was nothing but the truth, Tom figured, just not the whole truth. What would he tell Sally?

The next morning, after confirming her flight home, Tom asked, "Mother, may I read your medical report? My friend Dr. Ben Levi could recommend an Arizona oncologist for you. He could even set it up."

"No, thank you, son. I also told the hospital that. You reading that bunch of papers won't make me any less a goner, will it? But thank him for me. Please."

At the airport, when they got to security, she grabbed him in a clinch and didn't let go. She whispered into his ear, "Thank you, son. Almost like old times, wasn't it? And you're a real hunk now."

When Tom pushed away, she jerked her cosmetics case from his hand. "Don't you get huffy with your own mother." She turned and shot back over her shoulder, "You were always easy pickings, Tommy."

That afternoon Tom called Ben and told him of her depression over the cancer diagnosis. Was there some way Ben could help him ensure her proper care by checking the diagnosis and recommending an oncologist in Phoenix? Ben assumed that her doctor had already done that, and although her records would be confidential, he'd do everything he could to find out.

At the University Club squash courts the next evening, Ben and Tom showered and sat in the lounge in terry robes drinking Perrier with lemon.

"So, Ben, how did the detective work go?" Tom sat forward, hands kneading both arms of his chair.

"Well, this is all off the record, but it's good news —she has no malignancy, like you feared before she came. She has chronic bronchitis, yes, but she's in good shape for her age."

"What?" Tom gripped Ben's forearm. "You're sure that she doesn't have any malignancy? Liver? Nothing that even hints at it?"

Ben looked Tom in the eye. "Absolutely not, and Dr. Whittaker assured me they were looking for it. I'm curious why she misunderstood the cancer-free diagnosis. Why she was so depressed when she got what she wanted. I was baffled by that."

Tom wasn't baffled. And she did get what she wanted — twenty-thousand dollars' worth of clothing and medical care. Then, because she was in tears in the airport taxi over her "dreadful diagnosis," he promised a big increase in her monthly stipend. He couldn't believe it; his own mother had set him up and deceived him again. Ben watched him with concern. Tom struggled to keep his disbelief and outrage from turning into tears.

When Tom got back to the office after Ben's revelation he pulled his "Johnny Bench Crosley Field souvenir" bead chain from his center drawer. He detached the brass cross from the Matchbox Jeep, miniature Ohio license plate, and Buckeye football and laid it in the center of his desk. He phoned his mother while he viewed the cross, the one souvenir in his life from her. She answered and was off and running.

"I want you to forget what I said to you at the airport, Tommy, just forget that. I was so anxious with my cancer and that airplane trip, I didn't know what I was saying."

"You lied to me again. You stole dad's insurance money when I was fifteen, now about your cancer — lies, lies, more lies."

"A lady's got to have nice things, Tommy. I never had, not in that hellhole of a trailer in Kokosing your dad rented, never; I had to get out. And here recently I have been sick, really, don't have much time left."

"Well, you're not going to get another dime from me. The gravy train is over."

Silence. Would she break down, apologize, and ask for forgiveness? Somehow, he didn't want that. And yet . . .

"Well, you're not the high 'n' mighty know-it-all you think you are. That money you sent me for your wedding to get fixed up; well, smart guy, that kept us going at the Golden Nugget for a week. My sun doesn't revolve around no accidental son, I'll tell you that right now, mister, never has. I can get along without you, did for years, and Ricky takes good care of me. Why, he gave me a thousand bucks to spend on that trip, but I didn't need it, did I? Oh, yes, we'll do fine without you, Easy Pickins."

Dead line.

Tom picked up the tiny brass cross with baby aspirin-sized blue "jewels" and milky inserts that used to glow in the dark above his praying head when he was five. He crushed it inside his fist, grimaced with pain as the sharp edges bit into his palm, and tossed it into the wastebasket. That left the rest of the bead chain with Bench's wide mug facing up on his desk. A flushed Tom smiled down at it while he blotted the blood from his hand.

So, he was finally rid of his maternal albatross. And his maternity. "Are you?" Dr. Becker would predictably ask.

Could one escape the smothering cloak of family background, even if what that meant for him was decidedly different from what it meant for the wellborn? Or was it? There was rot at all levels, more than enough to go around.

CHAPTER 71

Cattivo was having a glass of orange juice in the kitchen. He'd follow it with a toasted whole-grain bagel, plain, and black coffee. Georgie came in and joined him in the orange juice that would launch him into several courses. This summer while his mother was away, he got up early to have breakfast with Dad. A first. He also had black coffee, and Cattivo liked to think the boy finally wanted to be like him. The kid was attacking a bowl of honeyed cocoa flakes when he opened a sleeve of waffle fingers to use as his pusher. And as always, he tried to regale his father from a half-filled maw of glazed gluten with the latest news from his socially challenged cohort of school techies. Then, midway through his first brown sugar cinnamon Pop-Tart — earlier that summer he showed his dad it had "low fat on the label" — he changed course entirely.

"Dr. West sure had his hands full with his mother the other night. Matt and I helped her . . ." chew, chew. Georgie had netted Dad before he added the details.

"Yes, son?" Whoa, don't scare him with your sudden interest in his drivel.

"Well, did you know that Dr. West grew up in a trailer park? He told

Matt last week after his mom and Dr. West came home from Amsterdam engaged. Matt's really happy."

"That'd be Matt Ernst, the soccer player, right?"

"Ya," he barely managed through the gloop.

"Well, why would he be 'happy' about that trailer park business?"

"Because look how far Dr. West has come, Dad. You always tell me that's a good thing — that I oughta have to come up the hard way, like you did."

"How do you know all about this trailer park? And what was that about Dr. West's mother?"

"From my friends, dad."

"What friends? Wait! You mean that *Chronicle* outfit? That bunch of arrogant shits who got the school sued for libel?"

But Dad, you always tell me that anyone can sue anyone anytime. And you should see the Columbia journalism awards on the wall of our office. Look, I've told you a hundred times that I'm the new Tech Editor — don't you remember *anything*? And they've been showing me the ropes. I like them." Georgie finished his assertion with his lower lip out.

You just about blew it, asshole daddy. "Oh, well, Georgie, that's fine, I guess.

Yeah, good for you. And have you guys got some new ideas for the school paper?"

"Yeah, Dad. Maury and Matt will be gone, but Cat says I have *carte blanche* — she'll even let me second-guess David Pogue in *The Times*. See, he comes out every Thursday, and we have a deadline later that day, so I can check his work, write about it, and be published the next day. And I've been poking around Verizon, with the help of a friend who works there in tech. I think they're vulnerable on identity theft and I could expose that from inside!"

Chip off the old block after all, thought Cattivo.

"What a great idea! You're going to knock 'em dead this year at the *Chronicle*. I'm so proud of you, Georgie!" He paused and watched his son blush, then reach for the cream cheese and jam to spread on his white bagels. "Now, what was that about Dr. West's mother? And did you say that the Ernst boy said his mother was *engaged*?"

Cattivo poured coffee for them both and pushed the Limited Edition Confetti Cake Pop-Tarts Georgie's way.

"Richie, I need your help. As you know, Wither Bramston is up in Maine with his family. So, you and I are the survivors here in the city."

"The 'dynamic duo,' more like," said the Reverend Dr. Philips, sucking on the rim of a club tumbler. Cattivo noted the Rev's subtle way of indicating he needed a refill. He snapped his fingers and pointed at his guest as the waiter looked over.

"Yes, of course. And that leaves just you to carry out a critical job."

Philips stirred in his seat, looked at the ceiling, and leaned on his dimpled elbow. "Not that I'm uneasy or anything, but it's always easier to have some company when undertaking the Lord's work or a critical job. If you get my drift."

Cattivo sensed that the Rev was jittery about any new project without the support of his Senior Warden Bramston. Cattivo leaned forward and patted Philips' well-tailored sleeve. "Not to worry, my friend, you could do it in your sleep." He eyed the uneasy cleric and sat up straight. "But first things first — I'll get to my thing later. Richie, I followed up on your youth ministry project."

The club waiter delivered Philips' drink. He sampled, approved, and was all attention. "So, Bob, what have you done about my youth vision?" This had better be good, Cattivo told himself. Philips has to take the hook in deep. "Well, I was telling Babs on the telephone — she's up in the country for a couple of days — about your hope for a renovated gymnasium and kitchen in order to provide . . . what did you call it in your sermon? 'A real neighborhood youth center.'" No doubt for the kids who are staying with their parents at the Carlyle hotel, reckoned Cattivo. And the Rev couldn't have done a feasibility study yet.

"Well, whadid she think?"

"That you're one fine pastor and leader of the young, that's what she thinks. And she told me to 'get in on the ground floor on this.'"

"Basement, more like," said Philips.

The literalist has struck again. "Yes, of course, she was only throwing one of my phrases back at me. Even she knows the gym is in the basement of the Parish house, Richie. So, how would fifty thousand do to get you started on a marketing survey to determine how the neighborhood would respond?" Philips had wanted $500,000 last Sunday for the first building stage; Cattivo would get off cheaply for the feasibility that would conclude Philips' off-the-cuff pulpit wish list wouldn't fly.

"Oh, you think I should do a feasibility on it, do you?"

"Richie, you know the church vestry will ask you to do the same thing. This way you can go to them loaded for bear."

The Rev gravely swirled his dark brown liquid. Drank. More thought. Was he playing with the Golden Goose? He drank again and looked up, refreshed and decisive. Cattivo found himself nervously fingering his key.

"You're right, Bob. Absolutely right. And I'll take it. With my ever-loving thanks. But you know I'll be back at you when the vestry approves my vision." He scrunched down in his chair and looked up almost playfully. "Now that you've come through, what can I do *you* for?"

"I like your Christian honesty, Richie. Now I'll return the favor. I'd like you to take a chance for me on a critical matter. Critical and delicate. I want you to help me do some seeding of a seedy fact: that we have trailer trash running our Christ Church School."

That got the Rev's snout out of his tumbler in a jiffy.

"What? Did I hear you right?" said Philips. "'Trailer trash,' as in Bill Clinton's gubernatorial hanky-panky?"

"Yes, but not in Arkansas. Tom West came from Ohio, and his mother visited him last week. Stayed at his place. And I have an eyewitness account of her getting out of the taxi with Tom and falling down drunk. The *Chronicle* editors were coming down the street. They saw it and helped get her inside as she struggled and vomited. Imagine the effect on those nice kids to have to see and participate in that scene!"

"But, Bob, you said those editors were not to be trusted."

"Oh, we've cleaned house — new, much improved staff for next year. Lots of new blood, believe me, but can you imagine what those kids must have gone through picking up the dead-drunk mother of the headmaster from the public sidewalk?"

"Well, that's sure not a pretty picture. Do you want me to work it into a sermon?"

"No, that might be too public, don't you think? Why not just season your lunchtime conversation with some of our colleagues on the CC trustees?"

Philips took another thoughtful draw on his diminishing supply of Wild Turkey Rare Breed. "This is just off Madison, then, right in front of Tom's door? And the kids helped him get her into his house? Then what happened?"

"One of the editors said their headmaster told them that his mother had been in town for a few days visiting."

"What did she look like? A touch of detail adds to credibility, you know."

"Guess she's quite a number. Young-looking. Blonde. Apparently she made a pass at the boys, wanted them to crawl into bed with her. My reliable informant was embarrassed about the whole thing, so I didn't want to press, of course you understand."

"I'd still like to know some details, makes a better story. Now, who told you?"

"Richie, you'll understand I've got to protect the minor in this case."

"Yeah, I do. And you can bet your life I'll be pleased to apply my Christian candor in letting some folks know our school is being run by trailer trash." The cleric shuddered. "It's unbelievable — so unholy, so profane — Jesus Christ, for the head of the oldest Episcopal school in North America!"

Cattivo knew he could count on his man of the cloth. Now he'd call Babs up in Westchester to give her the welcome news — she'd also know what to do with it.

CHAPTER 72

The summer meeting of the Christ Church School Parents' Association Executive Committee had gone off beautifully. Sally held it at Sarabeth's, so the members could have an afternoon tea while they discussed the coming year's meetings and speakers. It was her final task as president. It had gone beautifully because her old friends on the committee were thrilled when they discovered that the diamond she wore came from a fellow they all knew — Tom West! All seemed genuinely pleased at the development.

And then the bottom dropped out. Her two closest friends on the board, Mindy Halpert and Alison Gibson, stayed after the others had departed.

"We've debated for days about this, our staying to talk to you, Sally," said Mindy, a history professor at Barnard with three children currently enrolled at CC.

"And we didn't really decide until we got here," added Ali, a tall, horsy brunette who still rode in Central Park.

"Umm, now you've got me very curious," said Sally. "What is it? We're old friends, out with it."

"Well, we heard some disturbing news," said Alison.

"Yeah, that's right," said Mindy. "I heard from a CC alumna, one of my history majors—"

"And I heard from a Christ Church vestry member at a Junior League meeting," interrupted Alison. "But it was really Bob Cattivo's wife Babs who made it official, when she told everyone at yesterday's Kip's Bay reception. And, well . . ."

They both stopped, seemingly so uncomfortable they couldn't continue.

Sally tried to rescue them. "Oh, come on, you two. Please, tell me, and if it isn't perfectly dreadful, I'll be disappointed."

She wasn't disappointed.

Sally waited until after dinner that night when she and Matt were doing the dishes.

"Matt, I heard something today that disturbed me. Because it took me by surprise.

Have you heard anything from Cat or any of the *Chronicle* kids about Tom's mother?"

Matt took particular care with the rim of a plate, drying, adjusting his towel, and drying. Sally turned and looked at him. "Well?"

Matt hazarded a glance up from his dishtowel. "Ah, what about Mrs. West?"

"I know you knew that I'd met her early last week. Did you guys also see her or something?"

"Yeah, Georgie and I met her, sort of. And so did Cat and Maury, less sort of."

Unpeel all that, Sally. She stopped washing and turned to face him. "Please tell me, Matt — where, when, and how did you happen to meet Tom's mother. Sort of, and less sort of, because he didn't mention it."

"OK, Mom. It was last Wednesday night. The four of us were walking past Doc's door when he and his mother got out of a taxi. She introduced herself and they went in."

Sally was mystified.

"Honey, give me some details. What did she look like? How long did you talk?"

"She looked young for being his mom, I guess. And probably tall. Didn't talk long. I think we were all in a hurry."

Still mystified. But not for long. "'Probably tall' — did Mrs. West fall?"

"Uh, yep. Never saw her standing."

"Was she drunk?"

"No more than a skunk might be that time of night."

Sally laughed, although she hadn't wanted to. Matt looked relieved.

"Out with it, you devious, crafty son of mine. You've covered for Mrs. West long enough. What happened?"

After Matt filled in the details, they sat and drank coffee together. He stirred, licked the spoon, put it in his mouth, took it out, and ran out of things to do with it.

"Mom, I didn't want you to know. Didn't want it to affect you and Tom. And me. And that night he told us about her sad medical visit and hinted that she was an alcoholic. Plus, the other Irregulars felt the same way. Cat even said, 'Hey, that was Matt's future step-grandma — so not a word about it.' But how did you hear?"

Sally repeated her friends' reluctant trailer trash revelation. When they compared that with Matt's eyewitness account of helping Tom pick up and carry his mother inside, it all seemed to jibe. But when she repeated Babs Cattivo's story of Ethylene West's being arrested at Saks for shoplifting, she lost Matt.

"Where did *that* come from, Mom?"

They looked at each other in wonder.

"Yes, I think I know," said Sally. "From inside one of those Cattivo heads. And either one would be more than capable."

"Do we tell Doc about it? The whole thing?"

"Well, he'd want to know. But it wouldn't do him any good, the scene was bad enough for you all to go through, he would have been heartbroken, I know. See, since she left, he discovered that she has been very, very dishonest with him, even to the point of lying about her cancer diagnosis. He was devastated. They're now estranged. We'll tell you more someday if you wish."

"I won't. But I can believe anything about that woman after seeing her."

"Tut, tut," said Sally with a shaken forefinger and grin. "Remember Tom said she compared me with Penelope Cruz after we met at the Met, so she can't be *all* bad!"

"Hey, but then she said you were 'very dark' and that your nose was too long!"

"Or, was it that my upper lip was too tall?" They both laughed.

"Now, time to get serious, Matt. I need your advice."

"Yeah. Do we tell him all about this gossip and that crazy shoplifting story?"

They both sat and stared at the scarred oak grain of the table.

Sally spoke first. "I don't think we should say a word. Yet. But I do know he'd be deeply moved by your Irregulars' protection of him. He's been through enough, and he's getting desperate with his fundraising."

"Yeah, he looked really tired that night with his mother. OK, Mom. But I still wonder how the Cattivos picked all that up. Georgie wouldn't tell, I know — he wouldn't risk it, with the rest of us. What we'd think of him."

Sally gave her son an extra squeeze as they said good night.

As he left for his room, she talked to his back. "'No more than a skunk might be at that time of night.'" He turned to her with a grin as she finished. "You're nuts and certainly ready for Williams, but I'm not sure Williams is ready for you!"

The next day, Matt reported to the Irregulars that the story of Mrs. West's sidewalk fall last week had somehow found its way into Manhattan park bench and cocktail conversation. Two of his listeners were baffled, but Georgie put his head in his hands and confessed that he knew how it got out — he'd told his father.

"See, I figured Dad would sympathize with Doc West having an alcoholic mother all those years, because he told me last year that his mother was one. And we were having a wonderful talk, maybe the first ever, and he was so interested in me, and you all, and our plans for the *Chronicle*. I mean it, it was the best talk we ever had, course it was like the first one, you know. I didn't dream Dad would take what I said and come up with that 'trailer trash' story. You've got to believe me, Matt, it was the best talk Dad and I have ever had and look what came of it. Cat, please don't tell me you guys don't trust me anymore. Please." Georgie wiped his eyes, but his head was still bowed.

Cat reached over to pat her tech reporter, thought better of it, and pulled her hand back. "Don't worry, Georgie. We should have . . . no, *I* should have told you about your dad leading the charge on Doc West. You were only trying to have a good talk with him."

"But there's more," said Matt. "Your mother has been telling everyone that Mrs. West was arrested at Saks for shoplifting. That's out there, too."

"Fuckin' Christ! The hell of it is that I can believe Mom would do that, oh, yes. See, for years I've thought *he* was the good guy and *she* was something else. That's what Monica and I thought, anyway. But now, both of them — what's wrong with my parents?" He stopped. The others were silent. "But I'll deal with them. Or, at least Dad. Mom's always in the country; I never talk to her."

"So, Georgie, you did your best with what you knew at the time," Cat said. "He lured you in on that and then double-crossed you. Not so unusual — it's standard parent behavior."

"God, what a world," said Georgie.

Cat gestured toward Matt and Maury and summed it up. "These guys are almost out of here, but you and I have to fight to keep Doc here for our senior year. This means war, Georgie, and you're in charge of the tech side."

CHAPTER 73

Cattivo knew his daughter Monica and her brother Georgie were in weekly contact since she went to college, but this was the first time she called with a warning.

"Daddy, Georgie is very angry with you. He says you betrayed him."

"What? I haven't seen him. What's he told you?"

"Something about you and Mom gossiping about Doc West's mother being trailer trash. That's all I know. But Dad, that's enough."

Robert Cattivo liked to be in charge of the world around him. And he usually had control of that world. But he had begun to lose control after Monica's call from Ann Arbor. Things began to appear a little jumbled.

The thing to do, he had told himself, was to handle this as he handled business problems: review Monica's and Georgie's excited charges and solve whatever needed solving.

Cattivo collared his son the next morning as he tried to leave without breakfast. Well, actually, Georgie collared his dad — he immediately accused him of betraying his confidence over Mrs. West's fall. When Cattivo said he'd watch it next time and why didn't they go to the Yankees' double-header next weekend, he could arrange box seats, right next to Steinbrenner's, Georgie became furious.

"Forget it. No more bribes accepted. You should be ashamed of what you did to Dr. West. And think what you've done to our school's reputation, Dad! And you know you can't capture all the shit that's now out there about his mother and him."

"My only defense is that I didn't think people like the Reverend Dr. Philips and your mother would spread rumors."

"Yeah, sure. You figured those two would change their genetic imprint?" And then Cattivo's only son had stormed out of the kitchen. Why had Cattivo thought things were simply "a little jumbled"? Goddammit, they were fucked up royally.

But what had Georgie meant, after Cattivo said he'd handle Babs' outrageous shoplifting story and get her under control? The kid said, "Oh, sure, you will, Dad. Except you haven't had her under control for years." Georgie did finally agree to have dinner with his dad that evening at his favorite restaurant before he tore out of the house.

Cattivo knew he'd have to respond to his son's feelings and defense of his school. And even his defense of the headmaster. The kid needed some fresh air after a summer of working ten-hour days on that tutoring project. Maybe Georgie would like one of those wilderness adventure trips to the Grand Canyon for a couple of weeks. Or Cattivo's investment group had enough equity in Apple to place Georgie on one of those personalized Steve Jobs tours at the new headquarters. The kid would jump at it. Any computer geek would.

But his overriding problem remained. He'd still have to deal with Babs at the other extreme – her son wanted to save West, she wanted to kill him.

And she had seemed so distant when he called to tell her to stop peddling her Saks shoplifting story. Now he'd have to tell her she'd overdone the Tom West vendetta, she'd lost perspective, and that even Dr. Philips said that her shoplifting tale was so absurd it blew their credible trailer trash one out of the water. Why had this campaign figured so large in her life? Everything she had done over the past five years in Manhattan came up roses — records set with every one of her charities — even Bill Cunningham of *The Times* always managed a photo of her on what was left of the society page. Babs Cattivo had it all. And yet, she went to the country June, July, and August and was unavailable for him. And he couldn't go up there with his deals percolating all over the country. Cattivo would lay it out to her — he couldn't take a single weekend off or he might lose a major deal, and then there wouldn't be funds for her extravagances.

Who was he kidding? This was the Goddamnest Goddamn fucking mess Cattivo had ever seen. Just as his Hoboken allies were lined up, just as he unloaded his white elephant in Miami, just when he had the Countess's European boutique financing set, and just when he felt he and his son were at long last embarked on a solid relationship, this Goddamn thing came up.

Bob had promised Georgie he'd shut down the trailer trash operation.

Well, he pulled Philips off the campaign to tar the West family, but that cost him another quarter million for a fucking stained glass window restoration — that guy always had his hand out — and when Cattivo then asked him acidly if he would also like a spare set of hymnals, the damn fool said yes, about 800 of them would do it.

Next, he had tried to convince Babs to stop the smear against West.

She got a little testy when Bob ordered her to come back to town to be with him during the week so they could talk.

"No thanks, you're always gone, anyway; Jacksonville, Montgomery — all kinds of exciting places. Quick, what's the name of a world-class museum between Houston and Miami?"

"Maybe the High in Atlanta?"

"Ever been there?" Silence.

"See? Next you'll be telling me that the Ringling museum has something besides elephants and clowns in Sarasota. And I didn't even ask about theater!"

So, Babs refused to come home so they could talk and was a little elusive when he told her to stop spreading the trailer trash and Saks shoplifting stories.

"What? You tell me to pull the plug on the best way we've ever had to get Tom West? You're out of your mind, Bob. We've finally got him nailed to the cross with his drunken mother and you want me to pull out? Fuck you, paper wolf!"

CHAPTER 74

His worst fears were becoming reality. He'd have to look at his allies more carefully. Machiavelli, again: his allies had used his largesse to turn on him. He'd seen it with Philips and Babs. Now he'd have to regain control. Georgie was right about Babs — she was beyond his control. And he'd thought the key to controlling her was the same as for anyone else — money. He'd set up a secret "dream account" for them both in the Cayman Islands years ago. He had pumped money into it ever since, but hadn't a clue where it was now. Or what the password was any more — she'd changed it years ago. But Georgie might find the key to a lot of things. His dinner that evening with his son was assuming huge importance. Cattivo looked down at his busy fingers on the object that proved his worth and consoled him. God, he'd been giving his key a real polishing recently — the finish was coming off.

Cattivo hated to eat crow. But, he reasoned, short-term crow was worth it if it meant long-term pheasant in Champagne and truffle sauce. And he had discovered in the half-dozen setbacks he'd had in thirty years of success that mounting a sudden mortar attack *from cover* assuaged his feelings while he waited for that truffle sauce. He made an early call to Wither Bramston in Maine. He persuaded him to send a letter to all members of their CC trustee executive committee regarding Tom and Sally's "secret engagement." Bramston was about to sail for Nova Scotia, so he deputed his corporate attorney to do the draft after he sketched the basics for him. The attorney had the letters in the bike messenger's bag by twelve noon. To my fellow members of the Executive Committee:

> It has come to our attention that two members of our board of trustees have become engaged, one of whom enjoys a salaried position at the school. We join all in sending the felicitations the occasion warrants to Dr. Sally Ernst and Dr. Thomas West.
>
> We would be derelict in our duties as officers of the eleemosynary corporation, however, if we did not call attention to the clear and graphic conflict of interest this development presents. Hence, we shall look forward to the early reception of Dr. Ernst's letter of resignation from the board or of Dr. West's resignation from the school.
>
> Yours faithfully,
> Wither Bramston, V
>
> CC: Dr. Thomas West, Dr. Sally Ernst

The ailing Bishop dictated a response to Bramston with copies to the others after cooling down Tom and Sally:

> Your letter of cautionary felicitation is received. The felicitation was necessary and proper; the dictate to action was neither — Dr. Ernst has already concluded her excellent tenure as per the school bylaws. It would be helpful in the future if you would inform yourself before firing.

Damn! Cattivo said to himself. He knew he should have done his homework on the bylaws regarding the ex officio Parents' Association president. But he was hurt after Georgie attacked him, and he simply had to attack something. Thankfully, the stupidity of Bramston's lawyer's pretentiousness would not adhere to Cattivo — it'd be seen as business as usual for Bramston. Now he'd have to figure out how to handle the Bishop — the old goat was beyond belief. Philips claimed he was dying. Good riddance on the board, but Cattivo would have to get to him regarding the Brook Club, where he chaired the membership committee, before that happened. God! It was easier building out-of-code skyscrapers in Miami and Hoboken than simply getting the headmaster fired.

CHAPTER 75

Tom and Sally, who had felt personally attacked by Bramston's letter, now almost felt that the Bishop's riposte settled the matter.

Meredith Ross was still in China making headlines in the *Wall Street Journal* and *Financial Times* and didn't respond to Bramston's epistle or to the Bishop's response. The Bishop enjoyed reentering the CC fray, as he had been out of action for weeks with another round of radiation. Sally and Tom had increased the frequency of their visits to him. As the Bishop was recovering, he told them one of his top goals was to be able to perform their wedding on schedule before Matt went away to college.

With only a few weeks before their informal wedding at the Levis', Sally did her best to prepare for settling in with Tom in the head's quarters, even though there remained a cloud over the whole enterprise. Space or convenience wasn't the problem; his school apartment was twice the size of hers and was closer to her museum office. But it was difficult to feel settled when Tom's job was on the block and they would not know the outcome until the October meeting. She initially made a show of preparing to move in such quantities of kitchen ware and clothing that Tom would be assured that she was planning on a permanent stay, but he was on to her game during the first load.

"It's alright, just bring over your essentials," Tom said. "I don't mind. It makes sense, really." He was standing at the master bedroom closet watching her hang up some out-of-season dresses and suits. Two suitcases lay opened and empty on the bed.

"Just your essentials," Tom repeated. "After all, who am I kidding — I'm raising some bucks now, but I'm still five million short. Barring a miracle, well, Matt may never get his wish to bunk in that back bedroom with the bookcases. We may all be over at your place by Thanksgiving."

"Well, I already have more than enough transferred then, I guess." She closed the closet doors. "And if it comes to that, I'd like to think we've done all we can. In every way, now, while we can."

"You've lost me," said Tom.

"I'll lay it out, then. I know you love me, but my request might be a big challenge for you."

He motioned to the lavender and gray silk Queen Anne love seat under the window that had come with the school apartment. He'd never liked it — it was more than precious. "Here, let's sit down, I've never used this, except to sort clothing." She smiled. They sat and turned to each other. Now she looked hesitant.

"Out with it," he said.

"Tom, do you remember when you met Oliver Chase at lunch that day?"

"Yes. The honest art dealer who helped you in Amsterdam."

"Well, he came in the other day. He was pretty down."

"Does this have to do with the honest art dealer's grandson's admissions application?" Tom knew he shouldn't have raised his eyebrow. But he had.

Sally was hesitant no longer, but Tom could see that she was bewildered, maybe even miserable. "Yes. Simon 'bombed' his interview, according to his grandfather. Mr. Chase heard about my connection to CC and came in yesterday for advice. I really felt for him, because for the first time he told me his daughter has undergone a bitter divorce and that's why she plans to bring the boy back to New York from London. She told him she was 'very keen' on CC because her son had his heart set on it. Mr. Chase is quite vulnerable on this. He didn't want to say anything, and yet he wanted to do everything he could to help her and Simon, his only grandchild."

"I see."

"Tom, I know I was high and mighty about this before, but I had to say *something*. I hope at least *you* understand, even if I'm not sure that I do."

"Well, the boy didn't exactly wow the Admissions Office, that I know."

"You do?"

"Yes, I do." Tom let the silence build. He watched Sally carefully, but with a smile.

"Yes, I have followed the application and read the interview report. I do watch a good portion of the applicants who make it to the interview stage, ever since I began my mad rush to raise money."

She remained nonplussed. He took her hand.

"So yes, Simon had an unimpressive interview, but the director said he was notably distracted, no doubt with the breakup and the move. I rang his headmaster in London, and we reviewed the folder. His record at Westminster School was spotty and the supporting letters described an on-again, off-again application to his studies. The headmaster did say that when Simon is on, he's brilliant. In short, he's a risk. They won't hear officially until next week, but you're free to tell Grandfather Chase that he needn't worry further — I like to take risks with brilliant grandchildren."

Sally exhaled. "My, there's so much yet for me to discover in Thomas Sylvester West."

Tom leaned into her and inhaled her Shalimar, behind a perfect ear. "And for me in Estrella Malka."

Without a word, they stood and each removed a suitcase from the bed.

CHAPTER 76

Cattivo and Georgie spent the evening over Nebraskan Wagyu steaks at the boy's favorite restaurant — Le Bernardin. During the leisurely meal, Georgie's dad had discovered how much he coveted his son's respect and affection. He found that emotion unfamiliar and overwhelming. Georgie continued to ask questions about his dad's early years while they awaited their chocolate-olive oil dessert.

"So, it was risky, tough for you from way back, Dad?"

"Worse than I can tell you, Georgie. Yep, tough on the way to this Phi Beta Kappa key, which I did the hard way. I withdrew from two colleges because I was working thirty hours a week so I could pay my bills."

"But didn't your dad, your family, help?"

"No, Father was climbing out of bankruptcy and his credit was shot. Whatever he had, your uncle Dave had already taken to Yale."

"But Dad, you've told me so little about your family — just that your dad and brother died young. I never knew any of your family."

"Well, I've tried to forget getting the short end of that family stick. Tried to help my older brother, even when he didn't do anything with his Yale education."

"It doesn't seem fair, Dad. You ended up saving your dad and brother when they went under. That had to be tough, real tough. And you've always given Monica and me everything we ever wanted. Mom, too."

"That's life, son, at least in my fast lane. But maybe all that tension from way back helps explain why I've done some of the things I've done recently. The stuff that made you angry with me. At least I hope it does. And I've already put a stop to what Dr. Philips and your mom have been spreading about Dr. West. You have my word."

Georgie looked at him evenly, but didn't peep.

"You have to realize that when a guy makes it to the top from the very dregs, like I did, sometimes I guess I can get a little rough. I do my best, son, to make you and Monica happy — to give you everything I didn't have. I love you so much that I'd do anything to make that possible. And that includes getting rid of Dr. West, who's running the school into the ground with his deficit spending. Liberals are like that, of course. You've got to believe me on that, even if it doesn't show around the school and your friends can't see it. But the trustees and I see it."

The boy nodded, but still didn't speak. Cattivo was uneasy about it, but he had to carry it through.

"So, tonight I wanted us to have a good dinner together so I could apologize for messing you up with your friends at the *Chronicle*. I'm sorry for the grief I caused you, and I hope you can believe in your old man again. And maybe have some room in your heart for him."

Georgie could only bow his head and nod across the table.

"Now, Georgie, I need your help more than ever. I have reason to believe that your mother is being blackmailed. She has done so much for so many through her charities that she may have got herself exposed too much. She says she's desperate and about broke, but she cries when I ask why and how I can help. I think the attack has been on her personal Cayman bank account that I set up with mucho cash, and I've regularly made whopping deposits in it. But I guess she's too proud to ask us. So, you can see why she needs help. You seem to have some pretty good ins with those hackers you've told me about. I need to check on her account without her knowing, and I remember you gave her advice on passwords a couple of years ago. Do you think you could give it a try?"

"Sure, Dad, I'd do anything for you. Just like you've done for me."

Georgie was proud to tell his editor Cat all about his wonderful evening with his dad. It was clear that Georgie was a new and happy fellow now that he understood his dad's difficult rags to riches story. She tried to be pleased for him, but it was a hard go. He detected her skimpy enthusiasm for his resurrected relationship with his dad and his hair-trigger temper warmed up.

"Cat, what's your problem?"

When she didn't answer, he pushed. "Are you maybe jealous of my family? Especially after how your mother treats you and your nonexistent dad?"

Cat drew back as if she'd been slapped, and she didn't speak for a while. She did pull out a Ticonderoga #2 and beat a rhythm on her knee familiar to him.

Georgie refused to show any mercy. "Huh? Is that your problem?" No response. "Cat got your tongue?" he said with a nasty smirk.

"I'm sorry you said that, Georgie, but I understand. At least a little. And I hate to say this, but there's something you really have to know."

"Oh, big mystery! Fire away, Miss Cat that ate the canary! Or was it the cream? Shoot, do your worst."

Cat looked at her tech editor directly, but with care in her eyes. "Okay. When you became depressed over your father's taking advantage of you earlier this week, I decided to do some casual searching. Of Robert George Haverford Cattivo's family and career. I started with your parents' *Times* wedding announcement, then Crain's New York Business archives, Bloomberg News, and stopped after *Who's Who in America*, because that information is attested to by the subject himself."

"So? What's your point?"

"Simple: either all those sources are inaccurate . . . or your dad lied to you last night."

CHAPTER 77

Tom was lonely. Sally had left on a week's curatorial visit to Chicago and Dallas, and Matt was up at a pre-season soccer camp at Williams. Tom dished up the formerly frozen tray of spaghetti with marinara. He, Sally, and Matt ate together whenever they could manage it, and he loved those meals. Matt ate with Tom when Sally was away, the two of them amiably collaborating on tinned corned beef hash and fried eggs. Matt had the same rigorous summer schedule he had pursued for years: 5:00 A.M. newspaper deliveries in Queens and a gopher job at Conde Nast during the working day which sometimes ran to 8:00 P.M. The boy's attempt to work and save for college reminded Tom very much of his own struggles in Ohio.

This week Tom barely noticed his spaghetti because, as a solo diner, he always read. That meant the meal could be a shirt cardboard-saturated with olive oil and pepper and he would probably devour it without comment. But as an adopted New Yorker, he'd always insist on extra virgin oil and freshly ground pepper.

He propped his *New Yorker* magazine against a pile of unopened bills and catalogs anchored by keys and a box of Grape-Nuts. He gave up reading after browsing the cartoons, feeling more and more dejected because his fund-raising campaign was in peril. The day had been the most discouraging one since his campaign started, and he couldn't believe it — he had actually *lost* two and a half million dollars. A month ago, he would have retreated into a bottle of Scotch and a pack of Marlboros. But now he was trying to hold out after a couple of good talks with Sally in Amsterdam. She had convinced him that his way would be much clearer without the props.

The first blow had been delivered by the New Jersey trucking czar whose son had won the classics prize at CC last year. He revealed over breakfast at the University Club that his promised gift of $500,000 would not be coming for six months, if at all.

Number two was the real killer: Serena had asked him to lunch at Jean Georges — "Oh, you must come, you must, Tommy, I've got some exciting news about your capital campaign." Tom knew that could only be about her pledged gift of two million to match the one she gave to Natasha's new boarding school. He had been counting on that gift to make the twenty million goal possible.

They had a splendid lunch and a nice talk about Chris' theater internship and Natasha's school. Then she regaled him with her plans to launch her stores in London, Paris, and Rome. He was impressed with her grasp of strategic plan and details. He was sure she was saving the good news for Christ Church School over dessert. The chocolate creation was finished and they were having coffee before she made her pitch.

"Tommy, darling, I could hardly wait until I give you the first crack at an idea I've come up with. I really think it's an offer you can't refuse, because it will save your lubricious bacon at CC." He remembered another such offer last Christmas Eve.

"I've heard about your endowment mountain to climb and, frankly, I feel indebted to you for all you've done for my Chris and for prying my daughter into Miss Jessups. I'm on the board there now and getting very interested in how schools work. So, I've come up with my idea on how to revolutionize private school funding in America."

Tom encouraged her by leaning forward, his hands cradling his cup.

"I suggest we follow the H-Y-P fundraising hypocrisy and use it as a model," she continued. "Harvard, Yale, and Princeton have some professorships and buildings named after the families of kids who were admitted with substandard SATs — I lived in such a named hall at Princeton and they all do it. Nonetheless, everybody still wants to get into those three institutions — *nothing was lost, save temporary honor.*

"Look, since your board is already contemplating selling trustee seats, why not sell *a few*, notice my careful qualifier, *a few* student seats every year."

She handed him a creamy envelope and ordered more coffee. The envelope contained a single embossed stationery page that he read. It was from "From the Desk of the Countess von Konigsberg."

Christ Church School Nirvana in Fifteen Years

By applying a cost/benefit model or integrated price/worth/ Harvard-Yale-Princeton admissions payoff ratio (i.e., CC provides the best odds in America for getting a child into H-Y-P), an open-market place at Christ Church School in 2007 will be worth upwards of six million dollars to the Manhattan upper class (I speak entirely of economic class here — don't want you jumping down my throat!). That would be a one-time only payment for admission. Of course, all students admitted under this program would have to fall within the current admissions spectrum, but since you educators have already reduced everything to the numbers — ERB, SSAT, SAT, ACT scores — and minority admissions have extended that spectrum, this policy would be entirely defensible (unlike some of the historic fundraising admits at H-Y-P — ask me sometime).

My future projection is that at five 'special' places in each 7th and 9th grade class (your major intake classes), you could realize a total of sixty million new dollars every year without noticeably diluting the quality of the classes (2 classes x 5 students x $6 mil per capita =

$60 million). The six million, it must be said, is a minimum estimate for open-bids at a discreet Christie's auction, especially given the recent entry of scores of hedge fund and private equity billionaire cowboys into the Manhattan private school market.

And here's your payoff, Tom, you'd get your fondest wishes: you'd have funding for twenty new full tuition scholarships for each incoming seventh and ninth grade class every year (thus leaving the other schools in the dust on diversity). And you'd be able to pay your faculty 30% over the going rate and grow your endowment principal by forty mil every year without running a damn capital campaign every five minutes. At the end of fifteen years, Christ Church would be the richest school and have the best-paid faculty and the most diverse students in New York.

Tom knew he should have waited thoughtfully, run his eyes over the paper appreciatively, sit back and admire the woman who was capable of such a plot. Nope. No can do.

"Jesus, Serena! What a tacky, seamy, evil scheme." He inhaled. "'*Nothing was lost, save temporary honor*'— as in temporary virginity? God, you've outdone yourself."

Serena colored almost scarlet and choked on her sip of coffee. A waiter appeared at her side with a fresh napkin as she coughed into her own. When she came up for air, she was teary and angry.

Minutes passed as they both recalibrated. Tom put the paper back into the envelope and tucked it into his jacket. Serena sipped from her water goblet and stared fiercely around the handsome, understated dining room, her teeth clamped. Then she eyed him severely.

"Well, Tommy darling, you leave me with much to think about. I still believe my plan is honest and direct. Guess I'll have to try it out on some more of your trustees."

"I'm sorry if I angered you, even hurt you, Serena."

"So, you've already rendered your hasty decision. And I've just made my decision. There was no need to mollify me — unless you wanted that two mil." Serena checked her watch. "Got to run, my bankers await."

CHAPTER 78

It was just as well that Tom had his weekly golf round with Lulu the next day. He didn't play well, but neither did she as Tom told her about the crumbling of his campaign. After they returned to her house, she broke tradition by serving Scotch rather than their accustomed iced tea.

"Let's have some of the Bishop's favorite — Talisker, eighteen-year-old. He claims it has the essence of smoke, peat, and salt air in it. Don't know about all that, but I like it anyway."

They settled on her long screened porch overlooking the back cottage garden, but it was as if neither noticed the garden that day because they were thinking overtime. For five minutes, they sat and thought and sipped. Then Lulu broke their understanding silence.

"Do you remember my mentioning an old classmate, Roderick McBain, early in the summer?"

"Yes, and at the time I passed your 'mystery' on to Sally. Hmm."

"Guess I should fill you in a bit on my mystery. Roderick and I were Christ Church class of forty-eight. He was my boyfriend for years, and I thought he was the most intelligent, handsome boy in school. We both thought it would be forever." Tom nodded and smiled, and she liked that enough to blush a little.

"Rod was also the top athlete and the only student to go to Stanford. I remember no one else wanted to go out there, it was so far and we thought it was some kind of junior college because it was called 'Leland Stanford Junior University.' Do you remember?"

"Yes, and it's still officially called that."

She giggled. "So, Stanford it was. Rod always had a mind of his own, and he wanted to go where Herbert Hoover had studied engineering and then on to make his fortune. Well, Rod did the same, except he didn't get elected

President, which Hoover could have dispensed with, too. And Rod loved his golf all along and wrote me regularly. Certainly more steadfastly than my husband kept out of actresses' dressing rooms." She sighed and sipped from her glass. "And before Rod retired he began to experiment with the engineering of golf clubs. Said he wanted to make his game longer at the same time that he was getting shorter." She chuckled to herself.

Tom chuckled with her. "And every golfer knows what he came up with. Many call him a genius."

"I mentioned that I'd already told my genius about you and your St. Andrews connection and your current campaign," Lulu said. "Things have moved along since then, and now, well, I think that bachelor's still got a crush on me. He said he hasn't been active as an alumnus and that maybe he should join me since CC gave him a proper start, said he learned more about the things that mattered there than at college."

"We do hear that a lot," said Tom.

"Well, I struck while the iron was hot — told him I had been in the same situation until the Bishop introduced you to me, and that I was planning a gift. That smoked him out. He immediately said that he'd only give to a CC headmaster who could play a decent round of golf with him on the Old Course."

"Lulu, you didn't smoke him out — you smoked me out!"

She chuckled again. "Don't worry, Tommy, he said he'd be gentle."

"Oh, Lord, Lulu! But he does sound intriguing." Tom glanced at Lulu and discovered that she was already watching him closely.

"Roderick never was one for blather, as he calls it. Always direct. So, I took it seriously when he said this week that if you ever get over there, he might match my gift. Then he came clean — he sold his company recently and said that he could use a tax break."

Tom turned and looked levelly at her. "Do you want me to go?"

Lulu didn't hesitate with her answer.

CHAPTER 79

Tom slit the unmarked manila envelope, which was identical to the last one, and looked at the single sheet. Until Jo had suggested the first one might have been planted on his desk by Maury, Tom hadn't given it another thought. *Robert Haverford Cattivo greases Hoboken* was the title. Below was a single internet site for Farmers and Merchants Associates Bank, Grand Cayman with RHC and PW listed alongside.

Tom entered the bank's site and tried the account password. Immediately, a series of transactions came into view, all with "Hoboken Ten" prefixes and followed with names of ten local New Jersey politicians. My God! he thought. Could it be authentic? He sure hoped so.

"Jo, who was it this time?"

"Still don't know. I was in brewing coffee."

"How long ago?"

"Five minutes. Right before you came back. Maybe three minutes. Cat had been in earlier, but I don't think the envelope was on your desk after she left."

Tom called Cat in the *Chronicle* office to come by. When she arrived, he had a question for her. "Cat, when you were in my office earlier, did you see this envelope on my desk?"

Cat took her time. Then answered quickly. "No, I didn't see it there when Georgie and I checked your *Dictionary of American Biography*. Excellent entry on Fielding Yost, by the way. Monica Cattivo has been bragging to Georgie about that famous Michigan coach, so we checked. Thanks for letting us use it."

"Anytime," said Tom, eyeing her. She dropped her eyes, wheeled, and was gone.

After Cat left, Jo said, "I don't believe it. I didn't even see Georgie come in with her. I'm not sure of anything anymore having to do with those manila envelopes. By the way, are they worth anything?"

"More precious than rubies, Jo."

Later, Tom took a taxi up to the Cathedral Close and compared notes with the Bishop. He sat up in his leather Chesterfield sofa that served as a daybed. A weathered tartan shawl surrounded his stooped shoulders. If his movements were deliberate, even halting, his mind was as keen as ever.

"Dynamite, Tom," said the Bishop. "No, make that nitroglycerine."

"Yes, clearly. But I can't use it."

"Why not?" asked the Bishop.

"I suspect Georgie, maybe Cat's in on it, too, because they were both in my office earlier. But I can't finger Georgie — if I used the tip his dad would know immediately, I'm sure. But how that kid broke into his dad's Cayman accounts boggles the mind. You remember, even Meredith Ross's top techies couldn't get past that firewall."

"And yet," said the Bishop, "wouldn't the IRS investigate an informer's call on their own and it would never rebound on Georgie? Surely Bob would suspect a business rival first — he's made hordes of enemies."

"I guess you're right, but then the issue for me is, do I want to give Georgie and his older sister Monica a jailbird dad?"

"It's your call, Tom, but if you can't make that twenty million, you may have to reconsider."

"'Situational ethics,' it used to be called, and isn't that simply a cute modern update on Machiavelli?"

"I've told you — not necessarily. And Machiavelli isn't the enemy. He merely illuminated the reality of the human condition, of eternal human behavior."

"I'm still uncomfortable," said Tom. "And this gets more complicated. You won't believe this: last week I had to go up to Williamstown,

Massachusetts to pursue some Thorndike money. It was Lulu's lead, you remember — her cousin, Jim Thorndike, met me in at the old seventeen-ninety-seven pub for lunch."

"Oh, yes, Jim's active at St. John's parish up there."

"Well, he was gracious and generous, but the thing that I most remember was what I saw later. I took a nap in the car before the drive back to the city. Well, when I woke and was about to put the seat back up, there was Babs Cattivo coming out of the restaurant with a beefy man in his early forties. He seemed to be promoting some sketches under his arm, and I remembered that Bob used to claim that she did a country house redo every other year when she got itchy. Well, they got into the guy's BMW sedan parked at the edge of the lot with overhanging branches. And they went into a clinch in the front seat."

"And you didn't follow their car?"

"No, but I did notice he had a Connecticut plate in a Danbury dealer's cover. That would be convenient to Pound Ridge, where the Cattivo country pile is."

"Admirable restraint, Tom. I would have pulled up my trench coat collar, tugged my fedora down, mumbled into my wrist radio, and followed, at least across the highway to that seventeen-ninety-seven motel!"

Tom smiled and shook his head.

"But yes," said the Bishop, "I'm sure you're right on the inferences. I know that restaurant, and I guess those two figured one hundred and twenty miles away from home on a weekday was a safe bet. So, what are you going to do with this bit of serendipitous, damaging intelligence?"

"Nothing. I won't use it," said Tom. "I simply couldn't."

"Or, is it that you can't think of *how* to use it?"

Tom sat and drank. "Yeah, maybe, but I honestly don't want to be responsible for breaking up the Cattivos' marriage."

"And yet isn't the marriage already broken?"

"I admit I have no love for either Bob or Babs. It's that I don't want to leave Monica and Georgie with warring parents into the future."

"You're certainly taking the high road, Tom, in both instances, but you may want to reconsider next month before the big trustee meeting."

CHAPTER 80

Bramston and Cattivo opposed the idea of Tom's six-thousand-mile journey to woo American-Scottish money. "Not at the school's expense," ruled Bramston when Cattivo alerted him to Tom's plan. Only when Tom vowed to pay for the trip himself if he came back dry did they relent — Bramston by phone from Nova Scotia, Cattivo by email from Miami.

Tom didn't like their attitude; on the other hand, he was making no guarantees to himself about how realistic the whole scheme might be. Counting on a reignited sixty-year-old high school romance to deliver major donations from two graduates who had never made a donation before was patently absurd. But he had two compelling reasons to make the attempt, one "professional" and one personal. He believed in Lulu because he had to — she was his only remaining major prospect and she had tied her gift to her classmate's. The personal reason was that Tom had grown fond of her, and when she had answered his question, "Do you want me to go?" she concluded with, "I'm counting on you."

Things moved quickly when Tom talked with Roderick McBain on the telephone because Lulu Leonard had laid the groundwork well. Retired global engineer and golfer McBain's development of a titanium head and graphite shaft driver had received worldwide press in the 1980s. He was now bursting with pride after having sold out to an Oregon sporting goods company.

His invitation to Tom was unequivocal. "Now, don't you worry yourself over that compulsory golf round with me, I seldom break eighty these days."

Tom's heart stopped; he'd never broken ninety.

"I've slipped a lot, so you can chase me around the Old Course a time or two. It's my daily circulation medicine now that I'm retired, doctor's orders, along with whiskey. I do love that Scottish doctor."

As Tom drove the final stretch into St. Andrews, he saw the familiar fifteenth century university towers and the tenth-to-twelfth century castle and cathedral ruins rise above the "wee grey toun" and its golf courses along the North Sea. It was a storybook setting and always thrilled him. He was soon having a drink with Roderick McBain at the Royal and Ancient Golf Club overlooking the Old Course and the sea.

McBain looked quite the Scot; in fact, remarkably like Andrew Carnegie, the native Scot who grew up in the same county and later served as student-elected University Rector. McBain was short and stocky with a ruddy complexion, white hair, and a knurled knob of a nose. The man was brisk and candid, exactly as Lulu described him, an enthusiast by disposition, and was no doubt used to carrying people along with him. He seemed delighted that his old school's current headmaster was a St. Andrews man, but he was disappointed when Tom confessed he had only that summer begun playing golf again.

"But didn't you work on your game while you were here all those years?"

"Only twice in three years. Too busy studying."

"God, man, what a waste!"

Despite that reservation, McBain gave every indication that he enjoyed Tom's company. Tom tagged along as the inventive golfer played the Old Course — he chattered away about the "engineering" challenges of the links course, continually plotting revenge on its severe layout with his new driver, but never breaking eighty. And when Tom rented an identical side-saddle tall putter to the one Lulu had bought him at home, McBain shook his head at the sight and muttered, "Is nothing sacred?" When Tom broke ninety, McBain approved with warmth: "My God, I can't believe Lulu talked you into that monstrosity! But if you shoot your best rounds with that overgrown croquet mallet, you're quite the man!"

Their friendship solidified over dinners at McBain's stone house overlooking the harbor. On the third evening, when they retired to the parlor after dinner with a bottle of twenty-five year-old Lagavulin, the old alum made an uncharacteristically lengthy comment.

"Tom, I like your plans for the school, especially your goal of greater diversity in the student body and faculty. I've done engineering projects all over the world and I'm firmly convinced that it has been left to American education to solve the problem of segregated housing and work patterns, much as you put it yesterday on the seventeenth."

Tom was astonished. That Road Hole was the toughest on the course, and McBain had seemed not to be following their conversation very closely as he struggled to hold par. Moreover, he thought he'd blown it when McBain questioned him sharply over what he termed Tom's "social engineering" at the school.

"And I appreciate your coming all this way simply to deliver my invitation for alumni weekend." He looked at Tom contemplatively. "Can't think of any other reason for you to traipse all this way." He broke into a grin. McBain looked into his glass as he ran the liquid slowly up the sides. "You did say Lu promised to attend?" It was his first mention of Mrs. Leonard.

"She has her heart set on it," said Tom and smiled at his host. Then a little hesitantly, "She did tell me she could use an escort."

McBain looked at his guest over the top of his specs, shook his head, and smiled. "Let me brighten that up for you." He took both their glasses over to the liquor cabinet, poured, served Tom, and returned to his chair.

"Tom, let's make a deal. If you fulfill two conditions for me, there'll be a two million dollar bank transfer to the Christ Church School endowment the next business day. The first condition can be public: that the current headmaster promises to undertake an educational program quite foreign to him, but one that will be conducive to the physical and mental health of all concerned."

A wary headmaster checked his enthusiasm. "Ah, Roderick, what might that be?"

"That he undertakes a campaign to conquer his golfing illiteracy."

"I promise."

"Hmm. Now, I thought you might agree to my first condition a little too easily, so I emailed an old friend today who is the pro out at the St. Andrews Golf Club in Westchester. He'll be calling you in a couple of weeks to come pick up your set of McBain golf clubs and take the first of your fifteen lessons. He claims he can have an old rugby back breaking eighty-five by the first snowfall. Are you still game?"

"Absolutely."

"Done then."

McBain settled, or tried to, tugging at cushions, leaning back, and crossing his legs. He was nervous.

"Now, the second condition must remain between two gentlemen." He drew long and thoughtfully on his cigar. Then a careful sip of whiskey when Tom nodded. "I've always been partial to Lu Thorndike. Had some plans in mind when I went west to Stanford. Then her head was turned by that Yalie missionary's son who carried her off from Vassar. But I kept in touch even when I was abroad for years and she was going through a tough patch with that skunk. Now, even with my golf I'm a little lonely. I get a hint now and again that Lu Thorndike Leonard is, too."

McBain paused and colored. The old bachelor was on unfamiliar territory. "Now, how did I put that first condition if you learned to play?"

"Conducive to the physical and mental health of all concerned," repeated Tom.

"Well, there you have it. That's what I want from you."

Tom bought time by shifting in his chair and sipping. "I'm a little slow, Roderick. Am I to provide some diplomatic help toward . . . well, toward a resolution of that mutual loneliness?"

"That's the general idea, but *you're* not slow — *I'm* slow — sixty years slow. And Lu says you're like the son she never had. So, I'm counting on you to speed things up. Neither one of us has any time to waste."

CHAPTER 81

Cat was trying to put the finishing touches on the first *Chronicle* issue of the year, but a major worry kept getting in her way. When all her staff had left for the day, she turned to her new tech editor at the adjoining desk. She'd assigned him Matt's old desk so she could keep an eye on him.

"Georgie, I'm worried about those envelopes you asked me to leave on Doc's desk. We've heard nothing about them. I know he's gone to Scotland this week, Ms. Wilson told me, but she didn't say anything about the envelopes either. Do you mind reviewing this whole thing — why haven't we heard anything about those envelopes?"

"Okay, first, Dad's original purpose was to find out if my mother had been blackmailed. Wow! I loved the assignment, *carte blanche* to be the family cyberpunk!"

"Yeah, you sneaky adolescent, I know you loved it." She pulled out a fresh Ticonderoga pencil.

"I got into their account, except she changed the password long ago so it was, in a way, hers. If you want, I'll tell you how I did it with my Verizon contact's algorithm and an anagram thing I came up with."

"Spare me, no, never — you know how I hate math. I'm more interested in what was in that packet."

"I didn't feel right about sharing the details of that account, but after what I found later about my father, I don't mind who knows all of it."

"Yeah, Georgie, but don't get reckless with that kind of stuff. Honest. Be careful; it is family."

"There's that word, 'honest,' again. The only time my parents use it is to cover the lies that follow. But if you promise not to tell anyone, I'll let you see what was in those envelopes you left for Dr. West."

"Promise." Cat got up, locked the office door, and pulled the blind closed. "Let's go." She pulled her chair over next to Georgie's.

Georgie opened his MacBook Pro, found the Farmers and Merchants Associates Bank, Grand Cayman site, punched in a twenty-four unit password, another few tweaks, and turned to Cat for approval.

It was enough to make Cat forget her drumming. And there it all was. Cat bent into the screen: Ms. Cattivo had funneled a fortune to a Walter Saroyan in New York — over $7,400,000 in the last three years. Cat also saw that the only other people who received checks from Babs were Christ Church School teachers Ruth Soros and Pat Osborne and two men's names.

"Soros and Osborne, we know. But who's moneybags Saroyan, and the two guys — Pierre Gallosh and Robert Chandler?" asked Cat as she sat back in her chair.

"Mr. Saroyan's some big honcho up in Bedford at the country club — Mother made me take riding lessons from him. I told Dad about the Soros and Osborne checks and the two other men's names, but kept the Saroyan news to myself. Then Dad, after he blew up about the teachers' checks, found out that Gallosh and Chandler are private detectives — the best, he said. 'That proves she's been blackmailed in some way, Georgie,' he said. 'See, she's fighting back, but she won't tell me anything.' But Dad didn't seem very sure of himself. I've never seen that in him."

"That sucks, Georgie," said Cat, shaking her head. "But what did you find on your dad?"

"I don't know what it all means, except a lot of bucks by 'courier deposit' into his many accounts down there. It's complicated because some of his hidden accounts have hidden accounts. But my hacker at Verizon said that it could be money my dad didn't want to divulge, maybe drug money. He's seen it before."

"No, I for one don't believe that about your dad. He's famous and already rich — why would he get into that?"

Georgie frowned. "Or, we figured it might be some kind of Caribbean secret income. I know my dad has hotels and some big villas down there in the Caymans. Maybe hidden so the IRS wouldn't know about it."

Cat stroked her Ticoneroga absentmindedly, then stopped and looked up at her tech editor. "Back to my original question: what has Doc done with that stuff? We would have heard something from Matt by now for sure if Doc was out of the woods with that threat from the trustees. Matt is only days away from having him as a stepfather and they're all really close, so he'd be told by now."

Georgie frowned again. "Maybe Doc didn't believe it all. It is hard to believe. Hey, why don't we just ask Matt? Kind of roundabout, you know?"

"Aw, he'd be onto us immediately. And then he'd ask why we asked about it all of a sudden. Don't think so, if you want to keep what you discovered only between us."

"Yeah, you're right. That wouldn't work."

"So, what's next, Cyberpunk?" asked Cat.

CHAPTER 82

Tom was overwhelmed with school preparations and idiots when he returned to New York. Why did teachers wait to inform him of their pregnancies and request leaves the week before school started? And why did the soccer coach decide to have his elective knee surgery a day before he was to direct the ninth grade orientation retreat when he could have used the entire summer to rehab?

Tom had called Lulu as soon as he was back despite the school madness.

"Why don't you come up for lunch," she urged. "We'll take a good walk and you can report on your journey to your alma mater." Not a word about Roderick McBain. Tom knew she was hedging her hopes. He decided Lulu's hopes were far more important than anything at school.

Tom arrived a little late for the lunch date, after working on several "emergencies" involving teacher anxieties that ranged from family crises to classroom decor to late textbook arrival.

"We'll go down to the river and loop back by the old ice house, it's about two miles," Mrs. Leonard said. "Then we'll deserve our bloodies."

Tom resolved to address only what she had requested on the telephone: his journey to his alma mater.

After five minutes of his enthusiasm over the St. Andrews student drama society's *Macbeth*, she wheeled around and held him by the arm. "Tommy, you've been teasing me. I'll let you spout this piffle out over the Hudson to the gulls while I have my drink and Lobster Newburg by myself if you don't *tell me how Rod is right this instant!*"

Tom squeezed her hand and told her of Rod's playing golf every day, some detail of the charming seaside house, and of his kindness to his New York visitor.

She wanted more. "Yes, that's pretty much as he has described it. But is he happy, contented?"

"I guess so." Tom continued. "I think he is content with his well-deserved, very active retirement."

"Those can be two different things, can't they?" She nodded. "He's content, but maybe not happy?"

Pushing aside his discomfort with playing matchmaker, Tom told the truth.

"That's it — he's busy and pleased with his company sale, living in St. Andrews — all that — busy and pleased with it all. But Lulu, I don't think he's all that happy and fulfilled."

"That's me, Tom. That's me all over again. And I'm lonely, Tom." She took his hand shyly and patted it, looked him in the eye. "Now, tell me the truth, do you think Rod's lonely?"

The moment of truth. And surprisingly, she had made it easy.

"Yes, Lulu, I know he is. And that's where you come in."

CHAPTER 83

"I don't care if you've got appointments lined up your wazoo. You have an obligation to get your ass down here and tell me how that Scottish boondoggle went. After all, you musta spent two thousand bucks of school money going and coming."

Cattivo was frosted that Tom had brushed him off for days after he returned from Scotland. But when he heard that McBain had come through with two million and Lulu Leonard had followed suit, the trustee surprised Tom with his response.

"Hell, I thought it was a wild goose chase, a thinly-veiled golf holiday. In fact, that's what I told Bramston. But two million from McBain, Shit-Marie! I've got a set of his overpriced clubs up in the country, didn't help *my* game. Figured he was a tight-fisted Scot, taking advantage of all these American Anglophiliac assholes. God, four million big ones and we didn't have to make them trustees!"

Tom was on guard; he was almost sure Cattivo was aware he remained short of his goal and could afford to be expansive. Damn! With Cattivo he was never really, truly, lead-pipe-cinch sure about anything.

Cattivo picked up one of the three landlines he still kept on his desk and growled, "Get me some of that old Ballantine's I've never cracked."

He listened to the response. "No, not that one — the one with the royal seal, in the tall purple box with the Duke of something's approval on it. Two glasses. The Edinburgh Crystal ones shaped like a thistle."

Two of Cattivo's personal assistants were soon in the room, serving the Scotch and setting up a luncheon table.

"I'll drink to tight-assed Scots, including that McBain, and even to you,

Tom!" He drank quickly and held his glass out for a refill. Tom had never seen Cattivo drink like that before and declined his own refill. Cattivo started on his second drink while eyeing Tom sharply. "But you're a couple million short, aren't you?" No wonder he's so jaunty, thought Tom.

"Maybe. But I still have a final gift I'm counting on. I'll be home free with that."

"Well, well." Cattivo sipped. "A dark horse, eh? Would I know the donor?"

"Perhaps. But that's my secret for now."

"You leave me in the dark, Tom." Cattivo looked puzzled but shrugged, swigging his drink. He spoke without looking at the PA behind his chair. "Clear this off, bring on the soda and the pastrami." He motioned for Tom to join him at a side table by the window. As they sat, Cattivo appeared pleased to note once again that he "looked down" on the Yale Club across Vanderbilt Avenue. He must have been rejected as an eighteen-year old, Tom figured.

"I made another deal this week in Jacksonville. Boomtown just waiting for this Yankee carpetbagger to arrive with financing to build dreams. And all I was thinking after spending one hundred mil there was, I still can't get a good bagel in Jacksonville." He laughed with Tom as his assistants laid out the food.

"Tom, we're more alike than you realize — if your frontal lobotomy was successful and you went into business with me, you'd make millions. Now, eat."

Tom had a glimmer of what he was getting at, especially after five months of persuading rich donors to give. Once you established the worthy goal to make CC School more diverse *and* excellent, you simply ignored the contradictory details and shaded the truth to make the pitch and clinch the sale. And maybe he wouldn't even need that lobotomy — he had learned something similar when he sold scores of encyclopedias years ago to military families who probably never made much use of them other than as a part of the living room décor. Those reference books were useful and reliable, but he was actually selling prestige and future security to parents

— the vision that those inert books not only said something about the level of family culture, they would also smooth the child's way to Harvard . . . or Slippery Rock. And he was still selling prestige and future security to parents — the vision that their endowment gift would smooth acceptance at the club, church or temple, and maybe even Harvard . . . or Harvey Mudd.

So, who was Tom West to sniff at nouveau industry and enterprise? Was it a part of his new "respectability," including frequent entrée into New York's most restricted clubs — the ones with a not so ancient history of a scattering of black and no women members? How, as a matter of fact, had the kid from small-town Ohio made it up the greasy pole to head one of New York's finest schools? Certainly not by counting the pastel bunnies on his jammies.

Tom was finally getting some kind of fix on this little dynamo. Bob Cattivo wanted people to feel mixed-up about him, to keep them off balance and vulnerable, but he could certainly deliver when it counted. When Jo Wilson's daughter Wendy lost her job in a corporate takeover, all Tom could do was shrug and commiserate. So had Bramston and the other trustees. All talk. But when Bob overheard Jo talk of her daughter's problem, he stepped in and engineered an even better job for Wendy at Chase International where she could use her French language skills.

Cattivo's grudging compliment about Tom's frontal lobotomy seemed to spur his further talk about work and family over their grilled pastrami on rye. He said his eighteen-hour days weren't "hard" any more, but he loved making the deals.

"Real estate rumor becomes a kind of reality," Bob explained. "If I've made it ripe and inevitable for the other investors early on, things happen quickly. I can always count on human nature — trustworthy, rapacious, predictable human nature takes over. I've got it down to a science, but that also means I get bored." He added, with a twinkle in his eye, "That's when I make the time to help you run the school."

Cattivo served them both seconds and seemed to be enjoying himself and his lunch companion. Watch out, Tom.

"Oh, and I hope you'll give my Georgie a fair shake in your class," Cattivo said as he looked the head in the eye. Tom was floored — he hadn't had time to check his new class list. "He insisted on trying your AP class. I'm not sure he can keep up, but he sure as hell needs it to get into Brown University. I'll tell Babs to keep her mitts off his teachers for a change. Should have done it years ago. Oh, I guess you still have to approve all enrollments."

Tom was speechless — Georgie applying to one of the hottest colleges outside H-Y-P? To turn Bob's comment from last spring back on him, what kind of "academic cloud-cuckoo land" did he inhabit? The admissions people there had assured Tom that President Carter's daughter and a long list of children of the famous got in strictly on merit. How in hell did Bob think he'd pull that miracle off?

Cattivo read Tom's hesitation. "See, let me explain," said Cattivo. "I know it'll be a squeeze, but I've got to get Georgie on the right track. I don't want him to take after me." Tom was noncommittal — he could still void the enrollment, but it made sense — the kid needed AP History to balance his four top science and math AP scores. He was always distinctly mediocre on the verbal side because he always said, with shades of his papa, that he "didn't give a damn."

Cattivo noted Tom's tepid response and must have thought that his family history might conclude the sale, so he launched into another world. His autobiography tumbled out as if he were laying out his soul for the head to see. Or perhaps the 130-pound guy who drank sparingly was liberated by five ounces of rare Scotch? Watch out, Tom.

He had been, he told Tom, the fat younger son who responded to paternal pressure by "eating and waddling through school with my silver spoon upbringing. Well, it was really three schools in Riverdale — Fieldston, Horace Mann, and Riverdale." Then he headed west and drank his way out of a few colleges deemed "almost acceptable" by the old man — Lehigh, Denison, Whittier; so, when he took aim at the University of Hawaii, his dad dumped him on the trading floor at the Exchange. "Last chance became Main Chance," Cattivo said, and after five stressful years he found he had millions in his jeans, and collapsed physically. After the hospitalization he became a spare, disciplined marathoner and moved his money to real estate. The family commodities brokerage was being run into the ground by his perfect Yalie older brother and by his father's new younger wife's needs. The only thing untouched was Bob's personal hoard. And it stayed that way: all his and growing rapidly thanks to his speculative schemes that other property hawks couldn't pass up.

Tom had never seen Bob look so grave as he swigged his soda and continued. "The reason I got into all this today, I guess, is that I wanted you to understand my tacky academic record and my feelings for my Monica and Georgie. Over the years, like all busy marriages, Babs and I've grown a little apart. And it's as if Monica and Georgie grew closer to me as that happened. Depends on your perspective, I guess," Bob said, "but if it's an either/or deal, then I'll settle for the change."

One of Cattivo's PAs came in to serve espresso. He served Tom one cup and his boss two. Tom decided not to interrupt the flow of conversation by asking. He knew Cattivo's answer already: "Because I'm paying for it."

"From the time we'd all get into my Benz wagon late Friday for the run up to Bedford, to the time I dropped them off at the front door Sunday evening, I was constantly with the kids. Constantly. Which is about forty-eight hours more than Babs could ever spare from the Pound Ridge Golf and Racquet Club."

Cattivo paused long enough to chug-a-lug his first cup.

"We had our battles with, and for, Monica before she got into CC. Her elementary headmistress, upholstered like a nineteen-forties physical education major, announced that Monica 'didn't seem to fit in,' even though she was the top student. I cursed the bloodless, blue-eyed families who made my daughter's condition permanent at her girls' school. I sure as hell remembered it when I finally got her and young Georgie into Christ Church. My father pronounced his grandchildren's new school 'more than acceptable' just before he died. Hell, Tom, that's the only time in my life I was part of anything my father approved of. That made me happy for about five minutes, you know, until I remembered the bruising that old man gave me and the lost years of my own adolescence. So, I vowed that the same Goddamned thing wouldn't happen to my Monica and my Georgie."

CHAPTER 84

Georgie left a manila envelope at his dad's breakfast place and left the house early because he couldn't bear to discuss it with his father. It was the rest of the report on Babs, the part he'd told Cat he hadn't shown his dad. It contained a sheaf of printouts of Cayman bank withdrawals, including wire transfers to Walter Saroyan. Perhaps most devastating of all, she had authorized the huge transfers on Cattivo's family account; "Caribbean Dreams," a secret joint account he had set up to be used for their twilight years. After ordering his accountants to sequester a yearly half-million in it, he and Babs had agreed to uncover their secret total only when he retired. Its bottom line was now less than $75,000. Nearly nine million had been moved to an account at Banco Santander in Bedford, New York under the name of "Walter Saroyan." When Cattivo opened the manila envelope and read the report he recognized Saroyan as the son of a bitch who was the Pound Ridge Golf and Tennis Club general manager.

Cattivo was shocked into a state of indecision and inaction for the first time in his life. He was only sure of one thing. The manila envelope had to have come from Georgie because he had tricked Georgie into hacking his mother's account. The boy had responded to Cattivo's plea that they had to protect Babs from blackmail, a possibility he had also tried to sell himself. Cattivo was at loose ends, but this meant war. He had to protect, no, *capture* his kids from their treasonous mother.

That afternoon he led the critical final meeting of investors that, as he put it several times, "solidified our Countess Serena von Konigsberg's launch into the European theater of dreams." His stakeholders were enthusiastic, even smitten, by Serena's presence and presentation of her final breakout plans. After his guests left their Champagne flutes and wended their way out of his suite, he asked Serena to stay. Cattivo couldn't help thinking, what would it be like to have a wife whom I respect: respect for her brains, her business sense, her success, her dreams? And who still has melons?

Cattivo, the Giant of Speculation and Bundling, fumbled his lines when she sat across from him. Serena knew he was hurting, so she waited with hands folded and wet, melting eyes. He apologized for mixing the personal with business. He hesitatingly told Serena of Babs' betrayal and finished, "You've gone through something like this, at least that's what I've heard." Cattivo looked bereft.

"My philanderer died while we were cleaning him out." Serena pushed her divorce lawyer's card across the conference table to him. "None better — you probably knew her father, the judge."

Cattivo looked at the card. "Oh, yes! I gave to his campaign." He looked better already, she thought.

She zipped her Slim-Serena Nile crocodile computer case and moved around the table as he stood. "You need a hug, Bobby Cattivo," she said and pulled him to her chest. She accompanied the clinch with a whisper. "There's a way out, Bobby, always a way out, and I can help." She pulled a business card and gold pen from her Secure-Serena shoulder bag in matching crocodile and wrote a number on the back. "There's my private line. I'd love to hear from you. Maybe I'll make you an offer you can't refuse." She leaned down and kissed him on the mouth. As she eased her way out the door, she thought, "Look who's solidified now."

Cattivo was left with the warm, musky scent of the Countess's own Seductive-Serena and a near-adolescent erection.

CHAPTER 85

Serena von Konigsberg invited Tom to Jean Georges for another lavish, Michelin-starred luncheon. Since their last fracas over her admissions auction plan, she had called twice. The first time, she announced proudly, "Mr. Cattivo loved my auction plan and he wants me to present it to your trustees in December." The second time, she asked advice in dealing with her son Chris, and finally asked Tom if he would host him when he was on break over the Thanksgiving weekend, as she would be in London launching her first shop. After checking with Sally, Tom rang back and agreed — he assumed that Serena's two million was on the way. She was the final piece in Tom's twenty million puzzle.

During their lunch, Serena was again happy to talk about herself, although she diverged from that briefly.

"Tommy, I was surprised to hear about your engagement to Sally Ernst. Not 'surprised' in the sense that I didn't think you two belonged together — I hardly know her — and she's such an active parent. You might have told me. At least told me something about her."

"Well, we didn't formally list in *The Times*, although I think Sally is going to do a wedding note in the paper." That was the best he could come up with. Tom didn't think it any of Serena's business and hadn't dreamed that she cared. In some way.

"I was the only one in my circle not to have known. I was a little embarrassed when the others all told me last week, since they all still refer to you as 'Serena's headmaster.'"

Tom couldn't be moved to respond, and Serena was soon back on to her expected boutique triumphs in London, Paris, and Rome. She waited until they polished off the four courses to return to anything involving him.

"Tommy, darling, I've waited until coffee so that you would have only your demitasse cup as a weapon."

Uh, oh, he thought.

"I apologize abjectly to you, Tommy, because I can't honor my pledge just now. Bobby Cattivo has threatened to pull his investment group out of my expansion if I give you the two million now. He says we're 'joined at the hip,' and I guess we are. He's been monitoring my spending and says I can't afford it. I know he's doing it for my own good, but I'm very, very sorry. Don't know why he came up with that objection now."

Tom was speechless. She had said "just now," which left the door open for the gift in a couple of months or years. Yeah, my successor will get off to a flying start. Cattivo wins.

Jo Wilson welcomed her discouraged boss back to the office, and they spent the afternoon toting up his fundraising totals — just over a million short with only a few long shots left.

EARLY FALL, 2006

CHAPTER 86

The 323rd academic year of Christ Church School in the City of New York kicked off with an all-school convocation in the neighboring church sanctuary. For Tom, that meant convoking *all* the school — 750 people — every last student, teacher, counselor, administrator, secretary, and custodian, even if it meant hiring temps to handle reception and telephones. They were all there, plus 300 parent interlopers who had heard about "the show" from their teenagers.

The program included music taken from the school's founding period, and the school archives recorded that compositions by Purcell, almost anything by Bach, and Telemann brass and string compositions were regularly used in the seventeenth- and eighteenth-century school. Hence, Tom insisted that annual Baroque horn fanfares, battling trumpets among the limestone nooks, and rumbling organ sounds opened every Christ Church school year in a way the kids remembered.

Tom sat beside Dr. Philips and watched Dean Levi and Student Body President Sturgis across the platform. Sturgis would need some help getting through the year with *his* habits, but Jane thought he was coming out of his fog. Tom felt for him — what chance had he with a psychiatrist father *and* mother?

The school hymn was "O God, Our Help in Ages Past," written in 1708 and used ever since. Its fifth stanza was Tom's favorite:

> *Time, like an ever-rolling stream,*
> *Bears all its sons away;*
> *They fly, forgotten, as a dream*
> *Dies at the opening day.*

Tom loved the historical hymn and that stanza always got to him as he looked over the sea of half-lit young and earnest faces sitting by classes seven through twelve. The students were interspersed with teachers, a few of whose silver tops carried the hint of a steely blush and blue finish from the high west rose window. Tom drew his hankie across his brow unnecessarily and then took a necessary dab at his eyes. He knew there were devils among the student angels out there, but he persisted in believing the latter outnumbered the former by a wide margin. He scanned the congregation where the parents sat. Yes, there she was, and simply the sight of Sally gave him strength for the day and bright hope for the morrow.

Tom took a final look at his outline. It was time for the "Head's Homily (Greeting)" in the program, a custom unchanged for centuries. Tom had added the parenthesis because "homily" had no meaning for kids in 2006 New York, and he didn't want to be too literal with its meaning. He figured that by the next generation "anthem" and "hymn" would require explanation.

Over the past few years in his homilies, Tom had used biographies in his attempt to inspire the troops to personal and academic excellence: Willie Nelson, who he suggested dryly was "the greatest composer of the twentieth century;" Willa Cather, who he noted was "a typical Nebraska country girl, Pulitzer Prize winner who had lived in the Big Apple and walked Yehudi Menuhin around the Central Park Reservoir on Sundays;" and William Allen White, who wrote "the best editorials in nineteen-twenties America even if he had only two-thousand circulation, including throwaways." Each of his bios featured their personal struggles for identity and recognition, and lasted about ten minutes. The students, aged twelve through eighteen, seemed to appreciate his brevity. The faculty, who had spent an average of six years in higher education and were aged twenty-one through seventy-four, simply agreed that homilies, a necessary evil, were best left to someone else. Like the head. And for this day, Tom knew he was taking a risk with what he had in mind.

The head did not ascend the pulpit or use a lectern and no mic was necessary in the crystalline space — he swung one leg over a wooden theater stool and spoke.

"I want to begin this morning with a kind of guessing game. If you can't immediately answer, I'll provide clues. We'll see which class can nail it. I have a common object in mind for my talk this morning, one that can probably be found in your kitchen or dining room drawer at home.

"Seventh graders," Tom said, addressing the twelve-year olds at the front, all of whom were new to the school. "We'll give you first crack and the first clue: this object is almost certainly forgotten most of the year, but becomes a crucial item at certain family events. What is it?"

A scurry at the front left indicated one of the seventh graders had raised a hand and then retrieved it in embarrassment.

"Eighth graders, this item is always present at weddings. What is it?"

"A bride!"

"A good guess, given your single clue. But no, not even in Manhattan where people are rumored to never be too thin or too rich, even our brides couldn't fit into a kitchen drawer."

Laughter.

"Ninth graders, this object can make people of all ages warm and fuzzy. What is it?"

Not a peep. Uh, oh. Tom knew at once that the clue was dynamite, if a smartass senior yelled, "Pot!" or "Booze!" he could chuck it in. He moved on quickly.

"Tenth graders, it is always present at Christ Church School Chapel services. What is it?"

There were no takers. Then a smattering of guesses, including the barely audible, "Bor-ing."

"Boring? Nope — we're after an object, a noun, not a prevailing condition whenever I speak."

More laughter. That was close.

"Eleventh graders, it is usually present at temple, church and home worship services. What is it?"

Nothing intelligible.

"Seniors, this object is present at romantic dinners. What is—"

"Candles!" one shouted. "*A candle!*" another amended.

"Absolutely right! Once again, demonstrating why the seniors will graduate this year and the rest of you will be kept for more seasoning."

General laughter. Tom let it die down and spoke into the quiet.

"My text for this new school year is taken from a very old Chinese maxim used by U.S. Ambassador Adlai Stevenson at the United Nations in tribute to Eleanor Roosevelt. I hope you'll remember it after today: 'It is better to light one little candle than to curse the darkness.'" He repeated it. "Now, I have three candles here this morning and each one represents something important in all our lives."

Tom brought a tiny pink birthday cake candle from under his gown and held it up.

"This is the familiar object that marks your birthday year after year — the one in your kitchen drawer at home."

Some rustle among the eighth graders. He ignored it.

"Now we'll honor it, put it center stage, and remember it as our birth candle."

He placed it in a holder on the stool and lit it with a pocket lighter. It was barely noticeable. The lights in the sanctuary then perceptibly diminished and the little candle appeared brighter. Tom was relieved that the custodian was on his side today.

"Some of you will remember the story that Rabbi Gilbert told us one day in chapel last year. She talked of how awkward she felt in middle school, sometimes even ashamed, of her family's compulsory Sabbath candles and meal every Friday evening while her friends began the weekend by going out. Later, some of her friends, both Jewish and Christian, confessed that they had actually felt envious of what her parents insisted on. They had provided a stable, loving family heritage week after week, and it started with the lighting of the candles. It was a lesson she never forgot and I hope it is one we can remember."

Tom moved to the white Sabbath candle resting on the side lectern. "I have always marveled that most religions on the face of the earth ask young people of middle school age — your age, seventh and eighth graders — to make religious commitments. That request is made at the same time twelve and thirteen year olds are undergoing the greatest physical, mental, and emotional changes of their lives since infancy. So, I'd like to dedicate this candle to your search for personal identity — the middle school candle." He lit the candle and the house lights dimmed again.

Tom walked over to the other side of the platform and stood behind a short, wide white candle resting on a carved marble seraphim.

"Of course, the search for your identity continues through high school, college, and adult life. And you high school students are more and more aware of community in your studies and life. Community candles are immensely powerful in our lives. Years ago when I traveled in Greece, I was struck that the Greek Church employed a candlestick modeled on the menorah, which, of course, came from the Holy of Holies of the ancient Hebrew Temple; the flame kept burning as a symbol of a people's calling and the holy presence. And the Roman and some Protestant churches also use flame to symbolize the holy presence. These faiths find the candle and flame symbolism vital." He prepared to light the candle.

"This is the community candle and we continue it in our civic world — witness the Tomb of the Unknown Soldier, the Kennedy grave, or the Trade Towers site. You are now of an age where you can increasingly make decisions not only about yourself — who you are — but also about the kind of community you want to be part of. Along the way you may participate in rallies and demonstrations to express your definition of that community. And you will find that candles may very well be part of that expression. Here, then, the community candle."

As Tom lit it and stepped aside, the electric lights were doused, followed by teacher concern and scattered student rustling, but then silence. Those in the darkened auditorium saw the candles forming an arc of light from one edge of the platform through the smallest candle on the stool and over to the other side.

"Think for a moment how ancient this candle symbol is," Tom continued. "The campfire predated it as that provided warmth and food preparation. Historians aren't sure, but probably our candle later over-lapped the use of oil lamps, animal oil at first, olive and mineral later. But the flame provided light and must have symbolized much more. I think that the primal fixation with flame may have been among the first intellectual symbols, or concepts, in the lives of early humans. Think of it, an object that transcended its literal use, that first imaginative leap to a new place in the human mind. And it probably occurred before pictographs on the cave walls, because the flame would have been necessary for lighting the artist's work. And somehow, 'hope' was a part of that earliest fire/flame symboliza-tion — it had to be. Once the candle was developed, its physical essentials were set, from pre-history down to our two-thousand-and-six: a wick core surrounded by a slow-burning fuel. But always, from the beginning, there was community and hope.

"This ancient tool, this homely contraption, this lovely apparition made of cotton, wax, air, and fire is a social giant. Where there is a candle, there will usually be more than one human. We know that candles help us ex-press the inexpressible and then draw us into the core, together toward the light. And *a single candle* can surprise. And teach."

Now to the part that Sally and Jane had warned him not to try.

Tom stepped to each of the side candles and blew them out. The effect was dramatic. The newly blackened space converged on the tiny birthday candle on the stool in the center of the platform. It shone bravely, blinked once and smoked slightly from the effort, but it pushed back the dark and illumined softly the entire cavernous space: from the deeply carved creamy marble screen overlooking the platform to the thousand upturned faces below and away to the back where organ pipes on the balcony reflected the spot of light in a myriad undulation of gold and silver. There was quietness without rustle. A willing silence. Tom finished.

"It is better to light one little candle than to curse the darkness."

CHAPTER 87

Cattivo was now stopping in about twice a week on his way to work and he jokingly told Jo it was "to help Tom run the school." She didn't break a smile. Neither did Tom, who soon realized that his trustee needed to be close to Georgie, to stake his claim on the boy, and was actually checking on his son's progress in Tom's and other teachers' classes. The Brown University goal had become his dad's fixation. Bob considered the college game a horse race that could be fixed and he was checking out his entry during the stiff morning workouts.

After a day that included a preschool Cattivo visit, a futile fundraising lunch, and a successful fifty-thousand-dollar dinner in New Jersey, Tom came home exhausted. Unless he found a sock under his mattress containing a half-million dollars, he guessed a new head at CC would soon be "nerving the race" by selling board seats for millions. Bob had sounded off that very morning, "Hell, maybe we'll also auction off admissions spots." With that, Tom caught a whiff of Seductive-Serena's influence. He'd already sorted out what their being "joined at the hip" signified.

There were some areas of school life, however, that Tom felt he could still control. As Georgie Cattivo's teacher, the head had a series of early run-ins with the boy who had become an expert at using his mother to cow teachers. Tom was having none of it, so he flunked the boy's first five-page essay and wrote on it:

> The cat's out of the bag, Georgie. This paper is almost uniformly poor as you can see from my comments. BUT the one fine passage I've noted shows what you can do when you decide it's worth your

time. Now that we've settled that the issue isn't one of ABILITY but of ATTITUDE, I shall expect excellent work from you from now on.

The alternative for you is not a pretty picture. Please come in to see me.

The boy came in, saw what he had to do, and began to produce. Tom figured that the boy's perception that the head had considerable influence in college admissions, even if inaccurate, contributed to his conversion.

Georgie began to drop in with the other students to talk about history and a little about life. Within a week he came in on his own, and soon it was a little about history and a lot about life, family, and Brown University.

"I'd sure like to see Georgie get in the game."

It was Bob Cattivo suddenly alongside Tom. Bob was eight inches shorter and turned out in an Italian custom-tailored palomino tan suit and chestnut Ferragamo stirrup boots. Tom wondered what the chances were that Bob had ridden in on Old Paint, then tore himself away from such thoughts — he should talk, standing there in his Church's suede chukkas and spiffy new hacking jacket he got at St. Andrews. And as a school head, his experience of horses was limited. To only one end.

The soccer and baseball games in the park were fall and spring fixtures in Tom's life, and he never tired of them. The fields were surrounded by outcroppings of schist and groves of oak and poplar trees, in turn backed by the silhouettes of tan, gray, and white apartment buildings and the soaring dark and shimmering skyscrapers hedging the park — it all gave a peculiar urban intimacy to the school kids as they played. For Tom, it was an example of this human community's triumph over nature — in this case, the nature of the world's greatest high-rise city — that in the very bowels of the metropolis there was a homely space for children to play their earthy games.

It was that afternoon in Central Park when Tom saw Cattivo as a desperate, perhaps loving parent, not simply as a mean, designing trustee. Tom also reminded himself that Cattivo certainly majored in the latter.

"Bob, Coach Jenkins was burned last year when he substituted in the fourth quarter to get everybody in because it's league and school policy to do so in the last few minutes. Well, the University coach didn't and we were beaten."

"Don't like the sound of that, you mean they cheated us?"

"You tell me. It was a long-time league 'understanding,' let's say a matter of sportsmanship."

"Hell, what kind of a world is it when a property developer is disappointed with the ethics of the school playing field? Shit, Tom."

"That just about sums it up. And our coach is going to send Georgie and the other subs in, probably only after another goal, to be safe."

The University coach was berating the referee again. And his players had picked up on it and would now have a patented excuse: we were robbed. Tom's sense of high-school athletics hadn't changed over the years. When the adults lost control and perspective, the kids followed. Nonetheless, he knew it'd be difficult for the University coach to excuse a three-to-one soccer defeat as CC scored again. And it was nice to see the CC coach substituting freely, including the marginally-skilled Georgie, although the other coach kept his starters in until the final fifty seconds.

When the game ended, the CC team was soon discussing the next day's math exam as they pulled on their warm-ups and the rookies scurried to pick up the equipment and carry it back to school. The parent spectators scattered to the West and East sides and Tom, after greeting both coaches and commending his team, headed toward Fifth Avenue with Cattivo tagging along. Frisbee play and pick-up touch football games covered the East Meadow as they gained the wide asphalt path and finally moved south on the bridle path. For five minutes, while walking parallel to the reservoir jogging track, Bob was uncharacteristically silent; in fact, he seemed to be brooding. No doubt about money or head searches. He soon recovered.

"I did want to say, Tom, that I appreciate what you've done with Georgie this term. Think he's on the right track."

"He's a good kid, Bob, I like having him in class. I think he's surprised himself with what he can accomplish. He can hold his own with some pretty sharp cookies. We knew his abilities in math and science, so it's nice to see him begin to work at literary skills. It'll make his college applications much more impressive."

Tom walked rapidly in his habitual way and looked to his side, where the shorter man was huffing and scuffing his Ferragamos in keeping up. Cattivo had his hands stuffed into his pants pockets, steeped in thought. Dark thought. Tom slowed.

"Georgie says he goes in to see you quite a bit. Swears by you, in fact, says you're tough, but fair. 'Doc West this' and 'Doc West that'— gets a little boring at times." Cattivo stopped, grasped Tom's elbow, pulled him to a stop.

"I'm bushed," Cattivo said. "Let's sit down." He led the way toward a bench that faced the reservoir track. They sat and viewed a colorful stream of joggers, runners, and a few chubby walkers on the raised track as New Yorkers took their stresses out on the packed earth surface at a steady thrum of one-point-five-eight-two miles per lap.

Cattivo was fixed on a stiff-maned blonde in black roots and a pink velour Bloomingdale's warm-up suit who was thumping along the track unconvinced and unconvincingly. He looked over and saw Tom's bemusement as he also followed the same apparition fluttering through the crosshatched shadows of the reservoir fencing from the setting sun.

"I'd give that fitness pilgrim 'A-minus' for effort," the head said.

"Hell, she reminded me of Babs. Except for the running part," said the trustee.

Tom didn't add that it had occurred to him as well. For the moment, Tom envied the runners for their exercise and heard the fidgety entrepreneur beside him clear his throat. He had recovered his breath.

"I've also been thinking about you and Georgie. How you've maneuvered yourself into a position of trust."

"I can't accept that term, 'maneuvered,' Bob. That has never been my intention. And I don't know of any other CC teacher who operates that way, either."

"Okay, but I'll bet you and the other teachers hear a lot about the students' families. Maybe you overhear it or express curiosity about their lives, pry a little. That'd do it, I figure."

"Again, you're misjudging, or misunderstanding, what we do. But I will admit that we do hear a great deal. Every teacher does."

"'Hear a great deal.' Now that I can believe," said Cattivo, turning to look at Tom. "And I just wanted to say to you that, although I appreciate what you've done for my Georgie in class, it'd better never get into his family life. You may have noticed I'm a pretty tough operator — and I can certainly hand it out when I'm — I mean — when my family's crossed."

Tom began to rise, but Cattivo pulled him back down and he fixed the head with his cold, beady eyes. "I'll bet you and your buddy Levi get off on those family scandals you hear from the kids. You get tight with them and they spill the family secrets. Jesus, when you get right down to it, Tom, you're nothing but a shit magnet."

"Yeah, that's about it," said Tom as he stood. "And my present company proves the point." Tom took off.

Cattivo caught up with him at the terrace steps. As they walked toward Fifth Avenue, Cattivo looked sideways at the head with a jaundiced eye. At the Ninetieth Street traffic light, he flashed his standby Cheshire cat grin. Lots of teeth and gums. It scared Tom.

CHAPTER 88

Cattivo had thought about this reunion for weeks — so much had happened in his allies' absence. He'd reserved a table at his club for privacy. How to break all the news? Best to make a direct, clean breast of it and see how they respond.

"It's so good to be back right here," Wither Bramston said to Cattivo and Dr. Philips. "I've had a more than tolerable summer with my granddaughter

Kate, she's quite the sailor, or captain, so it's nice to be back in the city not taking orders."

"Same here," said a tanned, smiling Philips. "I didn't have to pay for a single round of golf or a single drink." He detailed how he'd wowed the Houston and Atlanta country club set during his August vacation, mostly former parishioners, on his annual summer tour of the Hilton Head golf courses.

"I've missed you two renegades," said Cattivo. "I've had no one to talk to. Really talk to. Thank God you're back."

"That's my cue," said Philips. "Same here. And if I keep repeating that, maybe our host will rally some liquid nourishment our way." They all chuckled at that, and Cattivo motioned for the waiter.

Cattivo had sparkling water while Philips had his usual Rare Wild Turkey and Bramston had what he called his "family martini." Still cut one-one with vermouth like great granddaddy, figured Cattivo, since no American since Herbert Hoover liked his gin that diluted. "I'd join you fellows in the real stuff but I've got a hot date later and I want to keep myself pure." Philips howled and clearly liked that more than Bramston, who appeared little refreshed from his nearly two months of sailing. He looked much more the aging, persnickety Puritan who had allowed himself too much pleasure. Might he be on the way out? Cattivo wondered. With no male progeny, the way would be open for the first non-Bramston trustee leader in over a hundred years. In the position that several commentators listed in the "Top Ten Most Powerful" charitable slots in New York. And there was only one highly visible candidate. But only if there were no scandals or gossip about sixtyish property developers being cuckolded for years by a sleazy aging beauty queen. Back to business, Bob.

"You two will expect a summary of my adventures at Christ Church School. Not much has happened on that front. Tom is still out begging with no chance of making his twenty million since his last chance donor pulled the rug out. And I'm pleased to report my son Georgie will be the first tech editor at the CC *Chronicle* in history—"

"Bravo, Bob, maybe he can bring some class to that rag," interjected Philips.

"Yeah, sure hope so, Richie. He's taking two AP courses and even Tom says he's a cinch for Brown this year."

"And I hear from my Harvard friends that Brown is right up there with the old trio," said Bramston. "But make sure Tom doesn't ruin Georgie's chances out of spite."

"I've got that covered," said Cattivo.

Bramston had become more energized — probably the effect of a weak martini. "So, all good news," he said, "Glad to hear it. And I have some of my own. Our management consultant is raring to go and will have his report to us before the big board meeting."

"You're beating par on every round, Wither!" said Philips, his mind still on Hilton Head.

Cattivo saw that both his guests had drained their drinks. That was intolerable, with his next item looming, so he motioned to the waiter. When the man returned and the table was refueling, Cattivo broached his least favorite topic.

"Gentlemen, I do have one setback to report, not formally to do with the school or you two, really more personal." His two companions looked at him intently. Even Philips looked sober.

Cattivo twisted in his chair to ensure the nearby tables were empty. "I had a shock the other morning when a brilliant computer guy gave me the report I'd commissioned." Cattivo looked pained enough that his allies remained almost silent. The exception was the slow swishing sound of Philips' forefinger stirring the ice in his drink.

"I'm tempted to tell you more than I should," said Cattivo, "but I don't have anywhere else to go with it. And hell, you two are more than friends to me, more like priests — you won't blab."

"You forget, Bob, I *am* a priest!" chuckled Philips.

"Of course, Richie, but I meant that Wither here is like you — a man of discretion, who knows his personal interests coincide with mine."

Richie and Wither provided sanitary smiles to affirm.

"And that's why I have to tell you some things about Babs — Barbara Schiff, runner-up for Miss New York when she was only eighteen. From an old Five Towns, Long Island and *New York Post* family who pronounced their town, 'You-lett,' as in 'yuge' meaning large." After that beginning, things got easier for Bob's story. He related how his Philadelphia Main Line mother, divorced, remarried and divorced again, said at his wedding she'd never heard or seen the like.

"Well, Babs proved loyal in thick times and hinted at something else in tough times — that's when she looked thoughtfully over my shoulder during parties at the young male sharks on patrol. But as long as I could buy her a succession of houses in Cold Spring Harbor, Rye, and finally in Bedford to go with the town house off Fifth, she was loyal."

Cattivo traced some old scars on the surface of the oak table with his thumb. They waited and tried not to watch their leader too closely. Philips withdrew his chilled finger from his glass and looked at it.

"To make a long, sad story short, gentlemen, I am sorry to report that, after much agony, I have had to initiate divorce proceedings. Babs has hurt me deeply. Sadly, I discovered in that computer printout that she has been unfaithful. She's been taking money from our personal retirement dreams account and funneling millions to a man up in Bedford for the last seven years or so." Cattivo faltered, seemed unable to go on.

Bramston broke the silence. "My, goodness, Bob. Is that all of it?"

"Well, for God's sake, that's more than enough, seems to me," said the Rev, flexing his finger and reaching across to pat Cattivo's shoulder.

"Oh, yes," Bramston gushed. "I certainly didn't mean to offend, yes, that is more than enough, we don't need to hear more, any of the details, my friend."

"Unless you're raring to tell us," added Philips. "Then we could set people right about it, if this Jezebel story gets out. The devil is in the details, I always say, and that's really what people are most interested in with a case like this — details."

That seemingly brought Cattivo back to a kind of reality and he regained control. "Thank you both. I deeply appreciate your trust. I can only ask that you be as discreet with this as humanly possible," said Cattivo. "I certainly don't want to besmirch the reputation of the mother of my two children, or the reputation of our Christ Church School. We've agreed on terms, and I've been far more generous and Christian than my lawyer could believe. You may hear some pretty wild stories about our marriage in the next few months, but you know the truth now and I'd appreciate any defense you might have occasion to make."

"Your wish is our command," said Philips, finishing his whiskey.

"Yes, don't worry," added Bramston, following suit with his 1928 martini.

"No, not another word," said the Reverend Doctor. "Unless you want to share."

CHAPTER 89

After dismissing his Bramston/Philips class, Cattivo moved over to a quiet corner table when the usual noisy "hedge fund cowboys," as Serena termed them, came in. They pulled two tables together with a screech on the floor and settled into their gin rummy as their vodka martinis arrived. They'd be there until eight, when they would return home to their families, or what was left of them. Imagine: these heads of billions under management of investments and the speculative bastards couldn't even get their martinis right — designer vodka! He'd bet the Brook Club wouldn't let 'em in the door.

When the waiter came over and asked if Cattivo wanted another Pellegrino, he answered, "No, make it a Balvenie double." Serena had called earlier to say she would be held up and late for dinner, so she suggested he use the dead time to "excogitate," and she'd look forward to hearing the results. She was so cute like that. He could never take her for granted and she had made that clear. That was a first for him — a person he couldn't take for granted. After he looked up excogitate — he'd never admit it — he decided to take her advice. How did you not take people for granted when they were dependent on you? You had to, that is, you had to take them for granted in setting the boundaries if you wanted to control them. He realized that he had never sat like this and let his mind wander. Purposely. Excogitating. He signaled the waiter with a finger in the air — Serena taught him that — he'd always snapped his fingers before. She had informed him that she didn't want to be with a man who snapped his fingers. He'd decided right there he wouldn't go to the wall to oppose her. Somehow his need had made them equals. He didn't mind. His Balvenie was more delicious than he could remember, and he started on his second with enthusiasm.

He had no other equals besides Serena — no one else he couldn't take for granted. Well, one. Tom West. Yeah, West could hurt him with Georgie and he might know more than Cattivo bargained for. Tom might even act the spurned lover after Serena let him down on her two mil; why, he probably remembered that time last Christmas Eve when he tried to fuck her in his office and she cut him dead. Bless her for telling Cattivo everything; now, he'd protect her from Tom. Cattivo threw his head back and emptied his glass. Waved at the waiter. Excogitated some more. West was probably lying in the weeds waiting to lull Cattivo to let his guard down. Couldn't have that. But he could nurse Tom along, lull *him* to sleep. As his father of unsainted memory said at the commodity exchange, "Take no prisoners and never leave witnesses." And West was very much a witness.

Less than a week later, Cattivo was on the line for Tom.

"Tom, I've only got a few minutes but I thought I'd let you know some things that have been going on with Babs. Maybe you've heard?"

"A little, Bob, but I consider that your business and none of mine."

"True, but I thought you should know in case my Georgie starts to act up after discovering that his mother has been fucking the manager of our country club and stealing from our joint retirement account for years. I wanted you to know how I handled that bitch. And her candy-assed lover."

"Of course, I am concerned for Monica and Georgie."

"Well, that's the first thing I took care of. Set up humongous trust funds for the kids. She won't be able to touch them if I buy the farm."

"Well, please let me know if there's anything I can do for the kids and you."

"Yeah, okay, but don't worry for me, I can take care of myself. I've already got the best ally I could imagine: Serena. I guess you tried to get into that yourself last Christmas, using her kid to get at her — nice try!"

"Bob, it wasn't like—"

"Fuck it, Tom. No hard feelings," Cattivo interrupted. "Not another word, I understand — we're all adults here — I always say, may the best man win! Well, Serena's been my biggest supporter — she's been through the same damn shit as me. I backed her for years on that Europe boutique thing, and now she backs me when I need it. And get this: she knew two of the executive committee of the Pound Ridge club that I didn't, and we set it up so that turkey Saroyan's ass will be fired next month."

Well, Tom admitted to himself, he felt a creeping jealousy simply hearing of Bob's possessiveness of Serena. He wondered if crafty Bobby truly recognized the world-class craftiness of the Countess von Konigsberg. She'll make Babs look like Dairy Queen royalty.

Cattivo was off and running. "After I confirmed Babs' treason, I spent three days with ten lawyers at Skarpel & Flam — they even flew in two Cuban lawyers from Miami who know the Caymans cold. They set up those trusts for Monica and Georgie and put most of my property under secret accounts. That'll teach her to chase men."

Tom couldn't help remembering that odd, frightening encounter with Babs in the Plaza hallway. He had been both scared and turned-off by her attack. But mostly scared — it was in his first year.

"We got her recklessness on film, because my attorney hired a 'top of the line' private dick. Now, get this — turns out this dick, named Robert Chandler, used to work for Babs, because she hired a private dick to tail you for the last eighteen months! But, see, she didn't trust that private dick on you, so she hired Chandler to tail *him*, who is now my guy." Cattivo finally paused to get his breath. Tom could only think that Babs had more than her share of private dicks.

"Are you still there, Tom?"

"Oh, yes."

"Well, to top it all off, this Mr. Chandler gave us a deposition that further proves she's a nympho. With him! God! The race is to the swift, my friend, and nobody fucks with me — I've cut her off at the knees and thrown the stumps at Saroyan's feet."

I'd hate to be this guy's enemy, thought Tom.

CHAPTER 90

Tom felt it had been tough going about half an hour into the drive up to Massachusetts. It started out almost as natural as their weekend bookshop and sports expeditions. Then Sally's and Matt's conversation, or even attempts at it, dried up. Tom caught the contagion — his mouth was dry when he made a couple of inane comments about the weather and the traffic — after which he concentrated on his driving far more than necessary. He felt inadequate as the buffer for a mother who was about to lose her son and a son who had his own unexpressed concerns about college. Not to mention all of their memories of the wedding the day before.

Jane, Jo, and a few museum colleagues had witnessed the custom-made ceremony that the Bishop and his friend Rabbi Beth Gilbert hatched. Ben Levi had been practicing his old acoustic guitar for the event and provided continuity music drawn from Bach and Willie Nelson. Jane said he seemed more at home with Willie.

Sally was ready to believe in Williams; she had helped Matt choose it over her own Harvard ("Save Harvard for graduate work"), and she was not disappointed. The college made the day as painless as possible. Tom was impressed with the whole operation, especially how the deans managed the separation of the reluctant parents from their sons and daughters and freed the students to settle in the residence halls and begin getting acquainted. The president addressed a parents' reception and talked of the college's history, finishing with the challenges and joys that awaited their sons and daughters.

"I guess there's nowhere to go but home," Sally said as they left the gathering.

Tom had crossed the state line into New York when Matt's mother broke down. The heaving of her shoulders was followed by a series of tears and brave smiles assuring him she was "fine." Finally, she began weeping, deeply so, only coming up for air in great gulps before resuming. He reached across and stroked her shoulders and neck.

As they turned onto the Taconic Parkway, which Tom favored after his many trips on it to see Lulu, Sally sat up with resolution.

"Sorry," she said looking over at him with reddened eyes. "My God, what you got yourself in for today, this demonstration of my precarious nerves." She shook her head, looked bravely through the windshield and the scenery, only to put her hands to her face for another round of tears.

Tom soon pulled off and parked in a special area for viewing the Catskill Mountains to the west.

"Oh, this isn't necessary, I'll be okay in a while," she said.

"Well, it's necessary for me," said a misty-eyed Tom. "A good hug will work wonders."

Tom enveloped her, and she pliantly tucked inside his shoulder. He laid his cheek on her hair. They sat for many minutes, both mute, simply feeling the other's breathing.

"Thanks, darling," she said as they separated. "I needed that, even if you now know I am a big baby." She pulled down the mirror. "Ugh, with bloated face and red eyes."

Sally took his hand between hers for a spontaneous squeeze several times. They both loved the Taconic — a modernized simple path through the heavy woods following the natural line of ridges and valleys. It was a road not to make time on, but to regain one's soul on. And they agreed it was the perfect route for them that day. By the time they passed the Pough-keepsie-Pawling exit, Sally wanted to talk.

"Shall I tell you something that I shouldn't, dear *echtgenoot*?" It was her favorite Dutch word for husband among four choices and the one he couldn't pronounce.

"How can I resist an offer like that?" he replied.

"Well, after Matt was accepted at Harvard and Williams last April and he chose Williams, Jerry Stone volunteered to take us up to college in September. It's his alma mater." She hesitated.

Tom felt something pressing upward onto his diaphragm. "And?"

"Well, I lied. But only temporarily, as it turned out. I told him that you would be taking us." She bit her lower lip and looked at Tom.

Tom shook his head in wonderment. "What was his response?"

"Let's just say he got the message. It took you much longer."

CHAPTER 91

"Headmaster? I had you dialed so that I could tell you to cooperate with the management consultant I appointed. He'll be coming in for some records, he said."   Tom hated the Bramston interruption. He was struggling to keep his head above water as he met with new teachers, dealt with the unexpected resignation of an impossible-to-replace physics teacher, and scrounged frantically among disinterested donor prospects.

"And whom did you appoint?"

"Oh, we got lucky — I hired an insider — who insists on doing the report for free. Of course, he'll understand the ethos of the school."

"Who?"

"Oh, he's got quite a record," Wither continued. "Done work for some mighty high rollers, oh, and he was an All-American at LSU — started at Drexel Burnham, landed on his feet, became a consultant. Knows everybody. And now, he's also a Florida property developer. He even lectures at B schools. Let's see — LSU, Memphis, Troy State..."

"What. Is. His. Name?"

"Odd Shakespearean name. Michael Lear."

Tom was stunned. "Wither, you have appointed an 'insider' alright, but he's also an outsider. His younger son Brian is an eighth grader and doing

OK, but I expelled his older son last spring: second offense of drunken vandalism at a school dance."

"Why wasn't I told of this last spring?" Wither said.

Tom clenched his eyes shut so tightly his neck cracked. "Because you asked me four years ago to spare you the details of student discipline."

"Oh, yes, I recall I said I needn't be exposed to the nasty underbelly of the school. Got that from Churchill, you know. Marvelous aristocratic plain talk."

CHAPTER 92

Tom was gutted: he'd lost both the fund-raising goal and his job. On the morning of the day before the October board meeting, he sat down with Jo, Jay Erickson, and business manager Oakes Ames. They pulled together every last scrap of his fundraising: $19,220,000, including the recent four million from dear Lulu and her fiancé, Roderick McBain. Tom was four percent short of the twenty million. No excuses allowed — he simply hadn't made it. The trustees had sealed their February deal with Cattivo. Now Bob's plan to sell board seats and replace the head after the school management report was approved at the trustee meeting could proceed with no complications.

Despite the bad news, Tom and Sally wanted to keep an important lunch appointment that day. They took an insulated container of CC cafeteria sloppy joes up to the Bishop. He had told Tom earlier that he was planning to get out of bed to attend the board meeting the next day, but that he wouldn't be down to have his monthly sloppy joes with Tom. The bachelor cleric was the only trustee who read the CC monthly lunch menus and seldom missed stopping by for that dish, joining Tom in confessing to a lifelong love of the gloppy orange mélange. When they arrived, the cleric, only an engaging smile short of haggard, brightened and claimed he appreciated their pilgrimage. He sat up on the edge of his day bed to eat, with sunshine through a gothic window flooding his shoulders and newly bald head. After a few bites he pronounced it, "Ambrosia for the soul, the flesh is already mortified."

When the Bishop asked, Tom reported his four percent fundraising failure.

"Sorry, Tom. You've done very, very well in unfamiliar waters and you should be proud of that. Please remember that Lulu and I are deeply proud of you."

"Thank you," Tom nodded.

The Bishop looked Tom and Sally over. "But of course, you both are now worried about your future."

"Yes, especially since I've given up on that 'independent' management report on me that Bramston asked our most bitter parent to do."

The Bishop pulled his lips in and shook his head. "Yes, and after you told me about his appointment, I asked a trusted Wall Street friend to check Mr. Lear. He found that Lear barely escaped going to prison along with Milken and those other Drexel renegade traders. Also, that Lear is bidding on a Florida marina development and using the Bramston management name as a kind of white shoes bait."

"That explains it," said Tom, "because otherwise Lear is night and day from Bramston's world."

Sally looked over at her dejected man. "Is there any hope that you can see?" she asked the Bishop.

"Well, Bob Cattivo will call the shots, I'm afraid, so let's review where we are with him. I've discovered that he is one wily negotiator and as his personal situation changed, his demands have altered." He reached over to his bedside table, retrieved a file, and checked it. "At first, he wanted a seat on the Cathedral board. Now he insists that I add my matrimonial services to the deal, complete with the use of the Cathedral for a big 'in your face' wedding after his divorce comes through. We're still negotiating, but he's also inquiring at St. Paul's in London because Serena could use the publicity for her London boutique launch. Frankly, I don't think I've got enough that he has to have."

"No, it doesn't sound like it, because Serena will play hardball with him on that wedding — she's precisely the type," said Sally. She turned to Tom and smiled sweetly. The Bishop chuckled and slowly used a straw to sip from a water glass on the table.

"Yes, she's already playing it that way. And after all, Tom, he's played public hardball all along with you in front of the trustees — he'd hate to back down." The Bishop looked down at his file. "Oh, yes, he has asked me several times to sponsor him for the Brook; I reluctantly agreed, but only because we'd still need a second and the only exec member besides me that he knows slightly is Ned Ross, Meredith's banker husband. I thought I was safe on that score. On the other hand, I can't really read Meredith — I think she admires you, Tom, but if the management report is critical, what can she do?"

"The picture you have painted is very, very complicated," said Sally. "Your only possible hold on Cattivo beyond the cathedral is that he wants the Brook Club membership. Is that correct?"

"That's right," said the Bishop, "but he hasn't even suggested that he would do a deal to save Tom's hide. But remember, with Bob, it all comes down to setting the price, because he knows the price of everything and the value of nothing."

Tom and Sally had no response. The Bishop raised his forefinger and punched the air slowly. "Hold on. Bob told me last month that he would commit murder to get his son into Brown University. Tom, can't you engineer that?"

"It was tempting, but if Georgie isn't ready for Brown, his failure there would reflect on our other applicants later. Cattivo is certainly on a Brown crusade and has tried to fix it. He's also trying to deliver Brown for his son in order to alienate Babs further from the boy. But remember that Bob still doesn't know the dirt Georgie uncovered about his own papa during his papa-inspired hacking of mama."

"So," summarized the Bishop, "we don't really have Robert Harding Cattivo over a barrel because one, his request for my Cathedral wedding is hedged with Serena's request in London; two, his Brook Club passion is effectively out of my hands; and, finally, Brown University appears impregnable to any outside influence."

"I repeat, this picture is very, very complicated," said Sally. "And tangled. And dreadfully depressing."

Tom brightened. "But it isn't for Cattivo; it's how he operates every day of the year. And I'm sure he knows that all roads lead to Ned Ross. Meredith's husband holds the keys to Bob's heavenly kingdom of the Brook and Brown University. And up at Williams last weekend, a Brown history professor friend told me that campus rumor has Ned Ross as the most likely to be elected president of their board of trustees this week."

"It still may not do Bob much good," said the Bishop. "I know that he'll still have to come up with something quite dramatic to get Meredith's attention — Ned and she operate in their own worlds." The cleric sighed and eased himself back into bed. Sally rose and tucked him in.

"Thanks, Sally, sure wish I could afford your rates so I could have you around here full-time!"

She laughed and said, "We do all have our price, don't we?"

"Yes, indeed. Oh! In my present muddle, I forgot to tell you: in my latest phone call from Bob, he claimed that the logical extension of the sale of CC trustee seats would be 'the discreet sale of student places.'"

"And we know where he got that idea," said Sally.

The Bishop smiled. "Yes, his future bride is one determined woman with quite a burr under her saddle."

"And the future groom has no threshold of decency," said Tom. "Quite a combination."

"Oh, I'd say those seamy conditions run beyond the saddle and threshold and into the stable and living quarters. But I'm enjoined by all that's holy," said the Bishop with his trademark twinkle, "never to consider a soul unredeemable." The cleric laid back exhausted onto his pillows and said softly, "Or to mix metaphors."

Tom met that afternoon with Bramston and Cattivo to make his final fundraising report. Both trustees seemed distant, and the snarling wolf under

Bob's desk had never seemed more appropriate. The trustees completely ignored the headmaster as Cattivo asked Wither if he'd reviewed the management report.

"Mr. Lear said this morning it was at the printer's, but that they'll send it over in time for our meeting tomorrow."

"Well, I hope he's done a proper job. We should have vetted it, Wither. It's important to have everything finished and wrapped up for the meeting."

Tom had no doubt who was about to be finished and wrapped up.

CHAPTER 93

At noon the next day, Bramston called Tom. "Please add 'the Lear Management Report' to our agenda. I doubt you'll be partial to it."

When the report arrived, Tom read it and his blood ran cold. He forgot about lunch, cancelled all afternoon appointments, and asked Business Manager Ames and Jane Levi to join him. Ames met regularly with the financial officers of Horace Mann, Trinity, Dalton, and several other schools, and knew their budgets well. Jane brought over copies of the school records that Lear had requested when he came up to the school.

"I hadn't seen him since we expelled his older son last spring," said Jane. "When Mr. Lear came to my office last week, the only thing he said was, 'I don't have much time for this. Just give me the numbers. I'll soon tell the board if you're fat and overfed.'"

Tom had been overly diplomatic when he protested Wither Bramston's choice of Lear to do the school management report. Jane and he had tangled with the man repeatedly.

The divorced Mrs. Lear had called in tears over an earlier problem with the son who was later expelled. The boy had cheated during an exam, but her former husband refused to come in for what he said was a Kangaroo Court — he sent his lawyer instead.

Tom had insisted that Lear come in a month later after the same son had arrived at a school dance drunk and had torn a water fountain loose from the wall. Tom explained the case and his decision to expel the boy. Tom would never forget the dark look of detestation on Mr. Lear's face before he stalked from the room. Now Lear would be passing out his evaluation of Tom's leadership record at the board meeting.

Tom studied his notes and nodded to the late arrivals in the Cattivo Seminar Room: the Bishop, who had lost considerable weight but not an ounce of presence despite walking with a cane, and the elegant Board Vice-President Meredith Ross, who had been enlarging her Chinese operation in Shanghai for nearly three months. Tom heard Bob Cattivo say, "Ah, Meredith, 'invading the Asian market,' according to Forbes, eh?" She smiled and moved down along the table. Tom caught snippets of comments to her: "Give your Ned my congratulations, Meredith — great news this afternoon from Providence," and "Maybe Ned'll be giving Harvard, Yale, and Princeton a run for their money again!" Tom looked to his left and saw Bob Cattivo leaning forward, listening intently.

The entrance of Wither Bramston escorting Michael Lear into the room interrupted Tom's trustee scanning. Wither was as obsequious as Lear was imperious, ignoring Tom's offered hand as he sat.

Bramston had a quick whisper with Bob Cattivo, seated next to him, and got right to work; he called the trustee meeting to order at 5:05 P.M. and asked for the Headmaster's Report. Tom confined himself to his solid new enrollment figures, a summary of the few new faculty, and made his final plea for better teacher pay and his minority teacher academy recruitment project.

Bramston sighed heavily. "Now, we do have some major items on our agenda." The board president looked down to his notes to refresh his memory.

"First, our management study as mandated at the budget meeting February last. I am honored to introduce Mr. Michael Lear—"

"That's Mike, Wit," interjected Lear.

Wit? wondered Tom, nobody called him *that*.

"Mike is a Christ Church parent who insisted on doing this *pro bono*, and—" Tom saw Wither fumble to find his place on the bio sheet that carried Lear's letterhead. "He's both a virtual Phi Beta Kappa and basketball All-American and a point guard when it comes to rooting out incompetent management. Confidentially," Wither stumbled a bit, "he was the trouble-shooter for the biggest fast food takeover deal in history and he was the creator of the 'Pragmatic Public Advancement' campaign in Europe for America's software giant, and has been termed the 'Leading Edge Messaging Solutions Guru.'" Bramston ceased his wooden reading and scanned his copy. "I could also name the many business schools where he has taught." Wither looked up, "Let's leave it that he is a former investment banker who has been around the block. Mike?"

The very tall, smiling Lear immediately passed out his fifteen-page report to the warmed-up audience. It was bound in Christ Church silver and red with delicate white foxing and was printed on slick paper. Tom marveled over the binding and wished his school could afford something like that; then he recalled his business manager mentioning that afternoon that he had already paid the whopping printing bill Bramston had authorized.

Tom was impressed by Lear's profound confidence. He was a polished performer and escorted the trustees through the graph and chart-filled report at an easy lope with such dispatch that no questions slowed his final gallop and reading of the "Conclusion," set in CC's red and silver letters in the center of the final page.

> For even though parent, student, and faculty morale is ostensibly high, at least for the moment, that latter level of personal employee aggrandizement has been 'purchased' by Mr. West over the past five years at an usuriously extortionate price that Christ Church School cannot, in actuality, afford. Simply put: there is a tide of mediocrity over the horizon, the result of the erosion of years of uncritical faculty spending not necessarily related to the realities of skill-sets or staffing altitudes, of purposively profligate and secretional fiscal and staff management, of soaring programmatic costs primarily due to runaway faculty/customer index-ratios, and of reckless

infrastructure and circumstantial intra-strategies shot through with excessive corroborational tactical staff support, and the whole dependent on employee incentivizations foreign to comparable eleemosynary institutions.

The message is all too clear: This is a hell of a way to run a railroad.

Chairman Wither Bramston looked around the table as soon as a smiling, triumphant Lear sat. "Any comments on the report?" Cattivo looked pleased enough not to comment; he'd let the report have its effect.

Several of the investment bankers nodded affirmation and one pronounced, "Just like Bill Buckley would have put it." Another, whom Tom knew had never run anything beyond his office Super Bowl betting pool, said, "Harsh, perhaps, but 'reckless circumstantiation' — that deserves harsh."

No one else moved, but there was muttering about the "impenetrable verbiage" from the media lord educated at Oxford and "typical B-school pap and crap" from the Viennese conglomerater at the table.

Then a determined shake of the Bishop's pink head. He leaned forward to take in Lear's bold chalk-striped suiting and asked the wide knot at the top of his gondolier-speckled tie, "I confess I'm a bit at sea here. Three sentences, and I only understand the off-the-rails one." He placed his forefinger on the text and said, "Might I ask the meaning that 'excessive corroborational tactical staff support, and the whole dependent on employee incentivizations foreign to comparable eleemosynary institutions' is meant to convey?"

"Well," said a comfortable Lear, "it's this excessive tactical stuff, like the drama teacher's special theater fund so she can see theater in New York. And like that 'summer sabbatical' program where faculty are paid to go to England to see Shakespeare or, like, you know, to Civil War battlefields or to Yosemite to get acquainted with some Adams guy. Stuff like that."

"Yes, I can see that kind of personal contact with the Bard or Ansell Adams would be expensive to arrange — heavy airfare, no doubt, not to mention pricey theological intervention," said the Bishop, followed by muted laughter.

Vice-President Ross, without looking at Lear, calmly said to the air above the table, "I find the same sort of 'virtual reality' in this report as in the concept of 'virtual Phi Betas and All-Americans' — or, in this case, the reality of grammatically-surrendered BS. If I may address our 'virtual messaging guru,'" she continued, as she looked daggers down the table, "You should know, Mr. Lear, that the board not only was told of those annual expenditures, I for one, am very pleased that we have them. I chair the selection committee for the summer fellowships and I'm proud that such creative ways to offer tax-free educational opportunities to our underpaid teachers should remain, as this report puts it, 'foreign to comparable eleemosynary institutions.'" At that point, she leaned forward and turned full on the report-maker. "But you see, that's *their* loss, sir, and I hope Tom's excellent programs remain as foreign to them as they are to you."

Tom noticed Cattivo's change of expression — he clearly didn't like the way this was going. Meredith Ross had missed the last executive committee meeting and had been an unknown factor all summer. She had been out of sight, out of mind for the hassled Cattivo. The Lear report had been royally blindsided by the one person on the board that Cattivo couldn't afford to alienate.

"Oh, and don't bother to explain 'eleemosynary,' Mr. Lear," said the Bishop. "It's a household term, of course. Unfortunately, it was last used in Noah Webster's household about eighteen-forty."

"Hear, hear," said the press baron, who was attending his first meeting of the year.

Lear adopted a graver manner and warily checked the others, especially Cattivo.

Bramston intervened. "I believe you've had ample opportunity to review this, Tom?"

"Yes, I got the copy you sent by messenger at—" he looked at Jo's stamp on his binder — "Twelve-forty-seven today."

"Anything you'd like to add?"

"Yes." Tom stood.

"Those of you who were on the board when I arrived will remember that I requested a yearly evaluation of my work. I'm sorry it has taken so long for the first one and I admit that such assessments can be wrenching." Wither scratched his chin. The Bishop shifted painfully in his chair. Cattivo sat back and folded his arms, while Lear, looming alongside Bramston, was the only person at the table not looking at Tom.

Tom looked further around the table and picked up his Lear report. "There is more than a suggestion in this thick piece that the erosion noted in the conclusion has been brought about by a management with a con-spiratorial bent, although there is not a scrap of evidence provided. I would remind you, as Ms. Ross did, and as our minutes will show, at every point in my five years I have informed the Board of my administrative proposals and decisions about people and programs. As St. Paul might have put it, '*This thing was not done in a corner.*'" The Bishop smiled.

Tom continued, "Although I am not sure I understand the vocabulary and syntax at every tide and horizon of this report — what Cervantes might have called its '*beautiful perplexity of expression*' — I think that the entire conclusion is derived from the double-page chart on pages six and seven, "Faculty/Customer Index-Ratios."

Bramston looked at Lear. "Fair enough, Mr. Lear?"

"Well, yes. Substantially correct. Indubitably." He sat back in his chair as if he were pleased with that last word. Which wasn't the last word because he added wearily, "Like I always say, 'just give me the numbers.'"

"Continue, Headmaster," said Bramston.

"The first section of this report purports to contain 'a scientific review of the history of Faculty/Customer index ratios,' on pages three through five. Following that, the only faculty figures and enrollment totals contained in Mr. Lear's handsome report are cited on that double-page chart on pages six and seven. The numbers are indeed accurate. But the use made of them is neither scientific nor historical."

There was an immediate flicking of pages and a buzz around the table.

Several gray and white heads leaned toward the head, albeit with a sideways glance at a puce Lear and a keenly alert Cattivo.

"Mr. Chairman, I'd like to pass out my paper addressing the same issues." He passed his sheets in both directions. "It is one page and is written in our native tongue" — there was a stir as the sheets were passed and placed by each trustee atop Lear's booklet — "and I trust it is readable and will not disappoint with its brevity." Now there was outright laughter at several points around the table, most notably by Ms. Ross, the Press Baron, and the Bishop.

"My sheet uses the same enrollment and faculty numbers as the thicker report — those for the years nineteen-eighty, nineteen-ninety, two-thousand, and two-thousand-and-five. It does, however, come to a very different conclusion. The contradiction can be explained easily, reading from my statement. 'The Lear report overlooks two crucial factors: one, that Christ Church students are now taking a much heavier course load than ever before, in fact, an average of two-point-five more courses per student per term, a more than fifty percent increase compared with nineteen-eighty; and two, that given the marked change in our family and school culture, that is, the addition of mental and emotional counseling and learning disability diagnosis as a school function, the instructional ratio of teachers to students has eroded, if I may borrow that term, has eroded from one-to-seven to one-to-twelve between nineteen-eighty and two-thousand-and-five. The practical effect of that change, for example, is that many of our English classes have moved from the twelve to fourteen students of the nineteen-eighties to our current eighteen to twenty-two students per section; and the other departments have even larger numbers.'

"Now, since we are going to discuss the endowment picture later, I can honestly tell you that the real challenge to CC's generally solid morale of parents, teachers, and students is not maladministration, it is that we do not have comparable resources to our rivals. Our tuition is now the eighth most expensive in the city, and our competitor schools can afford a better faculty to student ratio and faculty pay because they enjoy more tuition *and* endowment income. Thank you."

Tom sat down and saw an extraordinary restlessness throughout the room. Ms. Ross was steamed, removing and replacing her half-spectacles twice, the alumni association president looked hurt, the international publisher's substantial upper lip quivered, the hedge-fund whiz's thin lips leveraged in and out, Cattivo doodled intently enough to snap his lead, the Viennese gentleman folded his arms and glumly looked only at the Katz paintings on the walls, and the Rev. Philips looked at least puzzled, and at most confused. Something was coming to the boil and Tom couldn't detect whether it was directed at him or at Lear.

Chairman Bramston, who appeared both wary and embarrassed, breathed airy assurances into the air regarding "honest differences of opinion."

The Bishop virtually cut him off. "I move that the panjandrum's 'management report' be stricken from the record and that Dr. West's literate, tempered, and informed comments — unique thus far this evening — form the basis for the upcoming main agenda item, the one on the endowment." Bob Cattivo surprised everyone in the room by quickly seconding the motion. Wither was ashen, but not so ashed he couldn't excuse Mr. Lear from the meeting with mumbled thanks.

Cattivo was the only person who spoke when Wither asked for discussion of the motion. "I agree with the Bishop and Ms. Ross that Tom has certainly set the stage perfectly for our endowment decisions this evening. I call the question."

The Bishop's resolution was passed easily, with only three investment bankers dissenting.

Tom was astonished at Cattivo's flip-flop. He had often warned Tom that he should consider himself "expendable," but the head never wanted to pursue his point. Now, Tom saw how expendable Michael Lear had proved to be and how deftly Cattivo cut his losses and used Tom as a transition to the next issue — Tom's flunking his endowment test.

Wither Bramston appeared confused and looked in vain for guidance from his agenda. Tom, sitting in his usual place at Bramston's left hand, could see why. The trustees had marched in a different direction from what the president had planned. His personal agenda had been neatly typed and ended with two lines in caps:

—MOTION TO RECEIVE LEAR MANAGEMENT REPORT — Dr. Philips

—APPOINTMENT OF HEADMASTER SEARCH COMMITTEE — RC, Chair

"Now, I wonder how we should proceed," Wither said, as if talking to himself. "We have now received the headmaster's report, and the management report, that was, but now isn't, received. Plus, we *have* received the headmaster's response to the now unreceived management report." He paused and looked over at the headmaster for help, who simply nodded kindly in return. Sort it out for yourself, you wily incompetent, thought Tom. He enjoyed the change to Bramston's plot. Perhaps if he was given more rope.

"So that's all done," Bramston continued and looked thoughtfully down at his notes, at the same time making an exaggerated check mark through his *MOTION TO RECEIVE LEAR MANAGEMENT REPORT*. He hesitated, glanced up at his favorite sconces above the other trustees' heads, and with a tired exhalation, turned again to Tom.

"Did you wish to tell us more about the school, headmaster? About the students, their sports results, hobbies? Something along those lines?" He checked the watch in his vest pocket, and that energized his persuasion. "We actually do have the time; the caterers won't serve dinner for another hour. Drinks in thirty minutes." The very concept seemed to revive him.

"I would generally be pleased to do that, Wither," said Tom. "But we still have to deal with the resolution that was passed at the last meeting, don't we?"

"Oh, yes, of course," Bramston said, recovering some equilibrium, "you mean the one passed at the annual budget meeting in February." He now turned to Cattivo. "Bob, you and the Bishop, actually all of us, agreed on it. What shall we do about all this?"

"Well, unfortunately, the late, unlamented management report does cloud the issue," Cattivo said. "But you got what you paid for it, didn't you, 'Wit'?"

"Ah, yes, so I did, so I did."

Tom felt better having someone else share the force of a Cattivo attack.

"Well," said Bramston, "I think the ball should be in your court, Bob. You take over."

So finally, the guy really running the show was now running the show. Just in time to announce Tom's failed fundraising and regain control of his project to administer the coup de grace to the head.

Cattivo seemed more cautious than usual. He took his time, turned away from Wither and looked around the table. He held up the Lear report.

"Well, first, our annual trustee dinner with guests can wait. Second, business before pleasure: maybe we can reconcile this 'non-report' with my February initiative." He flipped the report facedown into the center of the table. "I think there's a way. But first I want to tell you a little story." Tom couldn't believe the new, expansive Cattivo — where was the crafty guy going? He certainly had everyone's attention.

"Tom came down to my office to report on his fundraising yesterday—"

"I was there, too," said Bramston.

Cattivo ignored the interruption. "And when he said he had come up short, that he came out of his final sprint with over nineteen million dollars, well, I had mixed feelings, 'ambivalence,' he'd call it, but not a condition I'm usually guilty of." There were a few chuckles, labored ones, Tom thought. "Then I made a few calls — I checked with Jerry over at Dalton, John at Trinity, George at Collegiate, and other board leaders — and you know what? Our guy has raised more money than all of their heads combined in the last six months. Well, frankly, at the first of the year I'd given up on him as a fundraiser, which was the one thing he had taught us we needed more than anything."

"Yes, that's what I told him at the time," tossed in Wither. "Right, Tom?"

Tom said, "Yes. You told me that I had been successful in redefining myself out of a job." There was polite laughter all round.

Cattivo smiled and continued. "So, this evening after hearing his response to Lear's hatchet job, I've cured my attack of ambivalence. Here's what I suggest and so move: one, we keep this guy" — he looked at Tom and grinned — "for another year; and two, since he didn't raise the twenty million we goose the endowment further by carrying out our February agreement regarding the five million dollar passport to the board. And finally, as part of this motion, I gladly add my twenty million dollar gift to the endowment total, but with the stipulation that it is to be used exclusively by Vice-President Ross's faculty enrichment committee for disposal as she sees fit."

Bingo! Tom thought. Cattivo hit the jackpot: he'll soon be the newest trustee at the Cathedral and will have his flashy wedding there presided over by the Bishop of New York, the Brook Club is within reach, *and* he figures that Georgie has gained admission to Brown.

It was a clever move by Cattivo. A clear majority now supported Tom, but probably did not support selling board seats for five million. Except that was off the table — the die had been cast in February by Cattivo and now by Tom's flunking the test. Cattivo had written and directed the script. And just reviewed it.

Even as the motion was passed easily, Tom saw that Wither pressed his fountain pen's nib hard as he struck through the remaining item on his agenda: *APPOINTMENT OF HEAD SEARCH COMMITTEE.*

Tom hadn't realized that he had been breathing rapidly and solely from the top of his chest until he now gulped a deep breath and had to cover the sound. He checked to see if anyone saw his state. No, but the stately Bishop down the table had closed his eyes for a moment and winced in pain. When he became aware that Tom was watching, he recovered and gave a quick wink.

Tom tidied up the room after the trustees left for drinks and dinner; he didn't want stray papers or snazzy "management reports" left for the curious. He had been so relieved by being given another year at CC that the larger issue of Cattivo's complex resolution had almost escaped him. He stood at the table, his weight planted through his open palms on its surface. He saw his reflection in the black window: a drawn lug of a man, his relief at having a job now tempered by the dark thought that his selling the board on the necessity of a significant endowment had become the Golden Calf — the trustees might have just delivered the school to mammon forever. And the Countess' proposal to auction student places soon would be no further from reality than Cattivo's ear on the next pillow. A new battle would have to be joined.

"Tom?" The voice came from the doorway behind him.

He turned. Sally stood with her hand on the doorknob, and then pushed the door closed behind her. She walked toward him and embraced him without a word. Neither spoke.

Finally she whispered, "Welcome back to the land of the living, Headmaster."

The Bishop leaned heavily into Tom as they walked to the car where Sally waited behind the wheel. As he got buckled in, the Bishop revealed the brief conversation that he had just had with Cattivo after the trustee dinner.

"Bob asked me what my biggest Choir School gift had been. I told him twenty million. He said immediately, 'Not any more. I'll send you twenty-five million tomorrow.' So, Tom, take good care of him in there at your meeting when you go back in — that gift means a real opportunity for at least thirty more boys."

Tom shut the car door and watched a very happy Bishop be driven home by Sally. The head reminded himself that he must keep in mind how effectively Robert George Cattivo followed up on his prospects with the Bishop. Now, what kind of follow up did he have planned for Thomas Sylvester?

Tom joined Bob Cattivo at the head table in the deserted Great Lobby, watching the caterer's crew begin stripping the tables. Cattivo had told Tom he wanted a word with him after everyone else left. The trustee fiddled with a leftover silver spoon as he pursed his lips and spoke.

"We can bury the hatchet now, Tom. We're both winners after tonight."

Cattivo watched Tom warily. Tom didn't bite — mostly because his mind was elsewhere — on a future board of trustees composed of Cattivo clones who each paid five million for the privilege.

Cattivo pressed on. "So, we might as well be allies. But put my mind at ease — Georgie said something I couldn't figure out last night at dinner. At Le Bernardin. I guess I can still take my own son there without running afoul of you, eh?"

Tom merely smiled and said, "You'll have to do better than that, Bob. I'm waiting. What are you after now?"

Cattivo raised his chin and looked over at Tom. "Just this: Georgie and I are finding some common ground, but he still tries to challenge me. He even claimed that you might have known about Babs' mess before I knew. That's all he'd say. Maybe he was playing his old dad, but I've got to know. Know anything about that, Dr. Thomas West? If you do, you'd better spit it out."

Tom was surprised by that question. And then pleased. He could protect Georgie and tell most, well, some of the truth. He raised his chin and looked narrowly at Cattivo, trying for the mean look he'd just seen aimed at himself, but gave it up and answered.

"Strange his saying that. Yes, I did know something, because I witnessed it." It looked like he had Cattivo's attention. "But I would swear on your stack of Ayn Rand Bibles that Georgie couldn't possibly know about what I saw. It must be his shot in the dark to rattle you."

Tom related his sighting of Babs and the man in the Williamstown parking lot, not sparing the details. Cattivo was silent as he listened. When Tom finished, Cattivo bowed his head and shook it. Still silent. Tom would swear he saw Cattivo's head quiver. Tom looked away — it was too hard to watch.

"How long have you known?" Cattivo asked, his head still bowed, his fingers picking at nonexistent trouser lint.

"I was up there raising money in late July."

Cattivo looked up directly at Tom. "So, why the fuck didn't you use it to threaten me? Threatening to make the cuckold public?"

"Bob, you forget, I'm a teacher deep down. I didn't want to have any part in breaking up Monica's and Georgie's family."

Cattivo looked toward the heavens, "Goddamn, I don't believe it! I fucking don't understand you sometimes!" He shook his head in disbelief. He recovered by blowing his nose. And by fixing his new ally with his best grin. Still a lot of teeth and gums.

"I've got no beef with you, Tom. From the beginning I only wanted Christ Church School to have the best headmaster — it was nothing personal."

"You actually expect me to believe that?" said Tom.

Cattivo looked peeved, then shrugged. "Okay, so, yeah, guess my head was turned by Babs, who'd been after you since our reception — you know, the cheap faculty booze — I'd never have allowed her to do that if I'd known. See, over the years, I had to do everything I could to keep Babs; she let me know that, I'm older. She had me by the balls, but I didn't wake up until I learned what Georgie found out about that whore, and now, Jesus, learning what you saw up in Williamstown." Cattivo shook his head. "But that's all history, and when you set that fundraising record for the endowment, well, I had to go with you."

"Well, that and the little matters of Brown and the Brook Club and the Cathedral." Tom looked hard at Cattivo, then softened. "And I'm sorry about your marriage, Bob, I really am."

"Yeah, I know you are. You're one of the only SOBs in town that I would believe when they said that very thing. Maybe the only one. And Serena doesn't even say that shit — she says that 'unmasking the bitch led us to each other,' and I agree."

The waiters were clearing the nearest tables.

Bob looked quizzically at Tom. "You are one naïve, vulnerable, reliable son of a bitch, I will say that."

"Shucks," said Tom with a grin.

"Yeah. You are, but don't expect me to be the mushy pushover I am now after Georgie gets his diploma next June. Watch out — I'll come after you again when you get out of line, when you don't support me. I mean it."

The two men were momentarily distracted by the sight of two waiters struggling to move a large table; one stumbled and the table rammed into the carved stone wall. The headwaiter took a few minutes to ream out the duo with language that made even Tom's profanely-gifted companion sit up.

But Tom's mind was elsewhere, getting his response to Cattivo's threat just right ...

"No, you won't come after me, Short Stuff."

Cattivo glared at the headmaster. "What's that supposed to mean?"

"Let me put it this way, little man: I think you will be the most supportive trustee that I've ever had the pleasure of working with, instead of the strutting, morally stunted—"

Cattivo rushed in, "Fuck's your problem? What the shit—"

"Hold on, Tin Pot Napoleon," Tom said as he turned and grabbed Cattivo's well-padded shoulder. "I wasn't finished. Let's see, 'you will be the most supportive trustee that I've ever had the pleasure of working with, instead of the strutting, morally stunted' man you are. That is, unless you want the IRS to look at your hidden rental income in the Caymans. Or the FBI to check out your building permit bribes in Miami and Hoboken."

"You bastard, no, you're bluffing," said Cattivo, sitting up.

"Tut, tut, watch your language to the lucky bastard who could bring you down."

"How could you know? Where? Who? Georgie?"

"Try me." Tom rose, leaving Cattivo with a crumpled shoulder, and pulling the silver spoon from the little man's grasp.

"Since I know the kind of man you are, Tin Pot Napoleon, I'd better protect our school's reputation beginning now — I'll start by counting the spoons."

No, no, Tom said to himself and came out of his reverie — he would be leading Cattivo straight to Georgie — their relationship would never survive. He'd have to bide his time and he had plenty of that — the statutes of limitations on those charges were up to six years and he'd figure out a way to cover for Georgie when the time came . . .

"Earth to Headcase," said Cattivo as he shook Tom's shoulder. "Jesus Christ, you looked as if you'd lost it, and I wanted you very much to hear this. I was saying, watch out, Doc — if you get out of line, I'll come after you again. I mean it."

Tom knew he meant it. But the head also knew that someone had left another plain manila envelope on his desk yesterday. The envelope contained new material from Bob's hidden accounts at Farmers and Merchants Bank, Grand Cayman. It showed illegal campaign donations to Senators McCain and Clinton for their upcoming 2008 presidential campaigns. Fast Bobby hedging his bets. But Tom had already hedged his — he'd stashed the new envelope in his safety deposit box at his Seventy-Second Street bank. He placed it on top of two earlier envelopes that showed Bob guilty of failing to report nearly $900,000 in Caribbean rental income to the IRS over the past five years and the record of Miami and Hoboken bribes for building permits.

CHAPTER 94

"So here we are," said Sally into the grainy semi-darkness of the bedroom. "Our first liberated night here. Really *here*. In the head's house. Matt will love being in this house as much as I do. And we're here as permanently as any baseball manager or school head can expect."

"Yep. Do you remember our pillow talk in Amsterdam?"

"Sure. The only thing unresolved by the two ethical philosophers was whether the barbarians tending the school trustee gate would let you keep your job."

"Not quite, my luscious Defender of the Faith," said Tom. "The question at that point was could Ole Sylvester do his job."

"Okay, put it your way, but the answer is very much yes."

"No, only yes for a year. And you've *also* bought into your reptilian art world after discovering it's sometimes more primitive and raw than mine."

"Maybe. But what kind of competition is this?"

"It'll have to be our twilight zone."

"I think I prefer your 'chiaroscuro' of last month." She turned and stroked his face gently, outlining his lips with the tips of her fingers. "And how do you feel about going back to work? Are you ready to reenter the world of Cattivo's 'finagle factors' and Serena's 'discreet open-bids?'"

"Those are as nothing after that board meeting. I'm a new man and ready to go again. But only because I have my new diversion." He nuzzled her shoulder and pulled her close.

"Only one diversion in your life?"

"Well, technically two — you *and* Matt." He waited for her approval.

She was silent for long enough to make him wonder, then, "What would you say to three?"

He sat up and looked down at her in the semi-darkness, straining to read her expression. Puckish. Smug. "Darling, you have that 'Curator who took the Rembrandt home' look. Do you mean — is it possible?"

"It's early, but I've missed two periods — I guess love's labor wasn't lost."

THE END

ACKNOWLEDGEMENTS

It was the renowned editor Richard Seaver (one of my favorite school trustees), who first encouraged me to write this book. He also cautioned that I would find my background as an historian a hindrance because I would find it difficult to master fiction's casual chronological order and its pervasive mental complexity. He was right — it took this fast learner twelve years to write the novel. Editors Andrea Chapin, Dan Zitin, and Karen Shepard got me started, Jane O'Connor and Anthony Gellert added their keen readings, and Judy Sternlight, whom Peter Matthiessen described as "exceptionally intelligent and insightful," guided me to the finish line. Eliza Dreier and Katarina Manos did final corrections. Agent Carol Mann was unfailingly helpful and her colleague Myrsini Stephanides proved a skillful and sensitive partner.

Twelve years allowed time for me to solicit and receive aid from many teachers, former students, parents, trustees, and fellow public and private heads. The following lists are suggestive and hardly exhaustive. It is important to me that all these fine people and, in some cases, their heirs, keep in mind that all the characters in this novel are fictitious, critters of my fevered creation, but nonetheless recognizable to my colleagues who head schools across America and the United Kingdom.

I thank former teaching and staff colleagues Jane Mallison, Carole France, Pat Robbins, John Hanly, Caroline Roberts, Massimo Maglione, Jim Shields, Barbara Sherman, Janet Kehl, Audree Pospisil, Shirley

Schnetzer, Edith de Montebello, David Trower, Rick Fitzgerald, Sue Hunt Hollingsworth, Marianna Leighton, Daniel Heischman, Lenesa and Frank Leana, Al Romano, Jim Iredell, Cornelia Bauer, Elaine Fries, Tracy Franklin-Smith, Walter Johnson, John Gulla, Richard Blumenthal, Ed Lynn, Randall Dunn, and Dan Frank for warm friendship, encouragement, and critical appraisals. Gary Simons, founder of Prep for Prep, remained an adviser throughout. And thanks are due across the Atlantic pond, as John Thorn, headmaster of Winchester College, and John Rae, headmaster of Westminster School, always championed my effort.

William Wixom, Medieval Art Department Head emeritus of the Metropolitan Museum, Susan Galassi, Senior Curator of the Frick Collection, John Williams of the National Gallery, London, and many friends from the Boston Fine Arts Museum, the Rijksmuseum, the Frans Hals Museum, the Mauritshaus, and the Rembrandthuis, provided invaluable guidance on institutional, artistic, and literary matters.

I thank many of the school trustees from New York to San Francisco to Chicago to Minneapolis with whom I've worked over the years including Michel Fribourg, Broward Craig, Tony Heard, Bishop Paul Moore, Richard Nye, John Johnston, Elizabeth Allen, Ed Franklin, Chris Doyle, Carolyn Smith, Barbara Paul Robinson, Evelyn Lauder, Vartan Gregorian, Mildred Berensen, Bill Ziff, Terry Andreas, Martha Watts, Kathryn Piper, Edward Lorenze, Fred Copeland, Sally Crane, Blaine Fogg, Stephen Kaufman, Joseph King, Edward Schmults, William McGill, Virgil Conway, Rupert Murdoch, David Wescoe, Carl Morse, John Arnhold, Sandy and Joyce Brass, The Reverend Robert Parks, Charles Bluhdorn, Roger Strong, Steve Cobb, Marvin Deckoff, Douglas Tansill, Maurice Greenberg, Richard Colhoun, David Feinberg, Jordan Gruzen, Thomas Peardon, Jr., Charles Benenson, Arthur Rosenblatt, Mary Linda and Victor Zonana, Yani Tree, Jack Rudin, Susan Ulin, Osamu Yamada, Helen Fung, Jerry Hume, Glynna Freeman, Christine Murray, Sara Stassen, Theodore Tetzlaff, James Gidwitz, John Brooks, Bill Byars, Kris Erickson, Marialice Harwood, Edson Spencer, Tom Crosby, Steve Goldstein, Judson Dayton, and Whitney MacMillan — everyone of them exemplary in their service to their school and headmaster.

Finally, deepest thanks to my family: two sons — Robin Debevoise and James Robinson — who have cheered this enterprise through the years, and their mother, the person who has been my best friend, lover, wife, editor and map illustrator through more than a score of drafts, Helen Sargent Doughty Lester.

Robin Lester, the former head of Trinity School in New York, also taught and headed schools in San Francisco, Chicago, and Minneapolis. This is his debut novel. He has written OpEd essays for the New York Times and his award-winning history of college football, Stagg's University, was termed, "splendid" and "brilliant" by Arthur Schlesinger, Jr.

6002633R00186

Made in the USA
San Bernardino, CA
28 November 2013